**Nichole Severn** writes explosive romantic suspense with strong heroines, heroes who dare challenge them and a hell of a lot of guns. She resides with her very supportive and patient husband, as well as her demon spawn, in Utah. When she's not writing, she's constantly injuring herself running, rock climbing, practising yoga and snowboarding. She loves hearing from readers through her website, www.nicholesevern.com, and on Facebook, @nicholesevern

**Tyler Anne Snell** genuinely loves all genres of the written word. However, she's realised that she loves books filled with sexual tension and mysteries a little more than the rest. Her stories have a good dose of both. Tyler lives in Alabama with her same-named husband and their mini "lions." When she isn't reading or writing, she's playing video games and working on her blog, *Almost There*. To follow her shenanigans, visit tylerannesnell.com

## Also by Nichole Severn

*Midnight Abduction*
*The Fugitive*
*The Witness*
*The Prosecutor*
*The Suspect*
*Rules in Blackmail*
*Rules in Rescue*
*Rules in Deceit*
*Rules in Defiance*
*Caught in the Crossfire*
*The Line of Duty*

## Also by Tyler Anne Snell

*Reining in Trouble*
*Credible Alibi*
*Identical Threat*
*Last Stand Sheriff*
*Small-Town Face-Off*
*The Deputy's Witness*
*Forgotten Pieces*
*Loving Baby*
*The Deputy's Baby*
*The Negotiation*

Discover more at millsandboon.co.uk

# PROFILING
# A KILLER

## NICHOLE SEVERN

# UNCOVERING
# SMALL TOWN
# SECRETS

## TYLER ANNE SNELL

# MILLS & BOON

First Published in Great Britain 2021
by Mills & Boon, an imprint of HarperCollins*Publishers* Ltd
1 London Bridge Street, London, SE1 9GF

www.harpercollins.co.uk

HarperCollins*Publishers*
1st Floor, Watermarque Building,
Ringsend Road, Dublin 4, Ireland

*Profiling a Killer* © 2021 Harlequin Books S.A.
*Uncovering Small Town Secrets* © 2021 Tyler Anne Snell

Special thanks and acknowledgement are given to Nichole Severn
for her contribution to the *Behavioral Analysis Unit* series.

ISBN: 978-0-263-28341-9

0621

MIX
Paper from
responsible sources
FSC™ C007454

# PROFILING
# A KILLER

**NICHOLE SEVERN**

To Nana:

You always believed in my writing.
I hope I've made you proud.

# Prologue

Absolutely perfect.

Short brown hair, slender through the hips, with honey-brown eyes he hadn't been able to stop thinking about since the moment he'd met her. Yes. If he had to narrow down his type, Kara Flood ticked all the boxes.

The kindergarten teacher strengthened her grip on her dog's leash, and a prickling raised the hairs on the back of his neck as he pressed back into the shadows. Her footsteps in those ridiculous platform sandals echoed off the apartment building at his back. She was getting closer, close enough he noted the streetlamp's reflection off the sweat beading along her flawless neck. It was hot out tonight, humid. Hot enough hints of her perfume tickled the back of his throat as a breeze swept off the inlet. A frenzy coiled in his gut, and he breathed the combination of orange, patchouli and Turkish rose deeper. It was the only perfume she wore.

The dog, an intrusive white shepherd who'd kept him from getting to know Kara on a more intimate level, glanced his way, but he didn't move.

Nothing would stop him from having her. Nothing would stop him from showing them what he was capable of. This was *his* time. He left the cover of the alley and cut off her escape, curling gloved fingers into fists. Hesitation combined with a slight hint of fear in her expression, and a wave of anticipation flooded through him. The dog pulled back on the leash, trying to convince Kara to leave, but there was nowhere for her to run. Not from him.

"Hello, Kara. I've been waiting for you."

# *Chapter One*

"Seattle PD received a hand-drawn map early this morning from a witness who hasn't been able to reach her sister for over twenty-four hours." Supervisory Special Agent Miguel Peters tossed a thick manila folder onto the conference table, the scrape of card stock and wood cutting off conversation. A thick five-o'clock shadow stood stark against his white button-down shirt and showcased the exhaustion under his eyes. The supervising director of the Behavioral Analysis Unit pointed to the head of the conference room. "Now we know why."

The projector flashed to life at the direction of their tech guru—Liam McDare—at the opposite end of the table. A single image filled the screen. The bright seal of the evidence bag cut off the top two inches of a crude, torn piece of lined paper with penned outlines of vague, unlabeled buildings, sidewalks, a park and a large red $X$ off to one side. SSA Peters hit the remote in his hand, and the image on the projector changed. A woman—no older than twenty-five or twenty-six—sat on a commercial steel bench outside what looked like a wall of windows leading into the main floor of an apartment building. One leg crossed over the other, the victim looked as though she'd sat down to take in the sunrise from across Puget Sound to start her morning. Aside from the angry purple-and-blue strangulation marks around her neck and the red *X* carved into her right cheekbone, she'd been a strikingly beautiful woman.

"The map designated where the victim's sister could find the body." *Hell.* Special Agent Nicholas James leaned forward in his chair, a knot of dread knifing through him. No. It wasn't possible. Reaching for the folder SSA Peters had tossed in his direction, he pried it open and compared the crime scene photos to those taking up nearly an entire wall in the BAU's high-rise conference room. All the signs were there, right down to the positioning of the body. He locked his back teeth against the denial clawing up his throat without looking up. "Who is she?"

"Victim's name is Kara Flood, a kindergarten teacher who lives in the building you see behind her, and, in case you can't tell from the crime scene photos, she resembles a few victims we've come across before." SSA Peters pressed his palms onto the edge of the long conference table. "Director Branson wants this handled as quickly and as quietly as possible. We can't have the public panic. Agents James and Striker, meet your next assignment."

A kindergarten teacher? Nausea churned in Nicholas's gut. Gravity pulled the blood from his face as he memorized the woman's features.

"The X Marks the Spot Killer." Madeline Striker, the unit's kidnapping expert, unfolded her arms and set her elbows on the table. Dark, layered hair with golden highlights framed perfectly angled warm brown cheekbones. A hard light of dedication to find the missing echoed in her dark, rich eyes. Her flawless complexion made her look younger than her age, but any perp who had the guts to take advantage learned Striker had an uncanny ability to handle herself. "He chose women who were in their early to mid-twenties, single, with short brown hair, and were much smaller than him to make it easier to strangle them from behind. He was all about control, domination. She matches his profile."

Nicholas's ears rang as images of his childhood superimposed the faces of the victims from his first case assignment for the unit three years ago. He forced himself to take a deep breath, to come up with some other explanation as to why Kara Flood had been targeted, strangled and mutilated with an *X*. They'd found the killer. They'd put the bastard behind bars.

Confusion altered the clean lines of Madeline's dark eyebrows. "He hunted his victims in that same neighborhood, but Cole Presley was found guilty and sentenced to life behind bars. We need to contact the warden at Washington State Corrections to ensure Presley is still accounted for."

"We never released the details of the X Marks the Spot case to the public, and there haven't been any leaks in information as far as I can tell after the conclusion of the trial." BAU's resident cybercrimes expert, Dashiell West, tapped his hand against the table. The light from the agent's laptop cast shadows along chiseled features and thick beard growth. Two years older than Nicholas, West had more experience in the digital world, but serial cases would always default to Nicholas. Especially this one. "The only way this guy could've gotten the specifics of how the victims were killed is if he was involved in the case somehow. Maybe one of the original victims' family members? They would've been informed about manner of death."

"The X Marks the Spot Killer strangled and mutilated thirty victims over thirty years that we know of, every year on the same day. Assuming one of the victims' family members is involved, that leaves hundreds of suspects."

Only Nicholas had known the killer by a different name when he'd been a kid. Right up until he'd put the cuffs on a man he'd trusted his entire life. The bones under his knuckles threatened to break free from the calloused skin on the back of his hands. Kara Flood. He didn't know the victim or recognize her name directly, but instinct heightened all the same as he studied postmortem photos of the woman discovered this morning. He could almost see the resemblance, and a shot of warmth dumped into his veins. Dark brown hair, same shade of honey-colored eyes, possibly a similar face shape. Had the victim been related to Dr. Aubrey Flood, the medical examiner who'd performed the autopsies on the last three victims of the X Marks the Spot Killer? He scanned the file in front of him. "The sister found the body."

"Yes." The lines around SSA Peters's mouth smoothed. "According to her statement given to Seattle PD this morning, Dr. Aubrey Flood found the map taped to her door this morning, then immediately tried calling the victim. When she didn't get an answer, she followed the clues the killer had left for her. Forensics is trying to pull prints from the map and the tape, but the lab is backed up as it is. We won't have results for a few days."

"Dr. Flood was the ME in the original case. She performed the autopsies on Presley's last three victims." Nicholas licked his suddenly dry lips as a visual of the doc replaced the violent memories in his head. Wisps of soft medium-length brown hair highlighting a creamy complexion, a honey-warm gaze that had pierced straight through him and the voice of a siren tempting him to believe in something other than the worst in people.

He'd only met the medical examiner a handful of times to discuss the initial case, but there always seemed to be a forged intimacy between everyone involved in a serial investigation. Emergency responders, agents assigned to the case, the first officers on scene. Drowning in that kind of darkness brought out a need for safe human contact that even the most veteran investigators clung to, and Aubrey had been part of the team. She'd been professional, respectful and warm toward the victims under her scalpel, a miracle considering the kind of work she had to face on a daily basis as Seattle's chief examiner.

"She gave us the exact type of blade Cole Presley used to carve an *X* into each of the victims' cheeks by swabbing particles from the wounds and testing hundreds of blades. Without her insight, we never would've caught up to him. We can't discount the possibility her sister's death might be some kind of retaliation from one of his super fans."

"You think this killer might be trying to get the attention of the X Marks the Spot Killer by drawing out the medical examiner who put him away." SSA Peters centered himself in the light from the projector as the slideshow ended. The FBI seal tinted the antiterrorism expert's Cuban American skin tone blue.

"It makes sense, but I think there's more at play than we're seeing here. This is the first victim we've uncovered using a previous serial's MO, and something tells me it won't be the last." Not when Dr. Flood was quickly becoming a central element to this case. Nicholas studied the photos of the victim again. "It can't be a coincidence Kara Flood was strangled and marked after her sister became connected to the case, or that the killer delivered the map directly to Aubrey Flood's door. His target wasn't random."

Nicholas raised his attention to SSA Peters. The question was why. That was the specialty of the Behavioral Analysis Unit—to make sense of the incomprehensible, to get into the minds of humanity's worst killers to stop them from striking again. Cole Presley had strangled young women in their twenties with brown hair and marked them with an *X* to show the victims' family members where to find his treasure, his masterpieces, but Nicholas wasn't willing to risk Aubrey Flood's life in order to add to his profile of this killer. He closed the file in front of him. "He knew exactly what he was doing and whom he wanted to draw into his game."

"All right. I've got Caitlyn Yang meeting with Dr. Flood and the family now to fill them in on the investigation and explain where we go from here. Dr. Flood is one of us, and we owe her nothing less than the full support of this unit." SSA Peters straightened. "West, I need you to search through security footage from the good doctor's apartment building. There might be something there to give us an idea of when our unsub left the note so we can track his movements last night. James and Striker, take Dyson to check out the scene where the killer dumped the body. I want to know if anyone noticed our victim or her killer before she wound up in front of her apartment building."

"You got it." Nicholas pushed away from the conference table and headed for the double glass doors leading out into the main offices. Blinding hits of sunlight glimmered across Puget Sound through the floor-to-ceiling windows. Liam McDare, the tall, lanky IT tech with an easy smile, unplugged the projector from his laptop and nodded as he passed.

"Agent James, a minute," SSA Peters said from behind.

Pivoting, Nicholas let the team maneuver past him as he faced the supervisory agent. "Sir?"

"Dr. Flood specifically requested for you to work this case after your work together three years ago, but I know how close you were to Cole Presley before you discovered who he really was." SSA Peters stalked toward him, and Nicholas's defenses automatically bristled. "No one would blame you if you recused yourself from this case. It isn't every day we find out the people we trust aren't who they seem. The team is here for you. However you need."

His mind instantly snapped back to the moment he'd cuffed the man who'd taught him how to play catch, how to drive, who'd been the role model he'd needed in his life when his father hadn't been around. His next-door neighbor had turned out to be the X Marks the Spot Killer, the very same killer who'd inspired him to join the BAU. SSA Peters was right. He'd never be able to trust the mask people presented to the world, including the pretty face that'd been the key to putting Cole Presley behind bars. "It won't be a problem."

THE KING COUNTY Medical Examiner's Office had already taken possession of her sister's remains at her request, but Dr. Aubrey Flood could still see the exact position the killer had left Kara in. Low voices carried through the white noise of cars passing, the weight of Seattle PD's attention on her crushing what little oxygen she'd managed to hang on to since this morning from her lungs.

She stared at the bench where she'd found Kara this morning, knowing exactly where the map that'd been taped to her door would lead. She didn't know why she was here, didn't know what she'd intended to accomplish by coming back. Her sister had been strangled, carved up with a deep laceration in the shape of an *X* in her right cheek and left for her to find. A knot of familiarity twisted tight in her stomach. Dr. Archer Caldwell, her counterpart for the county, would've already done the preliminary examination by now with such a high-profile case, but Aubrey needed to be here. There were too many similarities between her sister's death and the first serial case she'd handled three years ago. She needed to find answers.

Wiping her damp palms down her slacks, she maneuvered through the crowd of onlookers and neighbors being kept behind the crime scene tape and flashed her credentials to the officer assigned perimeter security. "Excuse me, I'm Dr. Aubrey Flood with the Seattle Medical Examiner's Office. I was told Special Agent Nicholas James from the Behavioral Analysis Unit would be on scene."

Nicholas James, the serial expert who'd caught Seattle's most notorious killer on his first assignment for the BAU. She hadn't interacted with him more than a few times when he'd been present for the autopsies of the X Marks the Spot Killer's victims, but he'd made one hell of an impression. If anyone could give her answers about the details of Kara's case, it would be him.

"The FBI just arrived, ma'am." He lifted the crime scene tape for her to pass, and she ducked underneath without hesitation. Pointing behind him, he set the perimeter back into place. "Agents James and Striker are setting up the command center across the street. The King County ME already claimed the body, though. They must've sent you by accident."

Not by accident. Aubrey's office wouldn't take responsibility for this case due to the conflict of interest, but she wasn't going to sit this one out, either. Kara had been disposed of for Aubrey to find. Like so many others before her. She nodded. "Thank you."

The command center was nothing more than a generic shade canopy with two folding tables, a few chairs and boxes of equipment the forensics team relied on to collect their evidence. Only there wouldn't be any. No DNA. No particulates they'd be able to identify on or around the bench. Nothing. If her sister's death had anything to do with the X Marks the Spot Killer, the attacker would've been too careful for that. Her heart jerked in her chest as she walked toward the tent. She forced herself to keep her attention forward, not on the spot where she'd found Kara this morning.

Sea-salted air grazed against her face and neck as she caught sight of the federal agent she hadn't been able to forget. Nicholas James. Gull calls pierced through the hard beat of her pulse behind her ears. Sweat that had nothing to do with the rising temperatures of July in the Pacific Northwest beaded along her collarbone and slid beneath her shirt. Green-blue eyes—the same color as Puget Sound behind her—locked on her as though he'd sensed her approach, and a buzzing filled her head. His mouth parted, highlighting the thick, dirty-blond beard growth along his jaw and upper lip. Styled, equally low-lit hair protested the breeze coming off the water as he maneuvered around the table under the canopy. A perfectly sculpted nose with a dent at the bridge—presumably from a childhood injury—divided symmetrical features and deep laugh lines she'd never had the pleasure of seeing firsthand, but she imagined smiles were few and far between in his line of work. Just as they were in hers.

Aubrey extended her hand. "Special Agent James, you might not remember me, but I'm—"

"Dr. Flood." He took her hand, rough calluses tugging the oversensitized skin of her palms. His voice, smooth as one-hundred-year-old whiskey, slid through her and battled to calm the jagged edges of anxiety and grief tearing through her. "How could I forget? If it wasn't for you, Cole Presley would still be out there."

Her neck and face heated. He remembered her from their short interactions during the X Marks the Spot case, even with the added impersonal environment of her morgue in the basement of Harborview Medical downtown. She ducked her head to cut off eye contact long enough to get her head on straight and released his hand. This wasn't a social visit. This was a death scene, and it was taking every ounce of her being not to break down in the middle of it or in front of him. Swallowing the thickness in her mouth, she cleared her throat. "I gave you the specifics about the lacerations in the victims' cheeks and the blend of steel. You're the one who recognized the blade the killer used."

Warmth seeped from her hand as Nicholas pulled back. "Dr. Flood—"

"Aubrey." She folded her arms across her chest as if one simple action could deflect what he was about to say to her. "You can call me Aubrey, and I know I'm not supposed to be here. I just…" Her gaze wandered to that spot, the bench where she'd found Kara staring out across the street as though her sister had been sitting there waiting for her to arrive. Her clothes had been pristine, probably the same outfit she'd worn to teach her kindergarten class yesterday. Not a single wrinkle or an askew fold. Her face had been flawlessly made up apart from the deep laceration in her cheek. The lack of blood in the wound indicated she'd already been dead when the killer had taken the blade—or whatever he'd used—to her sister's beautiful face.

Aubrey covered her mouth with one hand to hide the fact her lips trembled under the visual. She sniffed to gain her composure and refocused on the agent in front of her. The man who was going to find her sister's killer. She blinked to clear her head, but there was no amount of emotional detachment that would erase the images behind her eyes. Standing tall, she tried to keep the professionalism she used with decedents' family members after completing the autopsies assigned in her voice when all she wanted to do was fall apart. "Have you found her dog?"

"The victim owned a dog?" Nicholas hiked his suit jacket behind his hips and leveraged both hands at his belt. A shoulder holster traced the long, lean muscle of his torso and highlighted the strength under the clean white button-down shirt and tie.

"Yes." Aubrey nodded, for something to do other than sob in the middle of a crime scene. "Kara walked her white shepherd every night at 10:00 p.m. Dr. Caldwell— the King County ME—placed time of death around then. That's probably what my sister was doing before she was attacked."

"We didn't find any evidence of a dog, but we're waiting to hear from the owner of the victim's…your sister's building to gain access to her apartment." A flash of regret colored his expression. "Is it possible she left her apartment on her own last night?"

"It's possible, but that wouldn't explain why Kara was out so late." She struggled to come up with another reason her sister would've been out. "She wrestled with five-and six-year-olds all day at school, and part of her winding-down routine included walking Koko. She said it helped her sleep better."

"When was the last time you talked with your sister?" Agent James asked.

"We talk every night before she goes to bed, around 10:30 p.m. We never miss a call unless something comes up, but we always let each other know in advance so we don't assume the worst. Our parents—" She closed her eyes as a wave of dizziness threatened to rip the world straight out from under her. "*My* parents are retired, and unless we force them, they're not interested in leaving the house much anymore. We take turns looking in on them. We bring them groceries, take them for walks around the neighborhood, keep them company, and we update each other on any changes or problems we had during the day."

Her blood pressure spiked. Seattle PD had done their due diligence and reached out to Kara's next of kin, her parents, after Aubrey had discovered the body and called police, and she hadn't been there with them. The public relations liaison from the BAU—Caitlyn something— had reassured her mother and father that the investigation was moving in the right direction, but Aubrey should've been there. Her eyes burned. This wasn't another homicide that she'd be able to compartmentalize at the end of the day. This was Kara, and she didn't know how to process the fact someone she loved—someone she'd been responsible for—would be laid out on a cold examination table and dissected for evidence.

"That's when you knew something was wrong. When she didn't pick up the phone?" That brilliant gaze assessed her every move, every change in her expression, and she suddenly felt as though Nicholas James was the only person keeping her anchored to the earth.

"Yes," she said. "She didn't answer when I called, and I kept trying to get through to her, but there was no answer. I was getting ready to go by her apartment when I found the note taped to my door."

"Do you recall hearing anything odd outside your apartment last night between 10:00 p.m. and 11:00 p.m.? See anything unusual?" The intensity in his body language slid down to his hands as he reached into his jacket pocket for a notepad and pen.

"No. Nothing like that." He had to ask. He had to go over the details multiple times to ensure investigators wouldn't miss anything. She'd told all this to Seattle PD, but as the lead investigator on Kara's case, she understood he had to hear it for himself. "Agent James, I worked the X Marks the Spot Killer case, too. I'm familiar with the way Cole Presley killed his victims and left maps for their families to follow the clues to the bodies, and Kara was…"

She cleared her throat to regain some sense of control. "You don't need to wait for the building's owner to give you permission to enter Kara's apartment. I have a key." She pressed a hand against her neck, rolling her lips between her teeth, and bit down. Unpocketing her key ring from her slacks, Aubrey held it out for him. She couldn't say it, didn't want to believe, but the proof had been there on her sister's body. The truth surfaced as she studied him. "I gave you the evidence you needed to make the arrest three years ago. I think Kara might've been targeted because of me."

*Chapter Two*

Nicholas turned the key Dr. Flood—Aubrey—had given him and pushed inside her sister's apartment. A folding door stood partially open immediately to his right, another door leading into the space's only bathroom and laundry combination to his left. Sunlight crawled through the ceiling-to-floor window down a long hallway from the main living space. It seemed the bedroom had been sectioned off from the rest of the studio, and he moved inside to get a sense of the space.

Clean. Uncluttered. Warm and airy. He could almost imagine the woman who'd been found strangled on a street bench this morning outside this same building coming home after a long day of being at war with kindergartners to escape. Little noise came through the single window straight ahead, giving the apartment an isolated feel. His shoes echoed off the laminate flooring running lengthwise toward the back of the apartment. No television.

Kara Flood had been a woman dedicated to education, to shaping young minds for the future. He scanned the bookcases along the opposite wall of the kitchen. Tingling in the tips of his fingers urged him to feel the countless spines as he passed, but while the victim hadn't been killed in her apartment, anything here could be used as evidence during the investigation. He stopped in the middle of the floor, a sliding door cutting off access to the bedroom to his right. One couch, a coffee table. No room for entertaining or company. Kara hadn't been a host or someone who'd gone out of their way to connect with others socially.

This was a haven, everything in its proper order and place with soft, neutral tones. Turning toward the front door, he faced Agent Madeline Striker and the BAU's intern, David Dyson. Serial cases had a way of taking years off an agent's life, but Nicholas had found Dyson smart enough, focused enough and determined enough over the past few months to warrant including him in the investigation.

Both waited patiently for him to make his assessment, but it wasn't his team or Aubrey Flood he imagined walking down the hallway. Kara Flood's translucent outline—his interpretation of her—didn't look his way as she walked past him. He followed her every move as she glided through the space and into the kitchen. Setting her purse on the left end of the kitchen counter, she smiled as she greeted the white shepherd Aubrey had described. Retreating here from reality every day once she was finished teaching class, the victim would've been relaxed. At home. Happy.

"You want to work serial cases for the unit, Dyson? Tell me what you see." Nicholas spotted a photograph— of the victim and the missing canine in a grassy area, a park—and envisioned the sound of the dog's nails scratching on the laminate, his tail out of control in greeting. The dog's kennel was clean, filled with drinking water and a handful of dry dog food.

"Yeah, okay." At only twenty-four, David Dyson had thrived at the top of his class, graduating with his doctorate in psychology long before his peers. As the youngest prospect for the BAU, the intern had proven himself a valuable asset and eager to learn anything he could from Nicholas in the six months he'd been assigned to the unit. Chestnut skin lightened in the rays of sunlight coming through the windows as Dyson scanned the victim's personal space, took in the layout, how Kara Flood had organized her belongings. "No dirty dishes in the sink, bed made, laundry folded and put away. From a cursory search, I'd peg Kara Flood as routine, someone who would feel off throughout the day if things weren't done in a specific order by a certain time. According to Dr. Flood, the victim walked the dog every night at ten as part of her evening routine, which raises the question of where is the dog now?"

"Very good." Nicholas turned back to the space.

"I'm sorry, but how does any of this determine who killed Kara?" Aubrey asked.

"Agent James is a psychological profiler." The weight of Madeline Striker's attention weighed between his shoulder blades, but he didn't have the concentration to confirm. "The best way for him and Dyson to get a sense of a killer is to find out what it was about the victims that attracted them."

Nicholas's heart beat hard behind his rib cage. There was something here he was missing. Something Kara Flood wouldn't have told her sister about. Something that might've gotten her killed, but he wasn't seeing it. Not yet. "Did Kara spend time with friends? A boyfriend? Anyone she might not have wanted you or your parents to know about?"

"What? No. She would've told me if she was seeing anyone. We didn't keep secrets from each other." Aubrey wrung her hands together, most likely battling a hint of shame she'd let his team inside her sister's home. But if they were going to find the person who'd killed Kara Flood, they needed to know everything about the victim. "As for friends, she has the occasional meetup for coffee, but for the most part, Kara was an introvert. She taught school, then she came home and read."

The victim's belongings had been recovered with her body. Jewelry, purse—untouched as far as the first responders had been able to tell. Whoever attacked Kara Flood hadn't carved an *X* into her cheek out of anger or hatred. They hadn't been motivated by financial gain. Her death had been methodical, as though killing her had been the first logical step as part of a larger plan.

"Your sister made a kindergarten teacher's salary, but she lived in one of the most expensive neighborhoods in the city." Nicholas raised his gaze to Aubrey's, facing her. "From what I understand, medical examiners earn quite a living. Were you assisting her financially so she could be closer to the school, or perhaps your parents helped pay her rent?"

"I… I wasn't helping her." Her gaze bounced between Nicholas, Dyson and Striker. Aubrey's bottom lip peeled from the top, the rise and fall of her shoulders slowing. She lowered both hands to her sides. "I don't know how she could afford to live here. When I asked, she'd laugh and change the subject."

"Is it possible she was seeing someone more well-off than she was or working a second job to supplement her income?" Striker asked. "Maybe she borrowed money from someone other than a bank?"

Color drained from the medical examiner's face as though she hadn't considered the possibility Kara could keep secrets from her. Seemed Aubrey and her sister weren't as close as the doc had believed. "No. Like I said, we talked every afternoon after she came home from work, even if I was at the hospital. No exceptions. She would've told me if she was in trouble. She would've known she could ask me for help."

"Dr. Flood, your sister was murdered sometime between 10:00 p.m. and 11:00 p.m. last night by a man, presumably in his late thirties, early forties, Caucasian, with extreme control, a hell of a lot of patience and an obsession with past serial cases." His gut twisted as she blanched, and Nicholas wished like hell there was a way to soften that blow. He closed the distance between them, his footsteps heavy as she straightened to confront his approach head-on. "This wasn't a random attack. Something about Kara appealed to her killer, and I have reason to believe she isn't the only one he has his sights set on."

"The way he replicated the X Marks the Spot Killer's MO suggests the killer has intimate knowledge of the case and possibly something to prove to Cole Presley," Dyson said.

The kid was right. "You worked that case, Aubrey. You were able to fill in the blanks when we had no other evidence or leads to follow. Without you, we would still be looking for him. What better way to get your attention than by targeting someone you care about?"

One breath. Two.

Aubrey shifted her weight between both feet then folded her arms across her chest. A defense tactic that had little power to ward off the truth. They weren't looking for a one-off killer here. She had to know that. She had to see the similarities between her sister's death and the X Marks the Spot case. "You both think whoever killed my sister is punishing me because I was able to identify Cole Presley. A family member for a family member."

"You told Agent James you believed that's why Kara was killed. We're here to find out if that's the case." Striker surveyed the apartment for herself, taking in every detail. "Dr. Flood, I specialize in missing persons cases, but some of the same profile points apply during a homicide investigation. Did Kara mention anything suspicious over the past few days? Someone who was paying more attention to her than usual? Was she visiting places she didn't normally go or receiving any threats?"

"She didn't mention anything like that." Aubrey's face smoothed, and Nicholas read the change in her demeanor for what it was. Denial. "But she told me Koko started barking in the middle of the night last week."

His instincts shot into awareness. "That's unusual?"

"Kara hired a professional trainer a few years ago because Koko was barking at anyone he didn't know. It took him a full week to get used to seeing me when Kara went out of town the first year she had him." Aubrey cast her honey-warm gaze to the floor, almost seeming to curl in on herself, and Nicholas drowned the urge to reach out. Emotions couldn't get involved in a case like this. Not if they were going to find the bastard who'd murdered an innocent woman last night. "She said he hadn't freaked out like that for months, like he was scared out of his mind. When she got out of bed to see what was bothering him, she found him trying to escape his kennel. He was barking at the door. She thought maybe he'd heard something in the hallway."

"Kidnappers and killers like to stalk their prey, learn

their habits and routines. They like to collect trophies, too." Striker leveled her attention on him, and an understanding passed between them. "I'll call in a forensic unit to run through the scene. Until then, you should search the apartment to see if anything might be missing." She headed into the hallway, careful not to touch the doorknob on her way out, with Dyson on her heels.

"Seattle PD hasn't reported any sightings of Kara's dog hanging around the scene. Officers are still knocking on doors to see if somebody saw something last night, but there's a chance he hasn't gone far. Is there anywhere you can think of Koko might go if he felt threatened? A neighbor he might've warmed up to over the past few months?" It was a long shot, but one they couldn't ignore.

"You want to see if he might have any evidence of the attack on him." She swiped her hand beneath her nose then pushed thick, dark brown hair out of her face. Another defense tactic meant to distract herself from the brutal images the doc would never be able to forget, he was sure. She extracted her phone. "Yeah, there's someone in the building who walks him when Kara's working. They have my phone number in case they can't reach Kara. I'll send you the information."

He gave her his number, and his phone pinged a moment later.

"Whoever did this—whoever killed Kara last night—it's a copycat, right?" Desperation combined with exhaustion in her expression, and his gut clenched. "Tell me we put the right man behind bars when you arrested Cole Presley, that I didn't make a mistake."

Heat burned down the length of his spine. The medical examiner was one of the most intelligent, compassionate, emotionally aware people he'd ever met, and he'd hate the day when her drive to find justice for the deceased ebbed. "You didn't make a mistake, Aubrey. I did."

"WHAT IN THE sweet potato fries do you mean?" This case had just started. How had Agent James already made a mistake? Aubrey battled against the pressure seemingly closing in from every wall of her sister's apartment and tried to take a full breath.

She shouldn't have come up here. She should've handed off the key to Kara's apartment and stayed downstairs like the good witness she was supposed to be. But some internal drive she didn't understand had urged her to insert herself in the case, to find out who'd done this to her family. Every book on those shelves stared out at her as though she were an impostor, someone who didn't belong here. She'd always watched out for Kara. Now it seemed as though her sister's apartment was accusing her of not being there when she'd needed Aubrey the most. Why Kara? If the killer was out to punish Aubrey for her role in the X Marks the Spot Killer case, why had he gone after Kara?

"What'd you say?" Confusion deepened the lines between the agent's dark blond eyebrows.

"What do you mean, you made a mistake?" Stress had an array of physical, emotional and mental effects on the body, but odd cartoon sayings had always had the ability to alleviate her stress levels. She shook her head and folded her arms across her chest. But no matter how many different sayings ran through her head right then, none of them would help soothe the grief bubbling under her skin. Muscle tension strained the joints at her elbows and shoulders. She'd found her sister dead this morning, had been within fifty feet of the killer when he'd taped the map to her door. "The King County Medical Examiner's Office hasn't even performed my sister's autopsy. There haven't been any chances for you to make a mistake on this case."

The muscles in his jaw ticked under the pressure of his back teeth. He stared at her as though trying to read her mind—profile her—but she'd developed an equal detachment from the deceased as he had with the living over the years. Nicholas James had been the case lead when they'd worked together three years ago. Despite his secretive, isolated demeanor, there was a vulnerability in his eyes, a need to prove himself. He'd spent his life studying the most minute psychological details that made up a person where she'd spent her career uncovering what made a person physically. They'd chosen different career paths, but in the end, they weren't so different. They both wanted to find whoever had strangled Kara.

"I knew Cole Presley personally."

Aubrey stepped back. She couldn't think, couldn't breathe. "I... I don't understand."

"My father left our family when I was five. Cole Presley was there for us when we needed him. He helped me with my homework after school. He babysat me and my sister when my mom needed to go back to school. He taught me how to throw a damn baseball and coached my Little League team." Disbelief wove through each word, his voice getting heavier and heavier. "I had no idea who he really was. Not until you described the kind of blade that'd been used on the X Marks the Spot victims. You'd found slivers of western hemlock in one of the women's wounds. What you'd described—Damascus steel with a nick about a quarter inch down the blade and an intricate design pressed into the metal—I could see it right in front of me. Because I'd seen that knife before. He used it to carve figurines from chunks of wood whenever we'd go camping together. I'd held it over a dozen times in my own hands without knowing how much blood had collected in the handle over the years."

Thirty years, to be exact. Thirty victims, every year on the same day.

Air caught in her throat. She wasn't sure what to say, what to do. Swiping her tongue over her increasingly dry lips, Aubrey countered her retreat, her feet heavier than when she'd watched him search Kara's apartment. Her pulse rocketed into her throat. A hint of soap and salt dived into her lungs. "When you said you made a mistake, you mean because you didn't see him for what he really was before. You feel personally responsible for what happened to all those women."

"Aren't I?" he asked. "The X Marks the Spot case was what inspired me to join the FBI, you know. I'd see the yearly newspaper article detailing how he'd strangled and mutilated another woman, how police were baffled he kept getting away with it."

She flinched at the manner in which he addressed the killer's MO—so insensitively—and severed eye contact as fast as she could.

"I'd tell myself I'd be the one to catch him someday. Come to find out, the killer was less than thirty feet from my own family." A humorless laugh burst from his mouth. "Guess I got my wish in the end. Maybe if I'd seen him for what he really was, so many people wouldn't have died. But I…"

"You trusted him." The same unsteady guilt in his voice clawed up her throat. She reached out, gripping his arm in a comforting squeeze despite the fact he'd bowled over the way her sister had died without a hint of regret. Then again, she'd always put others' needs first without acknowledging her own. Instant heat shot up through her hand, and she fought to chase back the weight crushing her from inside. "You gave me credit for bringing the X Marks the Spot Killer down, but the truth is, if it wasn't for you, Cole Presley would still be out there, hurting women. You recognized the blade he used to cut *X*s into his victims' cheeks. That's why I requested you to work my sister's case. You're one of the most focused, insightful and realistic investigators I've ever worked with, and I need you to find out who did this to her."

"I'll find your sister's killer, Aubrey. I give you my word." Sincerity laced his voice, and a shiver chased down her spine. "But what do sweet potato fries have to do with anything?"

Heat climbed up her neck, and she withdrew her hand. She pressed her palm against her throat in an attempt to stop the embarrassment from taking over her face, but it was a battle she'd never won in the past. "I tend to repeat odd Southern sayings, mostly food or animal related, from a popular children's cartoon character when I'm under stress."

"A children's cartoon character?" Agent James stepped back, turning his focus to the wall of bookshelves. Historical romances, nonfiction educational resources, science fiction. Her sister never had been one to conform to the traditional sense of a kindergarten teacher. "I wasn't aware you had kids."

Was that shock in his expression? Satisfaction exploded from behind her sternum. Considering he'd had more than enough time to profile her from head to toe and inside out, she hadn't been sure it was possible to surprise him, and she stood a little taller. "I don't, but considering what I do for a living, I'd rather not indulge in crime dramas, hospital comedies or true crime documentaries. I'm sure it's the same for you with cop shows and profiling entertainment."

"You're right." A hint of a smile tugged at the corner of his mouth.

Her fingers tingled as she studied Kara's apartment a second time, and a hollowness set up residence in her chest. She curled her keys into her palm and forced the edge of steel deeper. The oversensitive skin along the back of her neck heated. Agent James—Nicholas—had promised to find her sister's killer, but how many more family members would have to stand in the middle of their loved one's home to try to give the BAU a lead to follow? How many more victims would have to cross Dr. Caldwell's slab before this new evolution of killer was found? No. She wasn't going to let that happen. "It doesn't seem real. Kara not being here." Denial burned through her. She cleared her throat in an effort to bring herself back to the present and away from the growing familiarity between them. "I haven't noticed anything missing so far. Everything looks just like it did the last time I visited. Do you need to look at anything else while you're here?"

"No, I think we've got everything we need." He craned his chin over his shoulder, giving her a glimpse of the thick tendons running the length of his neck, as he took in one last study of the space.

"Good." Straightening, she gave in to the spread of confidence and headed toward the door. "Then we should check with Kara's dog walker to see if Koko has shown up."

His footsteps echoed off the laminate a split second before a strong hand threaded through the space between her rib cage and arm and twisted her into a solid wall of muscle. The color of his eyes deepened—physically impossible but evident in the intensity in which he stared down at her all the same. "I know it can't be easy for you to be here, Aubrey, especially given what you've already been through today, but I need you to let the BAU do their jobs without getting involved."

"I've spent my entire life bowing down to the needs of others, Agent James. I've dedicated my entire life to giving family members answers they needed as to how their loved ones passed. I've taken care of my parents physically and financially for years, even when I had nothing left to give. I've made the Seattle police, the FBI and, yes, even your unit my priority since I took over as chief medical examiner and have lost friendships and relationships in the process, but today, your needs don't concern me."

She tugged her arm from his grasp. Her elbow burned from the friction emanating from his touch, and she notched her chin higher, more defiant than she'd ever felt before. Her scalp tightened as she pressed her hand against his chest for room to breathe. Running her thumb over the notches in her sister's key, Aubrey stepped back. The rush of her pulse behind her ears died as logic returned. "Dr. Caldwell is a fine physician, but he's not me. He doesn't have serial experience, and you won't find another ME within four hundred miles who does. You want to find out who did this to my sister and keep more women from becoming victims? You're not going to be able to do that without me."

Nicholas steadied his gaze on hers. She could practically see the wheels spinning in his head as he considered the chances he had without her. His strong exhale deflated his shoulders as he stalked past her toward the door. "Then we're going to need some coffee."

# Chapter Three

Talking with the victim's dog walker had ended in a dead end. The neighbor hadn't seen the white shepherd or heard anything unusual leading up to Kara Flood's death. Uniformed officers had cleared the rest of the building. No sign of the dog or statements anyone had seen the victim last night.

"We've got a handful of possible evidence walking around the city, and no one saw a damn thing." Nicholas shoved his notepad into his back pocket harder than necessary, but he had enough self-awareness and experience to know the missing dog was only a part of the equation that could lead them to the killer.

Apart from the unit discovering his childhood connection to the X Marks the Spot Killer during the investigation and being forced to see the bureau shrink after the arrest, he'd never told anyone about Cole Presley. Yet he'd willingly offered the information to Dr. Aubrey Flood. He hadn't considered himself manipulatable. In his line of work, that kind of influence could get him or any one of his teammates killed, but apparently, brilliant honey-warm eyes, an IQ notches beyond his and a mouth to die for was all he'd needed to spill his guts.

Both Nicholas and Aubrey pushed through the glass

lobby doors of the apartment building and stepped into a thick coating of humidity. "Can you think of anywhere else the dog might go?"

Sorrow smoothed Aubrey's features as her attention flickered toward the bench where she'd found her sister's body this morning. She cleared her throat as though to bring herself back into the moment, but there was only so much she could do to distract herself before the pain caught up. As much as she'd claimed she needed to find Kara Flood's killer upstairs, there would always be a part of her battling to deny her younger sister had been murdered in the first place. That was how the human brain worked. It could only take so much trauma and confrontation before it would snap.

Aubrey recentered her anguished expression on him, and an internal sucker punch to the gut threatened to knock him off his feet. "He's been to my house a few times, but I wouldn't think it'd be somewhere he'd automatically go if he was in distress."

She'd lost her sister, one of the most important people in her world. While Nicholas couldn't do anything to undo that kind of violence, he'd sure as hell find the son of a bitch to keep her from looking at him like that ever again. "Better safe than sorry." He unclipped the radio from his belt and pinched the push-to-talk button between his thumb and index finger. "Striker, come in."

The radio crackled. "Go ahead."

"CSU is wrapping up down here at the scene, and no one has seen the dog. Where is my other team?" He surveyed the crowd of onlookers beyond the perimeter of the tape, memorizing their faces. Killers had a habit of returning to the scenes of their crimes, especially budding serials who may have just stepped into the violent crimes arena. The serials he'd investigated liked to see the damage caused, revel in the family's grief, relive the events that led to the life draining from their victim's eyes at their hand. But worse, some used the opportunity of being able to blend into a crowd to choose a new victim. Revisiting the scene kept them going just as solving the case kept Nicholas going. Any one of these onlookers could be the killer they were looking for.

"The second unit is twenty minutes out," Striker said. "You want me to wait for them?"

A flash registered from beyond the tape and pulled his attention to a single male, around six feet with dull red hair, a thick beard turning lighter around his temples. The man lowered a camera slowly, steady gaze aware Nicholas had spotted him.

"James, you copy?" Striker asked.

Aubrey followed his gaze toward the man who'd taken the photo.

He lifted the radio back to his mouth. "Dyson can wait for them. I need you and West to help Seattle PD wrap up the scene and oversee getting the evidence they've collected so far to the lab," he said. "I'm going to accompany Dr. Flood to her residence to search there in case Fido is waiting for her to come home and grab a few overnight items before relocating her to the safe house."

"His name is Koko, Agent James," Aubrey said. "Not Fido."

He released the push-to-talk button. Studying the man beyond the perimeter tape, he brushed off the awareness of the medical examiner's gaze, determined to burn a hole through his temple. An immediate detachment from the vulnerability she'd resurrected in him took control.

"Confirmed," Striker said. "I'm still waiting to hear

back from the warden at Washington State Corrections on Presley's location. I'll keep you apprised of any developments. Striker, out."

"You're taking me to a safe house." Aubrey shook her head. Anger intertwined with the fire burning in her eyes. Medium-length brown hair lifted off her shoulders and caught on her eyelashes. Pointing a finger into his chest, she stepped into him, her voice low. "You had no intention of letting me work this case with you, did you? As long as I'm in a safe house with some other agent from your unit, you'll be free to investigate my sister's case on your own, but I can promise you right now, that's not how this is going to work."

He met her intimidation technique with one of his own, closing the distance between them until her exhales brushed against his neck. "The killer knows who you are, Dr. Flood. He knows where you live, where you work, how many hours you spend in the hospital, whom you care about, your running route and your favorite places to eat. He knew exactly when you'd be home to leave that map on your door, and he knows you were the medical examiner assigned to the X Marks the Spot case three years ago. He's done his research, just as I've done mine, and if you have any chance of surviving what comes next, it will be because of me." Nicholas clipped the radio to his belt and extended an arm toward the perimeter tape and his SUV on the other side. "The way I see it, you have two choices. Agree to federal protection and help me find the man who killed your sister, or continue denying you're in danger and take your chances alone."

She didn't move, didn't even seem to breathe, and admiration knotted in his gut. Most suspects hadn't been able to handle the intensity he radiated during interrogations, and Dr. Flood—Aubrey—had given every single one of them a run for their money by facing off with him. She peeled away and headed straight from the scene toward his vehicle.

A smile tugged at the corners of his mouth as he followed her. Damn, she was something else. Warmhearted and friendly dosed with a strong helping of defiance and drive. Hell of a combination. Nicholas hauled the crime scene tape over his head and maneuvered through the civilians who'd parted to let her pass.

A strong grip latched on to his arm, and it took everything inside him not to reach for his weapon. He spun to face the man who'd grabbed him and wrenched away from the six-foot, redheaded photographer he'd noted earlier. Nervousness radiated from the man in waves, his hands shaking around his camera as he spoke. "You're Agent James, right? With the FBI's Behavioral Analysis Unit? You must be here to investigate a violent homicide if they called your unit in. I remember you from the X Marks the Spot Killer case."

"You're familiar with that case?" Onlookers and civilians shifted around him, hoping to hear insight as to what'd happened in their very own neighborhood. "What's with the camera?"

"Oh, I'm training to be a crime scene photographer for the Seattle Police Department. Simon Curry." He lifted the camera slightly, an old-looking device that'd seen better days, before extending his hand. Curry withdrew as Nicholas merely stared down at the photographer's hand. "And I'm not just familiar with the X Killer's case, I'm familiar with you, too. I've been studying your career since you started with the BAU, Agent James. The work you've done here in Seattle with serials is changing the way the FBI investigates violent crime." Disbelief widened the man's small eyes, and he stumbled back a step. "If you're here, that must mean you believe this is a serial case."

Gasps echoed around him, followed by a rush of whispered murmurs and questions. This wasn't his area. Caitlyn Yang, the public relations liaison between Seattle PD and the BAU, handled what information to reveal to the public and the timeline when that information would be made public. He raised his voice over the mass but doubted anything he had to say would ease the panic buzzing around him.

"All right. We are at the beginning of this investigation. The FBI is not ready to conclude that the death that occurred in front of this building this morning is the result of a serial working in the area." He caught sight of Aubrey Flood through the crowd, her light gaze steady on his, and a calm washed over him. "Once we have more information, so will you, and that's all I'm willing to say on the matter."

He wound his way through a barrage of questions and shouts and headed across the street toward his SUV. Unlocking the door remotely, he rounded the front of the vehicle and wrenched open Aubrey's door for her. Once inside, he collapsed into his own seat behind the wheel. He twisted the key in the ignition, keeping her in his peripheral vision as he pulled away from the curb. "You okay?"

"I think they were more interested in you than they were me." Aubrey slid her palms down her thighs, staring out the passenger-side window. "I left my car parked in Kara's lot. It's probably going to get towed, since I don't have one of those HOA stickers. She offered to get me one, but…"

"It felt like lying." Her honest nature wouldn't have let her take advantage of her sister's offer. "I'll have Agent West ensure it's secure and drive it back to your apartment as soon as he, Dyson and Agent Striker are finished at the scene. The farther you're away from your residence and vehicle, the better until we find out why Kara was targeted." An uneasy sensation surged through him, and he raised his gaze to the rearview mirror. A single figure stood in the center of the street as the mob of civilians dispersed along the scene's perimeter tape. Simon Curry lifted his camera toward his face, and a flash filled the mirror.

NOTHING AND EVERYTHING had changed since she'd found that map taped to her apartment door this morning. Her building looked exactly the same. Contrasting shades of gray highlighted six floors of lofts a mere two blocks from the heart of the city. But where she'd woken with enthusiasm and confidence for the day, hollowness had taken control. Kara was dead, and there hadn't been anything she'd been able to do about it.

The Space Needle demanded attention out Aubrey's passenger window as Nicholas pulled into her underground garage. She handed the agent her fob to the gate and sat back in her seat as the vehicle crawled forward into darkness. Kara hadn't just died. Her younger sister had become a homicide victim, something Aubrey dealt with day in and day out as the city's chief medical examiner, but this… This was different. This was personal. "The doorman should be able to tell us whether or not Koko came here when we get to the lobby."

"The building has a doorman?" Nicholas's eyes narrowed as he pulled the SUV into her assigned parking spot for her loft. His tone had leveled again. Nothing like the intensity he'd used in Kara's apartment. More inquisitive. He shoved the vehicle into Park. "Makes me wonder how the killer managed to get to your apartment."

The blood drained from her face and rushed directly to her chest, a flight-or-flight response automated by the body when faced with danger and fear. She hadn't thought of that. She wasn't an investigator in the way Nicholas was. She had experience with a serial killer's work through a single case, but it'd been years since she'd had to deal with emergency situations like this. Aubrey set her hand against the passenger-side door. He was right. She'd been so focused on what'd happened to Kara, her brain hadn't caught on to the fact the killer had walked straight into this building and directly to her door. He'd known where she lived, when she would be home. How? How had he known where to find her?

"You're looking a little pale there, Doc," Nicholas said.

"I'm dizzier than a donkey trying to dance." She focused on the way he called her "Doc," on the slight inflection in his voice when he spoke to her compared to his team or even those people at the perimeter of the scene. Her heart picked up the pace as he took a brick from the invisible professional barrier between them. *Doc.* No one had given her a nickname before. "I just need a minute."

"I've got to start writing down the stuff you say for future reference." Nicholas shouldered out of the vehicle. Faster than she thought possible, her door disappeared out from beneath her hand, and he was reaching over her for the seat belt. A combination of salt and man filled her lungs, and she breathed in as much as she could to hold on to his scent a bit longer. Strong enough to overpower the odor of decomposing bodies and formaldehyde. Soothing. Reassuring. "Come on. I've got you."

The seat belt released as he compressed the latch, and then his hands were on her. Strong, calloused—as though he reveled in manual labor in addition to catching psychopaths—comforting. She wound the straps of her purse around her hand. Butterflies twisted her stomach as Nicholas helped her from the SUV and closed the door behind her. Hand leveraged on the vehicle's frame above her head, he leaned into her while giving her the opportunity to slide out of his reach. "Most people never see a body in their lifetime. Sometimes it takes a while for the brain to process that kind of trauma."

"I feel like you should be aware of the fact we met during the X Marks the Spot Killer's victims' autopsies." The sarcasm earned her a smile that tightened her insides and brought the feeling back to her fingers. The world washed away into overhydrated watercolors under his focus.

"You're right. You're not most people." The curl of his mouth deepened the laugh lines etched from the middle of his nose and cut through the sharpness of his cheekbones. Thick eyebrows, matching his natural hair color, shadowed his gaze as he shifted his weight between his feet. He lowered his arm from above her head, and instantly, the spell was broken. Curling his hand into a fist, he tapped the side of the SUV as though punishing himself for letting her see the softer side of his personality. "That doesn't change the fact that the body you found this morning is someone you knew. Someone you loved. It's going to take time to work through the emotions that come with losing your sister like that, and you're going to need someone to help you through it."

She locked her back teeth against the urge to claim otherwise, to deflect her obsession with being everything for everyone but herself, to make it easier for the agent to remain comfortable and detached from her. But as easily as Nicholas James presented an intense, secretive and isolated mask to the world, he'd spoken from experience. He'd lost who she imagined to be one of the few people he'd let see the man hiding under that defensive mask. While Cole Presley—aka the X Marks the Spot Killer—hadn't been murdered as Kara had, and had in fact been the one to do the killing, Nicholas had lost that connection all the same. Aubrey broke eye contact, clearing her throat. "Coulter Loxley."

Nicholas took a step back, seemingly reminded of where they were and why. "Coulter Loxley?"

"The doorman. He would've been the one on shift last night when the killer came up to my apartment. We should talk to him, see if he remembers anything and ask if he's seen Koko." Aubrey clutched the straps of her bag tighter, the leather protesting under her grip. She checked her watch. "The only problem is he won't be on shift for another two hours."

Nicholas nodded. "In that case, I want to check your apartment to make sure there aren't any signs of a break-in and have you pack an overnight bag for a few days."

"Right." Because a killer had brought her into his sick mind game by tacking a map leading to her sister's body to her door last night. Her throat tightened as she led the way toward the elevators and hit the ascend button. Seconds ticked by, maybe a minute when neither of them moved or said a word. What else was there to say? The elevator dinged before the car doors slid open, and they both stepped in. She scanned her key card that would give the elevator permission to stop at her floor, then leaned against the handrail surrounding them from three sides. Pressure to break the silence stretching between them, to make a connection with the man so familiar with murder, spread through her. Aubrey clutched her bag in front of her, the steel of the elevator doors reflecting her vain attempt to protect herself back at her. Diverting her nervous energy to the LED panel above the doors, she silently counted off the floors as they rocketed to the top floor. The penthouse.

"Does every resident have one of those cards?" he asked.

"No. Just the ones who live on the sixth floor." She studied the card, almost as though reading his mind. The killer would've had to have had one to gain access from the garage. "But visitors can access the floor from the stairs once they're past the doorman."

Silence descended once again.

"You said the X Marks the Spot Killer case is what inspired you to join the Behavioral Analysis Unit," she said. "How old were you when you decided you wanted to hunt killers for a living?"

His muscled shoulders rose on a strong inhale. He stared straight ahead, never deviating from his own reflection in front of him. "Six."

"Most kids that age want to grow up to be cowboys and astronauts or robots." The pull on her insides increased as the elevator dared to defy gravity. "There must've been a specific moment or event that made you feel profiling serial killers was the right path for you.

Before you realized who your next-door neighbor was, I mean."

The tic of his external carotid artery just below his jaw increased. He dropped his chin a fraction of an inch and exposed her awareness of his every move. "I heard a woman scream."

A woman's scream? Regret cut through her as the implications of that single statement registered. Had he known who lived next door to him, even as young as six years old?

"I ran to the window to see what'd happened, but it was too dark. Every night afterward, for years, I'd wonder who it came from, why it occurred. I asked neighbors if they'd heard it that night. I started writing down their statements and seeing if my dog could pick up traces of blood around my house." He folded his hands in front of him. "Never found out what happened, but I knew then what I wanted to do with the rest of my life. I wanted to keep people from screaming like that ever again."

"Was it…" Aubrey licked her lips, trying to come up with another reason a woman might've been screaming in the middle of the night. "Do you believe it was one of Cole Presley's victims?"

The elevator dinged, pulling her back into reality as the car settled and the doors parted. Light fractured through massive windows and crawled across light gray hardwood flooring laid out in long strips designed to increase the visual size of the loft.

"I'll never know. I never found evidence he'd killed any of his victims in his home." Nicholas stepped off the elevator into her apartment and scanned the space like the good agent he was supposed to be. "It's unlikely the killer didn't know you'd need a key card to access this floor, which means he had to have come up the stairs to deliver the map he left on your door."

"The front door is around the corner." She motioned to her right as she stepped off the elevator and set her purse on the entryway table nearby. "The building's head of security should be able to give you any surveillance footage from last night if you ask nicely."

"I've already got Agent West working on it." Hands on his hips, he accentuated the shoulder holster and weapon under his jacket as he took in her living space. Nicholas turned toward the short hallway leading to the front door, and she followed. Unlocking the dead bolt, he compressed the door handle down and crouched to put the lock at his eye level. "It's just you here? No one else has a key? An ex-boyfriend, maybe?"

"Is that your way of asking me if I'm single, Agent James?" She kept her smile to herself, but tension crept across her back the longer he didn't answer. "No. There's no one else. I live alone."

He straightened, pointing toward the security ring on the outside of the door. "See these scratches here? Someone picked this lock recently, and I have good reason to believe it was your sister's killer."

SHE'D STOPPED BEING afraid of the monsters a long time ago.

Special Agent Madeline Striker couldn't look away from the little girl at the edge of the perimeter tape. Five or six years old, long, dark hair, brilliant, knowing eyes. The same age her sister had been the last time Madeline had seen her.

It wasn't because the monsters weren't real. The violence that'd led to the end of Kara Flood's life—and so many others during her five-year career with the Behavioral Analysis Unit—testified to that fact. They were out there, waiting for the right time to strike, working their mind games and preying on the innocent, but they couldn't control her. Not anymore.

She'd dedicated every day of her life to seeing how the pieces fit together, to connecting the dots in lost-cause abduction cases in an attempt to bring home as many victims as she could, but this case... They hadn't been prepared for this. It'd taken the entire BAU to identify and stop Cole Presley from taking another victim, but all they'd managed to do was create another monster. A copycat.

"Dr. Flood's vehicle is secure." Dashiell West slid into her peripheral vision. Dark, styled hair caught in the breeze coming off the sound. The five-o'clock shadow around his mouth and running up his jaw had grown thicker over the past few hours, highlighting the exhaustion under his eyes and in his voice. The tinkling of keys reached her ears as he tossed them her way. "You okay with following me to the ME's apartment to drop it off then giving me a lift back to the office?"

She caught the keys against her chest, forcing her gaze from the girl. To prove she could. A young woman matching the X Killer's preferences had been strangled and mutilated in front of her own apartment building eight hours ago, and no one had seen a damn thing. This wasn't an abduction case, but the clock was ticking down all the same. Copycats followed patterns, same as their role models. Whoever'd gotten to Kara Flood last night had already killed one victim. It was only a matter of time before he targeted another. "Yeah."

"Striker, you okay?" West leveled dark chocolate eyes

on her. The former hotshot from the tech development arena had only been with the unit for two years after a former colleague had set out to ruin his career, but he'd been a vital addition to the team ever since. Cybercrimes, decryption, hacking—if a BAU case involved computers, it involved Dashiell West.

Reality caught up. Madeline glanced in the direction where she'd last seen the girl, finding the section of tape where she'd been standing empty. She swept the scene, but the girl had most likely been whisked back to the safety of her home with parents who'd do anything to keep her close. Gripping her hand around the keys her partner had thrown, she shook her head as though the past would dissolve at her command. "I'm fine. Have there been any developments on the Seattle PD side?"

Faint barking broke through the ringing in her ears.

"Last I heard, their crime scene unit was taking a casting of a footprint they found in the soil around one of the trees lining the street," he said. "Could be our guy, but considering how careful the killer was to not be seen by witnesses and how there isn't much evidence to collect, the chances are low."

The barking continued. Madeline turned toward the sound. Nicholas had asked her to keep a watch for a white shepherd the victim had been walking at the time of her death, but the dog hadn't turned up in the building or in the area. No leash. No paw prints, blood or anything else that would give her an idea of where the dog might have run after the attack. Nothing. Except the barking. "Do you hear that?"

"What?" West asked.

"That barking." She headed toward the south side of the scene, and the sound intensified. Hauling the perimeter tape above her head, she moved slowly down the street, West close behind. Sweat pooled in her shirt. Summer in Seattle promised cooler temperatures considering the proximity of the Pacific but had really only delivered humidity that frizzed her hair and drenched her clothing.

The barking stopped, and Madeline froze.

Nails scratched on metal from somewhere nearby, and she spotted a white cargo van parked along the street ahead. If Kara Flood's dog had gotten back into the habit of protesting any time a stranger came near as Dr. Flood had said, it was possible the killer would want the dog out of the way before attracting attention during the attack. She nodded toward the van and unholstered her weapon. "West."

West understood, withdrawing his own sidearm, and stepped out into the street to approach from the other side of the van.

Nicholas had taught her some killers liked to revisit their crime scenes, that they enjoyed the hunt brought on by law enforcement, reveled in watching the police try to do their jobs and staying one step ahead. Madeline checked back over her shoulder, gauging how far she and West had walked from the crime scene. From the angle of the driver's seat, whoever sat behind the wheel would have the perfect vantage point of the bench where Kara Flood had been posed.

They moved as one, West on one side of the van, her on the other, until they met at the bumper. Her partner reached for the swinging door's handle, those dark eyes on her as he waited for her signal. The front seats were clear, but without windows in the cargo area, they had no way to tell what was on the other side of the doors. Madeline nodded, and West wrenched the door open.

Ear-shattering barking echoed off the inside of the cabin a split second before a white shepherd, matching Dr. Flood's description of her sister's dog, came into view. Spots of dirt stained the dog's once-pristine coat. Madeline holstered her weapon and showed Koko both hands, palms forward. "Hey, Koko. It's okay. I'm not here to hurt you." She turned toward West. "Let Nicholas know we found his missing piece of evidence and call Animal Control to take him in. Not Nicholas, the dog."

The canine whined, sitting back on its haunches, and revealed a numbered piece of paper under his paws. Something like the numbers she'd seen on the back side of photos. She pulled a set of gloves from her pocket and snapped the latex against the back of her wrist. One hand raised toward Koko, she collected the glossy paper from under the dog's foot slower than she wanted to go. No point in scaring the poor animal. He'd already been through enough.

He let the photo go, and Madeline pulled herself out of the van. Flipping the evidence over with one hand, she gasped as West brought his phone to his ear, her heart in her throat. She turned the picture toward him. "Then tell him we've got another victim out there."

# Chapter Four

The killer had broken into Aubrey's home, most likely
touched her personal effects and uncovered details she
hadn't wished to share with anyone else. Rage coiled low
in his gut as the forensic team he'd pulled in swept the
loft for fingerprints and anything that could give them
an idea of who'd gotten inside.

Floor-to-ceiling windows looked out toward surrounding redbrick buildings. Light furniture, hardly used as far
as Nicholas could tell, and pops of color in accents brightened the space. Black-and-white modern art pieces had
been paired in twos on almost every wall with a beautiful kitchen island and patio that finished off the luxury
feel. The aesthetic could've come straight out of a home
decor magazine, but it wasn't exactly reflective of the
kind of home he'd expected from the medical examiner.
Too…cold. Distant. Definitely not the haven Kara Flood
escaped to every night after work.

Crime scene techs worked their way across the loft,
including the bookcases on either side of a large television screen. In an instant, he imagined Aubrey curled up
on the L-shaped fabric sectional watching her favorite
children's show to unwind after a long day of autopsies,
facing grieving families and pathology reports. Not in

her bedroom packing a few days' worth of clothing and toiletries to hide in a safe house from a violent killer.

He scanned the titles stacked in neat color-coded rows on her bookshelves and pulled one from the pack. A romance. Flipping through the pages, he studied the pliancy of the spine. Not just a romance. A book worthy of multiple reads. A favorite. Nicholas placed it back on the shelf and continued down the line. More romance, some inspirational nonfiction. Where her sister had been firmly rooted in reality as an educator, Aubrey obviously craved escape from her day-to-day routine, and he sure as hell didn't blame her.

"There's a perfume bottle missing from my bathroom. I've given your people permission to search through whatever they need, but that looks like the only thing that might've been taken." Aubrey maneuvered into his peripheral vision with a crime scene tech delivering her back to the living room. They couldn't take any chances of altering or destroying evidence of the break-in. Not when the killer had obviously set his sights on the ME. She clutched the handle of her carry-on–size luggage. Her gaze then lowered to a book still in his hand. "Didn't peg you for a romance reader."

Perfume bottle. A possible trophy? But how had the killer gotten past the building's security measures? He set the novel back on the shelf and pushed the book between the others with one finger. "Guaranteed happily-ever-after, no matter how wrong things go? Beats reality any day. What's not to like?"

"I agree." A small smile turned up the corners of her mouth as he'd revealed yet another piece of himself without hesitation, and his insides coiled tighter. "The doorman should be coming on to shift right about now. The elevator bypasses the lobby and goes straight to the parking garage, so it's better to take the stairs."

"CSU is almost finished here. I'll make sure they lock up when they're done." He motioned her toward the front door and stepped into line behind her. His phone vibrated with an incoming call, and he pulled it from his slacks without missing a step. Dashiell West. Hitting the large green button at the bottom of the screen, he brought his phone to his ear as they left the apartment. "What's going on, West?"

"We found the dog," West said.

Nicholas slid his hand around Aubrey's arm and turned her into him. He lowered the phone between them and put the call on speakerphone. "You're sure you've got the right dog?"

"White shepherd, approximately three years old with a collar that says his name is Koko. We're double-checking the chip in his neck, but Striker and I are ninety-nine percent sure this is the victim's dog. Whoever killed Kara Flood last night had locked the animal in a cargo van less than a block from the scene. Damn cabin got to over a hundred degrees by the time we found him. If it weren't for Striker's superhero hearing, we might never have found him in time." Admiration tinted the former tech expert's voice. "The dog was dehydrated and a bit disoriented, but Animal Services is taking care of that right now. I've got Forensics collecting particulates from his fur, but it sounds like he's going to be fine."

Nicholas raised his gaze to Aubrey's in time to see pure relief slacken her expression. "Thanks, West. I'll get in touch with Forensics when they're finished. You did good."

"That's not all we recovered from the van," West said.

"After we were able to calm the dog down, we realized he'd been standing on a photo. A Polaroid."

Confusion quickly replaced the excitement buzzing in his veins. Nicholas switched the phone off speaker and raised it to his ear. He'd wanted Aubrey to know her sister's dog had been located safely from the source who'd recovered the animal, but the last thing she needed to hear were the gory details of Kara's case. "A Polaroid of what?"

"A body. A woman." Silence settled between them as dread pooled at the base of Nicholas's spine. Another victim. "We don't have an ID yet, but I'm running facial recognition as we speak. Nicholas, the woman... There's no doubting the photo was taken after she'd been killed. Whoever murdered Kara Flood last night used the X Marks the Spot Killer's MO. Strangulation, mutilation to the victim's face with a thin blade. He locked up the victim's dog in a cargo van reported stolen in the last three days and left a photo of his next victim for us to find."

A trail of bread crumbs for law enforcement to follow. Nausea churned in his gut as the next piece of the puzzle fit into place. A photo left with a victim's body, leading police to the next. Just as the Gingerbread Woman had done. He turned away from Aubrey and lowered his voice. "Are the woman's lips blue in the photo?"

"Yes, with her jacket positioned beside her," West said. "I've already sent a copy to Dr. Caldwell at the King County Medical Examiner's Office since he's taken lead on Kara Flood's autopsy. He's positive the woman in the photo died of asphyxiation within two hours of the picture being taken."

Damn it. Running his hand through his hair, he processed the details of the Gingerbread Woman case.

There hadn't been anything linking Irene Lawrence—
the woman who'd suffocated five rival colleagues for a
shot at partner within her law firm—to the X Marks the
Spot Killer. The cases weren't connected, but whoever
killed Kara Flood last night wanted him to believe they
were, that there was more than one killer they were hunting. He shook his head. No. His instincts said one killer,
two MOs. "The killer is testing previously used MOs,
trying to find the one that's right for him. He wanted us
to find Kara Flood first. He used the X Marks the Spot
Killer's MO because that's whom he looks up to the most,
probably because of how long it took law enforcement
to identify Cole Presley. He sees a thirty-year reign as
a sign of success. Now he's moving on to another MO."

"The Gingerbread Woman." West swore under his
breath. "Is there any way to tell whose MO he'll use next
or something that will help us narrow down the identity
of this victim?"

"This killer locked the dog up because he needed Koko
to ensure we recovered that photo. He's not fueled by
anger. He's not out to make these women pay. He wants
an audience like the good narcissist he is." Nicholas set
his forehead against the nearest wall and let himself slip
into the mind of the killer, pushing two separate cases
together in an attempt to find common ground. It wasn't
his soundproof office he'd turned into a dark room back
at BAU headquarters, but he'd done this exercise enough
times over the years to drop into the meditation-like frequency to separate himself from the world. There was
a risk to doing it here. If he pulled out too quickly, he'd
spend the rest of the day paying the price. Why had the
killer chosen those two MOs to kill his victims? If he
could solve that variable, he might be able to predict

which MO the killer would use next and narrow down a possible victim.

The chaotic organization of the forensics team burrowed into his head, and he mentally pulled out before he had a chance to dive deep enough. Damn it. He needed somewhere quiet. Somewhere he could control the setting. His heart thundered hard behind his ears. Different MOs meant there was no pattern for them to follow. The killer didn't have a preference in regard to the victim or a motive to want them dead. Whoever had killed Kara Flood and this possible second victim simply believed he could do his heroes' work better. "I'm going to have to call you back."

Nicholas ended the call, all too aware of Aubrey standing behind him.

"Are you all right?" Her voice, more sincere than he wanted it to be, slid through him and battled to soothe the haunted memories he carried from his previous cases. She maneuvered into his peripheral vision, concern and compassion clear in the way she tentatively reached toward him but never made contact. "I'll get you some water." She retraced her steps toward her apartment door, her luggage still in hand.

He curled one hand under her arm to stop her from leaving, and the buzz in his head died in an instant. His heart rate dropped. His breathing evened out. "I'm fine. It's…" Nicholas pried his hand from her arm, and the buzz in his head returned. Her hypnotic honey-colored gaze settled on him, encouraging him to explain. "I have a unique way of profiling killers. It's kind of like dropping into a meditation. Nothing exists for me outside what I see in my head, and I get disoriented if I pull out too quickly."

"Like when divers surface from deep water too quickly, they get the bends." Not a question, and a completely accurate comparison. Aubrey stepped toward him, raising her hands to his face. "You're able to disassociate yourself from everyone and everything around you. I've read psychological journals detailing the theory. Deep meditation has many benefits for the brain and physical body. May I?"

He nodded, not really sure what she was asking his permission for until she set her fingers around his neck. She tested his pulse at the base of his throat, and the warmth of her skin anchored him to the moment.

"Headaches, dizziness, disorientation, ringing in your ears, that kind of thing?" Aubrey raised her index finger a few inches from his nose, and he followed it back and forth. "Are you experiencing any of them now?"

Amazement spread through him as he ran a mental check through his entire body. He was beginning to see why the killer had come here, to take something of hers in an effort to get close. "Not in the least."

THERE WAS ANOTHER victim out there.

She'd overheard Nicholas's call with Agent West. A photo of a woman had been recovered after the BAU had located Koko in the back of a cargo van mere feet from the perimeter of the scene where she'd found Kara.

"We'll be at the safe house in a few minutes," Nicholas said. "You'll be able to rest, get something to eat, clean up."

"I don't need to rest. I need to find who killed my sister." Questioning the doorman of her building hadn't resulted in any new leads. Coulter Loxley specifically remembered an ambulance pulling up to the doors in response to a 9-1-1 call on the floor below hers around the time Nicholas had narrowed down the killer's entry into her building. He'd let the emergency responders inside without hesitation, leaving whoever'd taped the map to her door to use the distraction to his advantage. Only afterward had the EMTs informed him the call had been a hoax. No one on the floor below had needed emergency attention. At least, not that they'd been able to confirm. And the footage from the cameras positioned around the lobby between 10:00 p.m. and 11:00 p.m. last night had been compromised despite security's insistence that was impossible.

Aubrey curled her fingers into her palms, traces of his body heat still absorbed into her hands as they drove away from her loft through the blurred streets of the city. She hadn't been a practicing physician for three years, but helping those in need had been the reason she'd gone to medical school to study pathology in the first place. Nicholas had needed her help. Disorientation, slightly slurred speech. She stared down at her fingers and forced herself to release her grip. Crescent-moon indents lingered near the base of her palms.

A few seconds. That was all it'd taken to exterminate the cold deep that'd settled behind her sternum when she'd measured his pulse under her bare fingers. It'd been erratic and thready, as though he'd woken from a nightmare, his skin slightly filmed with sweat, yet he'd been conscious. Highly insightful, perceptive, even cerebral, Nicholas James wasn't like any other FBI agent she'd worked with in her tenure as Seattle's chief medical examiner. The muscles along her throat constricted, and she blinked back the involuntarily emotion burning in her eyes. If it weren't for Kara, she never would've made the career change from research into clinical practice. Ironic now that Aubrey would use that hands-on knowledge to find her sister's killer. "I used to make my sister pretend to be a corpse when we were little."

The weight of Nicholas's full attention landed on her, and her heart rate ticked up a few notches. "Is that one of those weird sayings you spout when you're in a stressful situation, or did you actually make your sister pretend to be a corpse?"

"Kara would stage her death all over the house, and it was my job to figure out how she'd died. It was a game we played. We called it Murder-Suicide. I was very good at discovering cause of death. It's one of the reasons why I became a medical examiner." A humorless smile tugged at the corners of her mouth as the memories washed over her. "One morning, I woke up and found her asleep with her head in the oven in an apparent suicide, but I proved it was murder."

Nicholas cringed, sinking lower in his seat with one hand still on the wheel. "What the hell kind of house did you grow up in?"

"My parents encouraged us to explore all kinds of knowledge. My father was a science teacher at the local high school, and my mother was an anthropologist." Her pride echoed in her own ears. "They ensured we followed a career path that would make us happy."

"And cutting up dead people makes you happy?" he asked.

The convulsion in her gut hit as though he'd physically attacked her. "Being a pathologist isn't solely about cutting up dead people, Agent James. It's about learning how disease works inside the human body so vaccinations can be made. It's about giving loved ones answers as to why their family member passed away in his sleep. It's about helping bring a murderer to justice by studying how he attacked his victim, how much force he used and whether or not it was a crime of passion or premeditated."

Her sister's words. Not many people understood her career choice—friends, extended family, the men she'd dated over the years—but Kara had. Up until the past few years, when they'd gotten into a habit of talking of nothing but their parents. No matter how hard Aubrey had tried, she and Kara couldn't seem to connect as they had when they were children. Of all the people who should see the connection they had in common, she thought it would've been Nicholas. She took the bite out of her voice and stared out the window as loss charged up her throat. The roller coaster of grief would be a never-ending ride of pain—for years—and there wasn't a damn thing she could do about it. "Kara was the one who convinced me to leave research and publishing to pursue more clinical work. She said if anyone could give the dead a voice, it would be me."

"We're going to find whoever did this to your sister, Aubrey." He maneuvered the SUV off the main street onto a paved one-way road that ran along the length of a few warehouses. "But you're right. I'm sorry. What I said was insensitive."

Salmon Bay glittered out beyond the windshield, rows of boats and waterfront condos bright against the reflection of the sky off the water. She hadn't realized how long they'd been driving north, lost in her own head as the case grew even more complicated. "To be honest, it isn't much worse than what I've heard from the men I've dated and my friends. People who aren't in the medical field or law enforcement don't really understand what I do. They see it more as morbid fascination than anything. It's hard for them to relate, so I tend to alienate conversation when I talk about my job. My career choice and my dedication to my work has ended more relationships than I care to admit."

"Sounds like you need new friends. As for the men you've dated, anybody who doesn't see you for the generous and understanding woman you are is an idiot." The SUV's shocks absorbed the speed bumps leading down to the waterfront, and Nicholas turned onto another side road, bringing them parallel to the bay before slowing. Parking, he studied the wide expanse of docks, boats and trees in front of them. "Here we are. It's not much, but it's more than enough to keep anyone from finding you for a few days."

Aubrey shouldered out of the car and dropped into pressed, tire-casted dirt. The wind blew her hair back behind her shoulders and kicked up the scents of salt, mud and algae. The industrial chic shipping container–turned–condo had been outfitted with oversize windows, sliding glass doors and a bright turquoise paint color that stood out among the rest of those on the same row. Lapping water reached her ears, and doubt curdled in her stomach. "This is a shipping container. The FBI uses this as a safe house?"

"Wait until you see the inside." Nicholas closed his door behind him and gathered their bags from the back seat with a wink in her direction. He hauled his duffel bag over his shoulder—something he must keep in his vehicle for any situation—and dragged her suitcase behind him. "Shipping containers are the new double-wide trailers, and if we get into some trouble, all they have to do is load us on a boat instead of a truck." His laugh fed confidence into her veins, and she realized he'd made a joke. "Come on, Doc. You've got nothing to worry about."

She studied the configuration of three containers, two on the bottom, one stacked on top, and followed him around to the east entrance. The punch of a keypad reached her ears before Nicholas pushed inside, a glint in his green-blue eyes.

Light gray wall paint with white trim registered as she stepped over the threshold. Equally light hardwood flooring ran the length of the two containers that'd been welded together to create a warm and unexpectedly inviting atmosphere. The kitchen off to her right with gray cabinets and a wood block countertop didn't compare to the one back at her loft, but it promised to do exactly as Nicholas had suggested. Not much but more than enough. A small breakfast bar with two stools met her a few feet into the home, with a hallway on the other side leading to a dining room and living space at the back. A set of stairs branched off to her left, which she assumed led to the bedrooms on the second level and most likely a bathroom.

Nicholas studied her with too much intensity—she couldn't hold his gaze. He wheeled her suitcase in front of her, handing it off. "As you can see, it's not hard to get the lay of the land. The bedrooms are up those stairs, and I use that term loosely. There are two queen-size beds on opposite sides of the house without doors. Feel free to take whichever your heart desires."

No doors. Just opposite sides of the shipping container he'd brought her to. Eighteen hours ago, her life had been as normal and routine as it could get. It hadn't been reduced to hiding from a narcissistic killer who'd murdered her sister and started a mind game she couldn't understand.

She pressed the bar of her suitcase into the lock position. Someone had broken into her home, had gone through her things, studied her. She wanted to go back to her loft, to her routine, to pretending Kara hadn't been strangled and mutilated by a sick murderer with a vendetta against her for helping put away a serial killer. Her voice shook despite the significant amount of control she'd practiced over the years. "Please tell me there's a door and a lock for the bathroom."

"There is." His smile sucker punched her out of nowhere, and Aubrey held her mouth in a tight line until she trusted herself to speak again. He didn't give her that chance. Nicholas's expression collapsed as though he'd read her mind, and he slung his duffel bag to the floor. Closing the distance between them, he reached out for her, but hesitated and pulled back. "Aubrey, this is temporary. We're going to find who's behind this, and we're going to make sure he can't hurt anyone else. Together. I give you my word. You're going to get through this."

She licked dry lips, and his gaze instantly homed in on the movement, shooting awareness through every cell in her body. He was doing this to keep her safe. She knew that, but she wouldn't be of any use here. She needed to see the photo of the second victim. She needed to help. "Agent James—"

"Nicholas," he said.

"Nicholas." She tested his name, felt the weight of it on her tongue and the flood of saliva from her salivary glands. Aubrey breathed through the burn of tears at the back of her throat. Kara was gone. Nothing would change that fact, but the agent in front of her gave her hope it was possible. Her gut clenched. No. This was a murder investigation. Her sister's murder investigation.

Whatever this…connection was between her and Nicholas wouldn't go beyond professional. It couldn't. "Maybe you're right. I'm not thinking clearly. I think I'll take a few minutes to myself, after all."

## Chapter Five

Nicholas watched the medical examiner ascend the stairs, her suitcase in hand. He'd been assigned this case as he had any other in the BAU. Dealing with the victims' families had always been left for the unit's public relations liaison, Caitlyn Yang, to tackle. Not part of his job description. He hunted serials. He got inside their heads, profiled their victims in an attempt to understand what set them off, but with Aubrey...

Something urged him to follow her up those stairs and make sure she was okay, even though he knew the truth. The doc was logical, understood life and death better than anyone he'd ever met, but losing her sister wasn't something Aubrey would be able to explain away. He held himself in place. No. He wasn't the person witnesses and families turned to for comfort. He was the one who brought the dead justice.

Retrieving his duffel bag from the floor, he cleared the safe house room by room, which took all of five seconds, because it was the size of a shoebox. He deposited his overnight bag onto the sectional and unpocketed his phone. He studied the photo Dashiell West and Madeline Striker had recovered from the cargo van near Kara Flood's death scene. They were still waiting on

Dr. Caldwell's autopsy results from the first victim, but he couldn't ignore the fact a second had already been killed. Discovered less than twenty-four hours apart. Whoever'd gone after Kara Flood would've already had to have killed the woman in the photo in order to leave the Polaroid in that van in front of Kara's apartment building.

Nicholas pulled his laptop from his duffel and logged in to the FBI's missing persons database. If the victim in the photo had been killed before Kara Flood, there was a good chance she'd already been reported missing. Brown hair, Caucasian, approximately five-six or five-seven. Business suit. He paused. The Gingerbread Woman had focused her retaliation on female colleagues within her law firm. If the killer who'd re-created the X Marks the Spot Killer's MO with such detail was, in fact, the same killer who'd gone after Jane Doe, he would've followed the MO to the letter. It was possible the victim in the photo was also a lawyer or worked in a law firm. He scanned the list of potential victims, singling out a woman who'd been reported missing two days ago by her mother. A woman who'd worked for a law firm in the city. "Paige Cress."

He swiped his thumb up his phone's screen and messaged David Dyson, the BAU's intern keen on following in Nicholas's footsteps, to tell him to run a background check on the potential victim.

"You found something?" Aubrey rounded into what passed for the living room and leaned against the wall sectioning off the space from the kitchen on the other side. She'd changed out of her business attire into a pair of drawstring sweatpants and a dark T-shirt. Her brown hair draped around her shoulders, and time seemed to freeze.

In all the times they'd been in the same room, he'd

only spoken with her in an official capacity. Autopsy reports, pathology, cause of death. Hell, he'd even read a few books by medical examiners to be able to understand her during their last investigation together. He'd gotten used to her hair pulled back in a ponytail, the professional distance she'd kept between them with her black slacks and button-down shirts she'd worn as though they emotionally protected her as well as a piece of armor. This was…something different. She was different.

A hint of desperation rolled her lips between her teeth. "Did you find something about Kara, or does it have to do with the other woman your team believes was murdered using a different MO by the same killer?"

"You heard my call with Agent West, did you?" He wasn't sure why he was surprised. Dr. Aubrey Flood had broken every expectation he'd had of her from the beginning. She was highly intelligent, yet more personable than most academics he'd met, including her counterpart working this case. She was sincere, warm and didn't believe herself better than anyone else. If anything, he sensed the opposite after her admission of bending herself backward for the benefit of others, how she described her job as helping the families of the deceased rather than a need for justice.

He leaned away from the laptop, not entirely sure how carefully he should tread. The good doctor had been vital in capturing the X Marks the Spot Killer three years ago, but investigating the cause of death of strangers compared to her own sister were two separate departments. "Listen, Doc, I'm not sure—"

"You think I can't handle the details of my sister's murder investigation." She crossed her arms over her small frame. Her humorless laugh penetrated through the silence settling between them before she raised her gaze to his. Aubrey pushed off the wall, shortening the space between them, and his body shot into heated awareness. She took a seat beside him. "To be honest, I don't blame you. It's hard for a lot of people to compartmentalize their emotions when they suffer a loss like I have, but I've been burying my emotions for a long time. Whatever relates to Kara's case, I can handle it."

He believed her. With an entire life of ensuring others' needs were met before her own, Aubrey had the emotional awareness of her feelings, but she wouldn't have acknowledged them in order to become the keystone of those who needed her. If anyone could compartmentalize that kind of grief, that pain, of losing someone they loved to such violence, it would be her. He turned his attention back to his laptop screen and away from the outline of her soft pink lips. He pulled up the photo forwarded from his team. "Agents West and Striker recovered a photo of a potential victim with Koko. A woman. At a glance, it looks as though she was killed using a different MO than the one used on your sister. The blue lips indicate—"

"Asphyxiation." Aubrey leaned against his arm to get a better view of the victim, and a hit of her light perfume—maybe even the same brand as the killer had stolen from her apartment—dived deep into his lungs. Something along the lines of jasmine and rose, maybe a hint of vanilla. "The victim was most likely suffocated, but I won't be able to know for sure unless I'm allowed access to the remains."

"The way she was killed fits an MO for another serial killer the press started calling the Gingerbread Woman. All the victims were attacked in parking garages at their law firm, suffocated with their jackets and left with a photograph of another victim." Nicholas splayed his fingers wide, palm up. "No witnesses. No surveillance footage. That led us to believe the killer was actually working inside the same building the victims were killed in. We were able to identify Irene Lawrence by a strand of hair that'd gotten stuck to one of the victim's jackets during a struggle. Five in all. All female, all working for the same law firm she did."

"She was leaving the photos of her victims like bread crumbs." A visible shiver chased across Aubrey's shoulders, and he drowned the urge to trail his hand down her back to soothe it. "The Gingerbread Woman was leading you to her next kill like the X Marks the Spot Killer was leaving maps for family members to find their loved ones."

"During an interview with a psychologist who was writing a book on female serial killers at the time, Irene Lawrence admitted she'd been inspired by the X Marks the Spot Killer. Just as our current killer seems to be. The only difference is, I believe whoever murdered Kara and this woman isn't simply inspired, he's re-creating the MOs of his heroes in order to prove he's surpassed them." Not simply a copycat. Something far more dangerous.

He turned the laptop toward her and switched screens back to the FBI database. "Paige Cress, a paralegal who worked for a firm downtown, fits the description of the woman in the photo and was reported missing two days ago. Given the fact her photo was recovered near Kara's apartment, it stands to reason she was killed before your sister in order to keep law enforcement playing the game. Does the name sound familiar? Did Kara ever mention a friend who worked in a law firm or have reason to reach out to a lawyer? Maybe they were friends?"

"No. Not that I can remember." Aubrey shook her head. Distance swarmed into warm eyes that urged him to get closer. "As far as I knew, most of her friends were other teachers from her school, and as I said before, she rarely went out."

"I have our intern, David, running a background check on Paige to see if there are any other connections." He studied the photo once again, searching for any detail that might give them an idea of where the remains had been left. The killer was playing with them, and Nicholas couldn't see the endgame—not yet—but that didn't unnerve him as much as the mesmerizing woman beside him. He scrubbed a hand down his face. One fact they could rely on: Paige Cress's remains would be another piece of the puzzle. One that would lead them either to the next victim or to the killer.

"The body was disposed of on top of what looks like worn wood, possibly a dock or a pier, but that's not enough to narrow down a location given Seattle is one of the largest coastal cities in the United States. There are hundreds of docks and dozens of piers."

"You said he's a narcissist. That's why he left Kara's body in such a public place, so he could show off his handiwork. It's about pride for him, and a need to be recognized as a master compared to his heroes. He'd want to do the same for this victim, too, wouldn't he? He'd leave her somewhere busy enough no one would be able to pinpoint when the body was dropped or give a credible ID. Maybe a dock or a pier that gets a lot of foot traffic."

She circled the photograph on the screen with her index finger. "This wood is distressed, as though it's been exposed to salt water for years. Assuming the victim has been kept within the city limits, only battering winds, tides and rains, most likely from a large enough source such as Puget Sound, would've been able to age the dock like this." She latched her hand on to his forearm, and a shot of heat bolted up through his veins. "The waterfront. The city had to close down one of the piers due to it shifting away from land last month. They're not scheduled to make repairs for another few weeks, but the piers on either side would still be open to the public."

She was right. Nicholas reached for his phone and hit Madeline Striker's number. Raising the phone to his ear, he nodded toward the stairs as the line rang. Her logic made sense. "I'll call it in. Grab your gear. We need to find that body."

EXHAUSTION PULLED AT her ligaments and muscles as she stepped out of Nicholas's SUV. Waves of heat gave the illusion of a dreamlike state across the pavement and long stretch of Puget Sound. One of the few thunderstorms of the summer had begun its approach from the north, dark clouds forming a few miles off the coast, and had cleared out most of the tourists and waterfront visitors. Despite the stereotype of Seattle's weather patterns, the city didn't see as much rain as most of the people in the country believed, but when the storms hit, they hit hard. And looking at the formation of clouds out across the sound, the BAU had a limited amount of time before the victim's remains might be compromised.

Another SUV parked beside them as Aubrey rounded the hood to meet Nicholas, and the two agents she'd noted at the crime scene this morning exited the vehicle. Agents West and Striker. She didn't know much about the male agent experienced in cybercrimes, with only a few short interactions between them over the years, but

Agent Striker had been quite useful in searching for serial victims over her career within the BAU. Without the missing persons expert, Aubrey doubted they would've recovered a number of victims before their killers had finished what they'd started.

She nodded to both of the agents and slid her hands into her slacks, feeling more out of place in the field than in her examination room. With its drains, exposed pipes, surgical instruments and refrigerated drawers, she felt in control there. This… This was something else. She wasn't an investigator. Not the kind that followed the clues, put the pieces together and saved the day. Not like Nicholas. The victims she dealt with on a daily basis came to her already deceased, but the guilt taking root inside, the kind that blamed her for what'd happened to Kara, wouldn't let her go back and hide in her comfort zone. She owed it to her sister to find whoever killed her.

Nicholas brushed against her arm, resurrecting that flare of heat and disorientation as he had back at the safe house. "Storm's moving in. I figure we've got about twenty minutes of search time before things get real complicated."

Heavy rains washed away evidence. If they didn't move fast enough, they could lose anything that might identify the next victim or the killer.

"Where do you want us?" Agent West's incredibly brown eyes flickered to her for the briefest of moments, telling her far more in that single instance than she'd asked for. He didn't approve of her being involved in the search or the investigation, and she didn't blame him.

She'd been trained in pathology and uncovering cause of death. Until they recovered a body, she didn't understand what she could contribute here.

"Our unsub wouldn't have left the body to be recovered by anyone other than the people he intended to find it. That's why he left us the photo at Kara Flood's death scene." Nicholas pulled his phone from his pocket and turned the screen toward his team, every ounce the lead case agent she believed him to be. Authoritative, in control, unrelenting.

"I believe this is the woman we're looking for. Paige Cress, a paralegal for a firm downtown, who fits the Gingerbread Woman's victim profile. He's using the breadcrumb MO to draw us in, possibly into a trap. Dr. Flood and I have narrowed down a possible dump site on Pier 58. She and I will search there, but we can't risk narrowing our focus. West, you take the pier to the south. Striker, the pier to the north. Gear up and keep in radio contact."

Nicholas backtracked to the rear of his vehicle, West and Striker doing the same. He pulled a Kevlar vest over his head and strapped in, then unholstered his weapon, released the magazine and pulled back the slider to clear the chamber. A bullet leaped from the top of the gun, and he caught it before it hit the cargo area of his vehicle. Green-blue eyes raised to hers. "You know how to handle one of these?"

Aubrey shook her head, unable to look away from the overtaxed muscles of his forearms. "No. Not really."

He offered her the weapon, the weight of his team's study burning between her shoulder blades, but Nicholas didn't seem to notice. As though in his world, she was all that existed. He set the grip of the firearm in her hand then maneuvered behind her, his mouth close to her ear. Positioning his index finger over hers, he directed the finger she'd use to fire the weapon should the moment call for it alongside the trigger.

"Safety is here." He pointed to the small button above the trigger. "Magazine release is here. You currently have fifteen bullets. To load a round into the chamber, you pull back on this slide." He brought her left hand up and set it on top of the gun. "Always use your nondominant hand to load and unload the weapon. That way you're not wasting valuable seconds switching hands. Go ahead."

She pulled back the slide and heard a distinct click that said she'd loaded a bullet into the chamber. Her hand shook. The weapon was heavier than she'd imagined it being. "Now what?"

"Now you take a deep breath before you accidentally shoot me." His laugh whispered along the underside of her jaw and sent a rush of warmth straight into her gut. His hand slipped from hers, and an instant coolness absorbed into her body from the breeze coming off the sound. Pulling what looked like another vest from the back of the cargo area, Nicholas handed it to her. "Put this on. Stay behind me. If anything goes south, you use me as a shield, then get the hell out of there and don't look back. You understand?"

His words registered through the haze his proximity had built, and all evidence of the bubble he'd created around them disappeared. "You think he's here. That he's watching the remains because he enjoys the rush of the chase?"

"This killer, whoever he is, has broken in to your apartment, targeted your sister and left a map to her remains on your apartment door, Aubrey. From what I can tell, he has an unhealthy obsession with you, and I will do whatever it takes to make sure I deny him as long as I can." He pulled a second firearm from the cargo area and reached up to the SUV's hatch and slammed it closed.

He lowered his voice. "Wear the vest, use the gun if you have to, but no matter what happens, do not leave my sight." Cutting his attention over her shoulder, he called to his team, "Let's move out. That storm is getting too close for my comfort."

Aubrey attached the holster he'd handed over to the waist of her slacks and fit the bulletproof vest over her head. The weight sank hard on her shoulders and stole the oxygen from her lungs as she followed behind Nicholas and his team across the parking lot.

The Seattle Waterfront centered on an atmospheric collection of piers filled with souvenir shops, amusement attractions, an aquarium, cruise ship boarding, seafood restaurants and the Seattle Great Wheel. Gondolas overlooked Puget Sound and gave postcard-perfect views of the coastline and the city all at once. On the weekends, the farmers market was packed with tourists and locals buying fresh produce and crafts, but as dark, swirling clouds moved in, visitors retreated to the safety of their vehicles as the BAU spread out. Agent Striker veered off to Aubrey's right, heading for Pier 59, with Agent West taking the pier to her left, leaving her with Nicholas.

She adjusted the Kevlar vest around her neck as they crossed the sidewalk clinging to the edges of the piers, the weapon he'd given her heavy on her hip. Blockades prevented waterfront visitors from crossing onto Pier 58, but Nicholas didn't pay them any attention. Following in his wake, she stepped onto the old, weathered wood that was a strong match for the wood pictured with the victim in the photograph. The combination of metal and wood seemed to groan with the addition of their weight, and her heart shot straight into her throat. "In order to keep the body from being discovered too quickly, I imagine the killer left Paige Cress protected from the elements. Out of sight. Possibly in one of the maintenance sheds."

"You're probably right." Nicholas unholstered his weapon. "We'll start there."

Her steps echoed off the planks under her feet. Cement stairs branched off the concave pier and led to the piers on either side. Movement caught her attention from the right as Agent Striker moved farther out toward the end of Pier 59. Sphere-shaped white lamps flickered to life as the clouds centered directly overhead. Spits of rain stained the planks around her and caught in her hair. The storm was just beginning. They were running out of time.

Water *tinked* against the frame of the Seattle Great Wheel at the end of the pier. There were too many man-made angles that kept them from seeing the expanse of the pier as a whole—too many places to hide.

Nicholas moved ahead of her, the muscles down his back rippling with every step as they closed in on the closest maintenance shed. Built from the same cement as the stairs, the shed had been graffitied over the years with bright red and yellow spray paint. Steel double doors had been raised enough to allow the planks to run into the space. If the killer had wanted to protect the body from being found until the right time, this would be an ideal location to keep Paige Cress to himself until he was ready to show her to the world. Nicholas tested the handle, and the door swung open.

"Holy hell," he said.

Hot waves of decomposition and baked flesh dived deep into her lungs, and both she and Nicholas stepped back to release the buildup of bodily gases. The outline of a body registered as her senses adjusted to the darkness inside. Aubrey crouched alongside the remains, her medicolegal kit thudding against the pier. "Female, approximately twenty to twenty-five years old, which falls into the description given of the victim. There is evidence of petechial hemorrhages in the face, edema in the fingers and blue discoloration of the skin, suggesting the victim died of asphyxiation." Aubrey memorized the face of the victim, down to the obvious perimortem bruising in her face. She pulled back, her heart heavier than the Kevlar pulling on her shoulders. "I believe we've found Paige Cress."

## Chapter Six

Nicholas stared down at the remains as Aubrey performed the initial study of the body. Heat had engorged
the skin around the victim's eyes, mouth and stomach,
but he agreed with the ME's identification. They'd found
Paige Cress.

"It'll be difficult to narrow down time of death in
these conditions. Cement holds heat, which will raise
body temperature, but the wood planks underneath the
remains are spaced far enough apart to allow the ocean
to cool the underside." Aubrey stepped back. "We won't
know anything until we can get her to Dr. Caldwell to
have him perform the autopsy."

The detachment in her voice as she spoke about the
victim who'd been suffocated and left to play a part in a
psychopath's mind game jarred him. This wasn't a body.
These weren't just remains to be cut open and studied.
This had been a woman who'd worked hard to land a
paralegal position in one of the city's largest law firms,
who'd been reported missing by a family who'd cared
about her. Doubt scattered the similarities he'd noted between them. He'd spent most of his life trusting a man
who'd murdered thirty women over the course of his life
until Nicholas had caught the son of a bitch. He couldn't

take anyone at face value. Not even Aubrey. He had to remember that.

"The killer wanted us to find your sister on that bench. He wanted us to find Koko in the back of the van. He wanted us to find the photo of Paige. He's been leaving us bread crumbs from the beginning. Taunting us because he likes the feel of the chase. Not only is he trying to prove he's better than his idols, but he's determined to outwit the investigators on his trail. This is a game for him, and he's got a front-row seat to the whole show." Nicholas unclipped the radio from his vest. "Striker, West, come in."

Static punctured through the frequency. No answer.

Aubrey searched the area for Madeline Striker. "I don't see Agent Striker. She was there a minute ago."

Warning knotted at the base of his spine. He hit the press-to-talk button again. "Striker, West, do you copy?"

Damn it. Nicholas attached the radio into place, instincts screaming. His team wouldn't have gone silent without specific instructions or a damn good reason. Something was wrong. He nodded toward the weapon now clutched in Aubrey's hand. They couldn't leave the victim unsupervised, but he wouldn't abandon his team, either. "You remember how to use that?"

She glanced down at the firearm as though suddenly aware she'd taken it out in the first place and widened her stance. "I remember."

"Good. Call this in. Don't let her out of your sight. Understand?" He extracted his phone and dialed SSA Miguel Peters. The line rang once. Twice. "I'm requesting backup, but I give you permission to shoot anybody who comes near you without official identification. I'll be back as soon as I can."

"I'll protect her." She nodded a split second before he turned his back and took the first few steps to head across the pier. "Agent James."

Nicholas twisted around, catching the full sight of her standing guard over the body with his backup weapon in hand, and his gut clenched harder than it should have.

"Be careful," she said.

The doubt that'd trickled past his defenses cracked. "You, too."

The ringing ended, and the call picked up. He pressed the phone harder against his ear. "You've reached Supervisory Special Agent Miguel Peters…"

"Damn it. Voice mail." Keeping low, Nicholas ended the call and took cover behind one of the cement columns making up the inclined roof of a carnival game booth. He shoved his phone back into his pocket and broke cover to search the pier. No movement. Nothing to suggest an ambush. "Where are you, you bastard?"

Straightening, he forced one foot in front of the other around the curve of the damaged pier toward Miner's Landing—a souvenir shop—and the Seattle Great Wheel. Muted catches of sunlight reflected off the ocean waves, the scent of salt water clearing the lingering odor of decomposition from his lungs. Gulls screeched overhead, and he looked up.

Movement registered in his peripheral vision then vanished, so fast he almost believed he'd imagined it. Almost. His heart rocketed into his throat. The shadow had disappeared behind the long stretch of the souvenir shop, and he picked up the pace. The killer didn't just want to prove he was better than the BAU assigned to take him down. He'd want to humiliate them by showing he held all the power. This was all a game, but one Nicholas was prepared to win. His legs burned as he closed in on the northeast end of the building. He pressed his back against the old wood and craned his neck around the corner, air lodged in his throat.

Empty.

Blue umbrellas adorned minimalist outdoor restaurant seating along the south side base of the Ferris wheel. Hip-height Plexiglas created a barrier that led toward the back of the building. His pulse pounded hard in his throat as he maneuvered toward the southeast corner of the building. Tourists had cleared the piers with the oncoming storm, but Nicholas still felt as though he was being watched. Air-conditioning units and storage prevented any chance of escape along the back of Miner's Landing. There was nowhere for the killer to run.

Nicholas crept past the restaurant with its gleaming windows offering perfect views of the sound and swung around the corner, weapon aimed high.

An elbow slammed into his face. Lightning exploded behind his eyes as he stumbled back. He fell into the Plexiglas divider around the restaurant seating. Pain ricocheted around his skull as he tried to focus. A hole of clarity spread, but he wasn't fast enough.

A second hit rocketed into his jaw.

Nicholas flipped over the half wall and slammed onto a glass table on the other side, his weapon slipping from his hand. Glass shattered under his weight and sliced into his forearms and the back of his neck. Stinging pain woke the nerve endings throughout his body, and a groan escaped his chest. He shook his head as the masked attacker vaulted over the barrier and landed beside him.

"Agent James, so good of you to join us. I was starting to worry you wouldn't get my message." The distorted voice beneath the mask grated against his inner ears. Muscular build, well over six feet, trained in hand-to-hand combat. No identifying scars or tattoos. The killer had been watching, waiting, for the BAU to recover Paige Cress in the maintenance shed.

"You've got some control issues." Nicholas hauled himself to his feet, glass crunching beneath his boots. His pulse pounded at the back of his head, and he swiped a fair amount of blood from a laceration. He struggled for balance as he faced the bastard who'd targeted Kara Flood and Paige Cress. "Where are West and Striker?"

"Always out to be the hero, aren't you, Agent James? Or should I call you Nicholas? It's not enough you took down the X Marks the Spot Killer or the Gingerbread Woman, but you have to save your teammates as well. I've always admired that about you," he said. "In a way, you and I are very similar. Each trying to rise above the circumstances we were dealt. But where you've chosen to hunt the legends responsible for so much pain and loss, I've chosen to become one. When this is over, everyone is going to know who I am, but don't worry, your teammates are alive. For now."

Nicholas struck out, fisting the attacker's black jacket, and slammed the killer into the reflective glass of the restaurant. The window cracked beneath the momentum and spidered out around the killer's head. "You don't know anything about me."

A low, steady laugh penetrated through the ringing in his ears.

"On the contrary, Agent James. I'm your biggest fan." Wrapping his gloved grip around both of Nicholas's wrists, the suspect twisted out of his hold. The pier blurred in Nicholas's vision as the killer kicked his legs

out from under him and slammed him facedown into
the shattered glass of the destroyed table. "You're one
of the best, and I like to honor my idols the only way I
know how."

A scream tore from his throat as pain unlike anything
he'd experienced before burned down the side of his face.
Nicholas rolled out from under the suspect's grip onto
his back and kicked out hard with both feet. He landed
a hit in the center of the bastard's chest and threw him
backward into an adjacent table. Shoving to his feet, he
pulled a piece of glass from the entry wound in his cheek
and tossed it to the ground. Blood dripped from his chin.
He swiped it away with the back of his hand. He spit the
copper and salt mixture from his mouth.

"You honor the killers you admire by becoming them,
by re-creating their kills to prove you can do it better
than they did and never get caught, but, the way I see it,
you're nothing more than a copycat playing dress-up."

"I am better." A hint of rage filtered through the killer's voice, and Nicholas inwardly cringed against the
pain of a smile.

"Seems I hit a nerve." He spotted his weapon a few
feet away. "You see, I had you pegged the moment I saw
Kara Flood's body. Using another killer's MO?" He shook
his head in disappointment. "What that tells me is you're
a run-of-the-mill narcissist. There's nothing special about
you. You're going to go down like all the rest of the killers I've put behind bars."

"That's where you're wrong, Agent James," the killer
said.

Nicholas lunged for his firearm.

Faster than he thought possible, the man in the mask
shot a heel out and slammed it into the back of Nicho-

las's knee. He hit the pier as the tendons along his leg screamed. An arm snaked around his throat, pulled him into a wall of solid muscle and squeezed. The killer lowered his mouth to Nicholas's ear. "Dr. Flood is one of the best, too, isn't she?"

His attacker strengthened his grip around Nicholas's throat and dragged him from the outdoor seating area of the restaurant. His boots caught on the old wood as he fought for dominance, but the killer had the upper hand. Pressure built in his chest as he clawed for escape. "Without her, you and your team never would've been able to identify Cole Presley as the X Marks the Spot Killer. Would you like to know how I'm going to honor her?"

No. Not Aubrey. Nicholas locked his back teeth as dizziness swirled through his head. He clutched the suspect's forearms, fighting for release.

"You see, I've been studying all kinds of MOs for a few months now, trying to get a feel for which one fits me best." The killer hauled Nicholas to the edge of the pier, the wide expanse of the bay glittering back at him. "I've got to say, I think I've found exactly how to introduce myself to the world, and Dr. Flood is going to be my masterpiece."

Darkness closed in around the edges of Nicholas's vision, just as his attacker threw him over the railing and into Puget Sound.

NOBODY CARED ABOUT a victim when they were alive, but people sure took notice once they were dead. The bruising along the victim's mandible and maxilla, combined with the cuts and scrapes along the backs of Paige Cress's metacarpals, told a clear story of an attempt at survival.

Aubrey had been instructed to stay with the body

until the BAU backup arrived, but every moment the internal heat of the maintenance shed baked the remains could lead to another piece of evidence lost. Evidence that might identify the victim's killer. The medicolegal investigators would normally examine and document everything on the body before getting it ready for transportation to her office, but time was of the essence here. She holstered the weapon Nicholas had given her for protection. Wood planks bit into her knees as she dragged the death investigation kit she usually kept in the trunk of her car closer. Popping the lid, she pulled the sterile cuticle sticks from the depths along with two evidence bags and a pair of latex gloves.

She'd trained to study the causes and effects of human disease and injury in order to investigate sudden, unexpected or violent deaths. Sometimes that involved visiting crime scenes, reviewing medical records and performing autopsies, but she considered collecting evidence to be used in court possibly the most important part of her job. Especially in a homicide. Aubrey removed one of the cuticle sticks from its container, a seven-inch piece of wood with angled tips at both ends, and curved it beneath the victim's right thumbnail. If Paige Cress had struggled with her attacker, as the bruises and contusions suggested, there was a chance she'd scratched the killer and collected his DNA under her nails.

After swiping the cuticle stick under each fingernail, one for each hand, she bagged and labeled the evidence with the black Sharpie from her kit. She secured both bags in the extra compartment at the bottom of her kit. She needed the victim's body temperature despite the fluctuations in conditions where the killer had dumped Paige Cress to be found.

Inserting the digital thermometer from her kit, she brushed the sweat dripping from her hairline away with the back of her hand. She noted the victim's temperature and the time taken. "It's hotter than a hippo dipped in hot sauce in here."

The victim's skin was already slipping out of place due to rising temperatures. She had to hurry. Swabbing the injuries on the back of the metacarpals, Aubrey bagged and tagged the evidence before moving on to collecting particulates from Paige Cress's clothing. Tweezers in one hand and a magnifier in the other, she leaned over the remains, and a hint of gasoline coming from the victim's clothing burned down her throat. Nicholas had said the Gingerbread Woman had attacked her victims in the parking garage of her law firm in order to take out the competition for promotion to partner. If the copycat who'd lured them to the waterfront had followed the serial's MO exactly, it stood to reason he'd attacked Paige Cress in a garage, too.

A guttural scream punctured through her focus, and Aubrey straightened. Her heart threatened to beat straight out of her chest as she stared across the pier for a sign of the BAU team. Instinct kicked in, and her adrenal glands triggered the release of adrenaline, honing her senses. She'd recognized that scream. "Nicholas."

He'd told her to stay with the body, to not let anyone come close to it, but the agent was obviously in pain. He might need medical attention. She replaced the tweezers and magnifier back into her kit and unholstered the weapon he'd loaned her. Waiting. Nervous energy licked up her spine, but she couldn't hear anything else. She glanced back toward the body, torn between following his order and the inner need to help. She'd collected evidence from under the victim's fingernails, noted body temperature, swabbed for injuries and gathered a few particulates from the remains. Paige Cress was already dead. There wasn't anything Aubrey could do for the victim, but she could save Nicholas. "Okay."

She pushed her kit into the cement shed with the remains and secured the door. Turning back to face the water, she sprinted across the pier toward the last location she'd seen him. Agents Striker and West would've heard the scream. They would know where to find him. The pounding of her feet against the pier reverberated up through her frame and intensified the sweat building at the back of her neck. She turned the corner leading into the walkway between Miner's Landing and the Seattle Great Wheel, pulling the weapon shoulder-level out in front of her.

Nobody was there.

Confusion rolled through her as she battled to catch her breath. That didn't make sense. She could've sworn this was where Nicholas had headed. Taking a single step along the walkway, she listened for something—anything—that would give her an idea of where he'd gone. Every second she wasted trying to find him was another second he might be bleeding out. She tightened her grip around the weapon he'd handed her. "Nicholas?"

No answer.

Warning knotted low in her belly as the sound of ocean waves lapping against the pier fought to override her pulse in her ears. Another step, then another. She followed the slight curve of the Plexiglas divider cutting the Ferris wheel entrance off from the restaurant's outdoor dining. He had to be here. Glass crunched under her shoes. Her insides clenched. Frozen, she retraced the trail of shattered glass until she located the source. A broken table on the other side of the Plexiglas divider. She studied the red stains ground into the debris. Blood. Nicholas's? One of his teammates'? From the amount of blood left behind, the wound had to be nonfatal, but that didn't settle her nerves in the slightest. The stains had created a trail of their own, and she tracked them over the divider toward the edge of the pier. The scream. Nicholas's scream. The hairs rose on the back of her neck, but she forced one foot in front of the other to follow the blood.

One hand on the railing, the other wrapped around the gun, she leaned over. And saw him. "Nicholas!"

Facedown, he swayed with the rocking of the waves and slammed into one of the pier's supports. Unresponsive. Aubrey discarded the weapon and toed her shoes off one by one. Panic clawed up her throat as she tried to calculate how long it'd been since she'd heard his scream. Two minutes, maybe three. Climbing to the top of the railing, she jumped out as far as she could in order to avoid landing directly on him. Air rushed up a split second before the water engulfed her.

Cold water shocked her nerve endings into overdrive. The waves rocked against her and tossed her to the right. Bubbles filtered up through her slacks and shirt, tickling her skin, as she struggled to right herself. Distorted sunlight beat down, lighting the first ten or fifteen feet below the surface, but she couldn't see him. She kicked upward and broke through the surface, an automatic gasp seizing her lungs. Swiping her hair out of her face, she spotted him only a few feet from where she'd last seen him and kicked her legs as fast as she could to get to him.

"Nicholas." She grabbed his Kevlar vest and flipped him onto his back. Water drained from his mouth, his eyes closed. No. No, no, no, no. He wasn't dead. She still had time. "I'm going to get you out of here. Okay? Stay with me. I'll get you out of here."

She kicked to keep her head above water and dragged him to the next support. Another wave roared before it crashed onto them and pushed her under the water. She held on to Nicholas's vest for dear life, churning in the water until the beat of the ocean let up.

They were going to make it. She had to believe that.

Breaking through to the surface, she searched for a low section of pier she could reach to pull them to safety. In vain. The tide hadn't come in. None of the piers would be reachable for a few more hours, and the storm had churned Puget Sound into violence. Desperation coiled behind her sternum as her legs burned with exertion. The long stretch of Pier 57 seemed like miles, but she wasn't going to give up. She couldn't. She hadn't been able to save Kara from a killer. She wasn't going to let Nicholas die at the hands of the same man.

Her shoulder screamed in protest as she swam for the southwest corner of the pier. Miner's Landing had to be able to receive their shipments of seafood from the boats. There was a dock on the other side, but cutting under the pier instead of going around was too much of a risk. She couldn't take the chance of a larger wave tossing them into the bottom of the pier. Waves battered and beat at her one after the other as she struggled to stay above water. "We're going to make it. I promise we'll make it."

She spit salt water and automatically tipped her chin back to keep her head from going under the surface. Pain lightninged down her legs the harder she kicked around the corner support. There. The docks were straight ahead. She pushed everything she had left into keeping Nicholas's head back as she swam. Thirty feet. Twenty. Tears burned in her eyes. "Almost there. Just hang on."

Her fingers clutched onto the worn, cold steel of the ladder, and she pulled Nicholas close. Wrapping her arm around the front of his chest, she heaved him into her as she backed up the ladder rung by rung. At the top, she fell, taking his weight fully, but she couldn't stop. She wasn't sure how long he'd been facedown in the water. She maneuvered out from under him as an imaginary metronome ticked off in her head. She ripped both sides of his vest free and hauled it over his head. Centering the base of her palms over his breastbone, she interlaced her fingers and administered compressions. "One, two, three, four…"

She pinched his nose and pressed her mouth to his. Salt exploded across her taste buds. No response. Counting off again, she repeated the compressions and filled his lungs. "Come on, Nicholas. Breathe!"

His chest jerked under her hands, and water spewed from his mouth as she rolled him onto his side. Nicholas's groan filled her ears, and relief washed through her. He was alive. He was going to make it.

Aubrey ran her fingers through his hair. "It's okay. I'm here. I'm going to get help, okay? Just stay with me, Nicholas. Stay with me."

"Hello, Dr. Flood," an unfamiliar voice said from behind.

Agony ripped across her parietal, the momentum slamming her into the dock. She stared up into the storm. Nicholas's hand pressed against hers, but she couldn't move, couldn't think.

The dark outline of her attacker blurred as he positioned himself over her. "I've been waiting for you."

# Chapter Seven

*Stay with me. Just stay with me.*

Aubrey's voice echoed in his head. He blinked against the onslaught of rain. The soft lapping of waves reached his ears, gulls calling to each other overhead. Old, splintered wood caught against his skin as he raised his head. He was soaking wet. "Aubrey?"

The right side of his face and the back of his head stung as he pushed to sit up. He was on the docks, but the last thing he remembered… The killer had started dragging him toward the edge of the pier. How the hell had he gotten down here? Nicholas pushed to his feet, every nerve ending in his body on fire. He gripped the hand railing to haul himself up the stairs. He could've sworn that'd been Aubrey's voice in his head, but he'd given her strict instructions not to leave the victim alone.

Wood protested under his weight as he limped across the dock toward the stairs leading back to Pier 57. His head pounded in rhythm to the waves growing choppier with the increasing winds. Rain mixed with the blood coming from the lacerations on the back of his hand and tendriled in dendritic patterns along his forearm. He bit back the groan working up his throat and retraced his steps toward the outdoor seating area of the restaurant.

Shattered glass, blood evidence—the memories of the struggle between him and his attacker revived the headache at the base of his skull.

Striker and West were still missing. The bastard had gotten to them first, but they hadn't been the killer's initial target. He'd just wanted Nicholas out of commission.

Dark shapes materialized in his peripheral vision, and Nicholas bit through the pain running down the right side of his body to get a closer look. The pair of dark women's flats hadn't been there during the struggle. He would've noticed them. A second shape took form through his distorted vision and cloud cover above. A gun. The gun he'd loaned her. Nicholas twisted his gaze over his shoulder, toward the maintenance shed where he and Aubrey had recovered the remains. "Aubrey."

Holstering the gun, he pushed himself through the pain. He sprinted across the walkway between Miner's Landing and the Great Wheel and backtracked around the corner where he'd first noticed the killer. Lightning flashed overhead, lighting his way, before thunder punched through him. The storm had arrived, brutal and demanding. Wet, uneven planks threatened to trip him up as he raced to the maintenance shed. The doors were closed, and he slammed into them palms first. Ripping open the heavy steel, Nicholas ignored the crash of the handle against cement, his heart in his throat.

The victim was still here. The ocean churned in agitation beneath the body, sea levels rising with the battering storm. In a few minutes, salt water would break through the planks and compromise any forensic evidence that might lead to their killer. A black tool kit sat a few inches from the victim. A forensic kit. Aubrey must've started collecting samples from Paige Cress, then locked the body and the evidence inside the shed to keep them secure. Why? Why would she leave the remains?

Realization hit.

Because he'd screamed. Aubrey had been with him. She'd come to his aid, armed with his backup weapon, in order to help, and must've spotted him in the water. She'd jumped the pier's railing and gotten him to safety at the risk of both of their lives. She'd saved him. She'd pulled him onto the docks. He rubbed his chest for the source of the ache under his sternum. Chest compressions?

*Stay with me, Nicholas.*

Then the killer had come for her. Nicholas searched the pier, thick sheets of water blacking out sound beyond a hundred feet. Streetlamps flickered but wouldn't do a damn bit of good. She was out there—alone, afraid—and he hadn't seen the threat coming soon enough to stop it.

He didn't have time to secure the victim or the forensic evidence Aubrey had collected. His team needed him. Aubrey needed him. Sealing the maintenance shed, Nicholas ensured the gun he'd loaned to the medical examiner was still loaded. The rising water levels guaranteed the loss of the evidence the killer might have left on the body once the shed flooded, but when it came to saving an investigation or saving his team, it wasn't a choice. He loaded a round into the barrel and headed toward Madeline Striker's last known position.

The Seattle Aquarium stretched the length of Pier 59, with the outdoor exhibits bleeding over onto Pier 60. Over twenty different areas and over a mile of waterfront to search. Nicholas didn't have time to waste. He tested the front door of the aquarium, surprised the double glass doors swung open. The area had been evacuated due to the incoming storm. No one should've been able to get inside the building. He stepped inside, instantly encased in glowing, blue light from the wall of glass and water to his right. Countless species of fish, coral and plant life swayed with the rocking motion of the water within the tank. The killer had lured them into his trap with the promise of another victim. He'd planned to take them out one by one to isolate his real target: Aubrey.

Nicholas crossed in front of the massive tank and around the corner into a narrower section lit with golden light from above. The items in the gift shop, locked behind thin walls of glass, cast shadows across the floor. His clothing stuck to his skin, weighing him down as he entered the crashing wave exhibit. Roaring water splashed against the clear tunnel constructed to give visitors the perfect experience of being caught under a wave without any of the danger, and his lungs ached in response. An exit to his right revealed the intensity of the storm outside, and the lights overhead flickered. He pinched the push-to-talk button on the radio still strapped to his chest, but the device didn't respond. Fried from his time in the water. He checked his pockets. No cell phone. "Damn it."

A quick search of the rest of the main building revealed neither Striker nor West, but the son of a bitch who'd taken them out couldn't have gotten far. Not when he'd had a much better target in mind. Rain battered against the door leading to the other half of the aquarium. The outline of the massive underwater dome on the other side of the pier materialized through the watery streaks against the glass, and Nicholas's instincts prickled. The killer was about proving he was better than his predecessors. Deadlier. More intelligent. Dangerous. He wanted the attention he believed he deserved. What better location to expose two BAU agents than the most popular enclosure on the pier?

He shouldered through the door and onto the walkway separating the outdoor area from the main building. Protecting his face against the violent waves cascading over the pier's railings and across the wooden planks, he sprinted for safety and down the steps into the underwater dome exhibit. The roar of the ocean died as he slammed the door closed behind him. The surface of the water visible through the grid-like construction around the dome churned faster with the intensity of the storm, but the creatures closing in on the glass showed no signs of panic. Shadows shifted across the floor as he descended deeper into the exhibit, weapon raised.

Warning climbed his spine as he stepped down into the lower level of the wraparound viewing point. The lights flickered once again then died, throwing him into a dark underwater world full of surprises and threats.

A moan reached his ears, and Nicholas turned to his right. He couldn't see a damn without the overhead lights and planted his hand against the cold glass keeping thousands of tons of water from crushing him to death to guide him. His eyesight adjusted to the shadows in slow increments, every sense he owned heightened to compensate. Heart thudding at the base of his neck, he recognized an outline against the inner wall of the viewing area. Unmoving. "Striker!"

Holstering his weapon, Nicholas dropped to one knee and patted the agent's frame for the tactical flashlight she'd clipped to her vest earlier. His fingers brushed over cool metal, and he hit the power button. The beam cast straight into the floor beside the missing persons expert but gave him enough light to see the sticky trail of blood running along one side of her face. Madeline's hands had been secured to the railing above her with zip ties. He wedged her chin between his thumb and index finger. Rich, dark eyes reflected the flashlight's beam, her pupils constricting in response. "Striker, can you hear me?"

"James…" The muscles in her throat flexed as she swallowed. "It was an ambush. He attacked me from behind. He knew we were coming."

"I know." Pulling the blade still strapped in his ankle holster, one of the few things he'd hadn't lost at sea, he straightened to cut through the ties around the agent's wrists. "Where are West and Dr. Flood?"

"He already had Dash when he secured me to the railing. He's over there. I tried to stay conscious, but…" Motioning with her chin up the stairs, she rubbed the inflamed skin around her wrists close to her chest. "Dr. Flood was with you."

A deeper groan punctured through the darkness.

"We got separated after we found Paige Cress's body." Nicholas hiked up the three steps to the main level of the underwater dome and caught sight of West zip-tied to another section of railing. Crouching in front of the cybercrimes agent, he cut the ties around West's wrists and caught him before he slumped to the floor. Striker moved into his peripheral vision, and the crush of failure to protect his team—to protect Aubrey—pulverized what confidence he had left. "The bastard took her."

"You think she's the reason the killer lured us here? That he's picking us off one by one to get her alone?" It was as though Striker had read his mind. She pulled West's head into her lap and smoothed the blood from his temple. The tough yet compassionate missing persons expert had gone out of her way to keep her emotional distance from others, but when it came to the BAU and the people she cared about, he trusted Striker to do whatever it took to protect them. She handed him her flashlight. "Go. He took our phones, but I'll get West back to the SUV and call this in over the radio. Find Dr. Flood. If she's the one he wants, then she needs you to have her back."

Nicholas headed back toward the main doors and out into the storm. "He can't have her."

IT WAS HARD to breathe.

Aubrey gasped as pain pulled her from unconsciousness. She jerked against the binding around her wrists and ankles, and the sound of chains hitting against one another echoed in her ears. Pressure built in her head and intensified the ache in her chest, like all her organs had been shoved up inside her chest cavity. She forced her eyes open and was immediately blinded by the bright light aimed at her face.

"Absolutely perfect," he said. "Just like your sister."

That voice. She recognized it from the docks, before her attacker had knocked her unconscious. Disorientation messed with her head, and she realized she'd been hung upside down. Cracks in the cement floor had been stained red beneath her. Aubrey tipped her chin toward her chest, studying the large, sharpened hook between her bare feet. The kind used in slaughterhouses. Fear clawed up her throat. Gravity battled the angle of her head, and she relaxed back into position. Her wrists had been secured before she'd been hung upside down. There was no escape. "You killed Paige Cress. You killed Kara."

"They were perfect, don't you think, Dr. Flood?" Footsteps echoed off the cement from behind. "It took me years of studying the X Marks the Spot Killer to get the marks he left on his victims' cheeks just right. You might think carving something as simple as an *X* would be easy, but you use too much force and the blade perforates the masseter muscle. Use too little and you don't get your point across."

The man in the mask stepped into her line of vision, hints of salt and sea diving deep into her lungs. Dim lighting came through a boarded and dirt-crusted window to her right, but it was nothing compared to the reflection of the spotlight from the blade in her attacker's hand. A nearby table registered. One he'd lined with surgical instruments. "I prefer a more human touch."

Masseter muscle. Most people who hadn't gone to medical school or studied anatomy would call it the cheek, but the killer seemed to have a medical background. When this was over, the BAU could use that information to narrow down possible suspects. Aubrey swallowed through the tightening in her throat and chest. When this was over…

She tugged at the zip ties around her wrists again. Nicholas had said this was a game to the killer, a show for him to get the attention he wanted from the public. Whoever'd killed Kara had fed off his victims' fears. He wanted them to know he had power over them and that he could use that power at any time. He wouldn't kill her quickly. He'd get more satisfaction from a slow kill, and that alone gave her hope the BAU—Nicholas—would find her in time. She just needed to keep the killer talking, give him a reason to talk about himself like any narcissist enjoyed. "Kara and Paige. They weren't your only victims. How many others have there been?"

"Patience, Dr. Flood," he said. "We have more than enough time to get to know each other."

"You must have a process of choosing who will become one of your masterpieces, then. Why Paige Cress? Why Kara?" She studied the room as he circled around behind her. Hooks heavy enough to hold the weight of livestock, cement, boarded windows. An abandoned slaughterhouse. The scent of the ocean said they were still along the coast, possibly north of the waterfront where he'd abducted her. In the warehouse district.

"Ah, beautiful, beautiful Paige. She had this unique habit of remembering funny moments and laughing hysterically in the middle of long silences, especially at funerals. Things no one else would remember or would think were funny." Her attacker tucked the scalpel behind his leg, out of sight as he circled her again. "She'd go out of her way to make the people around her laugh, just to bring a bit of sunshine to their day. Given the kind of work she did for one of the biggest criminal defense law firms in the city, it makes sense. She was trying to compensate for all the evil in the world, evil she helped spread by working for those lawyers. I think her outward sense of humor was her way of making up for it, but it was her smile that caught my attention the first time we met. Unfortunately, I couldn't make her my own masterpiece. No matter how many times I tried to turn her into something they would remember, she wasn't good enough for what I have in mind."

"So you used the Gingerbread Woman's MO instead." Aubrey curled her fingers into the center of her palms and pressed her knuckles together to test the strength of the zip ties. She'd been unconscious when he'd bound her, and it'd been impossible to ensure any slack in the ties, but despite what many people believed, zip ties could be broken with enough pressure. "You knew her. Paige Cress."

"Of course I knew her, Dr. Flood. I loved her." The killer stopped in front of her, cocking his head to one side. "I loved the way she talked about the books she'd read, how she'd tuck herself in at night by cocooning herself in heavy blankets, even in the middle of the summer. Sometimes, I'd watch her fall asleep through her bedroom window, and I'd get this glimpse of sadness right before she closed her eyes. The same thing happened when I suffocated her with her own blazer. You see, that moment, the one right before the light leaves their eyes, that's when you see someone for who they really are. That's when you get to know them the best."

Tears burned in Aubrey's eyes. "And Kara? Did you see who she really was before you finished strangling her?"

A low laugh shook her attacker's shoulders as he disappeared behind her once again. Pain exploded across her scalp as he fisted a handful of her hair and craned her neck back toward her spine. "I know what you're trying to do, Dr. Flood." His breath warmed against the side of her face, and she automatically flinched, but he held her in place. He smoothed his hand across her cheek. "But I can assure you, trying to get me to revel in my kills won't delay my plans for you. I chose you, Aubrey. Paige and Kara, they were exactly what I needed them to be, stand-ins until I was ready to make my own mark, but you… You're going to be my masterpiece. You're going to be my introduction to the world."

Terror increased the pain in her sinuses, and he released her. The chains holding her to the ceiling protested as she swayed away from her captor. Her plan had failed, but she wouldn't give up. She wouldn't stop fighting. "Why? Why me?"

"I know about your work with the X Marks the Spot Killer and the BAU, Dr. Flood." The killer turned his back to her, a mountainous mass of muscle across his shoulders and arms flexing as he moved. Directing his focus to the table, he studied the selection of surgical instruments as though weighing each option. "I know it was you who narrowed down the type of weapon Cole Presley had used on his victims, and I know why it was so important to you to find him."

Aubrey pressed her knuckles together as hard as she could, and the zip ties around her wrists snapped. She bit back the moan elicited by the shot of pain, and she jerked to catch the ties before they fell to the floor. The chains above gave away her movement, but she managed to keep the tie secure against her back. Her hands were free, but she'd have to lift her feet high enough to unhook the double-banded ties around her ankles. She curled her upper body toward her feet, gravity fighting against her abdominal muscles. She just had to reach her feet. That was it, and she could escape. "You've been watching me."

The man in the mask gripped one of the tools, bringing it to eye level. The spotlight bounced off the stainless steel and reflected straight back into her face. She wouldn't be able to move fast enough. Even if she'd managed to somehow curl up enough to grip the chains, her captor would reach her first, but she had to try. "Watching, learning, admiring. You devote everything to giving the families of the dead under your scalpel the answers they need. That was why you spent hour after hour trying to find a weapon that matched the *X*s on the victims' faces. You put their loved ones' needs before your own, no matter how exhausted you were or how many meals you missed. You wanted them to be at peace, and you sacrificed your own health and well-being to provide that for them. You're selfless and well-meaning, but there's a downside to sacrificing your needs for others."

The killer faced her, his shoulders slumping as though she'd disappointed him in trying to escape, and Aubrey uncoiled. He stepped toward her, the scalpel in his hand. "You believe if you give everyone you care about your complete devotion, they'll love you in return, but you know as well as I do, that's not how the world works."

Her stomach revolted. He was profiling her, just as Nicholas had done to him. Every muscle in her body burned. Her mouth dried as the truth surfaced. "You're lying. You can't possibly know that by studying me from a distance."

"You're right in a way, Dr. Flood." He took another step, slowly closing the space between them. "There's a reason I befriended Kara before transforming her into one of my experiments, you see. I couldn't get what I needed from your parents. They're getting older, they don't trust new people in their lives at this point and, to be honest, I don't think they would put up much of a fight when it came right down to it. Kara was my obvious choice to learn as much about you as I could, and she didn't disappoint in the least. Now, here we are."

Kara? Her sister had been strangled and mutilated as a tool to get to her? Bile pooled in her esophagus. "One of these days, you'll be one of the bodies on my examination table. Whatever pain you put my sister through, I promise yours will be much worse."

The killer raised the scalpel toward her neck and

pressed the blade into her skin. Stinging pain sizzled for the briefest of moments before blood trickled along the underside of her chin and dripped to the cement floor. "No, Dr. Flood. I won't. Because I need you to be my masterpiece."

# *Chapter Eight*

He'd cleared the entire aquarium. Aubrey wasn't here.

The storm battered against him and worked cold straight through muscle and deep into his bones. Nicholas spun on the spot, searching for movement—anything—that might tell him where the killer had taken her. Another wave crashed against the pier and dumped almost enough water to sweep his feet right out from under him. He couldn't stay out here. The storm was only getting worse. He had to think. "Where the hell are you, woman?"

Aubrey had been the killer's target all along. That meant something, but the buzz in his head and the panic clawing up his throat were getting in the way of rational thought. He needed somewhere quiet, somewhere he could deep dive and lay out the facts of the case without all the chaos and urgency closing in. He needed Aubrey.

One touch. That was all it'd taken for her to calm the rage and defeat he'd tried to control since learning Cole Presley had been the killer he'd imagined catching as a kid. The memory of Aubrey's fingers framing his jaw, of her honey-warm eyes staring straight into his, surfaced, and his nervous system quieted. Nicholas closed his eyes against the rage of the storm and turned his face up to the driving rain. "You couldn't have gotten far."

He recalled the fight between him and the killer, the way his attacker had moved, his voice, what he'd said. *Dr. Flood is going to be my masterpiece.* The son of a bitch wanted to make a show of introducing himself to the world. He was desperate for someone to take notice of him. No. He wanted the BAU to take notice of him, the unit that had brought down the X Marks the Spot Killer and several other serial offenders. The killer wanted to prove himself worthy, but that didn't give Nicholas a location.

Blood pulsed behind his ears, drowning out the roar of the storm. Aubrey's phantom touch chased back the deep cold flooding through him, as real as the apparitions of victims. As much as her abductor wanted to be in the spotlight, he would need somewhere private, possibly abandoned to make an example of the medical examiner, but not someplace so remote that the BAU would never find her. Sifting through his knowledge of the area, Nicholas opened his eyes and faced the storm.

Clouds rolled low over the warehouse district directly north of his position. He took a single step forward. The area was secluded, far enough from residential witnesses that might see or hear something suspicious. An old slaughterhouse had been abandoned due to a handful of lawsuits over the years. The swinery had been forced out by growing businesses around the property. It was close enough for a muscular man of the suspect's size to haul an unconscious woman on foot. "Gotcha."

Nicholas raced into the parking lot, heading straight for his SUV. He ripped open the door and collapsed inside. Within seconds, he'd started the ignition, fishtailed out of the lot and sped toward the warehouse. Hints of Aubrey's perfume filled his lungs, but they couldn't soothe the fear of what he'd find in that warehouse if he was too late. He'd already lost too many victims to killers like Cole Presley. He couldn't lose her, too. Because despite the little time they'd worked the X Marks the Spot Killer case together and her discovering her sister's body this morning, Aubrey Flood had already slid past his defenses and anchored under his skin.

The killers he hunted, the agents he'd partnered with over the years—they'd all had an agenda of their own, but not Aubrey. She'd sacrificed her own happiness, her own needs, in order to help strangers cope with their loss and to find the truth. Too many people wore a mask, pretended to be someone they weren't, but the sincere warmth in her eyes and her friendly demeanor had carved a massive hole through his trust issues. She was the light he'd forgotten existed in his line of work. From the way she used cartoon quotes to deflect the emotional turmoil she carried to the fact she'd dedicated herself to making others see the positive qualities in themselves. He'd been drawn to her almost the instant they'd met in her morgue three years ago, and there was no way in hell he was going to let her abductor extinguish that light. "I'm coming, Doc."

Rain hit the windshield the faster he pushed the SUV, the right side of his face stinging with embedded glass. The killer had meticulously planned how to isolate his prey. Whoever'd taken Aubrey was intelligent, patient and highly perceptive, and they weren't going to give up their prize easily. Nicholas slammed on the brakes as the outline of the old slaughterhouse materialized through the watery streaks in the window. He shoved the SUV into Park and called for backup and an ambulance with the radio strapped to his dashboard. Just in case. Armed with the backup weapon he'd loaned Aubrey, he pushed out of the vehicle and closed the door quietly behind him. A single door stood out among two stories of cinder-block walls and roll-top doors, but he wasn't stupid enough to believe the killer hadn't planned for an interruption to his game. He'd have to go around, come at this from another angle.

He kept low as he crossed the lot, sidearm in hand, and maneuvered around to the south side of the building. No entry points. Not even a window low enough for him to pry open. Clearing the next corner, he studied the old docks on the west side and located another door. Broken glass from a beer bottle crunched under his weight as he closed in on the entrance. Abandoned slaughterhouse with an entry to miles of open water. It was the perfect location for teenagers to test parental boundaries and escape the pressures of life, but from the thin coat of dust on the cement and the lack of footprints under the large concrete overhang, he surmised no one had been here in quite some time.

Doubt coiled low in his gut as he pressed his back against the wall. The killer could've taken Aubrey to any number of locations. If he was wrong, if he was too late… No. He shut down that line of thinking and tested the wide steel door. It swung open. Aubrey was alive. He had to believe that. She hadn't forced herself back into his life to be ripped away.

Humidity and an acid bite climbed down his throat as he stepped into the slaughterhouse. A combination of dirt, garbage and debris coated the floor in the large space. Exposed piping ran the length of the main room and groaned with the fight of the storm outside. Water trick-led down along the walls from unrepaired holes in the roof, but there was no sign of Aubrey. Not yet. He crept through the darkness, shadows clawing closer, hiding corners and ambush points. Dozens of cement columns supported the failing structure, but it was the rusted ma-chinery and lines of stalls that held his attention. Struc-tured with drains, heavy machinery meant to dispose of livestock, and privacy, this place was the perfect location to dispose of a body.

A hard thud echoed in his ears from the far side of the building, and Nicholas froze.

"You're not supposed to be here, Agent James." The voice bounced off the walls, became part of the shad-ows. Footsteps reverberated through the darkness, each seemingly coming from a different direction. "You're too late. Dr. Flood is already mine, and there is nothing you can do to save her."

His stomach soured. No. Not possible. He was going to find her. He was going to take her home. Nicholas couldn't see a damn thing in here, but using his flash-light would only give away his position. "Why don't you bring her out here so I can ask her myself?"

The killer's low laugh reached his ears.

A hand shot out and wrapped around his weapon. An elbow connected with the sensitive tissue in his right cheek, and Nicholas stumbled back. The glass still embedded in his face screamed from the impact, but it wouldn't stop him from reaching Aubrey. The out-line ahead of him separated from the shadows. Nicholas launched forward, securing the bastard with both hands, and rocketed his forehead into the killer's face. He tossed the man in his grip back into a large piece of machinery designed to haul livestock to the other side of the warehouse. "That's for forcing her to be the one to find her sister's body, you sick son of a bitch."

Dim sunlight penetrated through the boarded windows. A flash of a blade was all the warning he got as the killer struck out. Nicholas dodged the initial strike, but his boot caught on a piece of piping discarded on the floor, and he went down. Pain shot up through his back and elbows as his attacker arced the blade down fast. Catching the killer's wrist mere inches from where the tip of the knife threatened to carve into him with one hand, Nicholas used his other to search for his weapon. His fingers brushed against solid metal a few feet away. A pipe. He latched on to the heavy tool and swung as hard as he could. The crunch of flesh and steel registered in his ears as the suspect rolled off him with a groan. Hiking one leg over the killer, Nicholas rolled to position himself above the man in the mask and raised the pipe. "Where is she? What did you do with her?"

The killer swiped his leg up, wrapped it around Nicholas's chest and slammed him into the floor. Faster than he thought possible, Aubrey's abductor vanished into the shadows. The same low laugh pooled dread at the base of his spine as he struggled to catch his breath. "Do you know how long it takes the human body to bleed out from a nick in the exterior carotid artery, Agent James? Because Dr. Flood does."

Panic exploded through him. He shoved to his feet, clutching onto the pipe. "You cut her then left her to die alone."

"She's stronger than I gave her credit for. It'd be a shame if you wasted time trying to handcuff me while she might still be alive." The voice seemed farther away now, nearly imperceptible. "Ticktock, ticktock. Time is running out, Agent James."

Nicholas gripped the pipe, steel warming in his palm. The killer was giving him a choice. Arrest the bastard in arm's reach or save Aubrey from bleeding out. But it wasn't a choice at all. "I'm going to find you. You're not going to get away with this."

The killer's voice whispered from the darkness, "I already have."

COLD.

Her hand trembled against her neck as she applied pressure to the wound. A growing puddle of blood collected beneath her, and in the back of her mind Aubrey understood the more blood she lost, the sooner she'd go into shock, but she couldn't stop fighting. Saliva thickened in her mouth and throat as she stared up at her feet, still secure with zip ties around her ankles. "You can do this."

Exhaustion seeped into her muscles and stole her energy drop by drop. Black veins bled into her vision. Her heart beat hard in her chest, trying to make up for the loss of volume. Breathing hard, she used the strength she had left to curl up, reaching as far as she could with her free hand, but it wasn't enough. Muscle exertion increased the pressure on her lungs and intensified the headache at the base of her skull. She collapsed back with her head high above the cement floor. The chains protested above. Sweat built in her hairline as she relaxed. She couldn't think, couldn't breathe, but she wasn't going to die here. She wasn't going to let her sister's killer get away with murder.

She wasn't sure where he'd gone, but she couldn't wait

around for him to watch her bleed out. Blood worked through her fingers, and Aubrey closed her eyes, tried to slow her pulse. She estimated she'd lost about five percent of her body's blood supply, still well within acceptable limits before shock occurred. She had time. She just had to use it wisely and not overexert the precious energy she still had left. Forcing herself to take a deep breath, she ignored the slight uptick of her heart rate and curled as fast as she could toward her feet. Her free hand brushed against the zip ties around her ankles, but her strength left as fast as she'd summoned it.

A frustrated scream escaped her throat, and she fell back into her upside-down position. Kara's killer had nicked her carotid artery. She was running out of time. It wouldn't be fatal if she received medical attention in the next ten to fifteen minutes, but the added combination of being restrained and hung upside down accelerated her body's output. Staring up toward her feet, she tried not to let the sway of the chains distract her. This wasn't working. Without something to hold on to or someone to get her down, she couldn't keep pressure on the wound and reach for the zip ties at the same time.

The stain beneath her spread across the cement. Without the pressure against her neck, she'd bleed faster, but she had to risk it. Using both hands was the only way to reach her feet. After that...she wasn't sure what would happen. The edges of her vision grew darker, and a crystal-clear image of the agent she'd pulled from the ocean materialized.

Nicholas.

He'd faced off with the killer in an attempt to save her and lost. She'd managed to get him breathing on that dock, but that didn't guarantee he'd made it off the pier alive. Had she saved him at all? Her head and chest ached as her breathing shallowed. She had to get out of here. She had to make sure he and the rest of the BAU had survived. Aubrey released the pressure against her neck, her hand covered with her own blood. "Don't pass out."

Summoning every last ounce of strength, she forced her upper body to rise and stretched both of her hands toward her feet. Her fingers brushed the edge of the zip ties around her ankles, and with a last burst of desperation, she grabbed on to the bind. Plastic cut into the bare skin around her ankles. Blood blossomed in a straight line and trickled down under her pant leg, but a few added drops wouldn't throw her into shock. Using the zip ties to reach higher, she skimmed the solid steel hook securing her to the ceiling and clamped on. She sobbed with relief as she settled into the awkward fight of remaining upright. Blood rushed from her face and neck as she righted herself, but she still had to free herself from the hook without falling five feet onto cement headfirst.

Dizziness blurred her vision as she notched one hand above the other on the hook. "Okay. Okay." Her own words barely reached her ears as the world righted itself for the briefest of moments. She'd made it upright. She could use her weight to break the zip ties and swing her feet down. She adjusted her grip on the hook with damp palms. She climbed a bit higher and brought her knees to her chest. The edge of the zip ties angled down against the hook, but it still wouldn't break with her added weight. "Come on."

She kicked her heels down as hard as she could. Once. Twice. Groaning through the tear of skin along the outsides of her ankles, she kicked down a third time. The zip ties broke, and her fingers slipped from around the hook.

The spotlight distorted as she fell, and she hit the cement. Air crushed from her lungs. The crunch of bone ricocheted around her head. Pain exploded from her shoulder, ribs and neck. A silent scream ripped from her throat as she turned onto her side, but the spasm hadn't released her lungs yet. Her stomach sucked in automatically as she battled to calibrate the damage then released.

Oxygen charged down her throat and increased the agony tearing through her right side. Another scream escaped and combined with a nerve-racking sob. She curled in on herself, careful not to aggravate the guaranteed fractures to her scapula and right sternal ribs.

Footsteps echoed off the barren walls and machinery stained with the odor of flesh and death. The killer? Straightening one arm, she pressed her palm into the floor and tried to pull herself to the edge of light given off by the spotlight. The footsteps grew louder, closer, and Aubrey forced herself to her feet. No. He wasn't going to finish what he'd started. Keeping her right arm pressed against her chest, she stumbled to her feet and leaned forward, out of the spotlight and into the unknown.

"Dr. Flood…" The voice came from the shadows.

Aubrey pushed one foot in front of the other, one hand outstretched to keep herself from running into a wall or piece of machinery. Her body hurt. She was bleeding, but she had to get away from here. She couldn't stop. Not until she found Nicholas and the rest of the BAU. Her ears rang. The footsteps were following her, and panic clawed through her. Glancing back, she recognized the outline of a man inspecting the circle of light where she'd been hung upside down to die, but she didn't slow. Escape. Getting to Nicholas. That was all that mattered. Dim light penetrated through the dirt-caked windows and illuminated the long stretch of warehouse ahead of her. Tears burned down her face and clouded her vision, but she only pushed herself harder. She could do this. She was going to make it. He hadn't spotted her yet.

Blood pooled between her breasts the longer she exerted herself. Heightened heart rate increased the chances of blood loss, but she didn't have a choice. She wasn't going to be his masterpiece. Not like Kara. Not like Paige Cress. Her hair broke free of the tie and pasted to her face. Machinery obstructed a straightforward escape, and she wound around a massive machine in hopes she'd spot an escape on the other side. The tick of rain pierced through the thready pulse behind her ears. She followed the sound until her feet sliced through a puddle. There had to be an exit here somewhere. Anywhere. The roll of thunder seemed louder now, and a breeze wrestled to cool the sweat beading on her face. She was almost there. She could feel it, but her body had consumed the last bits of adrenaline. She was going to go into shock from blood loss and physical trauma.

The room tilted to one side, and Aubrey slowed. She was as dizzy as a merry-go-round manatee. A laugh escaped past her lips. That had to be one of her best quotes. Falling into the wall on her uninjured side, she forced one foot in front of the other until she cleared the door leading out onto the back docks of the slaughterhouse. Relentless wind pushed her hair away from her face, and she clutched the cold steel of the railing leading down the ramp. Puget Sound protested against the raging storm, spitting salt water into her face. The shock to her nervous system cleared the fatigue pulling her down, but she couldn't go any farther as the lightheadedness intensified.

She just needed to rest for a minute. Using the railing for balance, she slid to the ground and pressed her head against the vibrating metal. Her eyes fell closed as she clutched her right side with her uninjured hand.

"Aubrey," he said.

Instant anxiety flooded through her, but she recognized that voice. Alert, insightful, soothing, it slid through her and chased back the fear knotting in her stomach. She tried to open her eyes to see Nicholas for herself, but she was so tired. She couldn't run anymore, couldn't hide. The killer was going to find her. He was going to turn her into his masterpiece. Just as he'd done with Kara.

Another sob escaped her control. She'd thought she was ready for this, that she could bring down the man who'd murdered her sister. She'd tried to save Nicholas. She'd tried, but it hadn't been enough. She hadn't been enough, and now she was alone.

Strong hands secured her against a wall of warmth, and she struck out, kicked, screamed, but the pain from the fractures in her scapula and ribs limited her motion. "No!"

"Aubrey, it's me. It's Nicholas. I'm here. I'm not going to hurt you. You're safe. He can't get to you now." The warmth disappeared, and she curled into the corner where two sets of railings met. He set something soft into her hand. "I promise not to touch you, but I need you to apply pressure to the wound on your neck. I won't touch you. I'll just wait with you until the ambulance gets here."

"Nicholas?" Was this real? His dark outline distorted through the batter of rain and dizziness. That intense green-blue gaze cleared through the haze, and then there was nothing.

# Chapter Nine

Fractured shoulder blade. Two fractured ribs. Fifteen percent blood loss and a mess of stitches at her temple. Dr. Aubrey Flood had been through hell and survived. Nicholas wasn't sure how, but she'd escaped being hung upside down and drained of blood in that slaughterhouse with mere minutes of consciousness left, and he'd nearly been too late.

He memorized the pattern of bruising across the left side of her face as she slept through the sedatives her doctors had given her. A monitor on the other side of the bed tracked her heart rate while another administered blood to get her volume back up to normal levels. Pain pulsed in his jaw from a strike he hadn't seen coming when he'd approached her on that dock. Along with the rest of him. It'd been obvious she'd started shutting down and going into shock, but he hadn't been able to keep himself from touching her.

Nicholas tried for the sixth—or was it the seventh—time to read through the crime scene report from the warehouse. They'd recovered the zip ties that'd secured Aubrey's hands behind her back and kept her anchored to the hook by her feet. A good amount of blood tested positive for the medical examiner's DNA on the patch of cement lit by a portable spotlight the killer must've brought in, but there was no sign of whoever'd abducted her. No matter how many times he'd read the report in front of him, none of it processed the way it was supposed to. All he saw was the scared, traumatized woman the son of a bitch had left behind. Lucky for him, Striker and West had made it out with nothing more than bruises and a mild concussion between them.

The killer wouldn't get another chance.

"Aren't you cuter than a chinchilla's behind?" she asked.

Setting the report on the side table, he leaned forward in his seat. An immediate sense of relief replaced the anger burning through him, and he slid his hand beneath hers at the edge of the hospital bed. Nicholas scrubbed his free hand down his face. In all the years he'd investigated serial crimes for the BAU, he'd never sat beside a witness's or victim's bedside like this, but he couldn't forget the fact she'd risked her life in order to save his. If it hadn't been for her, he would've drowned out there at the pier. He had to remember that. "Hey, Doc. Welcome back to the land of the living."

"Not sure I'm staying. Whatever they gave me is very nice." Aubrey's mouth curled slightly at one corner. Her fingers jerked in his hand, and she leveled honey-warm eyes on the spot where he held on to her. "I thought you were dead. I was trying to escape so I could save you."

His heart threatened to beat straight out of his chest. "You did save me. You pulled me from the water. My chest still hurts where you gave me CPR, but it's nothing compared to the fact I wouldn't be sitting here if it weren't for you. I owe you my life."

"You've got something on your face." A laugh rippled

through her, and she groaned, presumably from the bone-deep pain of blunt-force trauma to her right side during her abduction. The sedatives had cleared any kind of filter from her thoughts and her mouth, and he couldn't deny the amusement coiling through him at the sight. "Ouch."

Awareness prickled along the right side of his face. "Yeah. See, I had a little accident before you pulled me from the ocean and gave me mouth-to-mouth. The man who took you ground my face into a broken table. Nothing thirty-five stitches and a lifetime of battle scar stories can't fix."

"Beats falling five feet onto cement. We can trade injuries if you'd like." Her smile disintegrated, and reality settled between them. She pressed against the pressure point between his index finger and thumb, and a heightened sense of comfort pushed through him. "You were trying to stop him from getting to me. You were trying to protect me."

"Yeah, I was, but I failed, Doc. I wasn't fast enough, and he got to you anyway." And he'd have to live with that truth the rest of his life. Because there was a chance with the damage done to her right shoulder blade and ribs, she might not be able to recover enough to do her job as Seattle's chief medical examiner. If she couldn't hold a scalpel steady, she couldn't perform an autopsy. The city would replace her as soon as they found a candidate, and it'd be his fault. Her entire livelihood, her dream of helping loved ones find comfort and answers, gone. "I can't imagine the terror you went through, but I need to get a statement from you when you're ready. I've gone over the crime scene photos. I've read the reports, but there's not a single piece of evidence the killer left behind that we could use to identify him. Can you tell me what you remember?"

The laughter drained from her eyes, and the effect drilled straight through Nicholas's detachment and into his gut. "I remember his voice, but it was distorted with the mask. I don't think he was someone I knew." She pulled her hand from his. "I can assume samples from under my fingernails have already been collected, and that your forensic team has taken my clothes as evidence, but I'm not sure how much help they'll be. He wore gloves when he kidnapped me. You won't find his DNA evidence in the zip ties or on the hook, and the ski mask would've prevented him from leaving behind saliva, sweat or blood."

Defeat washed through her expression, and she raised her uninjured hand to the outline of gauze at her neck. "He cut me with a scalpel."

Nicholas sat a bit straighter. They'd recovered the collection of tools from a cart near where she'd been strung up, but there hadn't been a scalpel among them. "A scalpel. The same kind you would use to perform autopsies, right?"

"Yes. He had an entire arrangement of surgical tools, most of which could be found in my own medical kit. His hand was steady when he made the incision, which suggests he has medical training." Aubrey studied the sling keeping her right elbow bent against her chest. "I remember thinking I was going to die, and that Kara must've had the same thought while he was strangling her. I didn't want to die."

"I'm sorry, Doc." Medical training and knowledge of forensics, at least enough for the killer to know he had to wear gloves and a mask when he abducted his victims to prevent leaving behind trace DNA. That could narrow down possible suspects. Nicholas pressed an unraveling thread from the edge of her sheet beneath his thumbnail. "He won't touch you again. I give you my word."

"You can't promise that. Even if we manage to stop him from taking another victim, he made it clear I'm the one he's chosen to become his masterpiece." She shook her head, and a tear streaked down her face. "That kind of obsessive narcissism, his need to prove himself… I don't think he's going to stop until he gets what he wants. No matter how many people get in his way."

"He won't touch you, because I'm not letting you out of my sight." Determination unlike anything he'd experienced before rocked through him. Aubrey had survived what dozens of victims hadn't. "He went after one of our own, and the BAU doesn't forgive that kind of offense. I'm going to do whatever it takes to keep you safe."

"I believe you." Aubrey tried to sit higher in the bed, flinching against the pain morphine couldn't touch, he was sure. "Did you find your teammates? Are they okay?"

"Striker's and West's egos are hurt more than their heads, but yeah," he said. "They're okay, and I had our public relations liaison check in on your parents. They weren't given specifics about what happened at the slaughterhouse, but they were made aware you were injured trying to solve Kara's case. They want to see you as soon as they can, but until whoever attacked you is in custody—"

"I understand. Thank you. I'm not sure how I would've managed to explain everything to them." She scrubbed her uninjured hand down her face. "Were your forensic techs able to test the samples I took from Paige Cress's remains or find something I missed on the body?"

This was where his choices would threaten a conviction once they caught up to the killer. Paige Cress's background check hadn't revealed anything or anyone that might've contributed to her death, and Cole Presley's every move had been accounted for by the warden of Washington State Corrections. "No. The storm… I didn't have time to secure the remains after I realized you'd been taken. By the time CSU arrived on the scene, the ocean had risen enough to compromise any evidence the killer might've left behind and destroy the samples you'd collected. Dr. Caldwell is performing the autopsy as we speak, but I'm not sure how much survived the storm."

"You chose to compromise the evidence and come after me?" Shock wound through her words and bled into her expression. "There could've been something on her body to give us an ID. You could lose your job for failing to secure the remains in a homicide investigation."

"I was willing to take the risk. We're going to nail the son of a bitch, Doc." He maneuvered to the edge of his seat, forcing her to look at him. "Sooner or later, that ego of his is going to force him to make a mistake, and when he does, you and I will be there to take him down. You're right. He's not going to stop. His confidence is growing, and he'll try again."

"Why? Why would you do that?" The muscles along her jaw clenched. "You had the chance to stop him."

"Because your life was worth more than losing the chance to stop him, and if I was put in the situation again, I'd make the same call." Didn't she understand that? The minutes between when she'd vanished and when he'd found her on the docks behind the slaughterhouse had been the worst of his life. Worse than discovering the X Marks the Spot Killer had lived next door to his family his entire life. Worse than seeing Kara Flood strangled and mutilated in front of her apartment building. If he'd lost her...there wouldn't have been any good left in the world. "You're more important to this investigation than you realize. I couldn't let him have you."

"I'm a pathologist. I'm not even allowed to investigate the victims in this case. I was expendable, and you..." She darted her tongue across her lacerated bottom lip, and his attention homed in on the small change. "You were brave to face him. You saved me. I'm not sure I could do much more than say thank you."

"You might not be allowed to perform the autopsies for the victims in this case, but that doesn't mean you're expendable." Nicholas soothed circles into the back of her hand. A deep-rooted shift crushed the air from his lungs as the truth surfaced. He'd gone out of his way to detach himself from the killers and victims in his past cases, but the idea of losing the woman in front of him had triggered a change of emotion he couldn't explain. He'd made a call. He'd let the killer slip through his fingers and the evidence be compromised, but in a career where he'd seen nothing but blood, violence and death, Aubrey had reminded him there was still good in the world. How could he have let that be destroyed? "Not to me."

NICHOLAS HELPED HER INSIDE, motioning her through the safe-house door.

The days had never slipped through her fingers as quickly as the past forty-eight hours. Pain pulsed along her right side as Aubrey stepped over the threshold. Fractured scapula, two damaged sternal ribs and most likely the end of her career.

Taking in the cramped, bright decor and neutral colors, she hugged her injured arm tighter to her chest with help from the sling, and the pain flared again. Nicholas's strong grip under her elbow anchored her from losing complete control, but the cracks had already started to show. Exhaustion and constant agony broke the strongest of the human race. She wouldn't be any different.

"I'll help you upstairs then make us something to eat." Nicholas scanned the small kitchen and living space down the hallway, his voice more soothing than any painkiller she'd been administered since the attack. "I'm sure you're probably tired of hospital food, so I had the BAU intern stock the pantry and fridge while we were waiting for you to be discharged."

She nodded, not really sure what she was supposed to say, how she was supposed to react. A vicious killer had tried to kill him and two of his agents then abducted her, hung her upside down by her ankles and nicked her artery to watch her bleed out. If it hadn't been for Nicholas, if he hadn't confronted the man determined to turn her into a masterpiece, she wouldn't have walked out of that slaughterhouse alive. "Thank you."

"You're safe here, Doc," he said. "Dr. Caldwell has Paige's and Kara's remains, and my team is going through the evidence from the scene as we speak. We're going to catch the bastard who did this to you."

"I know." Because the alternative meant living in fear for the rest of her life. The killer had studied her, chosen her. She might've gotten away from him once, but that didn't mean he wouldn't try to finish what he'd started.

They took the stairs together, Nicholas's hand never

leaving her arm, and rounded into the first bedroom on the left. She caught sight of her overnight bag on the end of the bed. Everything looked exactly the same as when she'd left it to help Nicholas and his team recover Paige Cress's body, but her entire world had been ripped away from her. Pressure built behind her sternum as his hand slipped from her arm, and an instant cold flooded through her as though she'd needed his physical contact to hold herself together.

"I'm going to make us something to eat." Green-blue eyes—the same color as the water he'd nearly drowned in—settled on her, and her self-confidence waned. "You'll be okay here?"

The scrubs the hospital staff had given her after the forensic unit had taken her clothing for evidence chafed against her oversensitized skin. She wanted nothing more than to change into her old college T-shirt and a pair of sweatpants—to find a small amount of comfort in the nightmare closing in around her—but the limitations in her shoulder wouldn't let her do it alone. Heat flared into her neck and face. Her knees threatened to give out as exhaustion pulled at her ligaments and muscle attachments. "I want to change into my own sweats, but I can't... I can't do it by myself."

Realization widened Nicholas's gaze. He threaded one hand through his messy blond hair, so different than the controlled style he'd greeted her with outside her sister's apartment three days ago. "Right. Okay. Well, Agent Striker is heading up the crime scene search at the slaughterhouse, but I can pull her off that assignment to come stay with you, if that makes you more comfortable."

"I'm comfortable with you." She regretted the words the moment they slipped from her mouth, but she wouldn't take them back. It was the truth. Aubrey wasn't sure when it'd happened. But somewhere between the relief she'd felt at knowing he would be the agent to take the lead on her sister's murder investigation and realizing he was the one holding her on those docks after her escape, a life-altering connection had formed. "It won't take much. I mostly need help changing out of this scrub top and getting my arm through my shirt. I can change into my sweatpants myself."

"I can do that." Nicholas reached for her luggage and laid it flat before unzipping the main compartment. He pulled her dark gray, oversize T-shirt from the top and set it on the end of the bed then did the same with her sweatpants. Facing her, he closed the distance between them, and her pulse rocketed into her throat. "Now what?"

"You'll have to remove the sling without jarring my arm." She peeled back the Velcro supporting her thumb and unclipped the mechanism that would give her access to the inside of the sling. Her breath shallowed as hints of his aftershave filled her lungs. Salty and comforting. He must've gotten a shower during his hospital stay. She braced as he slid his hand under her injured arm and helped her lift it out of the sling. Her heart beat hard behind her ears as Nicholas brushed against her hip. The clips around her opposite shoulder and midsection released with his help, but the pain never returned. "I need help taking my shirt off."

"I usually have to convince a woman to say that to me." His laugh tunneled past the tension and warmed parts of her she hadn't realized had gone numb since the last time she'd let a man get this close. Nicholas maneuvered her uninjured arm through the sleeve of the scrub top and pooled the fabric on the side of her neck before circling around to her other side.

"I doubt you've had to convince a woman of much of anything." Cool air slid across her stomach as he slipped the shirt over her head and wound it gently down her arm. Exposed in nothing more than her sports bra and scrub pants, Aubrey shivered against the inferno coiling in her gut, and another layer of emotional control stripped free.

He collected her T-shirt from the bed, one hand still supporting her arm, and reversed the process until the hem brushed against the tops of her thighs. So careful. "I tell people I'm an accountant."

"What?" A laugh escaped past her lips. "Why?"

"As much as people claim they love true crime and want to hear all the gory details of my job, facing the real thing is entirely different, and definitely not that romantic. But nobody asks an accountant questions about their job." Nicholas flashed a crooked smile as he secured her sling back into place. "All set, Doc."

"Thank you." She let her sling take the weight of her arm and turned to sit down on the end of the bed. Her energy drained as she filtered through the adrenaline-driven haze of the past few days. "I tell my dates I'm a pediatrician. Although it's been a while since I've had to use it."

He hauled her luggage off the bed and set it on the floor near his feet as he took a seat beside her. The mattress dipped under his weight, his arm brushing against her left side, and the lingering numbness of the painkillers her doctors had prescribed vanished. All she felt was him. "You mean autopsies don't make great pillow talk?"

"Not exactly." A humorless laugh bubbled to the surface. Aubrey picked at one of the threads unraveling from the hem of her old university shirt. Silence solidified between them, and the hollowness she'd pushed off since leaving the hospital charged forward. Twisting her gaze up, she studied the lacerations across Nicholas's face from his fight with the killer, and her gut clenched. The hospital staff had done a great job of stitching the wounds, but he'd be left with permanent scarring for the rest of his life. She'd spent her career and her personal life trying to help as many people as she could—Kara, her parents, the families who'd lost their loved ones—but right then, she needed someone to help her. Tears burned in her eyes as her control fractured. "I can see him when I close my eyes."

Nicholas slid one hand into hers, rough calluses catching on her skin. "I know."

"I can hear his voice. I can hear his excitement after he cut me and feel the fear suffocating me faster than I was bleeding out." Embarrassment and shame exploded from behind her sternum, and she sniffed, turning her attention back to her lap. "I know your job is to find the killer. Trauma isn't part of your job description, but I need to know. Do those feelings ever go away?"

"No. They don't." He pressed soothing circles into the back of her hand, and the invisible thread of connection between them strengthened. "But it gets easier, Doc. I promise. One day, months or years from now, you'll wake up and it won't be the first thing you think of in the morning."

The muscles in her throat strained. "Was that how it was for you?"

"After a while." Nicholas nodded, his gaze confident and warm. "It didn't happen as fast as I wanted it to, but yeah, it got easier."

A sob clawed up her throat as the last grip on her control shattered, and the tears slipped down her face. "Can you…can you hold me for a few minutes?"

"Yeah." He slid his arm around her lower back and tugged her into his side. The room tilted on its axis as he pulled her down onto the bed, encircling her in his arms. He smoothed her hair back away from her face, his exhales warming her scalp. "I'm right here, Doc. I'm not going to let anyone hurt you again."

The sob broke free, racking through her as he held her. She pressed her hand over his heart, counting off the steady beat in an effort to gain some kind of control. In vain. Forcing herself to take a deep breath, Aubrey angled her head up to look him in the eyes and pressed her mouth to his.

TEMPERATURES DROPPED WELL below comfort level as Special Agent Dashiell West descended the stairs into Harborview Medical Center's northernmost morgue. Thick double doors protested on old hinges as he pushed into the surgical suite. A wall of cold lockers, each labeled with names of the deceased held prisoner inside, reflected blinding fluorescent light from above two exam tables in the center. Tables currently holding the covered remains of Kara Flood and Paige Cress. The pungent kick of decomposition hit Dash square in the chest and knocked precious oxygen from his lungs. He coughed into the crook of his elbow, aggravating the wound at the back of his head. "Dr. Caldwell."

A man, taller than Dash, raised his gaze from examining the victim Nicholas had recovered from the waterfront pier. The clear face shield protecting the medical examiner from contaminating the remains revealed a long, straight nose, thick eyebrows and smaller-than-average eyes. The pathologist's elongated, oval face emphasized the man's graying temples and five-o'clock shadow around his jaw. Dr. Caldwell was more muscular than Dash had expected for a man who dealt with the dead, standing well above six feet as he straightened.

"You must be Agent West. Please, excuse the mess." The King County medical examiner set his instrument on the steel tray beside the slab then rushed to pull the sheet at Paige Cress's hips higher. Tugging his latex gloves from his hands, he tossed them into the hazardous materials bin near the lockers.

Dr. Archer Caldwell extended his hand. "I don't usually get much company down here other than my assistant."

Dash shook the doc's hand, and the dull pain at the back of his head pulsed. He and Striker had been taken out of the game almost immediately after they'd split up at the waterfront, leaving Nicholas and Dr. Flood to survive a sadistic serial killer on their own. Wouldn't happen again. "You said over the phone you had something to show us from both sets of autopsies on the victims."

"Yes. Although I assumed it'd be Agent James who'd want to see what I've found firsthand, but please." Dr. Caldwell motioned toward the two slabs where each woman rested. "I've confirmed cause of death for the first victim, Kara Flood, as strangulation. You can see here from the dark contusions around her throat, the killer used an object about two inches in width. I was able to pull a few fibers from where the edge of the murder weapon dug into her skin."

Dash studied the line of deep black and blue bruising around the victim's throat, his chest tight. Kara Flood had been an exquisite woman before she'd died, committed to education and learning, with an understated beauty. The forensics tests from her dog had come back inconclusive. They needed something to nail the bastard before he struck again. "Fibers? The murder weapon shed fibers while he strangled her?"

Dr. Caldwell nodded. "Yes. Blue nylon. I had the forensics lab test the fibers against the leash you and your partner recovered with the dog from the scene. It was an exact match, but that's not what I wanted to show you. Do you see these two darker bruises between the edges of where the leash stopped? They're thumbprints. I believe the killer used his hands to strangle the victim first then wrapped the leash around her throat and tightened it in an effort to hide the outline of his hands, but the lacerations to the victim's face—"

"Kara. Her name is Kara," Dash said.

The killer might have wanted to erase these women's identities by trying to hide them within MOs from two separate killers, but Dash wouldn't. He remembered them. He remembered all of them.

"Yes, Agent West, of course. I apologize. It's just that in my line of work, in order for me to do my job proficiently, I have to be able to detach from the person I'm cutting open. Sometimes that's the only way I don't take the victims home with me." The pathologist bent over Kara again, tracing the pattern of deep cuts across the victim's face with his pinkie finger hovering above her skin.

"As I was saying, the lacerations to the victim's face are consistent with the injuries Dr. Flood noted while she was performing the autopsies during the X Marks the Spot Killer case, as we expected given the killer's testing of MOs. But instead of a hunting knife, whoever attacked this victim used a scalpel to carve the X into her masseter muscle."

"A scalpel. Dr. Flood's statement said the killer nicked one of the arteries in her neck with a scalpel, that he had a whole collection of surgical tools on a nearby table." Dash's focus shifted to the spread of stainless steel tools Dr. Caldwell had laid out to perform both autopsies on the victims. "Are you able to determine the killer's hand size based off the bruising around Kara's neck?"

"Unfortunately, no," Dr. Caldwell said. "Given the fact there are no foreign epithelial cells around the victim's neck, I concluded the killer wore gloves when he strangled her, which changes the shape and size of the attacker's hands. Add in the element of the leash to hide the bruising altogether, whoever killed Ms. Flood ensured we wouldn't be able to narrow down any identifying features."

Damn. This guy had been careful. "What about the injuries on Paige Cress's body? You said you were able to recover something even after the ocean water cleaned the remains."

"Yes." Dr. Caldwell motioned him toward the next table, where Paige Cress rested as though she were asleep—apart from the Y incision stitched with dark thread over her collarbone and down the center of her chest. "There's evidence of rapid decomposition due to rising temperatures in the shed where the remains were discovered, which made it difficult to determine time of death. With the addition of salt water washing the remains, there wasn't much to go off. But I can definitively tell you this victim was killed eighteen to twenty hours before she was placed in that maintenance shed on the waterfront. And you'll be happy to know, I found this between the victim's teeth."

The pathologist handed Dash what looked like a petri dish without the colored goo in the bottom he'd used in science class in high school. "My assistant recovered human tissue, but I've so far been unable to match it to a wound on the victim, and given it was found between her teeth, I suspect it came from whoever suffocated her. I'll know for certain once the forensic lab processes the evidence."

"She took a bite out of her attacker." Dash studied the tissue through the clear container. He handed back the petri dish. Dr. Flood had insisted whoever'd abducted her and hung her upside down by her ankles in that slaughterhouse had to have had medical training. Not only to keep the scalpel steady but to know where and how deep to cut her to keep her from bleeding out too quickly. "This is good. Have you worked a serial case before, Dr. Caldwell?"

"What an odd question, Agent West. No. I haven't." Dr. Caldwell replaced the tissue evidence on the same cart as his surgical tools. "I'd hoped at the time my work would've spoken for itself. I have years of experience in homicide investigations and have taught forensic pathology at the university for close to a decade." The pathologist's expression neutralized as he studied the victim on his slab. "But the spotlight shines on Dr. Flood."

# Chapter Ten

He could still feel the warmth of her mouth pressed against his.

Nicholas listened to the doc's steady breathing as she slept wrapped in his arms. Exhausted from the trauma sustained during her abduction, her escape from a cold-blooded killer and the emotional implications of almost dying, Aubrey had fallen asleep in his arms the minute she'd kissed him. Hints of her light perfume clung to her ratty T-shirt, and he filled his lungs as much as possible.

He hadn't been able to sleep. Not with the updates filtering in from his team. Kara Flood's dog hadn't given up any viable evidence other than Koko's leash had been used in the attack, which didn't quite fit with the profile Nicholas had built so far. The killer had targeted the victim. Why then had he only brought the scalpel to use during the attack and not something to replicate the strangulation patterns on the X Marks the Spot Killer's victims? Cole Presley had used his favored belt on his victims. This killer had used his hands, making Kara Flood's death personal.

They had no suspect.

According to Agent West, the King County medical examiner—Dr. Archer Caldwell—had recovered a possible DNA sample from Paige Cress's teeth during her autopsy. She'd bitten her assailant before she'd died, but without someone to compare it to, they were back at square one. The clock was ticking down to the killer striking again, but he couldn't deny the sense of calm washing through him now.

"How many of your extremities are numb from staying in one position all night?" Her sleep-addled voice pricked awareness down his arms and legs, every inch of the right side of his body pressed against hers. Aubrey notched her chin higher. An upturn of her mouth countered the blood, violence and anger cascading in unending flashes of memory and cleared his head.

"Approximately fifty percent, I imagine, but it was worth it to be able to get you to slow down." Damn, she was beautiful. Even more so than he remembered from the first time he'd met her three years prior.

"I'm sorry. I didn't mean to fall asleep on you. You could've extracted yourself if you wanted to get into your own bed. I probably wouldn't have noticed." Pressing her uninjured palm to his chest, she struggled to sit up without the use of her right side and failed. She tried again and fell against him. "This is embarrassing, but could you please push me off the bed?"

"Sure thing, Doc." His laugh erupted easily as he straightened. Sliding his hands under her right hip, careful of her higher injuries, he rolled her onto her other side and pushed her legs over the edge of the mattress. "Nothing to it."

"Thank you." Aubrey hesitated to stand, her back to him. "I appreciate you staying with me last night. It probably doesn't seem like much to you, but I haven't let someone else take care of me in a long time. All my energy, everything I do, has been to help the people I care about and the families of the deceased who come in my morgue. I forgot how good it feels to put myself first for once."

His gut clenched. Nicholas pushed to his feet, studying the curve of her spine down her back. Her obsession with being needed had nothing to do with ensuring the people she cared about were happy or that their lives were made easier because of her. Demanding to be part of her sister's murder investigation didn't benefit anyone. No. To Aubrey, being needed equated to being loved. Being valuable and worthy to the investigation fulfilled her, but the consequences of giving herself completely to external sources had taken a vicious toll. He'd held her last night because he'd recognized the exhaustion and pain in her eyes. He'd held her because of her drive to be close to others. He'd held her... Damn it, he'd held her because he wanted to be the one to help her forget what she'd been through.

At no point in his career—in his life—had he felt more protective toward another person than he had the moment he'd found her on those docks. She'd been vulnerable, delirious from blood loss, physically weak. He'd sustained injuries of his own during the fight between him and the killer, but the minute he'd pried her desperate grip from the hand railing, he'd felt nothing but the need to care for her.

Nicholas maneuvered around the end of the bed. He crouched in front of her. Hands leveraged on either side of her hips, he memorized the angles of her jawline, the smooth skin of her neck. Every cell in his body tuned to every cell in hers, and the defensive guard he'd used to protect himself from trusting her crumbled. "You've spent your entire personal and professional life in the service of others, Doc. You took care of Kara. You take care of your parents. Hell, you even try to comfort the families of the people who come across your slab. I've never met someone so sincere, compassionate and patient, but there's only so much you can give before there's nothing left. It's your turn. Tell me what you need."

"You've done enough. You said I'm the one who saved your life, but you saved mine, too. You held me last night when I'm sure that's the last way you wanted to spend your time on this case." She shook her head, refusing to look up at him, and swiped at her cheeks. "I promise, you don't have to do this—"

"Yes, I do." He intertwined his hand in hers. Her tears streaked across his fingers. "Tell me what you need from me."

Her shaky inhale reached his ears, and a sense of emotional awareness entered her expression. "I need a shower and chocolate doughnuts with rainbow sprinkles and to watch some cartoons. I need my sweatpants, because these scrubs are too itchy, and to scream as loud as I can because of what happened, and I need..." She visibly worked to catch her breath, and she squeezed his hand. "I need you to put your arms around me again, so I don't feel like I'm going to shatter into a million pieces right here in the middle of this room."

Horror and a hint of embarrassment entered her expression, and she tried to pull back.

"All right then," he said. "Let's start with the shower."

"What?" she asked. "You were serious?"

"Serious as soggy underwear in the springtime." Nicholas straightened, offering his hand to help her stand.

Her laugh punctured through the low ringing in his

ears and worked to destroy the defenses he'd been holding on to since learning who Cole Presley really was. Aubrey slipped her hand into his, the bruises on the backs of her knuckles a small testament of what she'd been through in the past few days. But more than that, proof she'd survived, that she was as strong as anyone could be in her situation, and a swelling of admiration and attraction heated under his skin. "That was…"

"Worthy of a Dr. Flood favorite?" He pulled her to her feet, and she stumbled into him, her mouth level with his. A few centimeters. That was all that was left between them as she struggled to gain her balance.

"I was going to say graphic, but yes. Definitely worthy of making it into my top five sayings. I might have to use that one myself someday." Her smile accentuated the laugh lines around her nose, and he homed in on her lips. "Not sure of the context quite yet, though. I'll have to work on that."

She'd tasted of honey and vanilla last night before she'd passed out on his chest—a figment of his imagination, he was sure. Because the truth was, trauma affected people in a lot of different ways. It'd broken down Aubrey's obsession to be needed in less than forty-eight hours. Maybe his own trauma response triggered hallucinations, but the combination of her perfume and something inside told him he hadn't imagined that kiss at all. Sweet as honey, addictive as vanilla.

"Could you grab my sweatpants from off the floor for me?" She pointed to the pile of light gray material pooled at the end of the bed. "As much as I appreciate you helping me change out of my top last night, I think it's best if I manage this part myself."

"Take your time. I'll start the shower and work on get-

ting one of the interns to deliver some chocolate doughnuts with sprinkles." He bent and swept her sweats off
the floor then handed them off. Heading toward the bathroom positioned between both ends of this particular
container-turned-bedroom floor plan, he ran through
the list she'd given him over and over until her words ingrained in his brain. *I need you to put your arms around
me again, so I don't feel like I'm going to shatter into a
million pieces right here in the middle of this room.*

"I kissed you last night," she said.

His gut clenched tighter, and Nicholas hesitated half-
way to the bathroom door. His boots dragged against
the industrial-style carpet as he turned partially toward
her. Spreading his hands wide at his sides, he tried to get
the feeling back into his fingertips as she stared at him.
"What you've been through... It can have a lot of different effects on a person. I understand you didn't mean
anything by it. We can forget it happened and move on
with our lives."

He wouldn't. No matter how many times he'd tried last
night as she pressed herself against him, he'd replayed the
feeling of her softness dominating him from the outside
in. People weren't who they said they were. Cole Presley hadn't been the support system Nicholas had needed
growing up. He hadn't been the father Nicholas wished
had stuck around. Not really. He'd been a serial killer
who got off on proving his power over innocent women
for thirty damn years, and Nicholas had been too blind
to see it. He'd taken big measures to ensure he was never
fooled again, but Aubrey Flood had barreled into his life
and turned his world upside down with that kiss.

"And if I don't want to forget it? What then?" She

clutched her sweatpants a little too tightly at her side. "What if I meant it?"

Nicholas faced her. One step. Two. He closed the distance between them. Spearing his fingers through the hair at the back of her neck, he crushed his mouth against hers.

AUBREY DROPPED THE sweatpants and fisted her uninjured hand in his shirt, barely able to hold herself upright as he swept past her lips and explored her mouth with a primal possessiveness. He tasted of salt and man and fed into her rolling need for comfort the longer he refused to let her go.

It'd been so long since she'd let someone get this close, afraid as soon as they discovered what she did for a living they'd run in the opposite direction. It'd happened too many times before, the rejection, the hurt. But Nicholas didn't care about her career. The rough brush of his five-o'clock shadow shot awareness straight through her, and a moan slipped from her lips. He'd been willing to do whatever it took to help her work through the pain and fear clinging to her every thought. When was the last time someone had offered to help her with anything?

Her lungs struggled to keep up with her racing heartbeat, and Aubrey pulled away to catch her breath. She set her forehead against his, forcing herself to unclench her fist from his shirt. To prove she could. Fortifying herself against dragging him closer, she pressed her hand into his chest. "That was sweeter than apple pie on a Sunday."

"You say the most flattering things." His laugh rumbled up through her palm and straight through her chest. Nicholas circled his hand around hers and brought her fingertips to his lips. He kissed her middle finger, and she swore her knees gave out just a little bit. "I'm going to get that shower ready for you. After that, we can talk about doughnuts and cartoons." Stepping back, he stole the warmth simmering from his touch and headed for the rectangular-shaped bathroom planted in the middle of the open floor plan. "You're not alone in this, Aubrey. You still have people who care about you. No matter what happens, I want you to remember that."

No matter what happens? A rock materialized in the pit of her stomach. Her scapula and first ribs on her right side ached with the reminder the fractures had the potential to end her career. If she wasn't able to be part of police investigations as a medical examiner, would she and Nicholas even see each other when this case was closed? More importantly, what was she supposed to do if she couldn't help those families who needed answers? She nodded as the room started to spin. Whether from Nicholas's kiss, the physical trauma she'd sustained or the idea of losing everything she'd worked for, she didn't know. "I know."

He shouldered into the bathroom, and the sound of water hitting tile filled her ears. Within a few seconds, he'd directed her into the luxurious bathroom she hadn't expected in any kind of safe house. Least of all one made of shipping containers.

"This is…beautiful." She took in the glistening marble tile lining the edge of a massive jetted tub and climbing high above the top of the large glass-doored shower. A light gray vanity had been installed perpendicular to the tub, and she ran her free hand along the cold smooth surface. Steam tendriled through the air and settled against her neck and face.

"Not bad for an FBI safe house, is it?" He unclipped

the attachments around her midsection and over her un-injured shoulder and maneuvered her arm out of the sling as he had last night. He set the sling on the counter, but his body heat had penetrated past skin and muscle. Just as quickly as he had the night before, he helped her out of her shirt and offered her a robe from a nearby hook before he wound her free from her sports bra. "Take as much time as you need. When you're done, I should have a lead on some fresh doughnuts and coffee." He turned to close the door behind him. "Black, right?"

"Right." Hesitation hardened the muscles down her spine, but she'd never felt so wanted, so…loved as she did right then. "Nicholas?"

"Yeah?" He pushed the door open wider, settling green-blue eyes on her.

"I couldn't have gotten through this without you." That truth resonated deeper than she wanted to admit, and an array of emotion washed through her. Fear, anger, desire, exhaustion, grief. It tornadoed into something unrecognizable and foreign, but she didn't try to stop it. She didn't try to control it. There was only Nicholas, her anchor. Her partner.

"You're the one who kept me from drowning out there, Doc. I'm the one who owes you." He sealed her inside as steam built around her and worked to soothe the aches of the past three days.

Her bare feet stuck to the floor as she discarded the robe he'd given her. Every ache, every shot of pain threatened to resurrect the memory of how she'd been injured. A flash of her counting the drops of blood hitting the floor beneath her lit up behind her eyes, and she automatically brushed her hand against the gauze taped to her neck. She'd faced the results of violence in her career, but she'd never come so close to winding up on another pathologist's table before. She peeled the medical tape from her skin and examined the cut underneath in the mirror above the vanity. Straight, yet small. Deep enough to puncture her carotid artery but not deadly enough to make her bleed out in a matter of seconds. Whoever had abducted her, whoever had hung her upside down by her ankles and promised to turn her into his masterpiece, had known what he was doing. He'd had surgical instruments, medical training, knowledge of human anatomy. Same as she did.

Aubrey stepped under the shower spray, reveling in the sharp sting against her scalp. Pooling a large amount of shampoo in her hand, she methodically washed the scent of the ocean and thick sections of dried blood from her hair with one hand. The stitches on her temple stung with the added chemicals from the shampoo, but the pain only managed to keep her in the moment. Red-tinted water swirled down the drain near her feet. Bruising protested under her touch as she scrubbed the evidence of her walking nightmare from her skin, and another sob clawed through her chest. The scent of lavender filled the shower. The forensic techs hadn't wanted her to shower at the hospital. She could still feel the killer's hands on her, still smell his breath. Still hear him telling her how much he'd needed her to be his masterpiece.

The skin along her forearm reddened, and Aubrey let go of the loofah.

She didn't want to be needed anymore. Everyone had needed her, and she'd let them, even when it was in rivalry with her own self-interest and well-being. They'd needed her because they'd known she'd come through for them. Her parents had needed her to check in on them throughout the week. Her sister had needed her to call her every night to talk about her day. Her friends had needed her to stop talking about her work in social situations, before they'd stopped asking to meet up altogether. The men she'd dated had needed her to lie about what she did for a living. Everyone had needed her. With the horrendous details of her job, she'd gone out of her way to make others comfortable in an effort to feel closer to the people she cared about, but she'd suffocated her own needs and identity in the process.

Grief charged in uninvited, and she slammed her un-injured hand against the tile wall. The little energy she'd tried to hang on to vanished. She sank onto the built-in bench and brought her legs to her chest. She'd given them everything without any kind of expectation of support in return and called it love. A one-sided relationship wasn't love. Expecting her to drop everything and come running wasn't love. Being needed wasn't love.

Physical relief lightninged down her spine and released the pent-up resentment and anger that'd lived in her bones for years. Nicholas was right. She deserved to have her needs met for once, and if it hadn't been for what'd happened in that slaughterhouse, she might never have recognized she'd been running on fumes at the expense of everyone around her. She'd had to think of only herself to escape. Not Nicholas. Not her parents if they'd lost another child. Not Dr. Caldwell after he would've been assigned to perform her autopsy.

Aubrey straightened and twisted off the water. She was tired of sacrificing her identity, tired of lying, tired of wearing herself out to make others comfortable. It was time she put herself first.

Drying herself as best she could with one hand, she

robed slower than a sloth in South America but managed
to fit her sling back into place on her own. Water from
her soaked hair dampened the collar as she stepped back
into the sleeping quarters. She descended the stairs, following the sounds of the television from the main living
space. Familiar voices filled her ears, and she glanced
around the corner to see the characters from her favorite cartoon working together to fix another toy. Nicholas
had done exactly as he'd promised and gone through her
list of needs. What kind of person did that?

Movement registered from the kitchen, and she caught
sight of Nicholas at the stove top, a spatula in hand and
an apron tied around his waist. She leaned against the
wall for support, watching him, as the scents of frying oil
and pastry chased back the lavender soap she'd abraded
against her skin. Flour and chunks of what looked like
dough peppered the small countertop to his right, and
she raced to replace the nightmares at the back of her
mind with this moment. "You're making doughnuts,
aren't you?"

"Hey." He turned, a wide smile in place. "I couldn't
pull my intern off the case for a run to the bakery, so I
decided to give homemade doughnuts a try." He scooped
a chunk of unrecognizable dough from the pan, showing off the blackened edges of one ring. "I've got to tell
you, I've never been burned so many times in my life.
Keep in mind they may or may not be doughnuts when
I'm finished."

She couldn't help but laugh at the effort and crossed
the kitchen. Taking his free hand in hers, she smoothed
her thumb over the shiny spots of skin. First saving her
life from a sadistic serial killer then taking time out of

the investigation to help her work through her abduction and grief. Aubrey kissed one of the burns. She could get used to this. "They're perfect."

# Chapter Eleven

"So this little girl has magical powers that make her toys come to life, and she's a doctor?" Nicholas took another bite from the warped, sugary doughnut he and Aubrey had salvaged from the mess he'd made in the kitchen. Her body heat spread through his right side as she huddled closer under the thick blanket they'd pulled off one of the beds. "Got to admire that kind of work ethic in a kid."

"She has a magical stethoscope, and don't bash my favorite show. It's cute." She picked a collection of pink sprinkles off the top of her doughnut—sans chocolate glaze—and pressed them against the tip of her tongue. "Beats all those true crime and procedural shows. I get enough of that in the real world."

"I can see that. I can also see where you get all your crazy sayings." His arm pulsed with the weight of her head pressed against it, but Nicholas couldn't for the life of himself—or for the life of the investigation—summon the desire to move. Not with the amount of doughnuts he'd eaten or the fact Aubrey had allowed him to hold her again. Hints of lavender from her shampoo and soap battled to replace the burned odor clinging to the kitchen and living room, but it wasn't responsible for the sense of calm pulsing through him. It was her. The warmth of her skin, the brightness in her eyes, the way she put him at ease and rocketed his pulse into dangerous territory at the same time.

And all this suddenly seemed a little less temporary.

That smile made him hope for more, but more wasn't possible. Not with him. Not when he couldn't trust the masks people wore for the world and lied about who they really were on the inside. Not when Nicholas couldn't trust himself.

Once they'd solved this case, he'd move on to the next, and Aubrey would go back to the morgue to examine the next set of remains that came across her slab. He'd gone out of his way to help her deal with the rolling effects of what she'd been through for the sake of the investigation and her mental health, but now... Now he'd started envisioning mornings just like this. Where she'd wake in his arms. He'd make her breakfast, and they'd watch morning cartoons together to escape the real-world violence they dealt with on the job. He'd imagined joining her in the shower, kissing her senseless and exploring the curves under her oversize sweats and T-shirt.

None of that reinforced the detachment he'd held on to after arresting Cole Presley, and an invisible earthquake rocked through him at the idea. This wasn't him, and Aubrey deserved a hell of a lot better than what he had to offer.

The past few hours had slipped by in the blink of an eye, but reality wouldn't be ignored much longer. A killer waited outside these walls, one who'd already murdered two women and had targeted Aubrey to prove he was better than the veteran killers Nicholas had hunted, and so far the son of a bitch was right. Most serials followed a set of internal rules when it came to stalking their prey, compulsions. They had to kill, and they had to finish that kill a certain way or in a certain order, but this one… He'd never seen a killer like this. Unpredictable, far more intelligent than he'd originally believed and seemingly lacking those internal values that helped Nicholas construct a profile.

There was no order to the way this killer worked. Not in his MO or victim choice. Maybe that was the point. Kara Flood had been an elementary school teacher, her sister the city's chief medical examiner, and Paige Cress had been a paralegal who'd been attacked and put in the maintenance shed eighteen to twenty hours before the first body had been discovered. Everything had been meticulously planned, but Nicholas couldn't see the pattern.

Images of toys come to life and a little girl who'd taken up being a doctor phased to the back of his mind. There had to be a connection. If the killer had planned to make Aubrey his masterpiece—his own sick introduction to the serial killing world—then the other two victims had only been the start of his plan. Who knew how many other pieces it would take to solve this puzzle?

Nicholas unwrapped his arm from around Aubrey and leaned forward on the couch. Instinct pulled him to his feet, and he crossed to the dining room table, where he'd set his laptop before he'd burned the doughnuts.

"Nicholas?" His name on her lips tightened a knot of desire in his gut and threatened to pull him out of his thought process.

He hadn't been able to do a deep dive since those panic-filled moments on the dock, but he couldn't ignore the zing of intuition driving him now. Nicholas scanned the attachments in the latest email from the team. "Striker and West sent photos from the first victim's apartment while you were in the shower. I only had a few seconds to run through them, but I think I just figured out how Paige Cress and your sister were connected. That's the pattern. You might not have known Paige directly before she'd died, but she knew your sister." He skimmed through the photos until he found the one he wanted and stepped back. Pointing at a shelf of books in the victim's apartment, he faced Aubrey as she struggled to her feet. "There."

"Those four books." Disbelief graveled her voice. "I recognize them from Kara's apartment."

The books. Damn it, he should've made the connection sooner. "What are the odds a paralegal and a kindergarten teacher would have the same collection of four true crime books? That must be the connection between the first two victims." He bent down, dragging a photo from Kara Flood's apartment beside Paige's. "Each of these books has been published in the last year. They're new, and judging by the spines' condition, I'd say they were all bought around the same time, possibly from the same bookstore."

"You think they were reading them together." Aubrey's tongue darted across her bottom lip, and she raised her left hand as though intending to cross her arms over her chest, but the sling wouldn't allow it. "He told me he used Kara to get close to me, to learn about me. If Paige Cress knew my sister, maybe he did the same thing to her."

"Stands to reason he would've had to have known her." The adrenaline surge of following a lead exploded through him. This was what he'd been trained for. This was what he was good at, taking the pieces of the puzzle and fitting them together to make a cohesive narrative.

"We'll have to confirm through the victims' financials and track down the retailer where they were purchased, but there's only one reason two or more people buy the same set of books and read them around the same time. The victims could be part of a true crime book club."

"Kara never told me she was part of a book club or that she was interested in this kind of stuff." Aubrey stepped away from the screen. "Serial killers? Crime? I had no idea."

"Maybe she understood you wouldn't want to talk about it given how much you try to avoid that kind of entertainment when you're off the clock," he said. "I imagine broaching the subject with you would've been difficult for her."

"It's possible. I'm starting to realize she'd been keeping a lot of secrets from me. We still haven't determined how she was able to afford living in her neighborhood on a teacher's salary." She pointed to the screen. "Nicholas, look at the book titles."

He enlarged the images to read the text clearly on the books' spines. Son of a bitch. "*X Marks the Spot: The Hunt for Cole Presley. Not Your Average Fairy Tale: The True Story of the Gingerbread Woman* and *Eat the Darkness: Exposing the Watcher.*"

"If Kara and Paige were in a book club together, it can't be a coincidence the man who abducted me used two MOs of the same serial killers they were reading about these past few months." Aubrey circled out of his peripheral vision. "Do you think it's possible he'll kill more victims, given there's four books on Kara's and Paige Cress's shelves?"

*But First, Lipstick.* Nicholas recognized the fourth title from the shelves of both victims. The detailed retelling of the Extreme Makeover Killer, a man who'd given all his victims—redheaded women between the ages of nineteen and twenty-five—makeovers after he'd bound them and cut their wrists; an homage to his wife, whom he'd bound and killed after her attempt to leave the abusive relationship. Nicholas studied the illustrated stick of lipstick on the binding. The Extreme Makeover Killer had applied a bright red lip color on his victims, the same shade his wife had preferred, before he'd cut their wrists and watched them bleed out. Had the Extreme Makeover Killer been the inspiration behind Aubrey's attack in that slaughterhouse?

"It's possible he already has. The killer has replicated the X Marks the Spot Killer and the Gingerbread MOs so far, every detail in line with the original cases, but the only reason we discovered Paige Cress was a victim was because the Gingerbread Woman left photos of her victims with a fresh kill. He used Kara's crime scene to give us that clue, but the Extreme Makeover Killer didn't leave bread crumbs for the BAU to follow."

Dread pooled at the base of his spine as Nicholas ran through the details of that investigation. "He hid his victims underground, where no one would find them. Whoever abducted you wants to prove he can kill as well if not better than his idols. He wouldn't have experimented with only two victims. He would consider it hands-on research, a test of his capabilities and a gathering of knowledge. These books laid out the investigations for him and walked him through exactly how to kill his prey."

He tried to take a deep breath, but the pressure behind his rib cage built faster. "There are more victims out there, ones we haven't uncovered. I'm sure of it."

"We need to find where Kara's book club met," she said.

Nicholas scrubbed a hand down his face. "And who else is a member."

THE BUILDING'S SUPERINTENDENT twisted the key for Paige Cress's apartment in the door and motioned Aubrey and Nicholas inside. They hadn't found anything in Kara's personal effects that'd given them an idea of when and where the true crime book club meetings had occurred, but Paige Cress might not have been so secretive. An immediate wall of sunlight spread across the light brown flooring and beckoned them into a long hallway expertly furnished with a bench, hooks for jackets and cubby holes for shoes. The super offered Nicholas the key. "Paige was a good tenant. Never late with rent, always greeted me with a smile. Have you contacted her family to let them know what happened?"

"We have someone in the bureau who's keeping her parents updated on the investigation and giving them a timeline of when they can claim her remains. As soon as we get what we need here, I'll have them contact you about packing up her things. Thanks for your help. I'll let you know when we're finished." Nicholas took the offered key from the super and closed the door as the older man disappeared into the hallway.

Aubrey swallowed through the tightness in her throat as she studied the bright colors of Paige's bedroom directly on the left, the photos of the victim and her friends and family smiling back from their positions on her dresser. "I hadn't thought about what happens after you close this case. I haven't really had time, I guess. I'll need to make Kara's arrangements after Dr. Caldwell issues the death certificate. My parents will want a funeral, but I'll be the one having to deal with all the details and packing up her apartment. I'll be the one who has to explain to them why she was targeted."

Nicholas's boots echoed off the hardwood as he maneuvered around the end of Paige's bed, those green-blue eyes taking in every detail. A large cutout revealed a straight shot view into the main living space. The double sliding glass door leading out to the third-floor balcony was the only source of natural light in the one-bedroom, one-bathroom apartment, and highlighted the damaged skin along the right side of his face. He raised his gaze to hers. "You think they'll blame you."

"Yes." She hadn't realized how deep that fear had tunneled into the base of her core being. "And why shouldn't they? I do. I'm the end result, aren't I? His masterpiece. He used Kara to get to me, to draw me into this sick mind game, and she was the one who ended up paying the price. How am I supposed to live with that? How am I supposed to face my parents when this case is closed?"

"The same way you've faced everything else up until now." Nicholas stilled, every ounce of his focus on her, and a massive flood of appreciation filled her.

"With burned doughnuts, cartoons and my very own charming profiler to unload my emotional baggage onto?" Her attempt at a smile failed as her bottom lip trembled. He wasn't just a profiler. Not to her. Over the course of the past four days, he'd become so much more. Her friend, her partner, her anchor in a storm she hadn't seen coming, and a small part of her believed whatever was happening between them could survive this case. That what they'd been through together in that slaughterhouse had forged the invisible connection between them into something stronger. Something unbreakable.

"Don't discount the effects a nice hot shower can have on your mental and physical health, too, Doc." He hit her with a crooked smile, and her gut coiled tighter. "You think I'm charming?"

"Well, you haven't turned and run screaming after finding out what I do for a living, so you've got that going for you." Aubrey picked up the nearest photo the victim had set on top of her dresser near an open jewelry box. Paige's straight, white teeth flashed in a wide smile as she stared up at the man beside her. A boyfriend? From the position of the camera and the height of the victim, it looked as though the man stood at least six inches taller than Paige, putting him around six feet. Dark brown eyes glittered as he pulled Paige into an overexaggerated kiss, bending her backward with the support of both of his hands, and an instant ping resonated behind Aubrey's sternum. Paige had been happy in the photo. In love.

A brilliant diamond ring caught the light from the victim's hand, and she made a visual inspection of the jewelry box beside where the photo had stood. It wasn't there. Scanning the nightstands on either side of the bed, she found them bare. "If we want to find out where the book club met, we'll want to question Paige's fiancé. He might know when and where the meetings occurred."

Nicholas circled around the end of the bed, and she handed him the frame. His hand brushed against her own, resurrecting the delicious tendril of heat she couldn't seem to shake when he was near, and Aubrey wanted nothing more than to hold on to that a bit longer. "Her friends and family never mentioned anything about a fiancé or a boyfriend."

"This photo says otherwise. Paige wouldn't have kept a picture like this unless she was still seeing him, but that's not why I wanted you to look at it. Look at the ring." She pointed to the glistening diamond. "It's not in her jewelry box, and she wasn't wearing an engagement ring when we found her remains on the pier. Dr. Caldwell or his assistant would've noted it in the autopsy report. Medical examiners are required to account for every personal effect taken off the deceased, including cash, jewelry and phones. We have to call it out to our assistants and anyone else around so we can't be accused of stealing from the dead."

"I recognize this guy. I talked to him. He was outside Kara's apartment, behind the perimeter tape." The lines between Nicholas's eyebrows deepened. He turned the photo toward her as though he expected her to remember anything more than discovering her sister's body at that scene. "He told me he was training to become a crime scene photographer. Simon something. Simon... Curry. Said he'd been following my career since the X Marks the Spot case...then he asked about you."

A shiver solidified in her gut. She stared at the photo, willing her brain to take the memories of her attacker and fit them into this mystery man's profile, but she couldn't. Not without hearing his voice. Because no matter how many times she'd tried to bury that sound in a box at the back of her mind, it'd been permanently engraved. She'd never forget that voice, and she never wanted to hear it again. Pieces of conversation broke free from memories of the slaughterhouse.

"The killer said he'd loved Paige, that he was the only one who really knew her." She forced herself to keep her pulse even. She studied the redheaded, muscular man in the photo. Was Simon Curry the killer? "He knew the first victim intimately and was photographing the crime scene of the second. According to Dr. Caldwell, Paige was already dead by the time I discovered Kara outside her apartment, but Simon Curry didn't mention anything about his fiancée being missing?"

"No, and he wasn't the one who reported her missing, either. Her mother called the police after Paige failed to show up for her parents' anniversary party." Nicholas pried the photo from the frame and slid it into his back pocket. Circling back around the queen-size bed, he searched the opening leading into what Aubrey assumed was the victim's closet. "There's no evidence Curry was living here with his fiancée. No clothes hanging in the closet. No men's shoes or any toiletries in the bathroom. If Simon Curry and Paige Cress were engaged, they were keeping it from her family."

"They looked so happy in that photo. Why keep the news to themselves?" she asked.

"I'm not sure yet, but that will be one of the first questions I ask him when we bring him in for questioning." Nicholas stepped back out into the hallway, the same dead expression she'd noted in her sister's apartment smoothing his rugged features. He maneuvered into the main living space. His boots skimmed across the hardwood floor and seemed overly loud in her ears.

"Paige Cress worked a lot of long nights being one of the most requested paralegals in her firm, which explains the lack of a pet, decor and personalization other than the bedroom. This wasn't a sanctuary to her as Kara's apartment had been. This place was a necessity. Somewhere close to the office where she could sleep and shower then start fresh the next day." He moved into the kitchen lining one wall and opened the refrigerator. "Empty. Her work was her life. She loved her job. She was good at it.

Her friends said they hadn't seen her in months because of her busy schedule. So how did she find the time for a serious relationship?"

Aubrey followed on his heels into the living room. Pulling one of the true crime titles they'd identified from the photos taken by Nicholas's team from the bookcase, she opened the hardcover wide. A note in strong, masculine handwriting cut through the book's title page. "'To Paige, my Gingerbread Woman. Never stop searching for the truth. Love, Simon, the Watcher.'"

"The Watcher." Nicholas's voice dipped into dangerous territory as he took the book from her. "That can't be right. Ellis Hull has been behind bars for over a year after being tied to the deaths of twelve tourists, and our victim wasn't the Gingerbread Woman. Evidence proved Irene Lawrence suffocated those women in her law firm after she felt threatened they'd get in the way of her making partner."

"'My Gingerbread Woman.' It's his nickname for her." A flood of warmth raced up her neck. "Simon gave the victim this book. He meant it as an intimate gift. You said Paige's social life had taken a hit with so many hours put in at the office the past few months. Makes sense she most likely met Simon Curry in one of the places she frequents the most, and the connection between Kara and Paige is a true crime book club."

"Simon Curry is a member, too. He's signed his name as the Watcher for Paige." Nicholas studied the left-to-right slanted handwriting in pitch-black ink. "His nickname for her matches the MO by which she was killed."

"It sounds like Paige and Simon used those nicknames for each other." Aubrey pulled the fourth title, *Eat the Darkness: Exposing the Watcher*, from the shelf and read the back summary to herself. "According to this, the Watcher abducted tourists from public areas overseas without anyone noticing. Within a few months, police uncovered their bodies dismembered in a seaside cave. Twelve in total, but the Watcher was apprehended by Interpol within a few months."

She flipped through the book, noting highlights and notes written in feminine handwriting. "It's possible each member of the club took on a nickname inspired by one of the killers they were studying."

"Only Simon took it a step further." Nicholas closed the book, his eyes darker than a few minutes ago. "Claiming a killer's nickname wasn't enough. He was inspired by the real thing."

# Chapter Twelve

"I've never been in an interrogation room before. What's the special occasion, Agent James?"

Simon Curry took his seat across the table as Nicholas planted the case file in front of him. Dark eyes, nearly black, scanned the two-tone gray walls, the reinforced electrical outlet to Curry's right and the one-way glass that protected Aubrey from facing a possible suspect in her abduction on the other side. A thick red beard failed to hide the slight nervousness of the man's mouth. Curry's forehead wrinkles deepened as Nicholas sat across the stainless-steel table. At six feet, Simon Curry matched the musculature and height of the bastard who'd attacked him and Aubrey at the pier, but it would take a lot more than the suspect's frame to tie him to two murders. "Does the BAU need the photos I took at the crime scene the other day?"

"No, Simon. The photographer we have on staff did a great job. We have everything we need from the scene." Nicholas opened the file in front of him and pulled a stack of developed and oversize photos from Kara Flood's crime scene free, including those documenting the victim outside her apartment. Positioning them one next to the other across the table, Nicholas watched Simon's expression bleed from excitement to disbelief. "Do you recognize this woman?"

"That's X Marks... That's Kara." Simon pushed the photos back across the table as a tendril of anger surfaced. "She was the victim at the crime scene? Holy hell, why are you showing these to me?"

"You were going to call her X Marks the Spot, weren't you?" Nicholas asked. "The nickname she took on as a member of the same true crime book club you're part of."

Curry crossed his arms over his chest—defensive— and avoided looking at the crime scene photos in front of him. He raised one hand in a dismissive gesture, and hints of the man's aftershave filled the space between Nicholas and the suspect.

"I'm part of a book club. So what? We all take on the nickname we're assigned during our first meeting. It's tradition, and Kara... She was always so interested in the X Marks the Spot Killer case because her sister was the medical examiner assigned to the investigation. She kept asking questions, seeing if anyone knew something more than what was in the book we were reading, and the name just kind of stuck with her. She thought it would give her something to talk about with her sister, that learning about the case would bring them closer. She would always brag about how Dr. Flood was the one who gave the BAU what they needed to identify Cole Presley. She was proud of her."

Nicholas glanced toward the one-way glass, easily envisioning Aubrey on the other side. Kara Flood had joined the true crime book club to understand her sister, to show she cared about her, to show she loved her. With all the friends and family who'd turned their backs on Aubrey because of her work as a medical examiner,

Kara had been in the process of showing her sister how proud she was of her before she'd died. "And what about Paige Cress?"

Three distinct lines appeared between Curry's eyebrows. "What about her?"

"Paige was a member of the book club, too, right? And you and she were involved intimately? Although Paige's family and friends don't recall her having a boyfriend or a fiancé." He unpocketed the photo he and Aubrey had discovered in the victim's apartment and unfolded it before sliding it across the table.

"Where did you get this?" Simon asked.

"Paige's apartment. This, too." He tugged the book Aubrey had taken from the victim's bookcase and opened it to the title page. "This is your handwriting, right? Paige called you her Watcher and you called her your Gingerbread Woman."

"Why do you have this? Why do you have any of this?" Simon's voice echoed off the bare walls as he picked up the photo of him and the first victim. "What's going on here?"

"Paige Cress is dead, Simon, but I have the feeling you already knew that." Nicholas tugged another set of crime scene photos from the case file and spread them over the top of the first. "She was murdered and dumped in a maintenance shed at the waterfront up to twenty hours before you showed up at Kara Flood's crime scene. Suffocated. Just like the Gingerbread Woman suffocated her victims. I'm sure you know the case, considering your true crime book club read the book detailing the investigation recently. Paige was a paralegal, she was suffocated with her own jacket and a photo of her body was found at Kara Flood's crime scene. It all lines up."

"No. This…this isn't happening. Paige can't be dead." Simon pushed away from the table, his chair hitting the back wall, and every muscle in Nicholas's body hardened with battle-ready tension. Only this time, the son of a bitch wouldn't take him or Aubrey by surprise. In fact, he'd never lay a hand on the medical examiner again.

Curry speared both hands through his hair and fisted chunks. It was all a very good act. The apparent grief, the shock. "It was a stupid fight. She isn't dead."

Nicholas straightened. "What fight?"

"Paige was getting cold feet about the wedding. We hadn't told anybody we were engaged because her family wanted her to focus on her career before she settled down, but I didn't want to lie to them anymore. She didn't want to tell them until we were already married. She wanted to elope, but I tried to talk her out of it. She made me move my stuff out of her apartment that night and told me she needed some time to think about her future, but when I left five days ago, she was still alive. She won't answer my messages or call me back." Curry scrubbed a hand down his face. "And now…are you positive the body you found is her?"

"The county medical examiner confirmed her identity through dental records and a fracture Paige sustained when she was younger. X-rays don't lie." Nicholas gathered the photos back into the case file and closed the manila folder. "I need you to tell me where you were between nine and midnight the night after your fight with Paige, Simon, and I need the contact information of anybody who can corroborate your whereabouts at that time."

"Is that…is that when she… I knew I shouldn't have left her alone. We could've worked it out. Maybe if I hadn't pushed her, she'd still be alive." Confusion overwhelmed the grief in the suspect's expression. Curry regained a small amount of control, his shoulders rising on a strong inhale as he clutched the back of the chair. "That night. I, uh, I went back to my apartment. I spent the rest of the night drinking myself stupid in front of the TV. Alone."

"No one can vouch for you that you were in your apartment all night?" he asked. "What about a bite mark? Paige Cress bit her attacker before she died. Can you prove it wasn't your skin the medical examiner pulled from between her teeth?"

"Paige and I were engaged. We were sleeping together. Sometimes it got more passionate than we planned. She'd bite and scratch me all the time, but that doesn't mean I killed her." Anger strengthened the level of Simon Curry's voice again. "You said Paige was murdered with the same MO the Gingerbread Woman used on her victims, and from the photos you showed me of Kara Flood, she was killed with the X Marks the Spot Killer's MO. Strangled with an *X* carved into her right cheek. Both of them were killed with the same MO as their nicknames, so it had to be someone from the book club."

"I'm going to need a list of members, Simon," Nicholas said.

"I don't have a list. We don't… We don't know each other's real names or see each other outside the club. We call each other by our nicknames," Curry said. "We just met at some after-hours coffee shop called AfterDark."

"You and Paige shared your real names. You had a relationship outside the club. You were living together. The proof is right there on the title page of this book you gifted her." Nicholas wrote down the name of the coffee shop in his notepad and motioned to the book in front of him. "And you recognized Kara Flood."

"Paige and I were an anomaly. We didn't mean for it to happen. It just…did. I loved her. I was ready to spend the rest of my life with her." Curry enunciated his point with an index finger pressed into the surface of the table between them. "And Kara let her real name slip during a discussion a few months back. She wanted us to know she was related to the medical examiner who worked the X Marks the Spot Killer case, and Paige took advantage of it. They started a true crime podcast together. It was really taking off, bringing in a lot of sponsorship opportunities."

"Kara told the book club Dr. Aubrey Flood was her sister, then she and Paige went into business together?" That must've been how Kara Flood had been able to afford her apartment in that neighborhood, but she'd never told Aubrey, and the BAU hadn't found any evidence of recording equipment in either of their apartments. A coil of unwanted protectiveness twisted in Nicholas's gut.

Aubrey wasn't the only one who was afraid to close her eyes after what'd happened in that slaughterhouse, but he'd managed to get through his past cases alone. He'd do it again. "Funny you should mention Dr. Flood, because the same day we discovered your fiancée's body on that pier, someone about your height and weight attacked Aubrey Flood. Hung her upside down by her ankles in a slaughterhouse and nicked her carotid artery to make her bleed out." The anger Nicholas had struggled to contain before he'd stepped inside this room with Simon Curry flared. "That takes medical training, and it turns out you dropped out of medical school last year in pursuit of becoming a crime scene photographer. You see this photo?"

He extracted the Polaroid of Paige Cress's remains that'd been recovered in the back of the cargo van near Kara Flood's death scene with her dog inside.

"The killer left this picture of Paige at the crime scene where you were spotted hugging the perimeter tape with your camera. You had knowledge of that case, and you're good with a camera. The killer lured my team to the pier so we could recover her remains, knowing Dr. Flood would be invested in finding out the connection between Paige and her sister. You admitted yourself you were fascinated with Dr. Flood and her work on the X Killer case. The killer also used a scalpel to nick Dr. Flood's carotid artery with a steady hand. You have a medical background."

Nicholas pressed his elbows in the table and leaned forward, his gaze locked on Simon Curry. "I think you lured us there to get Aubrey Flood all to yourself, Simon. I think you've read so many books about serial killers, you've convinced yourself you're capable of outshining them all, but you needed practice first. So you killed Paige, and when that didn't give you the satisfaction you craved, you moved on to Kara Flood to complicate the game and draw her sister closer. It's the love of the chase, isn't it? That's what you crave. You want to prove you're better than the killers you've idolized all these years. You want to prove you're better than me and my team, but that's not how this is going to end, Simon. You're not better. You're just a copycat."

Simon pried his hands from the back of the chair and calmly took his seat across from Nicholas. He interlaced his fingers on the surface of the table and dropped his chin, severing eye contact. "I'm not saying another word without my lawyer."

THEY HAD HIM. Simon Curry had the means, the motive and the opportunity, not to mention a connection to both victims, but doubt curdled in her stomach. It was the voice. That wasn't the voice of the man who'd abducted and tried to kill her. She was sure of it.

Aubrey studied the suspect on the other side of the glass before the door to the observation room swung open. Goose pimples climbed her arms and puckered across her back as Nicholas settled that intelligent gaze on her. "All the evidence seems to line up against him, and he has no alibi."

"But you aren't convinced he's the one who attacked you." Not a question. He didn't need to ask. Nicholas seemed to see right through her, understand her, and the unexpected connection between them vibrated stronger. He faced the one-way glass, his reflection highlighting the stitches and deformities along the curve of his jaw, but the damage hadn't lessened her attraction. Nothing could. "He has a medical background, a connection to both victims and the knowledge base of how serials work. Hell, he even admitted his admiration for you."

It all made sense. She couldn't argue with that, and the people pleaser she'd allowed herself to become over the course of her life screamed at her to sit down and avoid rocking the boat. But she wasn't that woman anymore, and she wouldn't help put Simon Curry behind bars unless she was absolutely positive he'd been the one behind that ski mask. It would be easy to agree with Nicholas and the BAU about the man in the interrogation room, but she couldn't. "It's not him."

Nicholas shifted his weight between both feet, and the tension in the room notched higher. Lowering his gaze along the edge of the bottom of the large window, he turned his head slightly toward her, disappointment clear in his expression. "You've been through a lot over the past few days, Aubrey. Trauma alters memories of things we're positive happened or that we heard. It's possible you're misremembering details of your attack or you're afraid of confronting those memories fully in order to protect yourself."

He didn't believe her.

"You think I don't want it to be Simon Curry? That I want the man who did this to me to go free?" But worse than that, that she wasn't strong enough to face what'd happened to her? Uninhibited betrayal exploded through her as she stepped away from the window. "I've been at your side every step of the way on this case, Nicholas. I almost died trying to help you find the killer who murdered my sister, and now you're telling me I can't be a reliable source because of what I went through? I remember what he sounds like *because* of what I went through."

His expression remained cool, under control, when everything inside her wanted to scream and rail, and suddenly this wasn't the man who'd attempted to make her doughnuts, who'd held her while watching her favorite cartoon. Who'd kissed her and helped her realize she needed to put her needs first for once. "It's not me, Doc. Claiming that's not the guy who attacked you on the pier based off his voice isn't evidence, and it won't hold up in court. You know that."

Nicholas faced her, something along the lines of regret pulling the tendons between his neck and shoulders tight. "You went to medical school. You've seen the research. You've read the studies proving trauma affects people differently, and you have to admit the only reason you kissed me is because you needed someone to help you get through it."

His words registered as though he'd physically thrown a blow, and she backed up until her thighs hit the edge of a table positioned a few feet away for balance. Disbelief gripped her heart in a vise. Was that what he really believed? That she'd used him for her own selfishness and coping? What kind of person did he think she was? "That's not…that's not why I kissed you. You think that's why I kissed you?"

"All I'm saying is your memories of what happened might not be accurate, Doc. Simon Curry fits the profile, and he doesn't have anyone to corroborate his whereabouts when Paige Cress or your sister were killed," he said. "Do you want a jury to find him innocent after your testimony because one detail feels off to you?"

His blow struck again, harder, and if she hadn't been braced against the table, Aubrey feared she might've crumpled right there in the middle of the floor. Her heart jackhammered in her chest, pounding so wildly that the cracks around the edges started to shatter. She'd requested Nicholas James to solve her sister's case, but she'd stupidly taken his affection and promises to heart. She'd imagined them closing this investigation and moving on to the next. Imagined waking up to the smell of burned doughnuts and hearing the voices of her favorite cartoon each morning before they left for their respective jobs. Imagined them trying to top one another with funny sayings and laughing, committed. Together. Happy. She deserved to be happy. Why was he doing this?

Aubrey forced herself to stand a bit straighter, to retreat behind the barrier she'd built from having one more person take advantage of her. He wasn't going to be the one to walk away this time. Anger bled into her voice. "I remember everything that happened after I pulled you from the ocean, Agent James. Every second, every minute. I remember the pain as he knocked me unconscious with a wrench. I remember the pressure in my head and chest when I realized he'd hung me by my ankles. I remember what he smelled like, his voice in my ear and the way his gloves warmed against my neck before he cut my throat. I remember the agony I sustained after I hit the cement so I could make sure you were alive."

She pushed away from the table, closing the space between them. She slid her hand into his jacket pocket and extracted his SUV's keys. "And when you and I were in that safe house, I remember how good it felt for someone to put me first for once, and how I'd finally found someone I didn't have to hide myself from. Someone who I could imagine being happy with, but maybe you're right. Maybe I can't rely on my memories after all."

Aubrey headed for the door and swung it wide, stepping out into the hall. She secured the door behind her but didn't have the strength to release her grip from the knob as everything she'd recounted came into question. The evidence pointed to Simon Curry as her sister's killer, but she wouldn't be able to walk into a courtroom to testify unless she was sure.

There was only one way to prove he hadn't murdered Kara.

She had to see her sister's remains for herself.

Prying her fingers from around the observation room door handle, she wound her way through the FBI's Seattle office and out into the floor's lobby. Two bays of elevators pinged, and she waited for one of the cars to clear before stepping on, tears burning in her eyes.

The doors started to slide closed, promising escape, before a hand slipped through and triggered the automatic sensor. "Hold it!"

A familiar smile flashed back at her, and Aubrey moved aside to allow the passenger room. She almost hadn't recognized him without his lab coat and face shield, but the long, straight nose, thick eyebrows, and smallish eyes punctured through the haze of spiraling hurt. Graying temples emphasized his elongated facial structure, but his five-o'clock shadow instantly set her at ease. She smoothed her uninjured hand down her slacks. "Dr. Caldwell, I didn't expect to see you here. I imagine the FBI's case is keeping you quite busy."

"Dr. Flood, how good to see you. Yes, it's been quite the experience working this investigation with the BAU. Now I know why you've been keeping them all to yourself." His rich laugh hitched as the elevator descended from the penthouse. "I'd heard you'd been attacked. I'm so sorry. I didn't realize the extent of your injuries. May I ask the diagnosis?"

"Fractured scapula along with two of my right sternal ribs. It'll be a few months of recovery, but I'm managing. I should be able to return to work soon." The lie fell from her mouth easily enough, but she wasn't about to break down in front of a colleague, and sure as hell not in this building. Her gaze flickered to the security camera in the corner of the elevator car. No. She wouldn't give Nicholas the satisfaction of seeing her cry. Denial charged up her throat as Nicholas's accusation filtered through the county medical examiner's concerned expression.

"Always the optimist. That's one of the things I like about you. If anyone could force a fracture to heal quickly, it'd be you." Dr. Caldwell's voice lowered an octave, and the walls seemed to close in around her. "You always were the best. I imagine that's why the FBI chose you to work the X Marks the Spot Killer case over me three years ago."

"In perspective of experience and years dedicated to your work, Dr. Caldwell, you are obviously the choice the FBI should've made for that case. It was simply being available when the case agent needed a pathologist at the time. I believe you were tied up with another homicide investigation when Agent James invited me to investigate the case." His hint of jealousy spiked through her, and Aubrey forced herself to stare straight ahead at her reflection in the steel doors, but the weight of being watched pressurized the air in her lungs. She cleared her throat. "I was actually headed to your office. The BAU has a suspect in custody—Simon Curry. He had the means and opportunity to target both victims without a confirmed alibi, but I'm not convinced he's responsible. I'd like to take a look at my sister's remains, if that's possible. See if there is something that can tie Simon Curry directly to both murders."

"You think I missed something during the autopsy?" he asked.

"No. Not at all, Dr. Caldwell. I'd simply like to see Kara for myself. Call it a personal favor. I'd owe you." The elevator jostled as it descended to the parking level, and she clutched the keys she'd taken from Nicholas hard enough to bite the skin of her palm. The doors opened, and a wall of humidity settled against her face and neck. Relief coursed through her veins as she stepped off the elevator and added another few hundred feet between her and the profiler upstairs. She called back over her shoulder. "We could drive together, if you prefer."

No response.

Aubrey slowed her escape and looked back. The elevator doors remained open, exposing the empty car within. She searched the parking garage, but there wasn't any sign of him. The nearest vehicle was still a few feet ahead of her. He wouldn't have been able to reach his own car that quickly. She'd just have to meet Dr. Caldwell at his own office. Forcing one step in front of the other, she kept herself together long enough to reach Nicholas's SUV, but the tears were already breaking through. She hit the button to unlock the driver's-side door.

She'd spent most of her life feeling alone, unwanted. She'd get through this.

Pain exploded across the back of her head as she reached for the SUV's door handle, and she slammed up against the window. Inky blackness spidered across her vision as Aubrey battled to face her attacker, but it was no use. She was slipping to the ground and into unconsciousness.

# Chapter Thirteen

He hadn't seen the threat coming.

Nicholas tossed the case file onto his desk and slumped into his seat. Aubrey Flood had walked into his life and taken out his defenses with a sweet smile and an underhanded charm. And hell, he hated himself for it. He hated that he could be manipulated so easily, that he hadn't been able to protect himself against her warmth and patience before it was too late. Cole Presley had done the same thing. The bastard had used Nicholas's own trust against him then shattered his world when the truth surfaced. The X Marks the Spot Killer had worn a human mask to hide the monster underneath. How was he supposed to trust Aubrey hadn't done the same, that her mask wasn't as much of a lie as Cole's had been? How was he supposed to know if the vulnerable, intelligent, beautiful woman he'd grown closer to over this investigation was real?

His cell vibrated from his slacks pocket, and he pulled the device free, answering in the same move. "Tell me you were able to confirm AfterDark is the location the book club met and find a barista or a customer who can give a description of all the members."

"Yes and no," David Dyson said. "For a coffee shop, AfterDark prides itself on ensuring their customers' privacy. Neither the owner nor any of the baristas would talk to me, and they don't have any cameras. But I was able to match purchases from both victims' financials to purchases made at this location. I'm waiting outside to catch a couple customers as they leave. See if I can't get something more from some of the regulars."

"Good work, Dyson." Nicholas leaned back in his chair. "Let me know what you find."

He disconnected the call. The evidence pointed to Simon Curry as the killer, but damn it, Aubrey's confidence they'd brought in the wrong man tunneled through logic and straight past rationale. He believed her. It'd been in her voice. In the way she'd studied the suspect and held her ground. Any other victim would've collapsed after facing the possibility of being within arm's reach of the person who'd tortured them, but not her. She'd gone against his every instinct and demanded he see things her way instead of bowing down to the inner people pleaser she'd sacrificed herself for, and hell, he admired her for it.

Loved her for it.

"Well, call me a purple hippo." Nicholas ran both hands through his hair. He loved her. He wasn't sure when it'd happened, wasn't sure he cared, but he'd fallen for the medical examiner he hadn't been able to forget for the past three years. He'd been an idiot. Of course he'd fallen for her. Despite the fact she used to make her sister play pretend homicide victim as kids and her taste buds had stopped working, as evidenced by her eating the doughnuts he'd made her, Aubrey was the most generous, driven and unselfish woman he'd known. She'd gone out of her way to put others first, to the point of losing herself in the process, and he couldn't hold her newfound confidence against her.

If anything, her defiance to comply with his suspicion against Simon Curry only made him love her more. She'd stood up for herself, and damn, that fire in her gaze had been one of the sexiest things he'd ever seen. Until he'd doused it by using her mental trauma after her attack against her. Nicholas set his elbows on his desk, staring at the case file without really seeing anything clearly. "You sure are a son of a bitch."

He'd taken his own fear of trusting again and weaponized it against the one woman who'd calmed the uncertainty he'd carried all these years. It'd been easy to discount her claim of Simon Curry's innocence, especially given the evidence seemed to line up against Paige Cress's fiancé, but Nicholas had never felt more wrong in his life. The past three days had shown him a life he hadn't imagined for himself. Aubrey had single-handedly broken through the doubt he'd held on to since discovering who Cole Presley really was that day. She'd looked at him as though he were the most capable, most intelligent and innovative BAU agent, to the point he'd started believing her. She'd done that. She'd given him the confidence and forced him to look at his positive qualities rather than focusing on his failures, and he'd thrown that service in her face.

He had to find her. He had to make this right.

The atmosphere in the office ratcheted higher. A swarm of agents jogged to the other side of the building. Nicholas rounded his desk, leaving his office, and spotted SSA Miguel Peters shouting orders from behind the conference room glass. Something had happened. He could feel it.

Nicholas caught sight of Dashiell West circling around the doors and wound his way through the maze of agents. He pushed through the wall of the FBI's finest, threaded his hand around West's arm and spun the cybercrimes agent toward him. "West, what's going on?"

"There's been an attack in the parking garage." Color drained from the cybercrimes agent's face, and dread pooled at the base of Nicholas's spine. The surrounding agents stilled, the weight of their attention burrowing deep in his chest. "Security reported the camera in one of the elevators had been disabled. I went through the footage leading up to the blackout and discovered the surveillance in the garage had also been shut down. They've swept the garage, but the only evidence they were able to uncover was a book near your SUV."

Air caught in his chest. "What book?"

"*But First, Lipstick*, the true crime book detailing the Extreme Makeover Killer's investigation." West seemed to prepare himself as though Nicholas would attack at the news that came next. "There was only one other person who got on the elevator with her, Nicholas, and we can't locate or get in touch with him, either. It was Dr. Caldwell."

Son of a bitch. Aubrey had been right. He replayed the interactions between him and the killer. The bastard's size, medical knowledge, his obsession with Aubrey. Hell, narcissistic behavior was common among medical professionals because of their overwhelming God complex of having lives in their hands. His background as an army combat medic, medical school and years on the job accredited the pathologist with enough experience around a scalpel, and the jealousy West had picked up on was more than enough motive to put Aubrey at the center of the killer's sick game. Simon Curry might've had the means, motive, opportunity and connections to kill Kara Flood and Paige Cress, but so had the King County medical examiner. Dr. Archer Caldwell was a member of the same true crime book club both victims had met with, and his jealousy of Aubrey being invited to work the X Marks the Spot investigation had pushed him to the edge. With Simon Curry in custody, it was the only explanation. Dr. Caldwell had claimed the Extreme Makeover Killer's nickname and left the book as a taunt. The parking garage. Nicholas released his grip on West. "Give me your keys."

"We don't have a location yet." West handed them over, and Nicholas raced toward the stairs. The agent's voice barely registered through the pounding of Nicholas's heart behind his ears. "How are you going to find her?"

"He's headed to the underground!" Nicholas had never been so sure of anything in his life. It fit the Extreme Makeover Killer's MO. Caldwell would see Aubrey's survival from the events at the slaughterhouse as a personal failure, possibly grounds to remove Aubrey as the one he'd chosen as his own masterpiece. If that was the case as Nicholas believed, the pathologist would retreat back to an MO he was familiar with, one he'd studied before moving on to look for another prize. One guaranteed to kill his victim. Samson Little had bound his victims before cutting their wrists and watching them slowly bleed out, but he hadn't wanted them discovered. Just as he hadn't wanted his wife discovered, but the dead always found a way to speak. Aubrey had taught him that.

Nicholas pushed into the stairwell and sprinted down the stairs. The snap of the door slamming into the wall behind it exploded like a gunshot above, and he looked up long enough to recognize Agents Striker and West and SSA Peters following close behind. They had a location. They were going to find her alive. There wasn't another option. Not for him.

Stale air slammed into him as Nicholas ripped open the garage-level door. Targeting his SUV and the security team sweeping the area around it, he called to the security lead as his team spread across the garage from behind. "Any progress?"

"No, sir. Not yet," the team lead said. "I'll report all findings to you as soon as we have something. We're doing a sweep for Dr. Caldwell's vehicle now and have contacted Seattle PD."

Nicholas ran for West's SUV as Striker and the cybercrimes agent loaded into hers. SSA Peters climbed into the passenger seat as Nicholas climbed behind the wheel. He twisted the key in the ignition and ripped out of the parking garage. Sunlight pierced through the windshield as he fishtailed onto Union toward Second Avenue and Pioneer Square. "He's headed for the Seattle underground. He's going to use Aubrey to re-create the Extreme Makeover's MO and leave her there for us to search blocks of underground to find her."

"This guy hasn't stuck to any one MO since he started. There could be a thousand locations within the city alone he's taken her if you're wrong about this." SSA Peters braced against the passenger-side door as Nicholas took the left onto Second above the speed limit. "What makes you so sure she'll be underground?"

"The book Dr. Caldwell left behind. Both victims were members of the same true crime book club, and one of the books on their shelves was *But First, Lipstick*, which gives an account of the Extreme Makeover Killer. According to Simon Curry, every member in the club took on a nickname of their favorite serial killer. Kara Flood was invested in learning about the X Marks the Spot Killer because Aubrey had been involved in the case. Paige Cress was the Gingerbread Woman, and Simon Curry claimed the Watcher."

If he hadn't pushed to put Curry in the dark silhouette of their perp on the murder board, he might've seen it before. There weren't more victims out there they hadn't discovered. Not yet. "Caldwell had to have been in the same book club. He would've known their nicknames. He replicated his idols' MOs to test his skills before he turned his attention to his real target."

"Dr. Flood," SSA Peters said.

"Aubrey isn't a member. I think he got tired of Kara talking about her sister during the meetings. He's jealous of her. He wants to make an example of her, to prove he's the better pathologist and that he should've been the one to handle the X Killer case. He's punishing her." Nicholas tightened his grip around the steering wheel, and he pushed the SUV harder. "He left the book for me. He wanted me to know his nickname was the Extreme Makeover Killer and that that was exactly how he was going to murder Aubrey once his own MO failed to kill her."

"It's public knowledge the Extreme Makeover Killer dumped all his victims' bodies in the underground. Why make the game so easy?" SSA Peters asked. "Why follow an MO to a tee when police already have the location of the dump site?"

"Because he thinks he can get away with it." The ego and arrogance had been right in front of him all this time. This wasn't about the manner Dr. Caldwell had chosen or with which he'd killed his victims. They'd been nothing but a convenience of which he'd taken advantage. Every move, every lead the BAU had taken uncovered nothing but pure narcissism.

"He craves the chase, and he's worked for the county as a medical examiner long enough to ensure none of the forensic evidence ties back to him. He's been involved in the investigation. He's had access to the remains of his two victims. He knows everything we had aside from the piece of tissue Paige Cress had between her teeth was circumstantial, and he's probably already destroyed it. This is one big game to him, and he took her because I let my own trust issues get in the way of protecting her."

And he feared Aubrey wouldn't be the last victim to pay the price if he failed.

HUMMING FILLED HER EARS.

There was no pressure this time. No crushing pain other than the constant ache in her ribs as she filled her lungs with cold, dry air, and the pounding at the back of her skull where her attacker had hit her. She wasn't upside down. Aubrey hauled her chin away from her chest, an old wooden chair protesting as she moved. The torn skin of her left wrist burned under the friction of rope securing her to the chair.

"Ah, Dr. Flood. Nice to see you again." Dr. Caldwell's outline darkened the spotlight shining into her face. He bent at the waist, coming that much closer to the point she caught hints of formaldehyde and cleaning agent. "While you were unconscious, I gained access to your recent X-rays after our first little meeting. Thank you for telling the truth about your diagnosis. Your fractured scapula and broken ribs, coupled with a change in binds, gives me confidence you won't be able to struggle this time."

She swept her tongue through her mouth to chase back the dryness and taste of dirt. The edges of the gauze on her neck pulled at her oversensitized skin. Mustiness embedded into her lung tissue as she rolled her head to one side. An exposed brick arch and cement flooring materialized as her eyes adjusted to the overstimulation from the spotlight. Strong pillars had cracked under the pressure of the slight bulge in the ceiling, and Aubrey felt as though she were deep underground. Far enough no one could hear her scream. "Dr. Caldwell—Archer—what… what are you doing?"

"I'm proving I'm better, of course." The voice that'd been stuck in her head since the attack grated against every fiber of her being, but she hadn't recognized Dr. Caldwell for the killer he was. The only explanation she had was his voice wasn't altered by a ski mask now. "You, of all people, should understand that, Dr. Flood. You've gone out of your way to become the FBI's favorite pathologist these past few years. Well, now I'm going out of my way to prove I was the better choice." Dr. Caldwell turned slightly, the spotlight highlighting the sharp angles of his face and illuminating a cruel smile. "And believe me, after I'm finished with you, they'll never doubt my abilities again."

Disbelief hardened the muscles along her spine. That was what this was about? Her sister had been strangled and mutilated because he hadn't been chosen to work the X Marks the Spot Killer case? "You were in the same book club as Kara and Paige, weren't you? You used their nicknames to replicate previous serial MOs, to show the

FBI you were better at killing than the originals, and set up Simon Curry to take the fall."

"Everything would've gone according to plan if Paige Cress hadn't bit me while I was trying to suffocate her with her own jacket, but as the official pathologist over this case, all I had to do was compromise the skin sample my assistant discovered during the initial examination. The lab will never be able to trace the DNA in that skin sample recovered from Paige back to me or connect me to Kara. Everything the FBI has right now is circumstantial." Dr. Caldwell smirked, and Aubrey pulled at the restraints around both feet and her left wrist. "But you... You had to go and be your own hero in the slaughterhouse. You had to attract the affection of Agent James and bring the whole BAU team to my door."

Nicholas. Her insides hollowed as the last few minutes of their conversation in the observation room hit her all over again. She'd been right about Simon Curry. The true killer had methodically made Curry the FBI's prime suspect while working under their noses from the beginning. Dr. Caldwell wasn't just intelligent, as Nicholas had suggested in his profile. He was a genius, and right then Aubrey couldn't see a way of escape.

She followed the exposed pipes above to the end of a long corridor. The headache at the back of her skull intensified the harder she tried to map an escape route, and she rolled her injured shoulder back to test her rotation. Her right hand was the only extremity that hadn't been bound to the chair, still useless in the sling. If she could distract Dr. Caldwell long enough and work through the pain, she might have a chance. "You used Kara to get to me."

"Would you believe me if I told you I'd joined the book club for the same reason as your sister?" His voice hitched as though paired with a smile, and her gut soured. "Kara was all too happy to regale me with stories of her big sister, the medical examiner who'd single-handedly taken down the X Marks the Spot Killer by narrowing down the kind of knife Cole Presley had used to carve his victims' cheeks. That was why she became a member of our little group. She wasn't sure how to talk to you about the investigation face-to-face, so she learned everything she could about the case in order to feel closer to you. A waste of time. Why study the pathologist assigned to the case when she could learn so much more from a killer?"

Kara had been trying to learn as much as she could about the X Marks the Spot Killer case in order to be closer to Aubrey. Simon Curry had said as much during his interrogation, but it wasn't until this moment she was able to process the information in the wake of losing her connection to Nicholas. Her body hurt, but it was nothing compared to the pain in her heart. All this time she'd believed Kara had never understood her, never wanted to understand her, but the opposite had been true.

Dragging a chair she hadn't seen until then closer, Dr. Caldwell took a seat across from her, his expression cast into darkness from the spotlight at his back. "Seems everyone just can't get enough of you, Dr. Flood, including your own family. I'll be honest, I don't understand the fascination. Kara's, Agent James's. You're an above-average pathologist from Seattle, dedicated to your work with little social life or hobbies, as far as I can tell. No serious relationships. If I hadn't known Kara was your sister from our conversations during book club or that your parents were still alive, I would've assumed you were utterly and completely alone. That leaves the X Marks the Spot Killer case. If it hadn't been for that investigation—for your connection to such a high-profile case—you'd be nothing."

"Maybe the fact that I'm not a psychopath has something to do with it." She blinked against the white lights developing across her vision from the unrelenting brightness of the spotlight.

"I underestimated you before, Dr. Flood." A low laugh punctuated Dr. Caldwell's rise to his feet. He turned away from her. He disappeared into the shadows fighting to close in around the pool of spotlight, his voice more distant than a minute ago. Shuffling sounds ensued from the darkness, a hit of metal breaking through. Another scalpel? "But I won't make the same mistake twice."

Aubrey secured her jaw against the bone-deep ache in her shoulder and ribs as she pushed her elbow toward the outer edge of her sling. Dr. Caldwell had been assigned to an investigation of his own making. Her heart rate rocketed into overdrive as the pain spread outward from her scapula and nearly pulled a groan from her throat. She forced herself to keep her breathing under control as she worked her injured arm free of the sling. Too much force and the tendons keeping her bone from separating completely would snap, causing irreversible damage. Too little and she'd never get free. The lining of the sling scraped against her heated skin, but she couldn't stop. She'd escaped Dr. Caldwell once before. She could do it again.

Nicholas had believed the killer was driven by his narcissistic personality disorder, desperate to prove himself better than the men and women he idolized. That desperation meant he wouldn't be able to turn down the opportunity to talk about himself. "You disposed of Paige Cress's body on the pier to draw me there. There weren't any signs she'd been killed in that shed. You had to have killed her somewhere else. The evidence on her body might've been compromised, but the scent of gasoline was still on her clothes when we found her. The forensic lab will be able to pick up traces."

A lie. The techs hadn't been able to recover anything after the ocean had washed the victim's clothes, but the Gingerbread Woman had attacked all her victims in parking garages. He'd stuck to every last detail concerning the X Marks the Spot Killer's MO. Made sense he'd do the same for the Gingerbread Woman's. "It was a garage, wasn't it? Agent James and the rest of the BAU will find which one. It's only a matter of time before he ties you to these crimes."

"Your profiler surely believes I'm a narcissist, and you've interpreted that to mean getting me to talk about myself and the way I kill will give you a chance for escape. You're wrong." Dr. Caldwell stepped back into the spotlight, and every cell in her body spiked into awareness. The outline of a blade in his hand, similar to the shape of a No. 11 scalpel used to make fine incisions during an autopsy, demanded attention as he stepped closer. He leaned into her, setting the cold steel against her cheek.

"You're forgetting I was the pathologist assigned to examine the victims, and I ensured none of the evidence the forensic lab tested would trace back to me. Cole Presley, Irene Lawrence, Samson Little—they might've been the inspiration for my masterpieces, but I've risen above them. Even if the BAU arrests me for the deaths of Kara Flood and Paige Cress, they'll never be able to prove it, and you won't live long enough to tell them what happened here today. I'm sorry to disappoint you, Dr. Flood, but I can't be beat."

The steel of the scalpel warmed against her cheek. Aubrey twisted her head sharply and bit down on her attacker's hand as hard as she could. Blood penetrated the seam of her lips and filled her mouth, triggering her gag reflex, but she only clamped her teeth harder. Her attacker's scream echoed off the brick walls, and he tore his hand away. But not fast enough. She forced herself to swallow as he held on to his bleeding hand, and a sense of accomplishment filled her. "Let's see you compromise that sample."

Dr. Caldwell arced the scalpel down toward her wrist bound to the chair and sank it deep through tendon, veins and muscle. Aubrey's scream rivaled her abductor's and intensified the pain in her head, but she couldn't pull away. His hand shook around the blade as he stared down at her. "Let's see how much you bleed."

## Chapter Fourteen

"All tourists have been accounted for and evacuated, Agent James." The Seattle PD officer's staticky voice barely registered from the radio strapped to Nicholas's vest.

Pinholes of light penetrated through the street-level grid-pattern glass skywalk above as he and the team descended into history. The network of underground passageways and basements in downtown Pioneer Square had originally been ground level when the city was built in the mid-nineteenth century, but the Seattle Great Fire had relegated a maze of shops and spaces to disuse. With fewer and fewer guided tours through the labyrinth, it'd been the perfect location for the Extreme Makeover Killer to dump his victims' bodies, but Nicholas wasn't going to let Aubrey become the newest resident.

"This guy is intelligent, beyond what we originally estimated, and dangerous. He's planned this out from the beginning, and he won't give Aubrey up easily. Stay alert, watch each other's backs and keep in radio contact."

"Striker, West, take the left corridor. James, you're with me." SSA Peters unholstered his weapon as they split at the first intersection of passages. "We want Dr.

Caldwell alive, but if you have to shoot the bastard to protect yourself or the victim, I won't feel bad about it."

"Copy," Striker said.

"See you on the other side." West laughed, following his partner.

Exposed piping above led them deeper into the manmade caverns, past shattered window fronts and through inches of dust, ash and debris. Nicholas angled his flashlight toward the ground, sweeping it across the broken, aged cement in an effort to pick up some kind of trail. Humidity worked deep into his lungs as he scanned the inside of the old store on his right. No movement. Nothing to suggest Dr. Caldwell or Aubrey had been here at all. His pulse ticked hard at the base of his throat. These tunnels ran the length of five city blocks in some areas and had become basements to galleries, restaurants and tourist traps on the surface. The killer could've taken her anywhere.

A scream resonated down the tunnel.

"Aubrey." She was alive. Nicholas bolted down the corridor in the direction he believed the sound had originated, his flashlight and weapon bouncing in his hand. His legs protested the harder he ran, but nothing would stop him from getting to her this time. The blueprint he'd memorized before they'd descended into the city's underworld stayed fresh in his mind as he came to another break in the maze, and he pulled up short. Two directions. Nicholas searched both passages, but he couldn't see a damn thing, couldn't hear her. If he chose wrong, it'd cost Aubrey more time. It could cost her her life.

Pressure clawed up his throat. He couldn't fail her again. His heart threatened to beat straight out of his chest. "Damn it."

The sound of footsteps fell into line behind him as SSA Peters kept close on his heels. The supervisory special agent studied the patterns in the dust along the floor. "Which way?"

"I don't know. He must've doubled back and covered his tracks." He aimed his flashlight and weapon down the right corridor. He kicked at an old crate and launched it down the tunnel. "She could be anywhere."

SSA Peters pinched the push-to-talk button on his radio and angled his chin down. "Striker, West, double back and meet us in the left tunnel." SSA Peters circled into his peripheral vision, heavy eyebrows outlining dark eyes in the flood of his flashlight beam. "You know this guy better than any of us. You're one of the best profilers I've ever worked with. You can get into his head. You can find her by knowing how he works."

"She doesn't have time. You heard her scream. That wasn't a scream for help. That was a scream from pain," Nicholas said. "He's torturing her. He's killing her, and I'm stuck here without a damn idea of how to get to her."

"Say...again... Peters?" Static broke through their comms. A gunshot exploded from the corridor behind them as the connection to Striker and West cut out.

His pulse rocketed higher. Warning lightninged through him as Nicholas turned back the way they'd come. The team was under attack, but he wasn't going to let Dr. Caldwell win this time. "The son of a bitch knows we're here. He's going to try to take us out one by one again, just as he did at the pier. He wants to lead us away from his victim in hopes of running out the clock."

Stepping into his path, SSA Peters gripped Nicholas's vest in one hand and shoved him down the right tunnel, his weapon in the other. "Do you remember what I said to you when you took this case?"

"What the hell are you doing, Peters? They need our help." Nicholas pushed against his SSA, but Peters wouldn't budge. Desperation to neutralize the threat knotted in his chest as the BAU team leader's words echoed in his head.

"I told you it isn't every day we find out the people we trust the most aren't who they seem, but what I should've said was, it isn't every day we let the people we trust show us who they really are. What Cole Presley did is unforgivable, but Aubrey Flood isn't the man who betrayed you, Nicholas. Don't let that old bastard keep you from finally being happy." SSA Peters released his hold, and Nicholas stepped back. "Go. Find Dr. Flood and get her the hell out of here. We'll handle Caldwell."

"Watch your back." Nicholas nodded. He knew who Aubrey really was. He'd known from the moment he'd met her during the X Marks the Spot Killer investigation, but his own fear of trusting the wrong person again, of not being able to see the threat coming, had shut down the possibility of something more between them. He wanted her. He wanted to trust her, to be close to her more than he'd ever wanted another human being. Cole Presley had shown him the worst mankind had to offer, but Aubrey had shown him the best, and without her, he feared he'd never let anyone get close again.

"Watch yours." SSA Peters disappeared down the corridor.

Nicholas faced two historical streets leading in separate directions. Peters would take care of the team. He had to focus on finding Aubrey. She'd been taken down one of these passages, and from the sound of her scream, time was running out. "Which direction, Doc? Give me another hint."

The calm space he used to deep dive into the case demanded focus, and Nicholas automatically went back to that moment in Aubrey's apartment building, the one when she'd framed his face between her hands and leveled those honey-warm eyes on his. Her voice faded in and out and settled the fire burning through him. Seattle's underground phased out as the details of the investigation pushed to the front of his mind. Aubrey. He forced stillness through his body and closed his eyes. His pulse steadied, his breathing evening out.

Caldwell's compulsion to kill was a combination of pride and a need for attention. The King County medical examiner had formed an unhealthy attachment to Aubrey. The pathologist felt as though she'd taken the limelight from him. He wouldn't kill her quickly. Not unless forced, but he would want to display his handiwork when he was finished. That was why he'd used the spotlight in the slaughterhouse. There was a chance Caldwell would want to do it again, which meant he'd need electricity.

Nicholas raised his flashlight to the ceiling. Different sizes of aluminum piping and electrical wiring ran through the rafters above. Broken light bulbs reached down from the ceiling in equidistant measurements. He wasn't looking for something as old as the shops and tunnels themselves. Caldwell would've had to upgrade the wiring to fit his needs. There. He separated a single bright orange extension cord from the darker, dust-covered collection, and followed it down the corridor to the right. Weapon aimed high, he listened for signs of movement as he searched each storefront before moving on to the next. "Come on. I know you're here somewhere."

The corridor ended ahead. There weren't any more shops to search.

He'd reached a dead end.

Nicholas lowered his flashlight and weapon but hesitated. The beam from his flashlight cut in half, one side highlighting the wall to his right, the other landing on the wall in front of him. Not a solid wall. He took a step forward, then another, before realizing the dead end wasn't the end at all. The brick turned a corner into a wall of brick that'd been disassembled. This section hadn't been noted in the blueprints West pulled from the city, but Caldwell had known about it somehow. Keeping his back to one wall, Nicholas ducked through the opening. More brick. More dust. More silence. Bright light hit him in the face, and he raised one hand to block the onslaught to his vision.

"Is someone there?" a soft voice asked.

"Doc, is that you?" He dropped his hand, trying to get eyes on her. He wasn't too late. She was still alive. "Where is he? Where's Caldwell?"

"I knew you'd find me," she said.

"Aubrey?" His eyes adjusted slower than he needed them to, then he saw her. Bound in a chair, her head slumped forward as though she'd simply fallen asleep. The spotlight reflected back from a scalpel buried in her left wrist. The blade had pinned her to the chair, and she couldn't use her other arm to get free. Nicholas holstered his weapon and crouched in front of her. Blood. There was so much blood. Not only running from her pinned wrist but from around her mouth. "Aubrey, wake up. Stay with me."

He wasn't a medical professional. He didn't know how to pull the scalpel from her wrist without putting her in more danger of bleeding out. "You need to tell me what to do, Doc. You have to help me get you out of here."

"Severed radial artery. Can't…pull it out." She lifted her head, those warm eyes brightening. The spotlight washed color from her features and intensified the dried blood around her mouth. "Caldwell killed… Kara. He killed Paige. He compromised the evidence, but… I have proof."

"That doesn't matter right now. I'm going to get you out of here. Okay? But first, you need to tell me how to stop you from bleeding out if I remove the scalpel," he said.

"I bit him. I swallowed…the evidence." Sweat built along her temple as she closed her eyes. She was losing consciousness. "You can prove…he did it."

Nicholas attached his flashlight to his vest and unholstered the blade at his ankle. He cut through the rope binding her wrist and both feet. "Come on, Doc. Don't give up on me now. Tell me how to stop the bleeding."

The spotlight lost power, throwing them into darkness.

"I'm afraid it's a little too late for that, Agent James." Archer Caldwell lunged.

HER FINGERS IN her left hand had gone numb.

Aubrey tried to curl them around the end of the chair's arm—to feel something, anything—but the scalpel hadn't only severed her radial artery, it'd most likely damaged the nerves in her hand.

She dragged her head over her shoulder, trying to locate Nicholas, but the spotlight had lost power. The only light came from a flashlight swinging wildly through the small area Dr. Caldwell had brought her. A fist connected with flesh and bone, and a deep growl registered through the dark. "Nicholas."

Dr. Caldwell would kill him if given the opportunity.

She had to help him. Aubrey forced her eyes open. She was losing blood for the second time in under a week. Her body had yet to recover from Dr. Caldwell's first attempt to exsanguinate her, but she couldn't leave Nicholas to fight this battle on his own. No matter what'd happened between them. He didn't deserve to die because of her. She leaned forward in the chair. The rope around her ankles and left wrist had been cut away and cracked under the weight of her feet as she straightened. The pain in her scapula and broken ribs tore a sob from her throat. The rotation in her right arm had been severely limited since her injury, but Nicholas needed her help. She wasn't going to let Archer Caldwell win.

Nicholas's scream filled the underground chamber and severed the detachment she'd forced on herself since their conversation in the observation room. Agony ripped across her back and down her right side as she cleared the rest of her forearm from the sling, and an answering sob ricocheted off the exposed brick.

"Do you hear that, Agent James? She's dying, and there's nothing you can do to stop it. No one can stop me." Dr. Caldwell's outline separated from the shadows with the help of Nicholas's flashlight strapped to his vest. He stood over Nicholas and thrust a hard kick to the profiler's rib cage. A hard exhale rushed from Nicholas's mouth, and he curled in on himself. Caldwell slammed his fist into Nicholas's face, and her partner's head snapped back against the concrete.

Nicholas went still.

"Stop. Stop it." Aubrey pressed her weight into her left elbow. Anger tore up her throat. It mixed with Dr. Caldwell's blood still coating her mouth, burning, twisting and carving her into pieces. No. She'd already lost Kara. She couldn't lose Nicholas, too. The past few days had broken her down to nothing, but Nicholas had gone out of his way to help her rebuild. He'd put her needs first, made her feel wanted. Made her feel loved. She didn't care if it'd surfaced out of the trauma she'd sustained from discovering her sister's body or nearly dying in that slaughterhouse. Her feelings were real. They mattered, and no one was going to take that away from her. Least of all a copycat killer who blamed her for his own weaknesses. "Get away from him."

She used her last ounces of strength and endurance to raise her right arm and wrap her hand around the scalpel pinning her wrist to the chair. The blade had most likely severed her radial artery. If she pulled it out without stanching the blood flow, she'd lose consciousness within thirty seconds and bleed out within two minutes.

Nicholas kicked out and shoved his attacker back into a standing tray of surgical instruments a few feet away, dislodging his flashlight in the process. The beam spun wildly across the floor then steadied on the collection of tools that'd hit the concrete. Her heart jerked in her chest as shadows consumed her partner, the fight growing more brutal, more violent. There. Dr. Caldwell's clamp had landed less than three feet away, but without the use of both hands, it'd take a miracle to reach it.

She had to try.

Blood trickled down the inside of her wrist. The only thing keeping her from bleeding out was the scalpel, but it was also what was killing her. Aubrey pressed herself out of the chair and extended her right leg. The agony in her wrist and opposite shoulder threatened to pull her back into unconsciousness, but she couldn't give up. Not until she and Nicholas were safe. Tears burned down her face as another sob broke free. She could make it. She had to make it. She slid her foot along the floor and stretched as far as her boot would reach. Her toes scraped along the side of the clamp but only managed to push it farther away. "Come on."

"You'll never lay another hand on her, you son of a bitch." Nicholas surged off the floor and attacked with a brutalness she'd never seen in person. He slammed Dr. Caldwell back into a pillar. Once. Twice. The pathologist's groan filled the corridor as Nicholas threw a right hook, then a left.

Her eyes adjusted as the fight unfolded. Blood sprayed across the floor and up her leg, and her heart rocketed into her throat. Whether it'd come from Nicholas or Dr. Caldwell, she didn't know, but the sight of those drops pushed her harder. She had to get to the clamp, but the fact she couldn't turn her wrist with the scalpel still pinning her to the chair put it that much farther out of reach. She pointed her toes as much as her boot would let her and swept her leg across the floor. The clamp skidded closer. A burst of relieved laughter escaped up her throat, and she pulled her leg back toward her. She could almost reach the instrument. Just a few more inches. Agonizing pressure built in her fractured shoulder as she crouched and straightened her arm. The pain stole the oxygen from her lungs. The tip of her middle finger glided across the clamp's handle.

The spotlight switched back on.

She closed her eyes and turned her head away, losing contact with the instrument.

"I haven't given you enough credit, Dr. Flood. Once again, I've underestimated your determination to ruin my plans." Dr. Caldwell swiped blood from his face with the back of a bloodied hand and stalked toward her. "You can't even die the way I want you to."

She gasped at the sight of Nicholas's prone outline across the room. He wasn't dead. She had to believe that. She had to believe Dr. Caldwell would stick to the MO and only kill his intended victim, but she wasn't an expert in profiling or psychology. She didn't know how far a killer would go to stop anyone who got in their way. It didn't matter. If she left the scalpel in her wrist, both she and Nicholas would die down here. "What did you do?"

Caldwell maneuvered around the spotlight, closing in on her. He wrapped his fingers around the scalpel and twisted the blade through her wrist. "Did you really think I was going to let him take you from me, Aubrey? How many times do I have to make my point? You did everything you could to keep me in your shadow, but now I'm the one with the power. I'm the one who is going to be remembered years from now, and you'll be nothing more than a footnote."

Her scream ricocheted inside her head, over and over, until she wasn't sure if she was still conscious. She slumped against the chair. Wood cut into her uninjured ribs, and the pain in her hand and wrist vanished. A crash of metal pierced through the haze suffocating her. The scalpel had shifted in her wrist. She was losing blood faster than before. The clamp. She needed the clamp.

"I'm not finished with you." Nicholas's voice chased

back the numbness clawing up her arm and into her chest. He sounded closer. Almost within arm's reach.

"I'm not...finished with you...either." Aubrey dragged her eyes open as another crash reverberated through the room. Nicholas and Caldwell battled for dominance, each trying to physically break the other, but she only had attention for the clamp. Reaching down, she didn't even feel the pain in her shoulder and wrapped her fingers around the stainless-steel instrument. She pressed her elbow against the chair and hauled herself off the floor. Blood pulsed out of her wrist, every second draining precious milliliters she couldn't afford to lose. She set the clamp on her lap and gripped the scalpel. She had less than thirty seconds to secure the clamp before she lost consciousness and never woke up. Shadows shifted in her peripheral vision, the ringing in her ears too loud.

She pulled the scalpel from her wrist.

Blood gushed from the wound and soaked the grain of the wooden chair and her slacks. The blade fell from her hand, the tang of metal against concrete barely registering as she grasped the clamp. She didn't have time to ensure it'd been sterilized. If she lived through this—if she and Nicholas made it out of here—the hospital could take care of any infection. Aubrey struggled to keep her eyes open as she inserted the clamp into the wound. The pain was gone now. There was only survival. She compressed the clamp's teeth where she believed Caldwell had lacerated her artery, and an instant exhaustion flooded through her. The bleeding slowed, but the longer the clamp obstructed blood flow to her hand, the higher chance she'd never be able to use it again.

Reality came into focus with measured breaths, and she caught sight of Nicholas. Her partner struggled to free himself from the pinning grip of Dr. Caldwell's hands around his throat. If the pathologist pressed down with too much force, he'd crush the profiler's larynx and the man she loved would suffocate in a matter of minutes.

The man she loved.

Aubrey slid from the chair, wrapping her hand around the scalpel she'd pulled from her wrist. The fractures in her shoulder had taken a considerable amount of strength from her grip, but she wouldn't need much. The best medical examiners made the best killers.

Caldwell had turned his back toward her. Nicholas's feet pressed into the floor to unbalance his attacker, but it wasn't enough. Those green-blue eyes she'd come to rely on widened as she arced the scalpel down and stabbed the blade through the occipital nerves at the base of Dr. Caldwell's skull.

The pathologist's body went rigid, and his hands fell from around Nicholas's neck. Faster than her blood-deprived brain registered, Nicholas rolled his attacker to the floor. His gaze dipped to her wrist, to the clamp hanging from the wound, then raised to her. "Aubrey, are you—"

The strength in her legs failed.

He caught her as she collapsed. Staring down at her, Nicholas swept her hair out of her face as he positioned her across his lap. Shouts echoed down the corridors and tunnels, but he never left her. "In here! Call an ambulance!" He hauled her closer, setting his forehead against hers. "I've got you, Doc. I've got you."

She closed her eyes, reveling in the warmth his body injected as the cold crept in. She tried to thread her hands through his hair, but her extremities wouldn't respond.

"Have I ever told you…your hair…is as pretty as a peri-winkle…flower on a pony?"

"Aubrey, come on," he said. "Stay with me."

She wanted to, but the blackness pulled her under.

## Chapter Fifteen

Archer Caldwell was dead.

The damage Aubrey had done to the occipital nerves at the back of his neck had instantly killed him, but the damage the son of a bitch had caused over the past few days would last for years.

Nicholas refreshed the glass of water on the side table beside the hospital bed and took a seat. Remote in hand, he turned on the TV and switched the channels until he found Aubrey's favorite show. The one with the toy doctor who could bring her stuffed animals to life. Monitors punctuated each beat of her heart as she slept.

The surgeons had been able to suture the severed artery in her wrist, but the amount of trauma she'd been through in the slaughterhouse, combined with the damage to her wrist two days ago, had forced her doctor to sedate Aubrey in order to speed her recovery.

"All right, the little girl with a magical stethoscope is having a hard time after making a big mistake at her clinic. She's wondering if her patients would be better off if she hadn't been there at all, but I think we both know how this one is going to end," he said. "Hell, you've probably watched it half a dozen times yourself, but I've got to tell you, I feel kind of bad for her."

Three quick knocks punctured the bubble he'd created inside the small room since she'd been released from surgery. The door swung open, and Dashiell West nodded. "How's she doing today?"

Nicholas turned off the television and set the remote on the side table near Aubrey's glass of water. "Her doctors came in about an hour ago to take her off the sedation meds. Her vitals are steady, but it's taking a while for her to wake up. They tell me it's nothing to worry about for now. If everything goes well, she'll be awake soon." He sat higher in the chair. "What's up?"

"Figured you'd want an update on the Caldwell investigation." West closed the door behind him softly and took the chair closest to the door. "Caitlyn has been keeping the families in the loop. The new medical examiner finished his reexamination of Kara Flood's and Paige Cress's remains and has released both victims to their families for final arrangements."

"That's good. You were there while he did the examination?" Nicholas studied Aubrey's sleeping form, her dark brown hair framing her face. The fractured shoulder blade, two broken ribs and the scalpel in her wrist hadn't stopped her from saving his life down in those tunnels. He'd see this through to the end. For her.

"Yeah. Seemed Caldwell went out of his way to make sure the evidence he recovered from both victims wouldn't tie back to him, but from what the new ME said, it's pretty clear who attacked Kara Flood and Paige Cress. The cast the pathologist made of Paige's teeth matches the wound on Caldwell's forearm, and the lab recovered epithelial cells from the dog's leash used to strangle Kara. He wore gloves, but the doc's sister must've struggled enough to scrape one edge of the leash against her attacker's neck. There are faint scratches under Caldwell's jaw."

West motioned toward Aubrey. "On top of that, the blood Aubrey swallowed after she bit Caldwell came back as a DNA match for the tissue the ME's assistant pulled from between Paige Cress's teeth. He tried to contaminate the sample, but the solution he'd used breaks down DNA over time. We caught it before there was too much damage. Forensics wasn't able to pull prints from the map he taped to Dr. Flood's door or from the Polaroid Caldwell left with the dog, but the shoe print outside Kara Flood's apartment is a perfect match and size to a pair of boots from Caldwell's apartment. Soil samples confirm he was there, and CSU found three bottles of perfume with both victims' fingerprints and Dr. Flood's on the glass from his bathroom. Looks like the bastard was collecting trophies from his kills. You'll also be happy to know Dyson found a regular from AfterDark who was willing to sit down with one of our composite artists. She described all four book club members to a tee."

"You should've seen her." Nicholas couldn't keep the admiration out of his voice. Even in the face of death, Aubrey had stood up against her attacker and killed him before the bastard could kill Nicholas. No matter how many times he found himself in awe of her determination and self-sacrifice, she surprised him. "Anything else?"

"I decrypted Dr. Caldwell's personal laptop drive. I found these." West handed over the file in his hand, and Nicholas forced himself to tear his gaze from Aubrey to take it. "Surveillance photos. Caldwell might've tampered with the evidence tying him to Kara Flood's and Paige Cress's murders, but he didn't get rid of all of it.

Seems I can break a serial killer's encryption, but proving my sister's innocence is beyond my capabilities."

West's sister. Arrested for embezzling funds from the investment bank where she worked as a hedge fund manager. Nicholas understood the obsession to protect the people he cared about and to use the very justice system he believed in to do it, but sometimes the law was out of their hands. He flipped through dozens of photos obviously taken with a telephoto lens. Kara Flood walking her dog, Koko, down the same section of sidewalk where she'd been found dead. Paige Cress outside her employer's office. Aubrey in one of Harborview Medical's hospital wings. He hesitated, his thumb tracing over the curve of her jaw in the photo, and lifted his gaze to the warm, real-life woman in the hospital bed.

He'd been wrong about her after Simon Curry's interrogation. He'd accused her of using the trauma she'd been through to cling to the next person who'd shown her any kind of attention, but the truth was, it'd probably taken everything she had to trust him with her safety and welfare. Aubrey had spent nearly her entire life putting others first, always ignoring her own needs in the hope the love she showed would be returned, and he'd thrown it in her face. He'd accused her of weakness when, in fact, she was the strongest woman he'd ever met in his life. Once again, if it hadn't been for her, Nicholas wouldn't have made it out of the underground.

He closed the file and handed it back to West. "We have proof that ties Caldwell to each of the victims. It'll be enough to close the case and give the families the closure they deserve. Great work, West. We got him."

"Thought you'd be a little more enthusiastic about it." West pushed to his feet, his gaze shifting to Aubrey. "But

I imagine you've got other things on your mind." The cybercrimes expert half saluted toward the hospital bed with the file folder. "Looks like she's coming around. I'll give you two some time."

The monitor on the other side of the bed ticked up in rhythm, and Nicholas shoved to his feet. The hospital room door clicked closed behind him as West exited. Sliding his hand beneath hers, he studied the subtle changes in Aubrey's expression as she battled to open her eyes. "Hey, Doc."

"Hey." She focused on him, and the world righted itself in an instant. Her tongue darted across her bottom lip as she scanned the room, took in the machines tracking her vitals, then came back to him. Her gaze dipped to the cast around her left hand, and his heart jerked in his chest. Aubrey Flood was—had been—one of the best pathologists in the country, and the tears welling in her eyes told him she knew exactly what the extensive damage to her wrist meant. "I can't feel my fingers. Nerve damage?"

Nicholas massaged his thumb into her forearm above the cast, but no amount of physical or verbal comfort would change what'd happened. "Yeah, Doc. Your surgeon did everything he could, but the damage Caldwell caused… They said there's still a chance of making a full recovery with physical therapy and time, but—"

"But I won't be able to hold a scalpel again. I won't be able to keep my job or help the people who've lost their loved ones find answers." Her voice deadpanned, her expression as neutral as her words. She pulled her hand away from his and set her forearm across her eyes. "Even dead, Dr. Caldwell got exactly what he wanted."

"I'm fairly certain he wanted to walk out of those tunnels alive. You made sure that didn't happen. You made sure he couldn't hurt anyone ever again." Nicholas brought his chair closer and took a seat. Tugging her hand back into his, he swept the tear that'd escaped from one eye away with his thumb. He had to be sure. He had to be sure this wasn't a dream, that she was alive, that she was really here, but hell, even if it wasn't real, he'd do whatever it took not to wake up.

"You saved my life. And my team's lives, Aubrey. You made sure we all got out of there alive. You might not be able to hold a scalpel again, but there are plenty of ways you can still help the people who need you. You're stronger than you think. No matter how many times you get knocked down, you stand back up. That's what I love about you."

Her gaze cut to his, confusion swirling through the honey depths. "What do you mean, that's what you love about me?"

"I mean I was an idiot." He shook his head, a humorless laugh filling the tension between them as their last conversation replayed in his head for the hundredth—or was it the thousandth?—time. "After Simon Curry's interrogation, I discounted your instincts about his innocence and blamed your attachment to me on the trauma you'd been through in the slaughterhouse. We had a perfectly viable suspect on the other side of that glass, but I was wrong, and I was wrong to invalidate your feelings. I didn't give you enough credit. I should've known after what you'd been through you were stronger than that, but the truth is, I was scared."

"It's hard to believe anything scares you," she said.

"Cole Presley made me believe he was a good man. Hell, he helped raise me and my sister. He took care of my mom when she didn't have anyone else to rely on, and he manipulated me into thinking he cared about us. But after the truth came out, I swore I wouldn't ever let someone manipulate me like that again."

Nicholas studied the fine lines of the sling on her right arm, heat rising up his throat. "Then you came along, and when you told me you'd finally found someone you didn't have to hide your true self with, I convinced myself you were manipulating me as he had. I convinced myself that you were wearing a mask to get what you needed from me before you left."

SHE DIDN'T KNOW what to say, what to think.

Nicholas had been through one of the worst betrayals a person could experience when Cole Presley had revealed who he was behind that friendly neighbor/father-figure mask, and her chest hurt witnessing the pain in his voice now, but she needed to know. She needed to know how they could move on from this. Because even though he'd crushed her heart in that observation room, a part of her still stood by what she'd said. She didn't have to hide pieces of herself from him. She didn't have to convince him she was a pediatrician or explain her need to autopsy human beings to give comfort to their loved ones. She didn't have to hide the fact she'd rather watch a silly children's show instead of the news or a true crime documentary or listen to a podcast all her colleagues and friends had become obsessed with.

"Do you blame me for being the one to prove Cole Presley was the X Marks the Spot Killer?" Aubrey willed her fingers to curl around his, but the signals from her brain had died the moment Dr. Caldwell had stabbed that scalpel through her wrist. The hollowness of facing the fact she'd never hold a surgical instrument steadily again had cut through her, but worse, the fear Nicholas would never be able to trust her hooked into her and pulled tight. "Do you resent me because you think I made a mistake on that case?"

The three distinct lines between his eyebrows deepened in confusion. He shifted to the edge of his seat and locked both hands around her cast. The dark circles under his eyes evidenced his lack of sleep, and it was only then she realized he'd slept in the clothes he was wearing. He'd stayed here. With her. "What? No. You did your job, Doc, and you're damn good at it. The evidence proved he killed all those women. You proved it. You're the one who showed the world who he really was, and I could never blame you for that."

"But you won't ever trust me." The pain of that statement sliced deeper than the fractures to her ribs and scapula. She'd trusted him. She'd trusted him to find her when Caldwell had abducted her from the pier, and afterward when he'd promised he wouldn't let anything else happen to her. She'd trusted him with pieces of her and Kara's childhood and to find the man responsible for murdering her sister. She'd trusted him with her heart, even at the risk of not being wanted in return. Tightness swelled in her throat.

"All I've done is trust you during this investigation, Nicholas. You made me feel wanted and worthy when you watched my favorite show with me and made doughnuts for me. When you held me and let me cry in your arms, I felt…loved. You showed me I was burning out by putting others first, but when I finally made myself a priority by telling you I didn't want to hide any part of myself from you, you reduced my feelings to an effect from trauma. It might not seem like much, but it took everything I had to convince myself what I felt was real—that I deserved to be happy—and it meant nothing to you. I am not Cole Presley, Agent James. That man manipulated and lied to you for thirty years, but there isn't an ounce of blood in my body that could do that to someone I love."

Seconds slipped by, a minute.

"You don't exactly know whose blood you have in your body now, but you're right, Doc. About all of it." Nicholas sat back as though she'd thrown a physical blow. He released her hand, and she swore the dead nerves in her fingertips went cold. Standing, he cast his gaze to the floor. "What I did had nothing to do with you and everything to do with fear of trusting someone who could hurt me again, and I'm sorry. I was falling in love with you, and losing control of myself like that scared the hell out of me. You're nothing like Cole Presley. I know the person I've spent the past week with on this investigation is who you really are, and I stupidly took it for granted. You're generous and sincere—a bit macabre, considering you used to make Kara play dead as a kid—but it took nearly losing you for me to realize you are everything I've been afraid of and everything I've needed in my life."

He pushed unkempt hair off his forehead and hauled a duffel bag she hadn't noticed until now from the floor over his shoulder. The stitches in the right side of his face shifted as one side of his mouth curled into a half smile. "I wouldn't blame you if you never wanted to see me after I leave this room, but you deserved an explanation."

Nicholas headed for the door.

Her heart rate ticked higher on the monitors as she struggled to sit straight in the bed. "You were falling in love with me?"

He hesitated, his hand on the door handle, every ounce

the BAU agent she'd fallen in love with. Intense, focused, protective. Craning his head toward her, he tightened his grip around the bag's strap until the whites of his knuckles materialized through bruised and lacerated skin. "I started falling in love with you the first time I met you, Doc. I just didn't realize it until I almost lost you to Caldwell in that slaughterhouse."

Heat exploded under her rib cage as time distorted into a comforting fluid, and she recalled their first meeting in the morgue at Harborview Medical Center. They'd met during an autopsy of one of the X Marks the Spot Killer's victims, and while she didn't exactly consider that a story worth telling to friends and family, she couldn't discount that case had started her on a path she'd never regret taking. Not when it'd led to him, to this moment. "Even surrounded by all those dead bodies?"

Nicholas unshouldered his overnight bag and dropped it into a chair by the door. A laugh rumbled through him, and those green-blue eyes brightened as he turned to face her. "You're a medical examiner. It would've been weird if there hadn't been any dead bodies."

"Well, isn't that sweeter than a sugar cookie in the supermarket?" She couldn't help but smile as she nodded toward the edge of the hospital bed, and he took her direction, sitting again. The mattress dipped under his weight, anchoring her to the moment. "In case it wasn't obvious, I love you, too."

"Does that mean you forgive me?" His smile notched her awareness of him higher just before he leaned into her, careful of her wrist, and pressed his mouth to hers.

She set her head back against the pillows. "Get me some real, unburned chocolate doughnuts with rainbow sprinkles and rescue Koko from Animal Services, and I might consider it."

"Anything for you, Doc," he said.

Hints of his aftershave chased back the antiseptic smell she'd become accustomed to over the years. She hadn't realized how much she'd come to rely on that smell, that it'd become part of her. Her smile faltered as she examined the cast. She wouldn't know the extent of her injury until she was able to discuss her diagnosis with her surgeon herself, but something deep inside said whatever came next, she and Nicholas would handle it. Together.

She tried to curl her fingers into her palm, but the tendons in her wrist needed a considerable time to recover. "It's really over, isn't it? I didn't imagine it."

"Caldwell can't hurt you anymore." He smoothed his thumb over the back of her arm, and the nightmares hiding behind her eyes seemed like a distant memory. The violent lacerations along the side of his face transformed the profiler into a rougher version of himself, one she couldn't seem to pull away from. "He can't hurt anyone. The new county medical examiner released Kara's and Paige's remains to the families. He was able to prove Archer Caldwell attacked both victims after you took a bite out of him and preserved his DNA. They're going home because of you, Aubrey. Once you've been discharged, we can put this whole thing behind us."

"Then what? What am I supposed to do if I can't be down in that morgue to give families the answers they're looking for?" How did she not let Caldwell win?

"You'll figure it out. You just need to take it one day at a time and know you're not alone. It's going to take time. You're going to want to give up, and it's going to be painful, but I'll be there with you every step of the way. As long as we're together, we can get through anything."

Nicholas swept his fingertips across her forehead. Bending at the waist, he reached down into his duffel bag and produced a white rectangular box. "Until then, we're going to watch every episode of your favorite cartoon and make ourselves sick with these."

Her mouth watered as he revealed the chocolate doughnuts with her favorite multicolored sprinkles, and a laugh bubbled up through her. He'd brought her doughnuts, and she found herself falling a little bit more in love with him. The grumpy profiler she'd called in a favor to be assigned to her sister's investigation had a soft spot after all.

Aubrey used his help to straighten and crushed her mouth to his. Her profiler. Her partner. Her everything. "You realize you're going to have to feed those—and everything else—to me for the foreseeable future, right? I have to warn you, the last man who put his hand near my mouth paid the price. Are you sure you're up for such a dangerous assignment, Agent James?"

Nicholas raised a doughnut between them and set it against her lips, his smile wider than she'd ever seen it before. "I've got to tell you that makes me happier than a dead pig in sunshine, Dr. Flood."

"I don't know what that means," she said.

He kissed her again, sweeping doughnut crumbs from her mouth. "Neither do I."

# Epilogue

*One week later...*

The pop of the cork exploded in his ears.

Shouts and claps filled the BAU conference room as Nicholas accepted the first glass of champagne from SSA Peters. It was over. The case was closed, and he couldn't help but celebrate the end of one of the most grueling, complicated cases of his career. Or that he'd walked away with the greatest prize he could've ever imagined—his future.

Aubrey flashed a wide smile up at him from her seat.

SSA Peters raised his glass, dark eyes brighter than Nicholas had seen them in a long time. "You might've cut it a bit close, Nicholas, but the FBI has officially closed the investigation into the deaths of Kara Flood and Paige Cress." He directed his attention to Aubrey.

"Dr. Flood, Director Branson has asked me to share her condolences. While it's impossible for us to ease your grief, I wanted you to know the BAU is here for you, and it's been a privilege working alongside you. To Nicholas James and Aubrey Flood."

Aubrey gripped her glass with the tips of her fingers and raised it as high as she could. Unable to mix alcohol with her pain medication, she'd chosen to stick with water for celebratory drinks with the team.

Madeline Striker, Dashiell West, Liam McDare and David Dyson all raised their glasses in tandem. "To Nicholas and Aubrey!"

"To Nicholas," Aubrey said. "The best partner I could ask for."

Nicholas took a gulp of his champagne, one hand on her uninjured shoulder, while the team dissolved into casual conversation. He caught sight of Liam McDare as the IT expert peeled from the mass of agents, answering his phone. Tension bled into the back of Liam's neck. Angry whispers cut through the echo of conversation from the tech guru's position by the floor-to-ceiling windows overlooking Puget Sound, and Nicholas closed the distance between them.

"No, Lorelai. You know I don't want them there. I told you that before we started all this planning." Liam ended the call, his rough exhale fogging the window. He turned back to join the party but pulled up short at the sight of Nicholas. Shock quickly transformed to faked enthusiasm, but Liam refused to meet his gaze. "Congratulations on closing your case, Agent James. I've read your report. It's amazing what you did out there."

"Thanks," Nicholas said. "Everything okay? And before you lie to me, I heard some of your conversation."

Liam shook off Nicholas's concern. "It's nothing. Lorelai is traveling with the director. We haven't seen each other in a few weeks, and it's starting to show. That's all."

"She wants you to invite your parents to the wedding." Because that was what most couples were supposed to do, share their wedding day with their loved ones, family and friends, but Liam McDare and his fiancée weren't most couples. They were members of the Behavioral Analysis Unit. Every emotion, every fear was amplified ten times because of the work they dealt with day-to-day. He had firsthand experience.

"She's trying to convince me I'll regret it if I don't invite them, but she doesn't understand," Liam said. "Her parents aren't on their third spouses. They've been married over twenty years and still laugh and love each other. Mine will go at each other's throats the minute they're in the same room together."

The tech expert swung his glass out to his side. "I don't know. Sometimes I think Lorelai is more excited about the wedding than what comes afterward, and then where will we be?" He took a swig of champagne. "Right where my parents are. Miserable, divorced and bitter."

Nicholas glanced at Aubrey as she talked with West. Honey-warm eyes lightened as she turned her attention to him at the same moment, as though she'd sensed the weight of his gaze. A flood of appreciation rushed through his veins as the future spread out in front of him. The injuries to her shoulder, ribs and wrist had threatened her career, but Nicholas had known the moment he'd found her in those underground tunnels, there wasn't anything he wouldn't do to give her the life she deserved. He turned back to Liam, slapping him on the shoulder with his free hand.

"Love isn't about who's coming or not coming to the wedding, color palettes, flower choices and bridesmaids' dresses, Liam. It's about the two of you. That's all that matters. It's about trust. It's about believing that even if you don't know what comes next, you do it together, and you support one another unconditionally. That's the only way this is going to work. Talk to Lorelai. Tell her the real reason you don't want your parents at the wedding. Everything will work out."

He slipped away from Liam and stepped into Aubrey's side. He wound one arm around her waist. Pressing his mouth to her ear, he inhaled as much of her simple perfume as his lungs allowed. "Time to go, Doc. You're going to be late for your appointment."

"Appointment?" Aubrey waved to West then allowed him to drag her toward the door, confusion contorting her expression. "My appointment with the hospital administrator isn't until next week."

"Not that kind of appointment." He led her through the BAU offices and into the lobby. "This one involves sweatpants, doughnuts and cartoons, and we've got all the time in the world."

"I like the sound of that." Aubrey punched the button for the elevators. "As long as you're not making the doughnuts, that is."

He couldn't help but laugh. "Picked up an unhealthy amount from the bakery just this morning."

The elevator doors opened, but Aubrey turned into him instead of stepping into the car. Her cast scratched at his jaw as she framed his face. She pressed her mouth to his. "Well, aren't you sweeter than a porcupine eating a pineapple. I could get used to this, Agent James."

"Good." He let the elevator doors close. "Because it's only going to get better from here."

And he couldn't wait to get started.

\* \* \* \* \*

# UNCOVERING SMALL TOWN SECRETS

## TYLER ANNE SNELL

This book is for the readers who have followed my characters and stories throughout the years. We've just left the Nash family in Tennessee and now we're meeting a ragtag group of misfits in small-town Alabama trying their best to make a difference. I hope you enjoy them all.

# Chapter One

Everyone in town went looking for Annie McHale when she first went missing. A year later and only three people went looking for Fallon Dean.

Detective Gordon was the third person to join the search. In his late fifties, he had been a week away from retiring and thought that Fallon had simply run away. But nothing had been that simple in Kelby Creek, Alabama. Not since the scandal known as The Flood had rocked Dawn County and nearly destroyed the small town. So, after conferring with the interim sheriff, he'd been encouraged to extend his stay to make sure nothing bad had happened to the twenty-three-year-old.

It had made the tired, grouchy man even more tired and even more grouchy. He'd done his investigation wearing an expression that looked like he always had a glass of spoiled milk stuck beneath his nose. However, worse than how he asked his questions during the investigation was the less-than-enthused answers he received.

The town had a lot of history it was trying to forget, but Fallon? He'd caused an accident that some weren't ready to let go.

Then there was Larissa Cole.

Before Detective Gordon had been assigned the case, Larissa had been first in line to help. The moment the

Dean family had come to Kelby Creek five years prior, she'd taken to them with an open heart and a maternal air that neither Dean sibling had felt in a long while. If she believed Fallon had left town of his own free will, it didn't matter because she was worried, regardless. She had become Millie's best friend and, while she loved Fallon like a brother, it was Millie who was hurting.

And hunting.

It had been six months to the day since Millie Dean had seen her little brother. In the time between first meeting with Detective Gordon to plead the case that something was wrong to now standing in her kitchen, looking out the window into the hot June daylight, only the smaller details had changed.

Fallon's lease on his apartment had expired, and all of his belongings were in Millie's guest bedroom. His cell phone was still paid for but had long since been off, just as his job at the newspaper had been filled. Even the rumor mill had gone on hiatus when it came to the Dean family.

They smiled and waved and had pleasant small talk with Millie at the grocery store or walking along the sidewalk of the neighborhood. They gave her the traditional Southern nod or half-wave when catching her eye while driving. They said it was about time Detective Gordon retired after only two months of searching, and they sure as the day was humid didn't offer to help look for him, not even on the six-month anniversary of his disappearance.

As far as Kelby Creek was convinced, although he was a grown man, Fallon Dean was a runaway. The name had stuck ever since he ran away as a teenager. And now everyone was convinced he wasn't missing.

Millie fisted her hand against the lemon-printed towel draped over the lip of the sink. Six months and one day ago she would have fretted at wrinkling the fabric. It was for light hand dabbing and decoration. Something she'd bought in the city on impulse because it had matched a sundress she'd once gotten a lot of compliments on at the grocery store.

But now?

Now she crumpled it in her hand like a wet paper towel.

Long gone was the woman in the lemon sundress. In her place had moved the sister who would do anything to find her only family.

Even if that meant starting over again.

She dropped the towel on the counter and turned on her heel. Her home had been built in the seventies but renovated by the owner before her. Nothing felt vintage about the two-bedroom anymore. It was all clean lines, whites, grays and wood, with accent walls of shiplap here and there.

One of those accent walls stood behind the eat-in table. On that wall was mounted a white board much too large for the space.

Millie traced her own handwriting across its surface.

Then she went to the coffee maker and started a new cup.

It wasn't until her phone rang hours later that she realized it had gone dark outside.

"Hello?"

Millie's stomach growled in tandem with her answering the call. Larissa's voice came through in a rush.

"Zach just called and asked who the man was moving into the rental next to your house. He said there was a moving truck out in front of it at the curb when he drove past to go to church and was still there when he came back."

Millie pushed out of the dining chair she'd nearly grown roots on as she'd gone over every detail of her own investigation into Fallon and made a path back to the kitchen window. A streetlamp stood sentry between her mailbox and the rental house in question, but its light showed an empty road.

"I didn't see a moving truck earlier and I don't see one now. Are you sure Zach saw right?"

There was motion on Larissa's side of the phone. She repeated the question to their coworker Zach, who must have been in the background. He responded but Millie couldn't hear him.

"He's sure. He said your car was in the driveway both times too so you must have seen him." Larissa paused. Millie could picture the forty-two-year-old perfectly despite the distance between them. Her round face arranging into a harmless, comfort-filled expression, glasses in need of being pushed back up the bridge of her nose and brown eyes that held more maternal concern than Millie or Fallon had ever gotten from their own mother. "What *have* you been up to today?"

Millie only ever felt guilt about her determination to find her brother when she decided to lie to her best friend about how determined she still was. Larissa had tried to take off work to spend the day with Millie, knowing it was the anniversary, but the truth was that Millie had woken up that morning with one goal.

To finally get answers.

No matter what.

Telling that to the levelheaded, good-intentioned mother hen who had seen firsthand how Millie had changed in the last six months?

It only made the worry in Larissa grow from her heart and fan out into her own life.

And Millie didn't want that.

So she lied and said she wanted to spend the day alone, lounging and catching up on her TV shows.

"I've been stuck in TV land all day," she said now.

"*Community* has six seasons and I was only on season two. You know I'm a completist when it comes to shows."

There was a hesitation again but then Larissa seemed to accept the fib.

"Well, make sure you get some food in you since I know how you can forget to eat sometimes when you're focused," she said. "I'm still coming over to drop off some cookies after my shift around ten. You better show me some dirty dishes to prove you ate." Larissa's soothing tone switched as quickly as the topic. "Now, go next door and find out who your new neighbor is. It's not every day someone moves *to* Kelby Creek."

They ended the call and Millie looked at the clock. She had a few hours before Larissa's well-meaning check-in.

That was plenty of time to retrace Fallon's last known stops around town before he disappeared.

Millie grabbed her purse and hurried out to the driveway. Just like the moving truck, she barely noticed the man walking parallel to her along the driveway next door, a box in his arms. On reflex she nodded a hello when their eyes met.

The light from his front porch showed him returning the gesture. Millie noted, the way one notes something when your mind was already filled with other pressing matters, the easy facts.

The man was young, at least younger than Mr. Tomlin, the tenant before him, had been. She guessed he was closer to her twenty-eight than Mr. Tomlin's sixty-two. Taller too. Built wider and sturdier if the large box he carried with ease was any indication. Millie couldn't get a good grasp of the color of his hair other than it was lighter than her black, and he had a lot of it. Shoulder length and with a matching beard. It felt hot just looking at it. Then again, it was summer in Kelby Creek. That meant even the night gave little respite from the heat and humidity that plagued

South Alabama. Past those quick flashes of detail, Millie didn't stick around to register any more.

She had a brother to find, Southern hospitality be damned.

Foster Lovett hadn't been back in Kelby Creek since he'd run off and married Regina Becker straight out of high school. Not the smartest thing he'd done in his thirty-two years of life but not the dumbest either. He and Regina had a good five years of married bliss before the dam of young insecurities, naive hopes and work had started to crack between them.

When that thing blew, the next five years of marriage had been all about surviving the flood.

They hadn't.

Now Foster was back in his hometown sweating through his jeans, cursing the mosquitoes and wondering who the woman next door was even though he'd sworn off the opposite sex the moment he'd signed the divorce papers and lost his house, his car and the dog two years ago. Sure, he'd gone on a few dates since that fateful day, but the lesson he'd learned from Regina was still seared into his brain.

Women were trouble.

And the woman who'd all but run and jumped into her car before speeding off? Well, he guessed she might be that with a capital *T.*

Foster was done with trouble. Or at least the woman kind. Professionally he had run back to Kelby Creek and jumped right into the sack with a damned mess. One he hoped he could help clean up.

He hefted the box of dishes high as he opened the front door to his rental home and jostled inside. The AC had been running since that morning, but the air was still on the stale side. He scrunched up his nose at it and slid the box onto the kitchen counter just as his phone started blaring. He eyed the oven's clock. It was almost seven at night.

The caller ID of a man whose first name was honest-to-God Brutus popped up on the touch screen.

Foster straightened and answered.

"Yello."

"Hey there, Love, sorry for calling when you requested some quiet while getting settled," the weathered and deep voice of interim sheriff Brutus Chamblin answered. "But I heard through the grapevine that you were being a grump at Crisp's Kitchen no more than half an hour ago, so I figured you were probably still up to no good."

Foster rolled his eyes and started to open the box he'd just put down.

"I wasn't grumpy, I just wasn't chatty. That's all."

"That's the same thing when you live in a town with only eighteen hundred or so people. You should know that already, or has living big in Seattle made you forget the niceties of being Southern?"

The sigh escaped him faster than the packing tape split on top of the box.

"I moved back to help redeem the image of this town and the sheriff's department. You'd think that would earn me a little leeway when I don't spend a half hour talking to Quinn Cooper about the fish he caught at the creek two months ago while trying to finish my dinner."

Brutus laughed.

*Sheriff Chamblin* laughed.

Foster was going to have to get used to the idea that his father's old friend was now acting interim sheriff until someone else was elected. That meant giving the man a little more formality than came naturally to him. Especially since Foster was now the lead detective in his department.

"Well, it might not kill you to fake the smiles and interest for a while. At least until things get a little more normal around here."

Foster started to pull out the plates while making a mental note to go out and buy new silverware. After the divorce he'd moved in with a buddy from the Seattle Police Department before segueing into a studio apartment. Somewhere during the different moves he'd lost more and more furniture, odds and ends, and, weirdly enough, forks. For the life of him he had no idea where they'd all gone to.

"I'll see what I can do," he finally said. "Just as long as you remember I'm not here to fake nice. I'm here to solve cases."

"Speaking of which…" Foster paused, plate in midair. He hadn't had an active case in almost two months. Just the thought of one got his blood pumping. There was a rustling on the other side of the phone. "I still don't have anything other than cold cases sitting on your desk. Maybe you can help make sense of at least one of them. Lord knows the people of Kelby Creek could use a win, and with a rockstar detective like you joining our ranks, maybe we can finally get them one."

Foster resumed his unpacking and nodded to himself. He never liked being called a rock star, but he was proud of his above-average closing rate that had made him somewhat famous within his career in law enforcement.

"I'll take a look at them first thing in the morning," he said.

"Good. I'll stop in to check up on you after my meeting with the interim mayor. He thinks since we're both temporary that we should be in constant talks about the town." Brutus sighed this time. "The man could drive a nun to drink, I tell you what."

Foster laughed and adopted the older man's earlier tone.

"Now, now, Sheriff. Don't you go forgetting your Southern niceties."

Brutus grumbled.

"Yeah, yeah. See you in the morning, Love."

The call ended, and Foster spent the rest of the night unpacking. The rental house was a two-bedroom but on the smaller side. At least for the town; for his studio in Seattle? Not so much. It wasn't until he was done that Foster realized the house still looked mostly empty.

It should have bothered him, he thought, but then again, when had he ever been a homebody?

Foster showered and then jumped into bed, mind already on the files that would be sitting on his desk in the morning. It wasn't until a few hours had passed and he got up for a glass of water that he noticed the woman from next door hadn't come home yet.

He wondered who she was again.

"You're wasting your time," he told himself out loud, empty glass in his hand. "You're here to work. Not make nice with the neighbors."

The small reminder was enough. Foster went back to bed. His routine kicked in after that.

He slept. His alarm went off and woke him. He ate. He dressed. He hopped into the used red Tacoma he'd bought a few weeks before and drove to work. His mind took in details around him in quick succession even though his focus was on something he hadn't even read yet.

He nodded to Libby at the front desk, said a few words to a deputy he hadn't formally met yet and passed by Brutus's closed office door before going to the end of the hall and hanging a left.

Detective Lovett was etched on a new nameplate next to one of two doors down the small hallway.

But his door wasn't closed.

In fact, not only was it open, there was someone sitting just inside it across from his desk.

Foster didn't recognize the dark curls, but he did recognize the concerned face as he walked around the stranger to his chair.

It was the woman from the night before. The woman in a hurry.

His neighbor.

"Good morning," he said, adding a question to his greeting. "May I ask who you are and why you're in here?"

With better lighting Foster was able to see just how beautiful the stranger was. Hair as dark as night, a mixed complexion that made her amber eyes even more bright as they took him in, and long angles that made him think of the description of royalty before he could stop it from popping into his head. Her long eyelashes brushed against her brown cheeks as she followed him with her eyes.

The woman gave what, he imagined, was a standard polite smile. But then it wiped clear from her lips. In its place worry so acute it made Foster's spine zip up to attention.

"My name is Millie Dean and I need your help."

# *Chapter Two*

Millie had bribed Libby and Deputy Park with chocolate chip cookies to get back to the detective's office and wait until he arrived. Libby was more than willing to let her back, but Deputy Carlos Park was huffier. He gave her a look she was all too familiar with but eventually took a few cookies back to the bullpen. Whipping up the yummy confections had been an easy price to pay for early access to the back hallway.

After a long night of trying to find the truth in the dark, she'd wound up home, defeated. Larissa had shown up soon after and given her an ounce of hope she hadn't expected to get.

A lead detective had finally been hired to take Detective Gordon's former position.

Which meant Millie had a chance.

And meant she had needed to talk to the new hire as soon as possible.

Yet, after introducing herself, Millie's nerves doubled. For many different reasons.

First of all, the Dawn County Sheriff's Department wasn't exactly beloved anymore. Not after a thunderstorm and a subsequent flash flood had caused the former mayor to wreck into a ditch. Not after the FBI agent responding to the crash found something that led to uncovering a town-wide conspiracy. Not after the corruption that had hollowed out the town and forced most of the Kelby Creek's high-ranking officials and employees, former sheriff and mayor included, into jail. Or sent some on the run.

The event itself was so widespread and complicated that the entire town nicknamed it The Flood. A name still said with as much anger and deep feelings of betrayal and distrust as it had been the day the news broke of the corruption.

Those who had been involved within the sheriff's department hadn't just broken the law, they'd shattered it. Their actions had given Kelby Creek a bad reputation that stretched countrywide and left the residents with a serious case of trust issues. Even with the new hires and transfers who had slowly been trickling in to restock the department and change its image for the better.

Millie didn't know if that was possible, but it was the reason why she was hopeful. Still, she didn't know the detective and that made her uneasy of itself.

Second, as Millie sat in the department, Fallon's MIA six-month anniversary felt painfully more apparent. Unable to be ignored. All the days between when she'd seen him leaving her house to now had collected together and they hurt. She hadn't gotten good news once, and now she was trying again to have a full-fledged conversation with a man with a badge. Trust or not, that made the vise around her heart squeeze tighter.

Third, and nowhere near the severity level of the other two points, was the realization that the new detective was the same man she'd seen carrying a box into the house next to hers the night before. Which had to mean he was the man who had rented it. Her new neighbor. One with groomed, dark blond hair, forest green eyes, and a jaw that set hard in intensity as she began to explain why she was waiting in his office.

"No one has seen my brother, Fallon Dean, since the beginning of December last year," she stated. "Yesterday was the six-month anniversary of his disappearance."

Detective Lovett put his coffee down and grabbed a pen.

"How old is he?"

"Twenty-three. Twenty-four in September."

"And why are you just coming to us now about this after six months?"

His expression hadn't changed since he'd come into the office. Millie wished she could read what he was feeling and she wished the part of her that wanted to know didn't also find him extremely attractive. That part of her was intrigued by him, despite the situation.

"This isn't the first time I've been here." She hesitated, hoping to find the magic words to keep him from dismissing her. "I reported it the day after he went missing."

"So it's an ongoing investigation?"

Millie shook her head. "He hasn't been found, but the case was technically closed four months ago."

That earned an eyebrow raise. His gaze flitted to the folders on his desk before responding.

"A closed case means a concluded case," he stated.

Millie mentally bit her tongue, stopping herself from going on the offense.

"The detective in charge of the case hit a dead end and gave up," she said carefully. "Fallon is still out there and—"

A knock on the side of the doorframe behind her broke Detective Lovett's attention.

Millie turned to the new face and felt her frown deepen.

Deputy Carlos Park, his dark buzz cut, and muscles sculpted from an obsession with the gym, had eyes only for the detective.

"Hey, Lovett, could I talk to you for a second?"

"I'm in the middle of something," came the smooth baritone. "Can it wait?"

Deputy Park dropped his gaze to Millie's. She instantly regretted bringing him cookies. He'd helped himself to them and taken several.

"No," he said. "I don't think it can."

The detective's chair rolled backward as he stood. Millie turned in her chair, away from the deputy, fresh anger coursing through her. Lovett's eyebrow rose again in question, but he didn't ask anything of her.

Which was good because she was already spinning a defense to give him when he came back. After Deputy Park tainted the image of her brother. Just like all the rest of the town would, given the chance. That was half of the reason she'd come in so early, hoping to catch the detective first.

A lot of good that had done.

"Be right back."

Millie nodded, tight and quick. It was only after he was out of the room that she realized she'd fisted her hands on her lap. Attractive or not, intriguing or not, new neighbor or not, Millie knew what was most likely going to happen next.

Still, she had hope that Detective Lovett would be different.

That he wouldn't listen to those who had been at the department five years ago. That he would give her, and Fallon, the benefit of the doubt.

People changed all the time. Fallon more than most.

Did some of the town refuse to believe that? Specifically, those in the department who were still around?

They sure did.

After The Flood, it was like the pot calling the kettle black.

"Sorry for the wait."

Detective Lovett appeared at her shoulder as fast as

Millie noted the change in his tone. He apparently was, in fact, no different from the colleagues he'd most likely just spoken to about Fallon.

Millie decided to cut the polite nonsense.

She didn't have time to dance around their past in the hope of being given a clean slate with the new hire.

"You're going to tell me that my brother ran away. That he's been labeled a flight risk. That he's an adult and that he didn't go missing, he just left." The detective kept his face impassive so Millie prodded him. "Am I wrong?"

Lovett threaded his fingers together into a steeple over his desk.

"I'm going off the facts, Miss Dean," he said, voice even. "Fallon has a history of running away, one that started before what happened once y'all moved to Kelby Creek." He looked down at the notepad he'd taken with him when he stepped into the hallway. There were several notes in tight, neat handwriting across the paper. "Four times between the ages of sixteen and eighteen. Then one time here where, in the process of looking for him, a deputy was struck by a car and forced to retire because of the injury." He looked up at her, his eyes a cool mint. "The former detective on the case found no hint of foul play, not to mention you buried the important detail that Fallon left you a note. One that said he was leaving and that he was okay."

The note.

The damned note.

It was the biggest reason no one took her seriously.

That no one listened to her reasoning behind not trusting it.

Now Millie was trying not to yell. Not to raise her voice in the hope that being loud would make him understand.

That it would make him see what she did.

Yet she wasn't fast enough to find the right words before he spoke again.

"You have to understand my reluctance here. Leaving isn't the same as missing."

Millie stood, Detective Lovett did the same. Now she could read him perfectly. He opened his mouth to continue, but Millie held up her hand to stop whatever it was he was about to say.

"You know what? I was an idiot to come here of all places looking for help. After what this department did? I don't know why anyone would ever come here looking for answers."

The detective's jaw hardened. His nostrils flared just enough to show her that she'd hit a nerve.

"What happened to the department, happened," he rebutted. "But that's not who we are now, and we're working very hard to prove that to the community."

"Just like Fallon has worked very hard the last four years to prove he isn't that kid anymore. He's not a thoughtless runaway. That what happened, happened, but that's not who he is now." Millie grabbed her purse and angled her body to the door. She was mad, sure, but she was also hurt.

She was also more than done with the conversation.

*She* was going to find Fallon.

*She* was going to save him from whatever bad had happened.

*She* didn't need the department, certainly not the detective who had judged her and her family without a second thought.

Millie paused in the doorway and cut the man off with a parting shot.

"You've known about Fallon for less than an hour. I've known him for twenty-three years. That note wasn't written by him, and he didn't leave because he wanted to." She almost left then, but six months of not knowing propelled the words out before she could decide against them.

"And not that anyone ever seems to care about this part

but when Fallon ran away when he was younger, it was always because he was running from our stepfather. But our dad is gone and has been for years. That's what scares me now. That's why I came here hoping to get the help of someone without any biases, knowing I'd probably still get turned away. If Fallon ran away of his own accord, then what was he running from this time?"

Detective Lovett didn't answer. He couldn't have even if Millie had given him time to respond.

He didn't know Fallon.

He didn't know her.

And now he never would.

THE COLD CASES on Foster's desk were still just as cold when he left for the day as they had been that morning. Some were from six years ago, others dated back to the late nineties. They were challenging, and he was more than up for each of those challenges.

But he'd be lying to himself if he didn't admit his focus hadn't been 100 percent since Millie Dean had stormed out of his office.

"Check into it if you need to," Deputy Park had said earlier. "But the last time the department went looking for Fallon he was out in the woods smoking pot and eating gummy worms. Because of him Deputy William Reiner was hit by a damn car while searching the county road. Hear you me, wherever Fallon is, he probably doesn't give a rat's backside that anyone is wasting their time looking for him."

Foster waited a few minutes after Park left before deciding to pull Fallon's file. He placed it on top of the cold cases he was *supposed* to be looking into and read the contents from first page to last during his lunch break.

What Park had summarized in the hallway was most of what was in the files.

Millie Dean had come to the department when she couldn't find her brother over a weekend. All she knew was that his car was gone too and that the note she'd found on her front porch wasn't from him. Detective Lee Gordon had been assigned to the case and, as far as Foster could tell by his language used in writing the report, he had mostly focused on finding the car.

He hadn't found it or Fallon. Not even a trace.

Foster moved the folder off to the side for the remainder of the day but, like the thought of his sister, Foster would catch himself glancing at Fallon Dean's life boiled down into three sheets of a paper and a picture that that same sister had most likely provided.

Foster was an only child, but that didn't mean he was apathetic to Millie's worry. Her pain. His career so far had shown him monsters, victims and survivors. He'd had to deliver devastating news to families just as he'd been able to deliver justice for what happened to them.

He'd also never gotten a case he hadn't closed, even if he didn't like the outcome.

It was the argument his captain in Seattle had used to try to keep him in the zip code.

*Every day you're doing real work here. That town? Everyone is already against you before you even put on the badge. It's like quicksand. Wouldn't you rather stay here where you know you can make a difference instead of rolling the dice and hoping for the best?*

Foster had answered with what he still believed to be true.

He needed a change of scenery, and what better way than to do that while also trying to help an entire town?

A town that included Millie Dean.

Eyes the color of sunlight shining on syrup.

The same eyes that had pleaded with him before narrowing in anger.

Now, hours later and sitting in his driveway, there Foster was thinking about those eyes again.

It didn't help that the woman herself could be seen through the front window, bustling around inside her house.

Foster didn't mean to, but he stared for a moment and replayed their conversation in his head. Then he did something he'd always done in his career. He put the memory of her from his office on mute and read her body language instead.

Anxious. Worried. Genuine.

She truly believed something was wrong. So much so she'd chanced going to a place she clearly didn't like, knowing there was a good chance she'd be turned away. Regret at that choice had tensed her body right before anger at being dismissed had. Then, before she'd even stood, Foster had realized it was him who had been dismissed.

And he hadn't liked it.

Not one bit.

Foster sighed, locked his truck and went inside his house. Belatedly he realized he could see into one of the woman's rooms from his small kitchen. He decided to avoid that window as he changed out of his dress shirt and slacks and into more comfortable clothes. He checked his email, thought about a few of the cold cases he'd looked into earlier, and finally gave himself permission to put all work matters away long enough to eat.

Corruption and conspiracy aside, it wasn't as though a small town like Kelby Creek was all that exciting. Not like Seattle had been.

So, Foster grabbed a beer, heated up a frozen meal and plopped down on the one chair he had in the dining room with every intention of forgetting about the outside world for a while.

But then he heard his neighbor's front door shut and curiosity made him go to his kitchen window, beer in tow. Millie Dean herself was hurrying out into the darkness to her car.

The motion sensor camera at the corner of her driveway came on.

"Oh hell," Foster breathed out.

Millie had a flashlight in one hand and a baseball bat in the other. She took both into the car with her. Foster put his beer down.

"Well, that can't be good."

# Chapter Three

The town of Kelby Creek was a warm place.

From spring to summer to Christmas Eve, there was a good chance its humidity was fogging up your glasses and making you sweat. It was at most times unforgiving.

The night was no different.

Millie's shirt stuck to her skin, her jeans wrapping her thighs with a cling that was wholly uncomfortable. Her curls were a ball of chaos atop her head in a bun, giving her neck the space to sweat openly instead of beneath the weight of her hair. Even the bat in her hand was starting to slide in her grip.

It wasn't pleasant.

Neither was the darkness around her.

The Kintucket Woods acted like a barrier between Kelby Creek and the outside world. Pine trees, oaks and wild underbrush had taken over most of the expansive boundary, but there was one section that Millie knew of that had a clearing.

One wide enough for a tent, a small campfire and a young boy in need of an escape.

Millie had long since left the beams from her headlights behind at the road. Now the flashlight in her other hand showed a path of dirt and roots and nothing else. No footsteps that she could see, no signs of someone else walking the same way.

Not that there was any other sign of life around her either.

The branches and leaves overlapping above hid the moonlight almost completely. Like the light switch had been flipped off on the world around her. It made the usually comforting sound of cicadas and frogs chirping an eerie one.

Millie held down a shiver of anticipation and fear as she marched on, hoping that the second she was at her destination, every worry about Fallon would disappear with his smiling face.

Though she knew it was an impossibly long shot.

*You're here because you don't know what to do next,* she told herself. Again. *And because this was his safe place.*

Millie took one step into the clearing and felt her hopes crash into the underbrush, despite readying herself for it to be empty.

She still tried. "Fallon?"

Her call fell flat.

There was no Fallon, there was no tent, there weren't even signs that a fire had once been used for warmth, light and a few s'mores.

She had hoped it would be that simple.

That Fallon had gone off on his own and now realized it was time to come home.

But it wasn't that simple.

Just like asking for help at the sheriff's department hadn't been simple either.

Detective Lovett had done exactly what Millie had been afraid he'd do. He hadn't listened.

Millie let out a defeated breath and moved closer to the center of the clearing.

If Fallon wasn't here, then where was he?

She let her gaze unfocus and let her mind wander. She propped the bat against her leg. The weight of mental exhaustion weighed her down.

But not so much as to keep her from jumping when a rustling sounded behind her.

Millie spun, taking her bat up again, and let the flashlight's beam scatter among the trees to her right. For a moment she expected to see her tall, dark and smiling pain-in-the-butt brother but, for a second time that night, her hopes were dashed.

Then fear took their place.

The man was tall and wispy. Like the wind could take him if it blew hard enough. He had on a pair of dark green coveralls and orange work boots. His dark hair was shaved close to his head. Millie guessed he might have been in his midthirties. What she couldn't guess was why he was out here, of all places, and at night.

Staring at her like he wasn't surprised that she was there.

Millie took a step back but kept the flashlight beam on his body.

He smiled. "Don't worry. I'm not going to hurt you," he greeted. His voice was stronger than he looked. "You work at Dobb's, right?"

Millie nodded on reflex.

She didn't recognize him from the grocery at all.

"I saw you there last week," he continued. "You had one of those big orange clips in your hair. Reminded me of my mom."

He took another step forward then stopped. A smile pulled up a corner of his mouth. Millie gripped the bat tighter. There was enough light in the clearing to lose the flashlight if she had to, but if she ran into the woods without it, she'd be in trouble.

Still, she readied to do it all the same.

Drop the flashlight.

Put both hands into swinging the bat with all the power that she had.

Run only after he was down and out for the count.

"Who are you?" she asked. There was no tremble in her voice, but there was also no emotion in it. The man's eyebrow rose.

"I'm just trying to be a friend is all." His smile vanished. "I'm looking for Fallon. But it doesn't look like he's here. Just you."

That put a temporary hold on her fear.

"You know Fallon?"

The man nodded slowly. "We go way back. I thought it was high time I do my part and help look for him. Because I don't know where he is." The man started to walk forward. "And I'd really like to."

The fear came back.

Millie felt like she'd been zapped by lightning. Every nerve in her came to life with a pulse of energy and one thunderous boom of thought.

No one knew she was out in the woods.

Not Larissa. Not Fallon.

No one.

Suddenly she saw what her trek into the woods alone was. Desperation of a terrified heart. Desperation that had led her into the darkness without a soul in the world knowing where she was.

Annie McHale's smiling face popped up into Millie's head, followed by Fallon.

Just another disappearance in the town of Kelby Creek.

So, Millie did the only rational thing left to do in the irrational situation she'd already gotten herself into.

She swung the bat with all she had.

Then she ran.

FOSTER LOST MILLIE right outside the neighborhood. One second he was watching her book it out to the main road and the next he was following her in his truck.

But she was fast and had a lead on him.

Once she was out of the neighborhood, it was like the world had gone to sleep.

He sat idling at the corner of Melrose Street and Lively Drive, trying to figure out which way the woman had gone. There was no car, no headlights and no Millie Dean behind the wheel, damn determined to do *something*.

Something with a bat.

Which was not good.

Foster looked off to his right. He mentally traced the road to the heart of town. He turned to his left and looked out at the street as it slipped off into darkness.

Not only did Millie have a bat, but she also had a flashlight.

She was going somewhere she didn't feel safe and somewhere she needed light.

*The woods.*

Nothing good ever happened at night in the woods.

What Kelby Creek lacked in big-city amenities and attractions, it more than made up for in back roads that looked straight out of a horror movie. Networks like reaching fingers branched off from the street Foster was on and led to the woods and the town limits. Some had older streetlamps, marking roads of gravel and dirt. Most had nothing but the moonlight to show their paths.

When Foster and his friends had been teenagers, they'd been fans of the twisting darkness with its almost-secret roads. It made their field and creek parties and hangouts private and easier to get away with when the law inevitably came to break them up. Or someone's parents. It was almost comical watching cars filled with teens scattering down different roads while the adults tried to remember from their own youth which roads led to where. Yet, as one of those adults now—and law enforcement too—Foster saw what a pain in the backside the most rural part of Kelby Creek really was.

It took him almost fifteen minutes to find the road that Deputy Park had said led to the clearing Fallon had been found in years ago. The same road that led to the spot where William Reiner had been struck by a car, effectively ending his career.

Foster should have found the road much sooner but he didn't.

And, when he saw Millie's car parked on a patch of grass along the shoulder, he hoped the delay wouldn't cost him. Foster didn't think Fallon was in trouble, but he couldn't deny his curiosity and concern had slowly turned into a sense of urgency.

One that pulled him out of his truck with his service weapon in his holster, his badge around his neck and his cell phone tucked into the pocket of his jeans. He didn't know what was going on, but he planned to ask Millie when he found her.

When he found her *safe* and sound.

Yet, no sooner had he thought about a potentially angry Millie asking why he was there than something happened that sent his sense of urgency blasting through the roof.

A scream split the night air.

A woman's scream.

It was brief but loud, carrying through the trees and up to Foster like a wave coming to shore.

He was off and into the darkness without a second thought.

Bark bit into his palms as he slapped his hands against the trees he passed, trying to keep from stumbling without losing his momentum. The light from the night sky left him wanting. Just like the flashlight on his truck's floorboard.

The gun in his holster was heavy against his hip.

Pulling it out now would only run the chance of accidentally harming Millie, and he wasn't going to risk that.

Foster kept on his trajectory for a few more seconds before realizing the world had quieted again. He slowed, tilting his head and trying to figure out where Millie was. When he heard nothing new, he called out.

"Millie?"

It didn't take long after that.

Something in the distance started crashing through the underbrush. Foster couldn't tell if it was coming to him or away from him but he strode out, ready to chase if needed.

"It's Detective Lovett," he yelled out. "With the sheriff's department!"

Whoever was making the ruckus ahead of him was keeping a distance between them despite the call. Foster might have grown up in Kelby Creek, but he was in uncharted territory at the moment. He tried to pull up a mental map of the area to figure out where Millie was running to or where the person who made her scream might be headed, but he was coming up short. There were too many variables and he had no idea what was going on even if there hadn't been.

That only became clearer as something barreled between the trees from behind him.

Foster skidded to a stop and pivoted, muscles already in overdrive.

In the dark he could barely make out the dark eyes of Millie Dean, wide and searching. The soft click of a flashlight caused the immediate area to come to life.

Millie had a sheen to her skin and a look that said she was somewhere in her flight or fight mode. She no longer had her bat.

When she spoke her words were strained and low.

"Wh-why are you out here?" she whispered.

Foster didn't have time to explain. He could still hear someone behind him running away. That had to be the reason Millie screamed. So he pivoted the conversation too.

"Why did you scream?" he asked. "Who attacked you?"

Millie's eyebrows turned into each other. Shadows transformed her look of panic into one of confusion. She titled her head to the side in question.

"I didn't."

Foster matched her confusion.

"You didn't get attacked?" he asked. "Then why did you scream?"

Before Millie could even say another word, Foster knew without a doubt that his first week back in Kelby Creek was about to get more complicated.

Millie shook her head. A bead of sweat slid down her cheek as she answered.

"I didn't scream. Which means there's someone else in danger in these woods."

# Chapter Four

"You weren't kidding when you said you were itching to get to work, huh?"

Sheriff Chamblin had his badge pinned to his belt and sleep in his eye. He'd also donned a pair of cowboy boots, something Foster hadn't seen the man do since he was a teen watching Chamblin and his dad heading out to go fishing.

The image was at first a flash of comfort, thinking of his father. Then that badge reminded him that the time between then and now had stretched and twisted. Chamblin was in charge and Foster wasn't some rebellious teen anymore. His expertise was valuable to the sheriff.

Even if that expertise wasn't exactly getting any answers at the moment.

"I told you when I came aboard that I was going to be as transparent as a thin sheet of plastic," Foster answered. "So here I am. Thin sheet of plastic."

Foster swept his arms out wide with the tree line behind him. His truck hadn't moved since he'd parked it two hours ago, and neither had Millie's Nissan. The only change of scenery was the addition of the sheriff and a patrol car with two deputies who didn't look any more enthused than they had when they'd first been called in.

Which was to say not at all.

Apparently Deputy Park wasn't the only deputy with trust issues when it came to the Dean family.

Now the sheriff moved his gaze to the woods right before a deep sigh rumbled out. Whether it was the poor lighting from his headlights or because the man had obviously just been woken up, Chamblin looked much older than he had that morning.

"So no one could find the woman who screamed."

It was a statement and one that Foster didn't like agreeing with.

"I couldn't find the man Millie said she talked to either," Foster added. "But I found a pretty decent footprint in the clearing. I took a few pictures while Deputy Park and Deputy Juliet looked around. But you know as well as I do that the Kintucket Woods are a beast all their own. I need a better search party."

Chamblin shook his head then lowered his voice.

"You think the woman who screamed is still out here somewhere?"

"I wish I knew," Foster said. "But if she isn't out there, then there's a good chance the man could have taken her. Which is even more reason for us to look for evidence or something that could lead us to one or the other." Foster let his voice drop so low that the sheriff leaned in to hear better when he continued. "As far as the public is concerned, this could be another Annie McHale situation in the making. A woman, now missing, in trouble in the woods? They'll eat this up if we don't handle it with every bit of attention we have."

The sheriff didn't like that.

"This is only an Annie McHale situation if I was the one to kidnap the girl and everyone and their dang mamas helped cover it up. And I sure as hell didn't do that," he said with a shake of his head. Disgust. Written across his expression just as it had been in his voice at the press conference announcing his acceptance of the role of interim sheriff. Anyone who respected the law and the duty to protect their people had deep anger and disbelief at those who had put Kelby Creek on the map for the worst reasons.

It was still a sore subject to the sheriff now.

Movement came from Millie's car. Before the deputies had shown up she'd been at Foster's side, helping him search the immediate area and clearing while recounting her conversation with the man in the coveralls. He'd already sent a description to the department but, like the deputies he spoke with in person, he'd been met with a hesitation once Millie's name came out. Since the deputies had shown up she'd gone to her car. Now she opened the door and stepped out. Yet she kept her distance.

Chamblin smiled her way but stayed in their conversation.

"We have no evidence that a crime was committed and a witness who has been labeled as suspect," he said matter-of-factly. "What if it was Millie Dean who screamed? What if she lied to you, Love?"

Foster had already had the thought. He wouldn't be a good detective if he hadn't.

Had Millie screamed? And if so, why?

To distract him from whoever was running through the trees?

Or had what made her scream been something she wished to keep secret?

It was easy to hope that everyone was good and honest, but the harder pill to swallow was to admit that everyone lied about something.

The question now became: Was Millie Dean lying about this?

Foster could give the answer he hoped was true but decided to play devil's advocate instead.

"And what if she didn't lie?"

Chamblin nodded. "Even if we wanted to, we can't ignore this. Not after Annie McHale." The sheriff pulled his phone back out. "Tell Juliet and Park to keep searching. I'll call Rudy in since he's pretty familiar with the area to help go over it again. I'd call in our K-9 unit to be fast but, well, there isn't one anymore."

"Another repercussion of Kelby Creek's fall from grace," Foster muttered. Chamblin nodded.

"Send Millie home but tell her to come in tomorrow to make an official statement. No use losing more sleep tonight."

"I can go in with Rudy when he gets here," Foster offered. Rudy Clayborn was the oldest deputy on the Dawn County Sheriff's Department's roster and an expert hunter. He had been longtime friends with Patricia Stillwater, the reigning champion of all things nature in Kelby Creek before him.

Before The Flood.

Now she was buried in the Kelby Creek Memorial Cemetery and Rudy was their go-to man when it came to combing the woods.

"Sounds like a plan," the sheriff responded, eyes trailing to his phone.

Foster felt the excitement of a plan start to unfurl within him. Plans either worked out or didn't. Either way, they got results. Still, Foster paused before enacting the new one.

"By the way, what's your take on her and her brother?" he asked. "Everyone at the department seems to already have an opinion."

It was easy to see what the others thought of the Dean family, but Chamblin had always been an introspective and politically conscious man. He didn't stir any pots unless he was sure of their ingredients.

The sheriff sighed, chest deflating. A look of sympathy folded into his expression.

"Whatever Fallon Dean did or didn't do, the fact is that there's always been one person who couldn't avoid the fallout." He glanced over to Millie. "And she's still standing. I surely won't be the one who tries to knock her down, so I'm going to keep doing my job. We need to get this all figured out ASAP."

It was a good answer. It was also the end of their conversation.

Foster went to the woman still standing.

Dark eyes watched his every move until he stopped across from her.

"We're going to keep searching this place, but you're free to go home," he told her. "I just need you to come into the department tomorrow to make an official statement. The sooner the better."

"I work at the grocery store tomorrow but not until lunch," she said with a nod. "I can come in in the morning."

"Good. That'll work."

A moment of quiet fell between them. Millie looked unsure of something and Foster could feel his own questions trying to convince him to interview her fully right now on the spot. But *unsure* wasn't the only feeling that came across her expression. Foster could tell she was tired, afraid and worried.

So, he decided to wait until the next day to dig deep.

He might not have known Millie Dean, but something in his gut told him although she was trouble with a capital *T*, she wasn't malicious.

He hoped he could trust her.

"I'll see you in the morning," he added after a stock smile.

Foster started to turn but a hand stayed his elbow. When he looked back at the woman, she dropped her touch and met his gaze.

"I was hoping Fallon would be here, that he had really

just gone on his own six months ago and had finally decided to come back on the anniversary. He's an artist, so I thought he might try to be poetic about it. But I knew deep down that he wouldn't be there. Still, it was nice to have hope." Millie's body tensed visibly. She glanced toward the trees, then back. "I don't understand why that man was out there looking for Fallon tonight, but I don't think he was out there looking for hope."

She smiled.

It was flash-in-the-pan quick.

Then she was getting into her car.

"I'll see you tomorrow, Miss Dean," he called after her.

She nodded through the window.

Foster didn't watch her go, but he couldn't deny there was a new weight against his chest as he heard the tires grind against the dirt.

His job wasn't to find Fallon Dean.

It wasn't his job to help Millie either.

He had to focus instead on the newest mystery to find its way to Kelby Creek.

The woman who screamed in the woods and the man who tried to attack a woman in the dark.

Not trying to heal Millie Dean's heart.


THUNDER RUMBLED IN the distance. Not enough to wake her, had she been sleeping, but there was enough power in the rumble that it rattled the old window next to her bed.

Millie rolled onto her side and stared at the glass.

It needed a good cleaning.

Just like the rest of the house.

The closer the anniversary had gotten, the more Millie had focused on everything but what should have been normal.

The window needed a good cleaning, but *she* needed Fallon home and safe.

Millie sighed along her pillowcase. Her alarm clock's digital readout let her know that if she stayed where she was, she'd see light of day splaying across her mint-green walls in less than three hours.

Another rumble and rattle of thunder made her mentally amend that conclusion.

A storm was on the way.

And Millie wasn't going to stay in bed, hoping sleep would take her.

She admitted defeat, sat up and placed her bare feet on the floor. The hardwood was cold. Goose bumps pricked up the sides of her arms.

Her mother used to hate having cold feet. So much so that her mom had a pair of socks in almost every room of their home growing up. It had been a point of teasing from Millie's father. He'd often joked that some people hated getting socks for Christmas but for Maryellen Dean, it was one of the best presents a person could be lucky enough to get.

Millie flexed her feet against the floor.

The only socks in her house were tucked tightly in her dresser.

The cold didn't bother her anymore.

She stood against the weight of being tired and grabbed her robe from the end of the bed. It was soft against her arms. She decided to pair its comfort with a cup of coffee and one of the leftover cookies she'd baked.

What a waste that had been. She wished she'd never offered the cookies to Deputy Park.

Millie had never been particularly afraid of the dark, but she couldn't deny she was clumsier in it. She had nightlights with built-in sensors plugged into a few different sockets throughout the house. The one in the hallway blinked on as she walked past. Normally she would have used the light to guide her into the kitchen, but something pulled her across the hallway instead.

The door to the guest bedroom was always open. Everything Fallon owned was either boxed up or in plastic tubs within the space. Millie could have closed the door, compartmentalized Fallon's disappearance by physically putting something between her and everything that reminded her of him.

But she couldn't.

Millie knew every object in the room by now like the back of her hand. What she wasn't familiar with was the sight out the window.

The window that pointed toward her neighbor's house.

Foster Lovett. Detective.

She walked to the window and looked out into the night. She could just make out the porch light from the front of the house. The garage was built into the opposite side, and she couldn't tell if his truck was in the drive.

Did that mean he was still working?

Was he still out in the woods?

The night-light in the hallway turned off.

Millie pulled her robe closer around her, the prickling sense of something being wrong making her want more comfort.

The sound of the woman screaming had been a vivid, haunting sound. A slap to the face in the quiet. A warning and call for help all at once.

Millie had gone to the woods in frustration, desperation and, like she'd told the detective, wanting nothing more than to feel hope. Even for a short while.

She'd left those same woods with three people caught in her mind.

The man in the coveralls, the woman who screamed and Detective Lovett.

Lightning forked high in the sky. The thunder that came next was louder than before.

Millie hoped they found the woman before the storm arrived.

She took a deep breath, but it caught in her throat.

Adrenaline moved through her faster than the lightning had the sky.

The hallway night-light was back on.

But Millie hadn't moved an inch.

# Chapter Five

*Throw everything.*

It was the second thought that ran through Millie's head the moment he stepped into the doorway.

The man from the woods.

The man in the coveralls.

And he was smiling.

Throw *everything.*

Millie's body went on autopilot.

It wasn't like being in the woods—this was her *home.* It was in the middle of the night. He was inside without an invitation.

Apart from those terrifying facts, the man was *close.*

Millie's home wasn't tiny, but the guest bedroom seeming to have shrunk to the size of the jail cell the second the man had filled the doorframe.

Unlike being in the woods together, this time Millie had only two escape routes. The door he was blocking and the closed—and locked—window behind her that she wouldn't have time to open and exit through.

Their close proximity with no options of an easy plan meant the odds of him hurting Millie faster than she could defend herself were high.

She just hoped the same could be said for him.

Millie pulled the lamp off the nightstand in one quick

tug. The force of adrenaline pumping through her veins made the throw that came next count.

The man grunted, seemingly caught off guard, but Millie didn't wait to see what damage she might or might not have done. There wasn't time for that. The second the lamp was airborne she had a thick, hardback book in her hands. She didn't even see the title of it before it too was a weapon soaring through the air toward its target.

The man cussed loudly. He staggered forward but not enough for her to get by him. Millie rolled over the bed to force distance between them, already reaching for something else to throw or brandish like a weapon.

"You little bitch," the man ground out. "I just want to know where he is!"

The closest thing to Millie was a garbage bag of clothes that hadn't fit in the closet. It wasn't ideal, but her motto was anything could turn into a weapon with enough willpower.

Though her practicality paled in comparison to the physical reality she saw as the man flipped the light switch on.

Millie squinted against the sudden brightness, but it was her stomach that twisted at the change in lighting the most.

The man in the coveralls had a gun in his hand, something she definitely hadn't noticed before.

This time she froze. If she hadn't been so scared, she might have felt silly for realizing she'd fought a gun with a lamp.

"Got your attention now, don't I?" the man growled. There was blood at the corner of his mouth. Maybe she'd counted out how effective the lamp could be too soon.

"I—I don't know where Fallon is," Millie responded, voice breaking from the new, insane rush of adrenaline at seeing his gun. "You can search the house and see he isn't here."

The man snarled. It reminded Millie of an angry cartoon character. He didn't seem real. A stranger standing in her house with a gun pointed at her... It didn't seem real.

As if he heard her thoughts, he shook the weapon. He was *too close* to her. There was no way she could fight or flight without running the risk of being hit by a bullet.

"You know," he started, "I asked around about you, about Fallon, and the town really doesn't seem to like either. Well, mostly him. They just seem to feel sorry for you. But, believe you me, they all agree on one thing and that's that you two were inseparable." He shook his head and winced at the movement. Maybe the book had done some damage too. "He may not be here, but I don't believe for a second that you don't know where Fallon is."

The man took a step forward. Millie clutched the bag of clothes against her chest. It was heavy, but wasn't a match for a bullet.

"I've been looking for him," Millie stated, eyes unable to stay off the gun. "Since the day he left, I've been looking. I have no idea where he is."

The man sighed.

He was frustrated; that much she could tell. Almost annoyed, even.

"You know, at first I believed that you really had no idea where he was." He used the gun to motion to the window. "I kept waiting for you to do something suspicious or out of character to show me you were putting on a show for the town, but you didn't. You just went on your boring way doing meaningless and routine things." His smile came back. There was no mirth, just vindication. A man who had won a bet and was about to collect his prize. "*Then* you went to the sheriff's department. And suddenly there you were rushing off into the woods."

A cold, creeping feeling threaded through Millie's stomach.

He'd been watching her, and not just that night.

"I went out there looking for Fallon," she told him. "I was hoping he was there but he wasn't. You saw that!"

The man shook his head again. That frustration was growing. His finger was so close to the trigger of the gun.

"I think you were meeting up with him and I interrupted too soon. So, now, we're going to try this again because I'd really like to get out of here." He readjusted the aim of the gun. This time it was pointing to her head. "Where is your brother and how do we get ahold of him?"

It shouldn't have happened, of all the times for it to surface, it shouldn't have done it there. Yet, standing with a bag of Fallon's forgotten clothes against her and staring at a stranger who very well could kill her, Millie felt it.

Anger.

Red-hot, unbridled anger.

No one was ever going to believe her, were they?

The town, the sheriff's department, even the newcomer detective couldn't take a beat to listen to her.

To hear her out.

To believe the words that she said.

Was that just her destiny?

To be the woman no one ever trusted?

That anger turned to indignation in one blink.

If no one wanted to believe she was telling the truth, then maybe it was time to start lying.

"Okay. Okay." Millie dropped her voice to an almost-whisper. Defeated. "I'll—I'll tell you what I know but only if you put the gun away. I'll just end up blubbering like a baby soon if you don't."

The man snorted.

"You have me cornered," she pointed out. "And all I have is laundry. *Please.*"

To Millie's utter surprise, the man obliged. He dropped the gun into his front coverall pocket.

He must have really wanted to know where Fallon was.

But so did she.

Millie took a slow step to the edge of the bed. It put her right across from him.

"Where is he?" he asked.

Millie's palms started to sweat. Her already-racing heartbeat went into overdrive.

She had a plan.

And it was probably a bad one.

"Not here."

Millie charged the man so fast that he didn't have time to do much other than put up his hands. It was a useless defense as she crashed into them, the bag of clothes acting as a bumper between their bodies. The force and momentum dragged and pushed them backward into the opened door.

Millie heard a *crack* but didn't want to stick around to see if that was from the man or the door.

The second his body was flat against the wood she let go of the bag and darted out to the left and into the hallway.

The night-light flashed on and, five steps later as she turned into the living room, a gunshot screamed behind her.

Millie wasn't sure if she screamed too, but by the time she made it to the front door her legs felt like Jell-O and any plan she had of escape dropped through the floor along with her stomach.

Her phone was in the bedroom.

Her car keys were in the kitchen.

A man ready to shoot her would have a clear shot if she didn't clear the porch in seconds.

She barely had time to register that the front door was already cracked as she grabbed the doorknob and yanked it all the way open.

Time seemed to freeze as two forest green eyes stared back at her, the porch light making his long hair almost shine and the gun in hand glint.

Detective Lovett didn't wait for an explanation or warning, which was good, since Millie didn't have time to give either.

The best they could do boiled down to the detective using his strength to push her to the side like he was the strongest man on Earth while Millie didn't resist.

She fell against wooden porch, pain radiating from her knees.

Then it happened.

An awful explosion of sound pierced her ears, followed immediately by another.

Gunshots.

Two gunshots.

Millie closed her eyes tight, knowing that even though the detective had pushed her out of the way, the bullet had still found her.

Yet no blinding pain came.

No darkness either.

Instead, she heard the sound of a falling body.

Scratch that.

*Two* bodies falling.

Millie opened her eyes and turned back to Foster. She gasped.

Detective Lovett was on the ground.

And he wasn't moving.

BEFORE HE'D EVEN set foot on Millie Dean's front porch, Foster had blamed his slow gut on sentimentally and nostalgia.

He'd spent the last few hours trying to see the same Kelby Creek he'd known growing up. Not seeing the town for what it had become after what had happened to Annie McHale. After The Flood. Not for what it was now.

He'd waited for Rudy, and then they'd gone over the stretch of woods that made up their surroundings only to find one more set of footprints. It wasn't a lot to go on but he hadn't wanted to stop.

Rudy, however, was tired. And not in the same sense as the sheriff had been.

He was the kind of tired that dragged every part of him down. Even his smile. Foster had seen that before in his career, and he'd seen the same look in the mirror once or twice. A part of Rudy had been hollowed out by the world and, sometimes, that hollow part got filled by the bad stuff that came after.

Rudy had seen bad and he'd also lost someone close to him because of it.

And, in those woods, he'd been tired.

Tired and ready to leave when they hadn't found much at all.

Foster empathized with him, but not the deputies who had been helping.

They weren't interested in finding the woman or the man. They had cleared the woods and announced they were going home the second their boots made it past the tree line and to their cruiser.

"Maybe you should ask Miss Dean tomorrow why she came out here with a bat tonight," Deputy Kathryn Juliet had suggested with a grin that had no right to be pulling up the corners of her mouth.

It had made Foster angry. Not just at another attack on Millie but for the fact that this wasn't the sheriff's department that he'd known growing up. The ones who were left hadn't really stayed. Their hearts didn't seem in it anymore. To Foster, it seemed like they were one foot out the door already.

If it wasn't a cut-and-dry case, then what was the point?

Annie McHale and The Flood had broken them.

*But that's why you're here*, he had tried to remind himself. *To help them. To find redemption.*

Foster had hoped that he was just being overdramatic, but he had driven away from those woods tangled up in his own thoughts and memories about what used to be and what was.

About wanting nothing more than to leave the town he'd grown up in and then leaving the good life he'd made as an adult behind so he could come back.

It wasn't until he had been turning into the neighborhood that his gut and his head had finally shaken hands and reintroduced themselves to each other.

The man in the coveralls had gone into the woods to ask Millie where her brother was.

But, if Millie had been telling the truth about not knowing him or even recognizing him, then how had he known she was there?

Foster's grip had tightened around the steering wheel as he'd answered himself out loud.

"He followed her, just like you did, Foster."

Foster had cursed beneath his breath and turned his headlights off. His gut had sent a shot of urgency through him. He'd pulled to the curb instead of into his driveway.

The neighborhood had been quiet. Thunder rumbled as he reached for his gun.

A part of him might have worried that he was being dramatic, that the red flags that had sprung up was just him looking for a lead because he hadn't found much in the woods, but then lightning had split through the night air and Foster had seen it.

Millie Dean's front door was open.

Not by a whole lot but by too much for a house in the dark.

That had been enough for him.

He had reached into his back seat, grabbed what his former partner in Seattle had dubbed the Just in Case.

He'd been haphazardly handling it as he'd hurried out of the truck and down the sidewalk toward the front porch.

Then the gunshot had helped him become something he hadn't in a long while.

He'd become calm.

Absolutely and 100 percent calm.

From drawing his gun, to Millie appearing wide-eyed in front of him, Foster had left his sense of urgency and found the only thing that would help him and Millie.

Focus.

So, as his gut let him know he should have realized Millie had still been in danger sooner, his head had taken over.

He'd moved Millie out of the way and pulled the trigger so the man couldn't.

But he had.

Foster's focus had gone and his gut and his head had quieted as the world went dark.

# Chapter Six

The rain finally came.

It hit the tin roof and sounded like hail instead of water droplets. Then he could hear the water spreading over the grass behind him. It was soothing, in a way. White noise attached to the irreplaceable scent of rain.

Then there was something else.

Strawberries?

Foster opened his eyes.

Light poured around dark, wild hair and the body of a woman leaning over him. For a moment, Foster forgot where he was, and it was just him looking into the amber eyes of someone concerned.

But then the pain in his ribs said, "How do you do?" and the memory of the gunman poured in faster than the rain falling around them.

"Is he down?" Foster grunted as he tried to sit up. "Wa-was he alone?"

Millie had a phone to her ear and, despite her darker complexion, looked pale. She also looked relieved.

"He's dead," she told him. Then into the phone, "No! Detective Foster isn't dead. He's awake now." He could hear someone on the other end of the phone call talking quickly. Millie nodded then handed over the phone. She helped him sit up as he grunted out his name, his position and the bare-bone facts to a dispatcher.

He'd shot and killed a man who had the intent to shoot Millie in her own home. He'd taken a bullet after giving out his own.

Normally Foster would have stayed on the phone, but he wanted answers. And he suspected the second that Sheriff Chamblin found out what happened, he would be shooing Foster to the hospital for a checkup.

Foster wanted to take advantage of his alone time with Millie before that.

He ended the call with an apology and a promise not to leave.

Millie didn't seem to approve. She'd run a gauntlet of expressions while watching him talk. From concerned to lost to an impassiveness that smoothed her face and down-turned her lips. She took her phone, the same one she'd run back inside to get once the detective had fallen, back from him but her gaze had fallen to his chest.

"The man. He shot you." Her voice softened tenfold. "I thought you were dead."

She reached out but didn't touch where the bullet had hit.

Which was good because it hurt like hell.

If Foster didn't have a set of bruised ribs, then he certainly had some cracked ones. Not to mention the throbbing pain at the back of his head, letting him know that he definitely had hit the floor after being knocked out by the impact of the shot.

Still, he'd been lucky as hell.

"And that's why I always keep Just in Case in my vehicle." He ran his hand over his bulletproof vest, grateful that he'd thrown it on when he did. Millie didn't look as appreciative. She eyed his side where the straps weren't fastened.

"It's not all the way on. You could have been killed."

Foster put his hands against the wood floor of the porch and pushed himself up. Millie stood with him, helping him to steady.

"There wasn't enough time."

Millie didn't seem to like that answer. He heard his own voice soften this time. "And his bullet hit exactly where it needed to, okay? I'll be all right, just sore."

The woman nodded.

"Now, what about you?" he asked, looking her up and down. As far as he could tell, she wasn't injured but, then again, she also had a robe on that covered most of her body. "Did he hurt you?"

She was quick to shake her head.

"No. But I hurt him."

Millie stepped him through the story of what happened from the time she got out of bed until she made it out onto the front porch. In between her recounting of the events and walk-through of the house, Foster made sure to keep himself between her and the man's body, shielding her from seeing him any more than she already had.

Much like the attacker, Foster's bullet had found the man's chest. However, unlike Foster, he hadn't had a vest to protect him.

Now he was bleeding across Millie Dean's hardwood and pink-and-blue rug, looking as out of place in the otherwise cheery home as the gun he'd discarded.

It was only when they were back on the front porch, the man's gun now in Foster's hand, that Millie underlined her biggest takeaway from what had happened.

"He was looking for Fallon," she said. "That was the only thing he was interested in. Fallon."

Her voice had gone small, nearly getting lost in the rain. Foster didn't like how it made him feel to hear it. Just like he was in no way a fan of the still-there anger for her attacker sitting against his chest.

"Is this the first time anyone has ever come to you looking for him?" he asked. "Any friends, enemies, or family?"

He could tell Millie was trying not to look back into her house. To the body on the floor.

"No. He had a few friends here before Annie McHale went missing. After that, like a lot of people, they ended up moving. I reached out to them when he first disappeared, but none have responded. As for enemies? Well, there's a town full of people who think he's an attention-seeking, self-involved guy with nothing better to do than waste everyone's time." Her words had a sharp edge to them. She caught herself and spoke more evenly when she continued. "And family? That's me. Just me."

For the first time since he'd met Millie Dean, Foster realized he didn't know if she had her own family aside from Fallon. Were there wedding pictures hanging on the walls that he'd missed? An engagement ring in a dish next to her bed? A boyfriend who she was hoping to call the second she could?

Surely a woman as beautiful as Millie had someone who would want to know she was okay.

Foster cleared his throat.

"Do you need to call someone? To let them know you're okay before this hits the news and gossip mill?"

Millie shook her head. The movement was as small as her voice.

"Normally I would have called Fallon."

Foster reached out and gently touched her shoulder. Pain at the move radiated up his side, but he held his expression firm.

"Well, I'm here," he said. "And we'll get to the bottom of this, okay?"

Dark eyes, searching and hard, traced his face. Whatever Millie Dean was looking for in him, he didn't know but she did nod.

"Okay."

THE SUNRISE CRESTED over Haven Hospital's well-kept but extremely small building hours later. The hospital was nestled between a flat park with a couple of benches and one grill and a town limits sign that had seen better days. However, the private hospital was pristine.

It had been created by the McHale family back in the eighties and had been one of the many gems they were proud to have their wealthy names on. But once their daughter had gone missing and then everything had gone from bad to worse to unfathomable, the McHale family had sold their shares in it.

Foster hadn't been to Haven since he was a teen. If the change in majority ownership had resulted in a remodel, he'd been gone too long to recognize any big changes.

All he knew was that while the sun was rising over the hospital, the morgue in the basement looked almost identical to every morgue he'd seen throughout his career.

Concrete. Cold. Weirdly bright.

Then there was the coroner. She was less standard with her blue-streaked black hair, bejeweled lab coat, and gum that she was smacking on as she introduced herself as Amanda Alvarez.

She pointed to the man on the metal table between them. His clothes were gone, in their place a white sheet that was giving off a powerful disinfectant spray smell. The doctor, who Foster didn't know much about other than she was a new hire after The Flood and that she was in her midthirties, motioned to Coveralls.

"So Sheriff Chamblin said he wanted me to call you if anything weird pops while I'm dealing with this one."

"Yeah, I'm working the case," Foster said. "But I'll admit, I didn't think you'd call me in here this quickly, especially since we know what killed him."

Dr. Alvarez's dark eyebrow rose.

"And I didn't expect for you to get here this quick. What were you doing? Sitting in the parking lot waiting?"

Foster sighed. The pain in his side moved with it.

"The sheriff finally convinced me to get examined. I was upstairs finishing the paperwork when you called." Alvarez still had her eyebrow raised in question. Foster motioned to the man between them. "He shot me."

The doctor looked him up and down.

"I've seen a lot of gunshot victims, and I have to say you should get a gold star for how you've fared."

Foster snorted. "I was wearing a vest."

She made an "ah" noise and pointed to the man.

"Well, our John Doe decidedly was not. You're the one who shot him, I'm guessing?"

Foster nodded.

He felt no joy or pride in taking a man's life, but he was confident that he'd made the right call. Especially after a search of his belongings showed plastic zip ties, a knife and a baggie of white pills in his deep pockets. The pills were being examined at the moment, but the zip ties alone had shown concerning intentions that the man had been harboring for Millie.

"Was that all you did?" Dr. Alvarez added. "Shoot him, I mean. Did you physically lay hands on him at all or any other contact?"

Foster shook his head. "No, but he was struck with a lamp, a book and was thrown into a wall by a woman holding a bag of laundry."

Dr. Alvarez tilted her head a little at the information. She didn't seem satisfied with it.

"First of all, I would love to hear that story in more detail. Second, that might explain his busted lip but a bag of laundry definitely didn't do this."

She moved the sheet down, revealing Coveralls' bare upper body. He'd been cleaned, but the bullet hole was still an angry red against his pale skin.

It wasn't the only thing.

Foster took a step closer and shook his head.

"Definitely not a lamp or book either."

Coveralls' torso had a smattering of black, blue and purple bruises across it. He looked like he'd been someone's personal punching bag. Foster pointed to his upper arm where Millie had claimed to hit him with the bat to get away in the woods. The spot had also bruised.

"He was hit with a bat in self-defense last night, hours before the second attack. But only on the arm and only once. I have no idea about the rest of these bruises."

Dr. Alvarez reached out with her gloved hands and hovered above the main cluster.

"Okay, so the arm bruising and the busted lip fits that timeline," she said. "But *these*, these have already been healing."

"Which means Millie had nothing to do with them."

"Not likely. That's why I called you in." She shrugged. "I can't tell you why it happened or who or what did it yet, but I *can* confidently tell you that probably around two days ago this man took one heck of a beating."

THE HEAT OF midday warmed the back of Millie's shirt and exercise pants. She was tired, hungry and nervous all at once, standing there in front of the door to her home.

She wanted to go inside and, at the same time, she wanted to do anything but.

If Detective Lovett hadn't been with her, she might have gone to work despite her boss telling her to take the day off. She might have also said yes to Larissa's offer of taking refuge at her home. She might have just stood there, staring on the front porch.

Frozen.

But the detective was there, and he'd already promised he wasn't leaving her just yet.

"I know you're probably ready to finally get some sleep, but I'd personally feel better if I could clear the house before I go to my own," he said. "If that's okay with you."

It was more than okay to Millie, but she didn't say it in that way. She didn't admit she'd been afraid and anxious just thinking about being alone in her house.

Instead, she unlocked the door and stepped aside to let him in.

"Thank you," she said to him as he passed.

He waved her off, his detective's badge around his neck swaying at the movement.

"It's the neighborly thing to do."

Millie stood in the entryway as Foster checked every room, window and lock. He looked good for a man running on no sleep, even better for a man who had been shot no less than a handful of hours ago.

Then again, he'd already managed to save her twice.

Twice on the same day that she'd dismissed him to his face.

Millie ran a hand across the back of her neck. Tendrils of exhaustion felt like they were coming up through the floorboards, wrapping around her body and pulling down.

That tug became more powerful when her gaze swept to the one spot she'd been hoping to avoid.

A man had died in her home.

Bled out in her living room.

Now the man was gone, but the blood that had seeped into the rug was still there.

A stain.

A reminder.

One that made her stomach tight and already-fried nerves almost painful. Her discomfort must have shown. When the detective came back into the room with an all clear, he pointedly looked at the rug.

"There's not a thing you can do to save it, I hate to say. No amount of carpet cleaner or stain remover is going to get it looking like new. But we can try if you want."

That surprised Millie. Not that the rug was ruined but the implication that he'd help her try to clean it.

She shook her head.

"Even if we could get it looking like new, I don't think I could ever *not* see him there when I looked."

Detective Lovett didn't fault her for the truth.

Instead, he surprised her again.

He took off his holster, his badge, rolled up his sleeves and picked up her coffee table like it was as light as a tooth-pick. He placed it on the bare hardwood floor next to the rug, then turned his sights on the couch.

"You don't have to do that," Millie said. "I can clean all this up."

He winced but shook his head.

"You've already seen a lot that you shouldn't have had to see. But me? I've been around things like this before. You deserve a break and I don't mind giving you one." The couch wasn't by any means a heavy item, but it was still impressive to watch the man push it out of the way like it too was weightless.

The detective might not have had muscles bulging through his clothes, but there was no denying that there was strength in him.

"Trash pickup doesn't come until Friday, but I can take care of it before then."

Millie watched as the man who had been told he had bruised ribs and a slight concussion by the ER doctor hours before single-handedly rearranged her living-room furniture, rolled up a bloodstained rug and then dragged it outside and into the bed of his pickup in the driveway next to hers. All without complaining one single bit.

His act of kindness, more than realizing he'd taken a bullet meant for her, did something to Millie.

When he came back in and asked where her floor cleaner was and then shooed her while he went back to the spot and cleaned it, that something turned into something more.

Despite that something, though, Millie couldn't help but ask the one question that had embedded itself in the back of her mind the moment the man in coveralls had appeared in the hallway.

"Do you think Fallon disappearing was because of that man? Or do you think I'm lying for my brother?"

They were back out on the front porch, the sun shining against the wet grass in front of them, the house smelling of Lysol behind them.

Detective Lovett's green, green eyes met hers.

He didn't look away as he answered.

"I don't think for one bit that you're lying, Miss Dean. Just like I don't think your brother left town for attention." He smiled. It was brief but helped her all the same. "And I'm going to do my damnedest to prove both."

That was it.

That was enough.

Millie closed the space between them with an embrace she hadn't expected to give.

The man was hard and warm against her body. His hands were soft, though, as one skimmed across her back.

"Thank you, Detective," she said into his shoulder. "Thank you."

She couldn't see his expression when he responded, but his tone was different. She just didn't know why.

And she didn't care.

Not right then.

Not when someone finally believed her.

His words rumbled from his chest into hers, melting away the layer of anxiety that had built up in the last day.

"Call me Foster."

# Chapter Seven

Rosewater Inn had been a tragic attempt at a bed-and-breakfast in Kelby Creek's early 2000s. Converted from a somewhat nice-looking motel into a fancier-looking motel, it had missed every mark on trying to be unique and charming. The inn had gone broke faster than Foster and Regina had when they'd first moved out to Seattle.

However, after they'd left Kelby Creek behind, the inn had been repurposed again, achieving the unique descriptor with the additional one of just plain weird.

Or, as Foster's mother would have said, *eclectic*.

The one-story rooms that stretched to the west and included the lobby had been gutted and turned into a bar. The rooms that stretched toward the east had kept their interior walls and been made into micro-office spaces. Only one was currently rented out to a Mrs. Zamboni, a palm reader whose real name was Helen Mercer. It was an upgrade from her previous spot in her parents' basement, that was for sure. The last of the rooms, set dead center in front of the long parking lot, still had the remains of the fancier version of the motel locked inside their rooms.

Foster spotted a bare box spring mattress and dust-covered wooden end tables as he peeked through the opening in a curtain covering the window of room 4A. He was surprised when a woman cleared her throat next to him.

Mrs. Zamboni herself was giving him a grin. Foster had to make sure he didn't stare too long at the crown of flowers she had woven into her dyed-silver hair or her very pregnant stomach. He knew from experience that commenting on either would earn him a one-way trip to confrontation town.

So, Foster went the safe, neutral route instead. He stood tall again and pulled a smile on. Not that smiling at his former sister-in-law ever put any points in his favor in her book.

"Hey, Helen, how are you?"

Helen rubbed a hand over her stomach and gave him a look that was all annoyance.

"I'm eight months pregnant during the beginning of an Alabama summer and my last client asked me if I could talk to the dead so he could apologize to his neighbor for being awful to his dog." She motioned to him with a wave of her hand. "Then on my way to get some snacks that I really don't need, I run into the son of a biscuit who took my sister away from her family and didn't even have the decency to bring her back when he was done with her."

Helen, all five feet of her, had always had a tendency to run hotheaded. She was two years younger than Regina and the most outspoken of the Becker clan.

Which meant she'd commented on every single milestone of Foster and Regina's relationship, most vocally their divorce.

Foster sighed, knowing there was no right response to avoid a talking-to from the woman.

The moment he saw the Mrs. Zamboni, Palm Reader, sign, he should have bolted.

"I had no say or right to tell Regina what to do after the papers were finalized. She's the one who chose to stay in Seattle with her new boyfriend. Talk to her if you're mad about it."

Helen snorted. Foster was immediately reminded of Deputy Park. He'd been acting like a disgruntled employee for the last three days. Helen looked like she was the one who wanted to complain to the boss now as she continued speaking.

"You know, when she said you were coming back, we didn't believe it. Dad said you'd have a lot of nerve to show back up anywhere within the county lines." She rubbed her pregnant belly again and smiled. "I guess I'm going to have some fun facts for him at family dinner tonight."

Foster wasn't an idiot. He knew a major drawback of coming home again would be largely attached to his former family-in-law but hope sprung eternal that he'd at least avoid the bulk of them for a while.

At least until he was settled in.

"You only get one hometown, so I thought why not come back and try to help mine," he said. "It's as simple as that."

Helen's demeanor shifted from annoyance to genuine interest as her eyes went down to the badge hanging around his neck. It was clear she'd forgotten his profession.

And now she was curious as to why he was there during the workday.

"Are you looking for someone?"

Foster shrugged. "More like getting reacquainted with the local haunts." It was a lie and a truth. Foster needed to do what he said but he was also looking for gossip on a particular person. Or the person in question himself.

William Reiner. A potentially angry man whose career had been ended by Fallon Dean.

Foster readjusted his stance and tried to look nonchalant.

Helen's eyebrow rose with her obvious suspicion of him.

"Does that have anything to do with what happened

over on Lively Drive Monday night?" Her eyes widened. "Wait. Were you the one who killed the home intruder?"

Foster couldn't help it; he took a jab.

"Aren't you supposed to be psychic, Helen? Shouldn't you already know?"

She rolled her eyes so hard Foster bet she came close to permanent damage.

"I read *palms*. I'm not a one-stop shop to everything psychic, so you can put that one back in your holster and shut it. But I'm guessing it was you since you didn't give me a straight answer."

"I can't talk about an ongoing investigation. You know that."

Helen didn't look impressed.

"This town is a fishbowl," she said with a shrug. "The truth will come back around whether you say a word about it or not."

Foster knew that to be true.

Which was why he'd had a stern conversation with almost half of the sheriff's department to make sure everyone was on the same page about *not* sharing information outside of themselves.

"Then you'll hear about it later." Foster wanted to end the conversation there but, despite his feelings about Helen, she'd grown up and grown older in Kelby Creek.

She knew its people more than most.

"Speaking of fish in this fishbowl, do you know William Reiner?"

Helen was faster to speak her mind than hide what she was thinking. She made a face.

"We're not social but I know of him. He used to work at the sheriff's department. He lost his little brother to The Flood."

That was news to Foster.

"How was the brother involved?"

"According to officials, he wasn't. According to the rest of town? Well, he sure seemed guilty of something. He up and left during the FBI's investigation. Put his badge and gun on his desk and ran."

Foster took his notepad out of his pocket and clicked his pen to ready.

"What's his name? Reiner's bother."

"Cole but, like I said, as far as I've heard he wasn't found guilty of anything."

"But you said he ran?"

Helen nodded. "He sure didn't take his time in leaving."

"Do you know if Reiner ever explained why?"

Helen sighed. "No, but, based on the fact that he came to me asking questions like I was some kind of crystal ball, I'm guessing he didn't know either."

Foster hadn't expected that either. What he knew of Deputy Reiner, which was mostly from his work files, was that he seemed to be a no-nonsense man. One who wouldn't go to a psychic or palm reader, let alone believe in them.

"And what exactly did he ask?"

Helen shook her head. "That charm might have worked with my sister, but you're not getting anything about my clients from me, Detective. I respect their privacy." She took a step out into the parking lot, hand doing a lap over her stomach again. "If you have questions for Reiner, then you've come to the right place. He's a regular at Rosewater Bar." Foster watched after her, his annoyance waning at the encounter. It seemed like everyone in Kelby Creek had to deal with the past, one way or the other.

Foster's phone vibrated in his pocket before he could leave his spot in front of the old motel.

It was Deputy Park and he got straight to the point.

"We found something."

MILLIE ANSWERED THE door with a crown of curls, a denim skirt and a blouse that dipped low and clung tight. Her sandals were flat, but her toenails matched the manicure that Larissa had given her after their shift at the store that morning. Millie had also gone bold with her makeup. Dark red lipstick that looked almost violet in certain lights complemented eyeshadow that told the general public this was an intentional outing, and not a spur of the moment one.

Though seeing a certain blond standing on her welcome mat didn't bode well for her evening plans when she opened the door.

"Detective?"

Foster had his badge around his neck and wasn't smooth in the least as he looked her up and down.

But he did catch himself.

"Hey, Millie, uh, sorry, did I catch you at a bad time?"

The heat of a blush was immediate. It ran up from her stomach and to her neck, promising to show the man that she was embarrassed.

Embarrassed that she'd been caught.

She laughed lightly, stalling.

If he knew about her plan, then he would probably point out it was at best useless, at worst a deeper hole that she'd find herself in.

If he *didn't* know about her bad plan, then there was no way anyone could trace any blame back to him for knowing about it before it was executed.

The devil on Millie's shoulder cheered at the thought of sidestepping the truth as a courtesy, yet the angel on the other told her to stare into the man's eyes.

Vibrant. Searching. The windows into the soul of the man who had taken a life to save hers.

Millie caved all within the span of two seconds.

"I was about to leave, actually. I'm going out. To the bar."

"Oh."

Millie didn't know why she wanted to, but she decided to let him know it wasn't a social visit.

"Alone," she blurted out. That blush found her cheeks and burned. She tried to be less awkward but sighed in defeat. "In all honesty, I'm hoping I can run into William Reiner and get him to talk to me."

In the last three days, Millie had seen Foster a total of two times. The first encounter had been the day after he'd taken the bloody rug from her house and promised her answers on the front porch. He'd been in full-blown work mode with a pad of paper in hand and a voice that sounded like a rehearsed recording. He'd broken down what he'd learned about the man who had come into her home after Fallon.

His name was Jason Talbot, according to his dental records, and Millie had never met or heard of him before seeing him in the woods. Past that, they had still been running down information on the, according to Foster, "surprisingly slippery" suspect. As for the pills that had been in Jason's pocket, those had been identified as a black-market off-brand of Paxil, an anxiety and depression medication.

"These popped up in a case I had in Seattle a few years back," he'd said. "Not the most common or popular of drug on the market, so we might be able to actually track them to the seller and see if we can get more information on Talbot."

He'd told her that was one of several new leads the department was working on.

"If we find out why Jason wanted Fallon in the first place, that can only help us get closer to what happened to Fallon," he'd added when Millie must have made a face. "We follow Jason, we also might find out who the woman in the woods is. Because so far no one in this county or the next has reported anyone missing or filed any reports of something similar happening. So, Jason is our goal right now."

The second time Foster had come over had been the day after that. It was less of an update and more of a check-ing-in.

"It's not an easy thing, being attacked. Same with see-ing a body," he'd said, standing on her front porch with his badge yet again. "I just wanted to let you know if you need me you can call anytime."

Millie had been running late for work then. Had she not, she might have asked him inside. For what, she wasn't sure, but the urge had been there.

Just like it was with him there on her porch for the third time.

Foster had been a hard man to read the last two visits, but now, it was clear she'd surprised him. He tilted his head to the side a little, eyebrows furrowing together.

"Why do you want to talk to Reiner?"

"I don't *want* to talk to the deputy, but, well, I was thinking about it and if Fallon did have one true enemy in town—someone who had a good reason to have it out for him—it would be Reiner. So I thought I'd see if he wouldn't mind casually talking to me about what he was up to six months ago…"

Suddenly Millie felt like a silly child.

If Foster felt the same way, he didn't say it. Instead, his forehead creased again in thought.

"You've never asked him before about Fallon's disap-pearance?"

Millie shook her head.

"Detective Gordon interviewed him, but other than him saying, 'He isn't involved,' I never got any explanations. Fallon and I hadn't talked to William Reiner or his family since he was forced to retire. And even then it was more of his wife yelling at Fallon while Reiner gave us the stink eye." She sighed. "It's been an unwritten rule of this town since then that the Deans give all Reiners an extremely wide berth."

"But now you think he might be involved."

Millie gave him the half-hearted shrug of a frustrated sister.

"Honestly, it's like I'm going out into the woods again looking for hope where there is none. I have no idea if Reiner had anything to do with Fallon disappearing, but he's one of the only stones I personally haven't overturned. So, I thought 'why not?'"

Foster was quiet a moment.

Thoughtful?

Trying to find a way to tell her not to go?

Regretting his move back to Kelby Creek and into the house next to hers?

Millie hoped the latter wasn't true.

Though she couldn't blame him if it was.

In less than a week he'd come to her rescue twice, been shot and had to shoot someone else.

That would definitely be grounds for a solid helping of regret.

However, instead of shaking his head at her, Foster's contemplation turned excited.

He nodded. "That's not a bad idea, actually." He flipped his wrist over to show his watch. It looked expensive, but the leather band was worn. "It's after five so I'm technically off the clock. Unless there's an emergency, of course. Do you mind giving me a few minutes to change?"

Millie felt her eyebrow rise. Just like a fluttering in her stomach.

"To change?"

"Yeah. So I can come with you. Actually, if you want I can drive too. I don't mind." He was already backing up, mind seemingly already forming a plan she wasn't privy to yet. "Meet you at my truck in five?"

"Uh, yeah. That works."

The words came out before Millie realized she'd said them.

Then the detective was off the porch and hurrying to his own next door.

# *Chapter Eight*

If Millie had known how the night would end, she would have stayed home. In fact, she would have not only stayed right there in her house, but she would have told Foster to join her.

To stay a while together, doors locked and the world firmly outside.

But Millie had no idea that her simple bad plan would be the start of a night that she hoped to simply survive.

Hindsight was twenty-twenty, and when Foster jogged back out to his truck, looking roguishly handsome with his black tee, Wrangler jeans and tousled golden hair that fell against his shoulders as he ran a hand through it, the only thought in Millie's head was to ignore how her body said, "yes, ma'am, don't mind if I do" at the sight.

Foster Lovett was a good-looking man even when he wasn't saving her life.

"You're not going to wear your badge?" Millie mentally cringed. Her words went up an octave like she was some schoolgirl nursing a crush. The detective made her nervous. She cleared her throat and tried again. "I mean, you know, if you need to ask questions in an official capacity."

Foster shifted the blazer he had draped over his arm. She could see his holster, gun, and badge on a chain beneath it.

"I'll bring them just in case, but I've found from experience that people are a lot chattier before you show them the badge."

He opened the passenger's side door and held his hand out to help her in. The skin-to-skin contact didn't help Millie's newly flared nerves. She hadn't intended to spend her time at the bar as a part of a twosome.

"So, do *you* think Reiner has something to do with Fallon?" she asked when he was seated behind the wheel. "I mean is that why you wanted to come along?"

Foster twisted around to put his blazer and gun in the back seat. Millie caught a whiff of a deep and delicious cologne coming off him.

She tried to rein in her senses and focus on his answer only.

"A lot of the older files at the department aren't exactly up to my standards," he said, careful as he chose his words. "That includes Fallon and Deputy Reiner's incident five years ago. So I wouldn't mind asking a few of my own questions. Plus it's been a long while since I've been back to Kelby Creek. I've never actually been inside Rosewater as a bar, and I'm curious as hell."

He gave her a grin and turned over the engine. It fussed a little showing its age, but Millie liked the sound. Growing up, her father had been a big fan of older trucks. It was the reason why Fallon had his 1979 Chevy pickup with its light dusting of rust across the bumper instead of something more modern. She suspected it was his attempt at staying connected to a father he had truly loved.

"You know, I have to admit that I didn't realize you'd lived in Kelby Creek before now," she said. "My friend Larissa said you even grew up here?"

Foster laughed, taking them out to the street and pointing the vehicle toward the neighborhood exit. For a famed detective he seemed oddly at ease and not at all as uptight as Millie would have expected. He seemed like a man you'd want to get a beer with instead of a man who went after criminals and worse.

"I did. Born and raised in a house not even ten minutes from here."

"So you have family here?"

He shook his head. "I used to, but after my dad passed a few years ago my mom moved to Huntsville to live with her best friend." He laughed again. Even in profile his smile was easy on the eyes. "I've *almost* gotten used to getting random drunk calls from them when they've had a little too much wine while watching one reality show or another. It's a special kind of awkward to be at a murder scene and have your mom call you upset that Bachelor Mark, or whoever, picked the wrong woman."

Millie couldn't help but join in with a laugh. Just like she couldn't help imagining the man at a crime scene, notepad in hand, and eyebrows drawn together in deep concentration. For extra effect she imagined his long hair slicked back while the dreary Seattle sky sat as his backdrop.

"Kelby Creek sure has to be a far cry from Seattle."

Foster slowed to a stop at a light. Night was falling and the smell of rain had followed them into the cab of the truck. South Alabama summers only ever had two modes: hot and humid or humid and thunderstorms. Millie hoped no showers were headed their way. The only thing she'd grabbed before leaving her house was a small purse. She could picture her umbrella perfectly in a holder by the door.

"I was eighteen when we first got out to Seattle. Life happened fast there, really fast, for two South Alabama teenagers who'd never been out of the state until then. We got swept up in that pace for a few years. School. Work. More Work. Repeat. I grew a lot, changed a lot, and when we got used to the pace, I realized two things." He ticked off both points on his fingers as he said them. "One, I love being a detective and, despite all of the bad things I've seen, I'd make the same career choice in a heartbeat." Millie heard his mood shift in his tone. Anger. "And, two, even though I left Kelby Creek in my rearview as fast as lightning, I still am extremely protective of it."

"The Flood," she guessed.

He nodded. "I had just wrapped up a particularly nasty homicide and the local paper covered the story. It went from stating the facts about what had happened to my victim's poor family and closing the case for them to how miraculous it was that someone from Kelby Creek could be in law enforcement and not be dirty."

"Ouch."

"Yeah. After that something just clicked for me," he continued. "I reached out to Sheriff Chamblin and said I wanted to help in the rebuild. A week later I had the job."

Millie wanted to say that was noble of the man, but something he said had her stuck so she looped back.

"You said *we* moved to Seattle? Did that person also come back with you?" Millie felt that blush again. She hurried to sound less like a curious teenager and more like a considerate neighbor. "I just mean I've only seen you come and go from the house."

Foster snorted as he turned on the street where Rosewater was located.

"My high school girlfriend and I eloped the second we were both eighteen. It wasn't until we both hit twenty-eight that we finally admitted that was a mistake. We're a whole lot better as friends now. I just wished we'd realized that sooner."

Out of her periphery Millie saw him turn his head to look at her. She didn't rightly know how to react. A part of her felt an unreasonable amount of jealousy surge at the idea of him being married for ten years while the other part of her was cheered at the fact that he was *no longer* married.

Then she thought of Fallon and Jason Talbot and William Reiner.

It was sobering.

"Well, I'll be honest. I'm glad you're here now."

Millie met his eyes. He gave her a small smile, but neither said anything until they were parked in the Rosewater lot.

Foster was all focus. He was already scanning the cars around them, no doubt trying to take in all the details.

Millie should have been too, but what he said next only made the bundle of nerves within her multiply.

"If Reiner is in there, let's not bombard him as soon as we're through the door. Let's treat this like a date and get our own table and drinks first. Then we can go from there. I don't want to spook anyone."

Millie's concentration shattered on the word *date*. It didn't have a chance to recover before Foster was retrieving his blazer.

"Sounds good," she agreed out loud.

Yet inside she was struggling.

*Pretend it's a date, Millie. No big deal*, the angel on her shoulder told her.

Whatever the devil had to say, Millie decided not to listen to it.

THE ROSEWATER BAR had been converted into one long and narrow room. The bar stuck out from one wall while the bathrooms had been tucked to one side at the back. The only door you could go into past those belonged to the kitchen, a straight shot from the former lobby's front doors. Most of the locals knew that through the kitchen was the office where Gavin Junior, current owner of all of Rosewater, did the mundane paperwork part of bar-owning while his bartender would occasionally use the space to smoke a joint.

Only a handful of people knew the secret that connected all three of the spaces.

He moved along the two-by-fours in the attic space above the bar with familiar precision. It wasn't his first time going high to listen to the chatter below, and it wouldn't be the last either.

That didn't mean he wasn't nervous when he walked above the heads of the patrons.

Once he'd misstepped and had seen what could have happened in his mind like a slow-motion horror movie.

One wrong step and he could have very well fallen through the Sheetrock and landed in the laps of the people he'd been listening in on. That, no doubt, would have resulted in him landing somewhere else.

Jail.

Or worse.

It wasn't like Kelby Creek always stuck with following the law.

Another time he'd shuffled along the beams with too much enthusiasm, knocking loose a thin sheet of dust that had floated down onto a table of patrons. Then he'd had to stand still for almost an hour to make sure no more dislodged and drew attention up at him.

Wouldn't that have been a kick in the pants? Everything he'd been working toward, and some ceiling dust gave him and his secret away.

So that night he was careful as he moved along the beams. Methodical in practice, attentive to every single move.

*Slow and steady doesn't win any race. Careful and confident does.*

He replayed this mantra over and over in his head until he was at one of the two vents that hadn't yet been closed since the renovation. They served no other purpose other than being a grated window that looked down into the bar.

Slowly he knelt, making sure no body part was in danger of slipping off a beam, and surveyed that night's crowd, hoping tonight was finally the night.

To say what he saw surprised him was an understatement.

Or, rather, *who* he saw.

Millie was seated at the most popular table along the right wall, situated beneath a neon sign that spelled out Danger, High Voltage and across from a man he didn't recognize. She was wearing her party clothes and had one of Rosewater's Pink Drinks between her hands. From his vantage point he was looking diagonally down at her but could see the smile she was sporting for her date.

He sat there for a while, trying to hear what they were saying but Millie and her companion had the good sense to keep their voices low. Most nights he was lucky to get loud patrons who only became louder the more they drank.

*Check the other vent.*

The mental reminder, since time got lost between the rafters when he became distracted, made him abandon his attempt at eavesdropping. He was careful as he pushed up and walked over to the vent opposite.

This one gave him a better view of the front doors and the middle of the main room.

And William Reiner's usual seat.

Since his wife had left him, William had been a constant at Rosewater. The same beer, the same small table and the same sour face. He never had another soul sitting across from him, and he never was interesting at all.

Tonight would be no exception, he decided.

Plus Millie was there.

And she'd never been there before.

That had to mean something, right?

He went back to the first vent, deciding to put his attention there for the night, but came up short when the table showed empty. He bent lower and tried to see the rest of the room.

Where had they gone?

Like a mouse caught in a maze, he scuttled back over to his only other view into the bar. Millie and her date were probably leaving, though they hadn't been there long. Still, Millie Dean had never been known to spend a lot of time in bars.

Maybe they were going to a late movie or—

"Well, I'll be…"

Millie and the man weren't headed for the front doors but had instead gone straight to another patron's table.

William Reiner's to be specific.

That couldn't be good.

Not after Jason's death.

He pulled out his phone, triple checked that the flash on his camera was turned off, and took the best picture he could through the grates. It wasn't as flattering an angle of Millie but it put her and her date side by side, something he knew would be interesting to his boss.

He tried to stay a while to listen but even with the addition of William the group's volume remained low.

Whatever they were talking about couldn't be heard.

Which made him nervous, and he bet he wasn't the only one.

# *Chapter Nine*

Millie opened her eyes. Pain hit her faster than clarity. The groan that left her mouth was instinctual; rolling over and finding a bucket in time for her Pink Drink to come back up was luck.

If she hadn't been so disoriented *and* in the process of emptying her stomach, she might have felt fear radiate up her spine as a hand touched her back. Instead, all she could focus on was the relief that came after a smooth, deep baritone spoke.

"You're okay. You're okay."

Foster.

It was Foster.

Whatever was going on, it felt nice to know that he was there with her.

But where *was there*?

He shifted behind her, but his hand didn't stop stroking her back until she was done getting sick. Millie would have normally been embarrassed, but confusion, pain and fear had put every normal reaction on the back burner.

She wiped her mouth on the back of her hand and shook her head. The pain that had made her sick swam from the top of her head to behind her eyes.

She didn't understand.

What had happened?

Why had she woken up when she didn't remember ever falling asleep?

Millie let herself be turned back over. Foster helped her to sit up. Her head was foggy. Slushy. Not able to put the clues from around them together to create a picture that made sense. A dim light was coming from a flashlight just beyond her feet on the floor. The light showed a small, small room around them. Not at all what Millie had expected.

Not that she expected anything.

"Wh-what's going on?" she asked, voice hoarse. "Where are we?"

The room was the size of a small bathroom or maybe a large closet. Metal walls had peeling and bubbled-up paint. The floor was cold and in the same poor condition as the walls. Old linoleum squares came up in places, bare in others. An opened box was turned over and empty just beyond the flashlight. A mop was against the wall next to a small window that had been spray-painted black. Then there was the bucket next to her.

That was it.

There was nothing else in the room other than them.

"Are you okay?" Foster didn't answer her question but, based on the blood across his face and his torn shirt, he might not have known how.

He took her face in his hands. It was a gentle movement that Millie appreciated, considering how she felt.

"I—I don't know. My head feels cottony? And it hurts."

"What about the rest of you? Anything else?"

Millie did a quick mental scan of her body.

"Everything else feels normal. What about you? You're bleeding."

He didn't let her face go as Millie reached out and lightly touched his cheek, beneath the blood. For the moment it was just the two of them touching, trying to make sense of something.

"My head also feels off but I'm fine." He ran his thumb across her cheek and let her go, only to then pause his hand in midair. "I definitely fought someone."

He titled his hand so she could see his knuckles. They were busted and bloody.

"I don't understand. *What happened?* The last thing I remembered was being at Rosewater."

It was like someone had rubbed the memory right out of Millie's head. One second she was drinking a Rosewater special drink and coming up with a plan to talk to William Reiner, and the next moment was just gone.

"I think we were drugged." Foster stood with a slight wobble. "I can't remember anything past walking up to Reiner in the bar."

Well, that was more alarming than Millie had expected.

"Drugged? As in things they do in the movies?"

Foster nodded as he walked the few steps over to the mop. Then he was back at her side, reaching down to help her stand.

"It would explain the gaps in memory and how our heads feel," he said. "I'm thinking someone could have spiked our drinks."

Millie was less of a wobble on her feet and more of a stumble. Foster wrapped his arm around her and turned them both around to face the only door in the room.

It was narrow and old, sitting at the top of two stairs. Two *plastic* stairs. The room didn't make sense, not that anything else did, but the feeling of queasiness that was still in the pit of Millie's stomach was familiar.

She didn't place it until Foster had her positioned behind him with the mop handle as her weapon and him with the small flashlight about to try to open the door.

"Foster. I think we're on a boat."

As soon as she said it, Millie knew it was true. The room wasn't a room. It was a cabin. Not only were they on a boat, she was as sure as her motion sickness could be that they were also on the water.

Foster accepted that line of thinking with an even more severe frown.

"The creek is only wide enough for a boat this big at, maybe, three spots. All of those are a good twenty to thirty miles away from anything useful." He shook his head. "It doesn't make sense why we're *here* and not bound or with a captor watching us."

For the first time since gaining consciousness, Millie realized Foster's blazer, gun and badge were nowhere to be seen. Which meant whoever had done this to them could be armed with something that had been meant to protect them.

Foster must have seen the new flare-up of worry.

He closed the space between them and leaned his head down. His forehead touched hers. Warm and reassuring. She could even still smell his cologne. With one hand he held her arm, with the other he motioned to the mop handle. His words came out crystal clear.

"If you need to use this on anyone, when you swing don't imagine hitting them, imagine going *through* them. Okay?"

Millie nodded. It hurt.

Foster's face softened, but he didn't say anything more. He turned back to the door. Millie readied the mop handle like a baseball bat.

She held her breath as Foster tried the door.

It was unlocked. He slid it open slowly but with ease.

Millie tightened her grip on the mop handle, sure someone would be waiting.

Yet, the only thing that came for them was the ambient glow of darkness.

And water.

Millie had been right.

They were on a boat.

A boat that, aside from them, was empty. It was also in the middle of the water. Foster shone the light along a bank and its tree line to their right and then to another bank with more trees to their left. Millie could make out the dark water ahead of them and behind.

"We're anchored," Foster finally said. He turned his attention to a chain off the side of the boat. Millie went to the captain's chair and looked at the engine.

Since she had to have Dramamine in her system to even think about being on a boat, she wasn't that familiar with their intricacies. Still, it was easy to see the key to the ignition was gone. She said as much, and the two of them lapsed into a confused silence. Foster inspected every nook and cranny while Millie tried not to get sick again.

When he seemed to be done, she asked a few of the several questions she was holding on to.

"Why would someone anchor us here? In the middle of the creek, at night, and alone?"

Foster shook his head then shone his light to the tree line to their left. The bank had more sand than the one opposite it.

"One time I got called to the scene of a homicide while I was off duty. It was pouring rain and I got drenched." Millie felt her eyebrow raise at the subject change but then he pointed to his shoes. "I was wearing these, and it took almost a full day for them to completely dry out." He ran his hand along the closest part of the boat to him. Millie realized belatedly that it was wet. It had rained. "They're dry now, which means we were inside when it rained. That might help us with a timeline later."

"I guess it also means we never were *in* the creek," she added. "So does that mean that someone either drove us here and left us or used another boat to get us to this one, which was already anchored?"

Foster shook his head again. Millie wished there was better light for her to see him. His expression now looked haunted, shadows across his features that pulled at her. She went to him, so close that she could smell that cologne again.

"What do we do now?"

Foster moved the beam of light back to the bank.

"We swim for it, go find help, and then bring the entire sheriff's department back out here to tear this boat apart to look for any forensic evidence."

Millie looked out at the dark water.

The motion sickness part of her loved that plan.

The terrified-of-water-she-couldn't-see-through-never-mind-at-night part of Millie got a little weak in the knees.

Foster must have recognized the shift in her.

He surprised her, a feat considering their current situation, and took her hand in his.

"I'll be right next to you the entire time."

Millie would have been lying had she said that didn't make her feel better.

She nodded and winced at the pain.

"If there used to be a ladder here, it's not on board anymore," he said. "Even with the flashlight I can't see the bottom, so I'm going to try to lower myself over so we can figure out how deep it is before you jump in."

"Would it be too much to hope that it's shallow?"

The dark water was a nightmare and a half, waiting with menacing calm.

"Based on the fact there's an anchor, I'm assuming it's at least six feet. I just don't want to take our chances and jump in and break our legs."

Millie conceded to that, even if she wasn't a fan.

He squeezed her hand and then let go.

"That's only about thirty seconds of swimming from here to the bank. We can do this."

Millie knew the pep talk was for her, so she gave him a smile to let him know it landed. In the dim light they had to work with, Foster's green eyes still penetrated with ease. She felt a pang of disappointment when they left her to focus on the task at hand.

The flashlight was passed over to Millie as the detective perched on the side of the boat and then swung his legs over. With an impressive amount of upper body strength, he used his arms to lower himself until he was no longer moving himself down but holding on. Millie leaned over and watched him let go.

The darkness went up to his shoulders before he started treading water.

"Can you touch the bottom?" Millie asked with hope clear in her voice.

He dipped down, the water going to his chin, before popping back up.

"No dice. Whoever picked this spot knew it was deep."

Millie's fear response might not have liked it but her stomach was reminding her that she needed to get to land sooner rather than later. She passed the flashlight down to Foster and finally let go of the mop.

She had never been the fastest swimmer, but she was pretty sure she was about to temporarily acquire Olympic-level speed as soon as she hit the water.

Knowing she couldn't do the cool, strong man way of getting in like Foster had, Millie sat on the edge and threw her legs over until she was sitting. Foster stayed close as she did a little hop off.

The water was surprisingly warm. Foster reached out to try to keep her above the water, but Millie's spaz level at being in the dark water made her move more than she meant to. Her head went under in an instant.

It felt like a second went by.

Just one.

Yet it was enough time to take their already tilted world and turn it upside down.

FOSTER WASN'T A MAN to believe in luck, good or not. It was an old fight he'd had with his ex-wife, Regina, from age fifteen when she had called him lucky to land a girlfriend like her to the day they signed the divorce papers and she cited their marriage had ended because of bad luck.

Good, bad, or anything in between, luck was just what you called the timing of something based on the outcome.

It wasn't good luck that Jason Talbot had found Millie alone in her home when he'd gone to question her about Fallon, just as it wasn't bad luck that he'd shown up minutes before Foster had.

Luck was the ripple effect of actions. Consequences of actions, whether accidental or intentional.

However, in the dark creek water, next to an abandoned boat he'd woken up on—after most likely being drugged—and treading next to a beautiful woman who had just resurfaced, Foster's disbelief in luck sank to the bottom.

Actual, physical ripples spread across the top of the water, diverting around Millie as she took a breath.

The ripples weren't coming *from* her but toward her.

Foster clicked off the flashlight.

Millie made a noise but something else farther off was louder.

Foster propelled himself backward in the water. Instead of turning toward the bank, he looked around the front end of the boat where the creek remained wide and snaked out of view around a bend of trees.

The fleeting existential crisis of bad and good luck warred within him as he moved back to Millie, careful not to move too much.

Millie's eyes were wide.

She'd heard it too.

It was good luck that Millie had gone overboard with as little sound as she had.

It was bad luck that they hadn't left for the woods sooner.

"A boat," he whispered, water lapping in his mouth while he took Millie's body in his arms and pulled her along with him. "We need to hide."

# Chapter Ten

The second boat had at least two passengers.

Foster could hear their footfalls as they stepped onto the plastic flooring overhead. They'd docked their boat alongside the craft Foster and Millie had woken up on.

Had they come back for Foster and Millie?

Why had they left them in the first place?

There were too many questions and, while Foster was quick to let everyone know he loved a challenge, this wasn't what he'd meant.

One set of footsteps came closer to their side of the boat. Foster felt Millie's entire body tense against him. He probably wasn't faring much better. His muscles were all working toward two purposes. To keep Millie against the side of the boat as best he could and to be ready if their hiding place was spotted. Though he wished he could tell her with confidence that everything would be okay.

That this was all just some weird misunderstanding. That help was on its way and everything would be fine.

But he couldn't.

They were in a wild, unpredictable situation.

One he couldn't have imagined had he sat down at his desk and been told to try.

So if he couldn't promise her a good ending, he was

going to make sure she knew he was going to fight for it at the very least. That included keeping her safe.

He pulled her against him with one hand so she didn't have to keep treading water and tightened his grip on a small, busted light protruding from the side of the boat.

However, even that play had its set of problems.

If the newcomers—whoever they were—looked out at the bank Foster and Millie had been about to make their way to, they would see nothing but water, sand and trees.

If they looked over the side of the boat and down, they'd see Foster and Millie trying to stay as still as possible in the deep, dark water.

Foster just hoped that they weren't that thorough. And that the other boat stayed on the opposite side of them.

"Be careful."

It was a man's voice, deep and with a thick Southern drawl that saturated the three short syllables. He was the one closer to them. Thankfully, he didn't seem too interested in inspecting further.

The other set of footsteps softened.

They'd gone down into the cabin.

It didn't take long for those same footsteps to come back topside.

"There's no one in there."

The second voice also belonged to a man. There was less twang to it. Foster also didn't recognize it.

"I don't believe it." The Southern drawl turned angry. His footsteps changed course as he must have gone to double-check his partner. He took a bit longer in his search and was none the happier when he was back outside.

"Someone got sick down there," he said matter-of-factly. "Which means *someone* was down there."

"Well, they sure ain't there now, are they?"

Foster stared into the warmth of Millie's eyes as the sound of a punch went through the night air. The receiver of the hit groaned. Foster's guess was it was the one who had less twang.

"You think this is all some kind of video game, don't you?" the Southern drawler said, voice raised so much that Foster didn't have to strain to hear him. "That every little damn hurdle we've hit is just a minor inconvenience. That all we have to do is go lay next to a beautiful woman and call it a day and everything resets in the morning."

There was movement again.

Foster wasn't sure but he bet it was another hit.

"This ain't a game, son. If it was, we'd be losing to a much better player." He muttered something, but it got lost in the distance between him and the water. Though Foster hazarded that it probably wasn't poetry.

A sigh broke the rant and seemed to help Southern Drawl calm himself down enough not to hit his partner again.

"That woman said she saw those two get muscled into the truck," he continued. "This is where he took Fallon, so this has to be where he'd have taken them."

Foster had dealt with the intersection of death and surprise for years during his career in Seattle. He'd been the one to notify a family member of their loved one's demise, and he'd been the one to take the confession of a killer in the interrogation room. Not every case was so cut-and-dried and not every one was about homicide, but from his time dealing with it all, Foster had picked up a skill that kicked into gear the moment Fallon's name had been said aloud.

It was knowing the gravity of the look on Millie's face at the mention of her brother.

That instinctual feeling a person had when something life-changing had been said. That piece of information or string of words that, once spoken, could never be unheard.

Millie had felt it.

And Foster knew the second she had.

Millie had a new lead to go on. An answer, just waiting for a question.

A question she was ready to ask, even if it meant putting herself in danger.

Foster leaned his head over so it pressed against her forehead.

*No*, he mouthed.

He wasn't sure if she saw it, but she kept quiet as the men kept talking.

"Someone puked down there so someone *was* here." This time it was the second man. The younger man, Foster decided. "He either came back for them or some drunk has been staying here and couldn't hold his liquor. Either way, what do you want us to do now?"

There was another sigh.

It deflated as fast as Foster heard the *third* boat.

The engine on it was in no way stealthy and sounded waterlogged and labored in the distance.

It also wasn't expected by the men above them. The younger one's voice split between obvious excitement and fear.

"Oh man, do you think it's him?"

The older man wasn't as thrilled. He also wasn't as loud.

Foster could hear that he was whispering but couldn't hear what he was saying.

Millie nudged his head with hers. He felt her shrug against him.

Even if they could talk, he didn't have answers for her.

Though that was going to change soon enough.

They waited as the men above them became quiet. Foster wasn't big on boats, but he knew enough to take a guess that the approaching one was much smaller than both crafts it was steering toward.

The person driving the boat stopped.

Ripples moved across the water.

Millie placed her hand against Foster's chest.

He didn't have to hear her to know she was thinking one thing.

Was Fallon the man on the other boat?

Or the man who had brought Fallon here before?

"Howdy there, guys."

Unlike the other two men, Foster recognized this voice in an instant.

Deputy Carlos Park.

"I was out looking for a buddy of mine and was wondering if you could help me?"

His voice echoed clearly around them. The same as Southern Drawl's.

"Well, howdy yourself, Deputy. We're just fishing, is all, I'm afraid. No one but us out here."

They knew the deputy?

Park asked exactly what Foster was wondering himself.

"I'm sorry but have we met before?" the deputy asked. "What's your name? The light on your boat isn't helping me get a clear view of you."

"Everybody in town knows who the law are," Southern Drawl replied. "You know, what with everything that's happened."

That took the conversation and made it stall. Deputy Park must have been trying to decide on what to do next. Foster wished he could see the men on the boat just like he wished he could see if they were armed.

Also, he might not have liked Deputy Park all that much, but he was a colleague. One who hadn't been found guilty or run during The Flood.

That should have counted for something.

And it did in Foster's book.

When the silence overhead saturated the air, fraught

with tension he could feel all the way in the water, Foster made a few decisions of his own in rapid succession.

The first required the risk of making noise, but he had a feeling that group of men were focused on their conversation more than the water. He held his breath as he moved the hand he had around Millie and pushed her gently closer to the boat than him.

The ambient light of night had put a slight glow on the woman. Her eyes were still warm in the shadows it created. They let him know in no uncertain terms that she understood what he was trying to convey. Slowly she moved her hand up to the busted light Foster was using as a handhold. He kept her floating until she had a purchase on it.

Then he let go of both her and the light.

The men on the boat had started talking about their lie of fishing while, Foster suspected, Deputy Park was doing his own fishing for information. Or more time.

He could have been stalling, waiting for backup.

Or he could see that one or both of the men were armed and wasn't comfortable in a shoot-out over the water.

Either way no one seemed to notice the lapping of water as Foster came free of the boat.

Which was good because he needed some surprise on his side.

*Stay. Here*, he mouthed to Millie.

She nodded.

It was all the encouragement he needed.

Foster moved as quietly through the water as he could, keeping his arms and legs beneath the surface while propelling him to the back end of the boat. Whatever light was on the strangers' craft was enough to show Foster Deputy Park's position.

And his body language. It might as well have screamed that he was about to pull his gun even though he was alone. His hand hovered by his holster.

It was now or never.

Foster went to the busted engine. Its casing was cracked and crusted. The lip around it that led into the boat wasn't in the best of shape. The abandoned vessel was definitely a junker. Foster just hoped when he put his weight on the lip that it didn't break off completely. Trying to back up the deputy only to fall *back* into the water definitely wasn't ideal.

But could he get onto the boat without making any noise?

Absolutely not.

Would his sudden appearance cause him to draw fire from the deputy he was trying to help and the two potentially armed men?

Probably.

Foster did it anyway.

One second he was in the water and the next water was pouring off him and into the back of the boat.

The lip of the boat cracked before he was standing tall. Foster yelled out he was from the sheriff's department, but he wasn't about to stop to make sure they heard him correctly.

The two men who had boarded were standing a few feet apart. One glance in their direction showed both had guns. The man closer to Foster—the older one judging by the gray hair in a halo around his balding head—had a holster on his hip while his partner, a stout man with black hair and an outfit that looked like he was about to go golfing at the country club, had a shotgun down and resting against his leg.

Deputy Park *was* waiting for backup. Or, at least Foster assumed that was the case because as soon as the deputy saw him, he was the first to react. Which was good considering the younger man went for his shotgun like he aimed to use it. Foster couldn't let that happen.

He used his momentum to go for the older man, hoping to use him like Millie had used the bag of laundry against Jason Talbot, but his shoes couldn't get any traction. Foster stumbled into the older man and hit him at the knees. Instead of bowling over into his partner, they went down to the deck hard.

Then Foster did something on instinct.

He put absolute faith in Deputy Park. Instead of scrambling to get out of the way of the younger stranger's shotgun, Foster turned his attention to fighting the older man to keep his gun in his holster.

When the gunshot exploded through the air but Foster felt no pain, he realized he'd made the right choice.

The younger man toppled over. The shotgun hit the deck with a clatter, but Foster couldn't go for it yet. He had his hand fastened over the butt of the older man's gun and was actively punching him in the gut. Foster had to give it to the man, he was tough. He took each hit with a grunt before delivering his own.

The sound of water displacing synced with the older man landing a frustratingly accurate hit. His fist went into the section of bruised ribs that he'd gotten from Jason's bullet. While it mostly didn't hurt anymore while doing mundane tasks, getting hit square in those ribs by a man desperate for his gun made Foster roar in agony.

Which was probably why he didn't realize at first that Deputy Park *wasn't* the new arrival on deck.

Millie drove her fist down from the heavens with such quiet swiftness that neither Foster nor the older man saw it coming. For the rest of Foster's life, he doubted he'd ever see such a beautiful hit.

The older man recoiled from the force and, to everyone's surprise, he went limp.

Millie Dean had just knocked out a man with a sucker

punch that was so precise that it could have taught its own class.

Foster wanted to praise her then and there, but he was hyperaware that they needed to get two guns away from the men.

"The shotgun," he breathed out, pain still radiating up his side.

Millie nodded, cradling her hand, and took possession of the discarded weapon as Foster pulled the handgun free of the older man's holster. She jumped back as the younger man groaned.

"Keep it on him but don't shoot," Foster directed her. He was slower to stand, but when he did, he was at her side, gun trained on the unconscious man just in case.

"Are you okay?" Millie asked, voice wobbling. Most likely from excess adrenaline.

Foster nodded. "What about you?"

"My hand hurts but I'm okay."

Foster snorted. "That was an amazing hit," he admitted. "Especially considering I told you to stay in the water."

Millie laughed. It too was a wobbling sound.

Someone cleared their throat.

Foster turned to see Deputy Park, gun hanging down at his side and mouth open like a fish trying to breathe out of the water.

He shook his head, eyes wide.

*"What in the hell, y'all?"*

# *Chapter Eleven*

Millie was ready to leave the hospital, the doctor disagreed.

"You're in observation until I say otherwise," he'd told her with quite a stern look.

The tone, and look, had been deserved though, if she was being honest. Since they'd been brought to Haven Hospital, Millie had been ready to go to the department and question the man who had spoken about Fallon. Being drugged, losing almost eight hours of memory, and waking up sick after being dumped out in an abandoned boat thirty miles away from where they'd started at the bar?

Well, those details were irrelevant in Millie's opinion.

The man talking about Fallon was not.

Millie had been itching for the sheriff to change their course from the hospital to the department while driving her and Foster away from the dock where Deputy Park had sequestered the small boat. He'd been a steadfast *no* against forgoing a medical exam.

Foster had agreed with the man, though Millie could tell that the detective wanted to go and detect.

She could also tell that he was in pain.

He'd opted to sit in the back of the truck next to her, saying it was to save the sheriff's passenger's side seat from their wet clothes, but Millie suspected he was still trying to protect her.

Not that she minded one bit.

There might have been a lot of questions in the air around them, but there was one point of fact that was easy for her to admit.

She trusted Foster.

That was a rare thing for Millie, a phenomenon that wasn't lost on her.

Still, once they were at the hospital she tried her best to hurry the process of being examined, despite the detective telling her that they'd get the truth soon enough. The sheriff attempted to reassure her in private before they left.

"I've known that man in there since he was a baby," Sheriff Chamblin had said to her. "He's not the kind of person to let something go. Most times that's a great asset for a detective but, for a man who's just been beaten, drugged and shot all within the last week, it's not helping him." Sheriff Chamblin had taken off his cowboy hat with an acute look of concern. "I know you aren't a fan of the department and have a history with a lot of the town, but that man in there? He hasn't let you down an inch since you've met him. I'm pretty sure if you asked Love to go take on an army right now, he'd do it. Return the favor and make sure he gets the care and rest he needs to get better. In the meantime, I swear to you that we will do everything in our power to get to the bottom of this."

Millie would have taken offense at the implication that she was the one standing in the way of Foster's well-being, but the sheriff's words were heartfelt and genuine. So, she'd decided to calm down on her own.

"I'll make sure he listens to the doctor," she'd promised. "But, when we're out of here, y'all better not cut me out of this."

Sheriff Chamblin had put his cowboy hat back atop his head. Then he'd tipped it to her.

"Yes, ma'am."

After that, Millie had been a good patient, all the while keeping her impatience as quiet as possible. She'd given Foster space while the doctor saw to him in his room.

Now, a few hours later, Millie's resolve was breaking.

She peeked out of her room and into the hallway. A deputy named Lawrence was stationed down the hallway in the second-floor lobby. Foster had said they'd been assigned someone just in case another attack came their way. Yet Millie now saw that same man distracted by his phone. Had she not wanted to sneak into the detective's room, she might have been offended. She padded across the short space and was inside the room without a fuss.

It wasn't until she turned around and saw Foster standing at the foot of the hospital bed in nothing but his jeans that Millie realized she should have knocked.

She was also painfully aware of her less-than-flattering hospital gown.

"I—I should have knocked," she said in a stammer.

Millie intended to avert her eyes from his bare chest but, well, that's not what happened.

Not at all.

Millie already knew the detective was attractive. She'd already admitted that to herself, and she'd already had some stray, somewhat inappropriate carnal thoughts, but standing there, caught in a candid moment, Millie couldn't help but stare.

After they'd gotten to the hospital and been put into rooms, both had taken showers. Millie's makeup was gone, her hair was free and frizzy, and her right hand was scabbed and bandaged.

Foster, however, was a sight to behold.

His hair was dry now and waved to his shoulders, wild and golden even under the hospital fluorescents. The color matched the stubble along his jaw and the dusting of hair that went from his chest down to beneath his waistband.

And that chest. Millie had felt the man's muscled body against hers in the water. Logically she knew how his body must have looked beneath his clothes.

Yet the lean muscles that went from biceps to abs gave her such great pause that, for a moment, she felt like she was caught in mental quicksand. Sinking lower and lower, in danger of getting completely lost.

Luckily, or not so much, it was the same bare skin that had her transfixed that pulled her out of her fascination.

"Oh my God."

Millie closed the distance between them with concern replacing appreciation in a flash. Her eyes locked in on his side.

"Is this where you were shot?"

It was unlike any bruise Millie had ever seen before. Dark and angry. Wide and unavoidable.

It looked absolutely painful.

Foster laughed. It was a light sound. It didn't feel right next to such ugliness.

"*And* where our friend Southern Drawl decided to hit me during our tussle. If I'd been a carnival game, he'd have walked away with an oversized stuffed monkey as a prize for hitting the bull's-eye."

He was trying to be funny about it, dismissive, but seeing the horrible mark made Millie realize just how bad it would have been had Foster not been wearing his vest.

She reached out and felt his warm skin beneath her fingertips. She was careful, gentle.

"You could have died." Millie's voice had hollowed. For the first time since he'd disappeared, the worry for her brother was moved aside. "You could have died because of me, Foster. And not just once. The woods, Jason Talbot, Rosewater, the creek... You wouldn't have been in any of those situations if it weren't for me."

His hand was warm as it enveloped hers. Together they

rested against his side. When he spoke, she could feel it through his body.

"You didn't pull the trigger, you didn't attack me and you didn't drug me and then dump me on a boat. Trust me. None of this was your fault."

"I'm the common denominator," she said simply. "And I'm so sorry."

Foster took his other hand and used it to angle her gaze to his. She noticed belatedly that he had a shirt in his grip. He could have been holding a flamethrower instead and she still would have kept her focus on his eyes.

"It's easy to blame yourself when you don't know who the real blame falls to." His smile was small. A whisper, almost. It brought her attention to his lips but not before being pulled right back up into those true green eyes. "And, by my count, you've been doing your fair share of having my back out there. Not many people I know, women or men, would take their chances at going against two armed men soaking wet. Never mind knocking one out cold with a picture-perfect punch. Who taught you how to hit like that anyway?"

Millie tried not to but she grinned.

"You did." Foster's eyebrow rose. "I just used what you told me to do with the mop. The whole 'imagine going through them' when you hit someone with a thing." She shrugged. "I figured it probably applied to humans too and not just mop handles."

Foster let go of her chin. His laugh lit up all of his features. Millie smiled along with him.

"Millie Dean, you are a surprise and a half. God sure broke the mold with you."

The warmth of a blush made its way to her cheeks.

"I don't know about that, but I'll take the compliment all the same." She cleared her throat as she pulled her hand away from the man. Then she took a small step back. She finally averted her eyes and motioned to the shirt he was holding. "Also, sorry I barged in here just now. I should have knocked. I didn't mean to catch you dressing. I guess I was starting to feel a little cramped…and a lot impatient just waiting around in bed."

Foster waved off her apology. Then he sighed. "To be honest I was considering a jail break myself. Since I already got some sleep to make the doctor calm down, I figured I could get away with leaving."

"Oh?" Millie forgot to give the man privacy again. She snapped her head back toward him so quick, her hair shifted against her back. "Did you hear anything new?"

It was a generalized question, but she couldn't figure out which one to present first.

"I've been told that they found some new information but not what. Yet." He took his shirt and started to put it on. "So I figured I'd be harder to sidestep if I was in front of them."

Millie watched as he looped the T-shirt over his head and then paused before pulling it down.

He was stuck.

Millie reached out again, this time uncertain.

"Do you—"

"I've got it," he said, cutting her off with unmistakable male stubbornness.

Foster curled the shirt down to his shoulders. His face contorted as he paused again.

"Are you sure?"

He nodded. "I took a bullet to the vest and fought a man two days later. I think I can handle putting on a shirt."

Foster struggled on.

Millie held in a giggle.

When someone knocked on the door, the playfulness went away.

Millie took the bottom of his shirt in her hands and pulled down to cover his stomach. Foster didn't fight it.

"Come in," he called when his stomach was covered.

Millie put more space between them but didn't get too far. Their closeness was enough to draw a glance between them by the new arrival.

"Deputy Lawrence said I could come in."

The woman was a bouquet of color. From her patchwork blouse, red slacks, blue-striped hair and purple lipstick, she ate up the drabness of her surroundings with ease. It made Millie once again self-conscious of her gown and its garbage bag vibes.

"It's fine." Foster motioned between Millie and her. "Millie Dean, this is Dr. Amanda Alvarez, Dr. Alvarez, this is Millie Dean."

The doctor's height allowed her less than three strides before she was shaking Millie's hand.

"You can call me Amanda," she said, all smiles. "I'm the new Dawn County coroner."

"Oh! I read about you in the paper when you were hired," Millie said. "You're the youngest coroner in Kelby Creek history."

Amanda laughed. "That wasn't a hard feat considering I'm pretty sure the man I replaced had a personal relationship with the dinosaurs."

Millie had never met the former coroner but knew he was one of the many who had lost their jobs during The Flood. He'd been suspected of doctoring some of his reports in favor of keeping certain friends in places of power. Though, on the spot, Millie couldn't remember the specifics past that. Still, she laughed at the joke. A lot of the first round of people fired or incarcerated had been Kelby Creek's older, more prominent members.

"So what brings you out of the basement?" Foster swept his hand wide to the love seat next to the bed, offering her a seat. Amanda raised her hand to decline without saying the words.

"I'm actually here because your doctor has the hots for me." Foster shared a confused look with Millie. Amanda continued. "When he confirmed you two had been drugged with the same meds that had been found in Jason Talbot's possession the night he died, he came down to the basement and asked if Jason had had the same meds in his system. Unlike my predecessor, I told him I couldn't discuss the details about an ongoing investigation. And that seemed to be all I needed to say for *him* to start telling me about the details he knew."

Amanda took a step closer. On reflex Millie and Foster took a step in closer too. The doctor didn't lower her voice when she continued, but there was a quickness to her words. An excitement.

"Most of what he said, I had already heard through the grapevine of nurses and deputies hanging around when you were first brought in, *but* he told me something I wanted to make sure you knew. But first, can I see your hands?"

The question was to Foster. Again, he shared a look with Millie. Then he held up his hands. Amanda was quick to take them in hers to inspect.

"I heard you don't remember what happened between the bar and waking up on the boat, right?"

"Right."

"But your hands were busted like this when you regained consciousness but not when you first arrived at the bar."

Foster nodded. "Right again. Though I fought on the boat after."

Amanda poked one of Foster's knuckles. Some were still scabbed, some were still in the process due to his most recent fight. She looked thoughtful for a moment.

Then she nodded, seemingly to herself. She dropped his hands.

"I'm no detective and I certainly don't know the full extent of the case and what's going on right now—"

"But?"

Foster went from friendly to professional in an instant. Millie couldn't blame him. He'd caught a scent.

Another piece of the puzzle.

Something that might lead them to the rest.

"You obviously hit someone," she said. "Hard enough to bust your knuckles. That suggests you either hit them so hard in one go that it broke the skin or, more likely, you dealt several blows."

"Yeah, I'm guessing I landed multiple hits. Why is that of interest?"

"Normally it wouldn't be, but from what I've heard? Neither of the men who were brought in with you this morning had any bruising or marks across their bodies other than the fresh hits."

Millie watched as realization dawned across Foster's face.

"What does that mean?" she asked, not quite there with him yet.

Amanda opened her mouth to answer, but Foster beat her to it.

"It means that whoever I fought during our missing gaps of memory definitely wasn't one of the men on the boat."

"If you have a suspect already, I'd also go see if they're sporting a new shiner," Amanda added. "Because I'm pretty sure a guy like you left a mark."

Millie's stomach went tight as she met Foster's gaze.

"The sheriff told us on the drive here that he had already questioned William Reiner when we went missing," she said. "But did he say if Reiner had any bruising?"

Foster broke their huddle and went to the hospital

phone next to the bed since their personal cell phones were still missing.

"No," he said, dialing a number. "But I'm sure about to ask."

# Chapter Twelve

"And then she rose out of the water like Swamp Thing!"

Deputy Park sprung up from behind his desk and waved his hands at this audience in the sheriff department's bull-pen for effect.

Foster cleared his throat.

Millie shifted at his side.

Deputy Park, however, didn't look like he'd been caught bad-mouthing the woman. If anything, he seemed excited to see them both. A distinct change from his past behaviors, that was for sure.

"Honestly, I've never seen anything so cool!" He was grinning from ear to ear. He addressed Millie directly. "I mean I had barely recovered from the detective here popping out of the water like a salmon going upstream, but then you rocked my world. It was some James Bond, spy-craft-type stuff if I ever did see it."

Foster smiled at Millie. Mostly because he agreed. He might not have seen the woman go through the motions, but he'd definitely benefited from her actions.

"I was just trying to help," she said shyly.

Deputy Park wasn't hiding his admiration.

"You didn't just help, you probably saved *someone*'s life out there."

Foster recognized the profound relief that flitted across

the deputy's face as he put emphasis on "someone." It was brief but poignant. He wasn't spelling it out to Millie but, had she not helped, there was a good chance that Deputy Park would have had to take a kill shot had one of the men, or both, managed to take up their guns. Which meant there was a high chance that she'd saved him from his first causality in the line of duty.

Now Park was grateful, and Foster wasn't at all surprised by that.

"And if you hadn't shown up, things could have been a lot worse for us," Foster pointed out.

Park shrugged.

"If the Good Samaritan hadn't seen you two get taken and called it in, we wouldn't have known you were missing for a while," the deputy said.

"But you took that extra time they gave you, found tire tracks, and decided to check the water. That's good work. No matter which way you slice it." Park took the compliment with a smile. Foster followed it up with a question he was itching to ask. "Is the sheriff in his office?"

To say they all had questions was an understatement. Foster had been compiling and updating his own list of questions since he'd met Millie. The last twenty-four hours had just extended that list to an uncomfortable length for him. Calling from the hospital to ask the sheriff about William Reiner was just another drop in the question bucket. Maybe that was why Chamblin hadn't fought Foster's desire to leave the hospital earlier than he was supposed to.

"We have questions and we have answers," Chamblin had said, heavy on the vague. "If the good doc is okay with you leaving, then I'd like to use that brain of yours."

Foster and Millie's doctor hadn't been that thrilled at the idea, but Amanda had stuck around to help convince him.

"They're going to the sheriff's department, not a rave," she'd pointed out. "Worst case they pass out among trained professionals, best case they figure out who did this to them and why. But if it sweetens the pot, I will personally go check in on them after my shift."

The doctor had relented—and complimented Amanda's outfit—and added in his off-the-record comment that he believed they'd be fine.

"There's no lingering effects of the drugs, and any physical injuries you obtained were only superficial," he'd said, trying to keep his gaze from settling on his coroner crush. "That said, my unsolicited advice for the near future? If you're looking for leads at a bar, maybe make your own drinks."

That had put fire in Foster's veins. Mostly because he'd been benched while the sheriff's department had gone over every inch of Rosewater and the boat. Including in-depth interviews of staff and patrons. Specifically the bartender.

Foster and Millie had been drugged at almost the same time and, since there were no needle marks anywhere on their bodies, it all boiled down to their drinks.

That was enough to make anyone's skin crawl or, at the very least, uncomfortable, so Foster had felt the need to offer Millie an out.

"I have it on good authority that Deputy Lawrence talks a lot but that he's a good man to have on watch," Foster had told Millie in the hallway after. "He can take you home and keep an eye out while I try to work this at the department."

Millie had been adamant in her short response.

"No way, bud," she'd been quick to say. "We're partners in this now, whether you like it or not."

Foster had had partners before back in Seattle but found that Millie's statement elicited a different kind of reaction from him. But he put that thought on the back burner. It was still sitting there, waiting for more time for him to think on it later, when Deputy Park nodded.

"He's in there with his fifth cup of joe," Park said. "In

my nonprofessional opinion? We'd all benefit if a shot or two of whiskey finds its way into his cup."

Foster bet he was right.

Chamblin had come out of semiretirement to become the interim sheriff to help his community, to help his home. To rebuild the department so he could leave it again and be happy with the results. Now he was drenched in a sea of unknowns, and Foster was sure he was getting mighty tired of just treading water.

"Let's drop our stuff off in my office," Foster said, turning toward his closed door.

Chamblin had taken the time to pack a quick bag for Foster when they thought they'd be at the hospital overnight. Larissa, Millie's best friend, had done the same for her. Both had had to use their hidden spare keys, considering Foster and Millie hadn't just lost their memory from the bar, they'd also been stripped of their keys, wallets and cell phones. Millie had mourned the abduction of her purse maybe even more than her own abduction. Then again, Foster understood the grief the first time she'd realized she'd probably never see her things again.

"Fallon's sixth grade school picture was in my wallet," she'd said, voice quiet. "It was my only copy."

Now she was quiet again. Though it was more introspective than upset.

"I can't believe I was sitting in here a week ago." She set her bag down on the love seat that was crammed into the corner of the office. The piece of furniture was worn and cracked leather, a welcome hand-me-down gift from Chamblin since he knew Foster sometimes spent the night at work when on a case. "It feels like a lot longer."

He chuckled because she was absolutely right.

"You know, growing up I thought Kelby Creek was the most mind-numbingly boring place on the planet. Now here I am with more excitement than a year in Seattle."

He checked the top drawer to make sure Fallon's file was still inside. It was. "I guess it goes to show you that even small towns aren't as sleepy as the movies would have you believe. I'd love some boring right now."

A smile passed over Millie's lips but it didn't last. Instead, she followed him down the hall to the sheriff's office, tension lining every move as she went.

They had answers to get. Foster just hoped they weren't all bad.

"Well, if it's not good to see you two up and about." Chamblin greeted them with his, apparently, fifth cup of coffee in hand. He used it to motion to the door. "Let's get rolling and go ahead into the interview room where we can start mapping this all out."

The interview room? Where they interrogated suspects?

Foster raised his eyebrow at that but followed orders. He got to the door first and let Millie in. Chamblin caught him before he followed.

"Hey, Love, I need you to do me something before we start." His voice dropped so low that Millie couldn't hear.

It tipped Foster off to the fact that he wasn't going to like whatever it was the sheriff was about to ask of him. Millie gave them privacy and took one of the two chairs on either side of the metal table.

Foster didn't like the look of her sitting in the same place criminals were usually handcuffed. He shrugged off the feeling and looked his boss in the eye.

"And what's that?"

"Did Miss Dean ever tell you why she believed the note her brother left was a fake?"

It was such an out of the blue question that Foster took a beat. The sheriff misread his hesitation.

"Listen, Love, I get that you two have been through more thick and thin together than most partners on the force, but I can't just let a civilian into an investigation.

Especially not knowing some pretty key facts, like the main reason why she's been looking for a runaway for six months only to have mud slung into the fan the first day we get a new detective in here. For all we know she can be in on this *with* her brother."

There was no hesitation this time.

"No dice there, Sheriff. I may not know what's going on yet, but I do know I trust her."

Chamblin ran his hand along his chin, thinking. The older man wasn't convinced.

"Give me some truth I can work with then. Get her to tell us exactly why she is the only one who thinks Fallon Dean has been in trouble for the last six months, and then I'll tell you why you might not be so quick to trust her."

IT HAD BEEN humid outside, hot too. The Alabama sun was nice to lay out in, but for Millie, that's where her love for it started and stopped.

Inside the interrogation room of the sheriff's department was surprisingly cold. Goose bumps rose up along her arms and pricked up across her legs beneath her jeans. She thought to let her hair down to give the back of her neck some warmth, but Millie wasn't sure the cold in her was all the air conditioner's fault.

Not after the stone-faced Foster took a seat in the metal chair across from her.

And the sheriff didn't come in at all.

Something had changed.

Foster had changed.

He'd gone impassive, unreadable. Just like the first day they'd met with her sitting across from him, frustrated and angry that no one would believe her.

Those feelings tried to come back now.

Millie tamped them down.

After everything she and Foster had been through, she couldn't imagine he didn't believe her.

Unless…

Had something happened while they were in the hospital?

"Miss Dean, I need to ask you something to help clarify a few things for us."

If Millie hadn't seen his lips move, she wouldn't have thought the monotone voice had come from the detective at all.

She glanced behind him at the mirror.

The sheriff must have been behind it. Watching.

Millie felt a wash of embarrassment at not catching on sooner.

They weren't just in the interrogation room to talk. They were in there to question her.

Millie tried to keep the hurt out of her voice as she relented.

"What do you need to know that I haven't already told the department?"

It might have been her imagination, but she could have sworn the detective's jaw hardened. Though the question that followed was a simple one.

"Why do you think the note your brother left you six months ago was fake?"

Millie couldn't help it.

She sighed. Not because she didn't know the answer but because she'd already had this conversation with Detective Gordon. Which meant that the department must not have believed her answer.

Would Foster?

A part of Millie didn't want to know.

If he didn't, then he was just like everyone else.

That was something she couldn't overlook, even after the brushes with danger they'd had together.

"Millie?" he prodded. His golden hair and bright green eyes were harsher beneath the room's hard light. "Can you tell me?"

"Yes. I can and I will, *again*." Her words were harsh too, but Foster was a stone wall. Unmoving and unfazed.

Millie made an effort to soften in comparison, though not by a lot. The story she was about to tell was a long, emotional one.

But it was also the only way to get to her reason.

The reason she knew her brother was in trouble.

"My dad once said that when he met my mom, for the first time, the entire world came into focus," she began. "That up until then the world hadn't been wrong, per se, it had just felt off. My mom was cheesier when she talked about them. *She* said that meeting my dad was like finding the part of her that had been missing, the part that made her whole. Basically they believed they were soul mates. And from what I can remember, I think I could believe that."

Millie paused, just enough to see if Foster planned on interjecting. Wondering why she was talking about her parents being in love, no doubt. Detective Gordon had fussed about it immediately when she'd first told him the story. Foster, however, nodded for her to continue. So, she did.

"That love really carried over to Fallon and me when it came to my dad. He wanted to be, and was, involved in almost every part of our lives. Even when work got in the way, he made sure to always let us know he was there for us. See, he was an adjunct professor of biology at the local community college. He was a big believer in expanding the mind. 'You should never stop trying to learn' was a big motto of his."

Pain, old and profound, started to wake up within her chest. A monster stretching after its hibernation. Millie rolled her shoulders back, trying to physically distance herself from it.

She knew from experience it wouldn't work.

Nothing really would.

"When Fallon was eight he came home so upset," she continued. "It was his first day of elementary school, and he'd found out that they weren't teaching cursive anymore as part of their curriculum. You know, me as a thirteen-year-old didn't get what the big deal was but my dad? He commiserated with Fallon and made him a Dean family promise. He'd teach Fallon cursive himself because you should never stop learning, you know?"

This time Millie couldn't help but shift her entire body. The cold from the room seeped deeper. It burrowed into her bones.

"Dad decided to start teaching Fallon before his Wednesday night class. Since it was a small campus and everyone knew and loved my dad, no one ever really cared that sometimes he would pick us up after school and let us sit in on his class until it was finished. He just really loved spending time with us, even if it was just being in the same room as we did our homework." Millie smiled. It didn't last. "I was out of town on a field trip the afternoon that Jim Mallory decided to take an assault rifle to campus."

Tears pricked at her eyes already. Her throat started to burn. Millie continued anyway while Foster remained impassive.

"He was angry and fast and made it to half of the science department classrooms before he was killed by an off-duty cop. In that time Dad took three bullets shielding Fallon, and he died before the ambulance was even en route."

Millie's vision started to swim. Her chest was tight. Some memories destroyed you, even if they weren't all yours.

"What about Fallon? Was he injured?"

Foster's voice had lost some of the even edge it had when he'd started. It helped bring Millie back to the present.

She cleared her throat and shook her head.

"No, but the damage was more than done," she continued. "It took twenty minutes for authorities to lock down and clear the campus. Fallon spent those twenty minutes holding my dad while he bled out. He wouldn't even leave him when the EMTs came in. One of my dad's colleagues had to physically carry him away so they could do their job." Millie felt relief that that part of the story was done. She knew she could make it through the rest with no problem now. "My mom... Well, she never recovered. I mean we were all devastated, but Mom, she just shattered. I didn't realize it until later, but she was just going through the motions of being a parent after that. She became more like a ghost who haunted the house. An echo of someone who loved us that faded even more every day. If it wasn't for Fallon, I wouldn't have started resenting her for it, but he was just a kid. A scared, traumatized kid who was trying to act like he was okay and his mom didn't even care. I was only thirteen and barely knew how to be a teenager, let alone a parent, and so I did the only thing I could think of to distract him. I decided to teach him cursive."

Foster was at least more engaged than Detective Gordon had been at this point.

"Did he like the idea?" he asked.

Millie actually laughed, her heart becoming lighter at the memory.

"He thought it was the best thing ever," she said. "Every night before bed we'd sit and write in his room until he got it. He likes art, so I think to him it was more like drawing than writing. After he mastered it, he was unstoppable. Every day until I went to college, he'd write me a note in nothing but cursive. That's a lot of letters from me being thirteen to leaving at eighteen, and even after I first got to school he continued to write me these script-filled letters. I told him I didn't expect him to keep it up, but he told me that if I took the time to teach him something, he'd take the time to use it. So, I got a letter every week while I was away. Until I didn't."

She turned her gaze toward the two-way mirror, assuming the sheriff was there.

"You can check the police reports about what happened next. Just like I told Detective Gordon."

Foster's eyebrow rose in question.

"What do you mean? What happened next?"

Millie decided right then and there that this was the last time she ever told this story in its entirety. If they didn't believe her? Well, that was their problem, not hers.

"My mom tried to fill the hole in her heart by marrying a man named Steve Conway when I was eighteen. Two years later and Fallon stops writing me. One day I get suspicious of how he sounds on the phone, then the next day my mom calls and says he's run away. Since he'd never done that before, I rush home and find him in one of his favorite spots in town. He had bruises all over him. You don't have to be a detective to guess what good ole Steve had been up to."

"He was abusing Fallon."

Millie nodded. "Turns out, not only was it *not* the first time he'd run away, but he'd also gone to the hospital *three* times with mysterious injuries." Millie was angry again. "I filed a report, but by then no one wanted to listen to Fallon. They assumed he was just some teen acting out and hating his stepdad because he wasn't his real dad."

"What about your mom?"

Millie snorted. "She wasn't much better. She went on record saying that she didn't know if she could handle Fallon anymore. Talked about possibly getting DHR involved to get him into foster care so she could get a break." Millie shook her head. "There was no way I was going to let that happen so I left school, got a job in town and made a deal with her that I wouldn't ask for any money from them if she let Fallon live with me until he turned eighteen. She agreed, and the last thing Fallon and I ever did in that place was sit in my car next to the town limits sign and blow out his birthday candle on a cupcake at midnight. Then we ate that cupcake and drove until I found the first Help Wanted sign in a window. We've been in Kelby Creek ever since."

Foster opened his mouth to say something, but Millie wanted to be thorough in her last attempt. She held out her hand to stop him.

"And before you point out that Fallon ran away after we first got here, I'll tell you what I told Detective Gordon. Mom showed up at the house while I was at work one day. She told Fallon she wanted to make sure I hadn't thrown my life away because of him. I got there just as she was leaving and realized Fallon was gone. My then-boss at the grocery store heard me panicking and reported him missing. But this time he had just needed some time to process. To breathe. But the rest, as you know, is history. William Reiner gets hit by a car while Fallon smokes pot in the woods. No one in Kelby Creek has liked him since."

The room filled with silence.

Millie hadn't realized how much adrenaline was pumping through her. She was no longer cold.

Foster was also no longer impassive.

He leaned forward, eyebrow raised again, and put emphasis on the first question he asked.

"And why did you think the note from him was a fake?"

Millie made sure her voice was as clear as crystal as she answered.

"Because it wasn't in cursive."

# Chapter Thirteen

"Steve Conway has been booked three times for domestic violence but no charges have ever stuck." Sheriff Chamblin tossed his hat onto a chair next to where Foster was standing. His tone said it all. Disgust at Millie's stepfather. "It seems that Miss Dean was telling the truth about that."

Foster had a hard time not snarling in response.

"I already believed her before she even said a word."

Chamblin sidled up to Foster and gave him a long look. Their reflections were slight in the two-way mirror. He could barely make out the imploring look from his father's old friend in the glass. What he could see clearly was Millie in the next room, tearing the paper off a water bottle and openly trying not to fidget.

Foster didn't like it.

He liked how he'd handled her even less.

"You know, I never thought I'd have to remind you of all people to be objective on a case, but here we are," Chamblin said. "You're working a case. That means asking questions even if it's uncomfortable."

Foster tore his gaze from Millie.

"I'm not uncomfortable with the questions, just how they've been asked and their answers ignored in the past," he countered. "I have no problem with being objective either, but I think that's what's been the problem for the

Dean kids since they came to Kelby Creek. Too much objectivity can turn into apathy if you're not careful, and if the law enforcement sworn to help and protect is too apathetic to you, then there's very little chance anything is going to get done the right way."

"Detective Gordon," Chamblin guessed.

"Detective Gordon," Foster confirmed. "Millie said she told him word for word what she told me in there, and he didn't even take the time to put it in his report. Let alone even entertain the thought that she was right about the note. If it had been me? If Millie had come in and told me that same story when Fallon first disappeared? I wouldn't have stopped digging until I hit something."

"So you think Fallon really didn't write it? The note I mean."

Foster crossed his arms over his chest. He was going into a hard stance that his ex-wife used to call Full Detective Mode. Defensive but ready to strike. Walls up, focus engaged.

"I can't say for sure if he did or didn't, but my guess? If he did, he purposely didn't use cursive as a way to tip Millie off that something was wrong. It sounds like she mostly raised him so he had to have known she would look for him. Either way, I think Fallon is caught up in *something*. I just don't know what yet. But I think it's time I finally talked to Gordon myself."

"You think he knows something."

"He's either incompetent or there's a reason he did such a bad job when he got the case. No matter which one it is, I want to hear it from him. Clearly he knows more than he put in his report."

Sheriff Chamblin let out a sigh so long that it could have rooted into the tiled floor beneath them.

"Gordon is going to have to wait. We have a few more pressing issues." He put his hands on his hips and didn't look pleased at all. Not that either man had looked pleased in days. "We finally identified the two men from the boat."

Foster's ears perked up at that. Since being in the hospital he'd only been updated on their medical statuses. The younger man who had been shot in the leg by Deputy Park had made it out of surgery and was in recovery. The older man had sustained a concussion but would be transferred back into custody once the doctor cleared him.

Past that, Foster felt like he'd been isolated on an island the last several hours while everyone else was on the mainland, so to speak.

"Donni Marsden is the older fellow and Wyatt Cline is the younger one."

Foster tilted his head, trying to jostle a memory loose at either name. Nothing came free.

"I don't think I've heard of or read about them before."

Sheriff Chamblin shook his head.

"I hadn't either, though Park said Wyatt sounded familiar. He went and did a search on social media and found an account for him on Facebook. It hadn't been touched in seven months, but we could see where he loved Auburn football, thought Bill Gates was trying to spy on us all, and frequented a bar in Mobile up until he stopped using the account."

Foster felt his eyebrow raise on reflex.

"Just from what we heard on the boat, I got the distinct impression that he didn't take whatever their job was seriously. And that Donni wasn't a fan of him. Do we know anything else? Mobile is a good drive from here, and Bill Gates does us no good in this situation."

The sheriff snorted and then went serious again.

"Both men have records that were pretty easy to pull up. Though old, Donni Marsden did time for manslaughter back in the nineties down the road in Kipsy and had time added on to his sentence after starting a fight in the prison cafeteria. It was a 'mutual stabbing' according to a guard, and one that left scars on both. After Donni served the extra time and was released, his daughter picked him up at the front gate. That's where Donni Marsden seems to disappear. We couldn't track down anything else aside from an address for his daughter who now lives in Georgia. We reached out to her but so far no luck there either."

Georgia was a state away. Kipsy was a city in the county over. A good drive too, just like Mobile.

And there Foster was thinking that Donni had been a local.

"And let me guess, Wyatt's rap sheet had a whole lot of 'petty' attached to it."

Chamblin gave him a questioning look.

"Petty theft, intoxication, simple assault and disorderly conduct from ages seventeen until last year at twenty-five. How'd you know?"

Foster sighed. "Just a vibe I got from the time on the boat. Plus, if Donni Marsden did time in prison where he got and gave his own hits, I suspect someone who'd only done quick time, if any, wouldn't be someone he respected all that much." That gave Foster an idea. "We might be able to use that. If Donni won't talk, I bet he'd believe Wyatt did. That could get us a reaction from him. He could slip and give us some real info. Have you talked to them yet?"

"Donni clammed up like the devil was trying to tempt him." The sheriff shifted his weight to the other foot. His tone changed to frustrated defeat. "And apparently Wyatt didn't react too well to the anesthesia coming out of surgery. He slipped into a coma."

*"What?"*

Foster hadn't seen that coming.

"It's rare, I'm told, but it happens. The doc said all we can do is to wait to see when he wakes up. If he wakes up."

"Leaving us with a man who might rather go back to prison than answer any of our questions."

"Unless we can find a way to hit a nerve, I'm thinking that's the gist."

Foster turned back to Millie. She had abandoned her project of stripping the label off her water bottle and was now tracing circles with her finger along the top of the table.

The details.

Foster was good at those. Or, really, he was good at distancing himself from them. So, he made a quick change to the interrogation room and let a new scene play out in his head.

Donni Marsden was sitting where Millie had been, his halo of gray hair centered beneath the harsh light, and Foster across from him.

Donni would growl. He would say that he *wouldn't* say anything. He'd go tight-lipped and he'd cross his arms over his chest, leaning back to show that he rather lounge in the belly of the beast than fret about his luck.

He wasn't nervous or afraid.

He wasn't angry.

He was resigned with a side of sass.

It wouldn't be the first time Foster had to deal with someone like that in a soundproofed room with a metal table in its center.

But that didn't mean it wasn't a challenge. Though at least it was a challenge Foster was used to taking on.

Unlike his and Millie's stint on the boat.

Foster slowly let the image of Donni fade.

Millie was twisting a long curl of her hair between her fingers.

"Is Donni still here?" Foster finally asked.

The sheriff nodded. "In the basement." He clapped Foster on the shoulder. There was a grin in his voice. "Waiting for you."

Foster nodded too. It was more to himself than his company.

"Good because I definitely have questions that need answering. And that woman in there? She deserves them too."

Chamblin turned to face the two-way mirror again. Like Foster slipping into detective mode, he'd gone right into sheriff.

"I'll admit I'm not used to having a case that has so many leads. You're going to have to delegate some of them or you'll just spread yourself too thin."

"And where do you want me to start, boss man?" Foster hadn't meant to, but the words came out with snark attached. Chamblin didn't hold it against him.

"I'd focus on who had the great gall to drug and kidnap a man of the law and his companion from a public place. You pull that thread and follow it, and you might just find out what in the Wild West is going on. And how Fallon might fit, especially after Wyatt name-checked him on the boat."

That was something Foster had spent time in his hospital bed thinking on.

Who was the better opponent that Donni had warned Wyatt about?

And was that the same "him" who had taken Fallon to the boat before Foster and Millie?

"Which means I need to have a lengthy conversation with William Reiner. Again. Preferably one I can remember after the fact."

Chamblin let out one last, long sigh.

"Oh, goody, you have some more news for me?" Foster asked, heavy on the sarcasm. The sheriff didn't take offense, but his mood had definitely soured even more.

"I didn't want to tell you until I knew you were okay and ready to leave the hospital, but we couldn't find him."

"Reiner? What do you mean you couldn't find him? I thought the Good Samaritan who called the department said that Reiner's truck was already gone when she saw us thrown into the one that took us to the boat? Did you send someone to his house?"

Chamblin crossed his arms. "I'm going to glaze by the fact that you're acting like I'm an idiot and didn't immediately look for the man *at his house* and put an all-points bulletin out on him, and instead I'm going to go ahead and dip right into an apology for lying to you earlier." Foster turned his entire body to face the older man. Like the night in the woods, he looked years older than he had the last time Foster had seen him. He nodded toward the two-way mirror.

"You trust her," Chamblin stated. "Why? You barely know her."

Foster didn't know why the answer came so easily.

But it did.

"I just do. Call it a gut feeling. Why?"

There it was. Something that the sheriff had been hiding their entire conversation. Something he'd already had before he'd even directed Foster and Millie into the interrogation room.

Something else had happened while Foster had been in the hospital.

Something that had shifted the sheriff's sense of duty from helping Millie to questioning her.

Now it was like the blindfold had been ripped off.

Chamblin went to pick his cowboy hat back up.

He wasn't a happy man as he spoke.

"Because, son, if you don't trust her, then this next part might get a little awkward for you." He lowered his voice despite there being no way that Millie could have heard him in the soundproofed room. Not even if he'd yelled. Though his words still rang loud in Foster's ears.

"The truck you and Millie were thrown into was none other than Fallon Dean's."

MILLIE DIDN'T KNOW who Donni Marsden or Wyatt Cline were when Foster reported they'd identified the men who'd drugged and kidnapped them, but she wished she did. If only for the fact that saying she didn't seemed to buy her a one-way ticket to Foster's office.

Since he'd gotten her out of the interrogation room, he'd done a spectacular job of avoiding her. Though if she was honest with herself, he was probably just doing his *actual* job.

And if she was keeping with her self-honesty thing, she was still a bit angry at having to relive the past again in the hopes that someone would do something in the present to help her.

Or she was disappointed.

Millie couldn't decide.

Either way she was quiet when Foster asked her to wait while he did a few things, and she was quiet again when the door to his office opened a half hour later.

"Donni Marsden didn't say a word." Foster ran a hand through his hair and rounded his desk. He pulled open a drawer. Tension lined his shoulders. "I mean, not even *one* syllable." He rummaged through the drawer, obviously looking for something, then abandoned the search altogether.

Finally, he met her eye.

A butterfly dislodged in Millie's stomach at the contact. She saw the man who had risked his life to save her, the one who had bloody knuckles and a cut along his cheek. She also saw the man who had called her Miss Dean before questioning her.

Foster was now a problem for Millie.

He was a distraction, and she didn't need any more of those.

She stood to distance herself from that one butterfly trying its best to sway her.

"And I'm guessing Wyatt hasn't woken up since you left me in here?" Millie overcompensated her attempt to act normal and went right into a bite. Foster didn't address it.

"Yeah. The sheriff said he'd let me know as soon as Wyatt was awake. *If* he wakes up at all."

"Could I talk to him then? Donni."

That earned the quickest *I don't think so* look Millie had ever seen. She felt her expression harden into defiance.

Foster shut the drawer and let out a breath.

"I don't think that's a great idea."

"And why not? Because I'm not a cop? Or is it because I'm a woman?"

Foster shook his head but was interrupted by a knock on the doorframe. Millie turned to see Deputy Park. Since what had happened on the creek, all hostility the man had once had for Millie had disappeared. Though Millie wasn't sure the feeling was mutual yet.

"I'm ready now, if you two are. Deputy Lawrence is already there."

Millie shared a look with Foster.

"Where is there?"

"Rosewater," Foster answered. "He's going to drop us off."

"Why? Did the department find something?"

Excitement became a soothing salve over the emotional turbulence Millie had been experiencing the last several hours. A lead? That was something she'd gladly take.

The tension in Foster's shoulders lessened. He grinned.

"They found something all right."

## Chapter Fourteen

"I know I don't have your years of experience in the field, but this isn't normal, is it?"

Millie was standing in the middle of Rosewater Bar, holding her cell phone in one hand and her purse in the other. Foster had his truck keys and phone in his own hands, brow creased in thought. He'd already put his badge back around his neck and his sidearm and holster across his hips. Even his blazer seemed to be in fine shape and was currently draped over a bar stool.

"I just thought whoever took us kept our things or, you know, threw them away," Millie continued. "Not put them in the lost and found box."

Foster ran his thumb along his keys in one hand while scrolling through his phone in the other. As soon as they arrived and Deputy Lawrence had shown them where their things were, Millie had searched her purse. As far as she could tell, everything was still in its place. Including Fallon's sixth grade school picture. The moment she'd seen it Millie had made a silent vow to make a copy of it as soon as possible.

"The whole thing doesn't make much sense," Foster said when he was satisfied with his phone.

He turned to where they had been sitting the night before. The place where both of their memories had run out.

"We decided on a plan with Reiner where you told him that I was your new neighbor and asked you for an introduction since I was the new lead detective at the department," he continued. "Then we went to his table, drinks in hand."

He walked over to where Reiner had been seated. Daylight from the front door streamed in, dust motes visible in the air. Daytime pulled off the mask that Rosewater wore at night. There were no colored lights. No patron chatter mingled with music from the overhead speakers. The bartender was gone, as were any and all staff. Instead of the smell of fries and alcohol, the place stunk of cleaning supplies.

During the day, Rosewater lost all its charm.

It certainly didn't help her overall opinion of the bar that the last time Millie had been inside she'd been drugged.

"I don't remember talking to him," she added, coming up to his elbow, careful to tuck her purse against her side. "I just remember walking. Do you think the drugs had already taken effect that fast? We were only seated for—what?—ten minutes?"

Foster was scanning the area around the table. He shrugged.

"The doc said that those meds can sometimes block out the time before they were even ingested, which makes figuring out a timeline a bit trickier." Foster bent down, inspecting the floor beneath the table. Millie leaned in, curious.

"See anything?"

Foster shook his head. Then his eyes were off to the door behind them, which led to the kitchen.

"After we were reported to have been taken by the Good Samaritan, two deputies were dispatched to question everyone here who had seen us." He was still crouched. It reminded Millie of an umpire about to be asked to make a call. The concentration made her own brow furrow as she tried to picture the bar the night before the best she could. "One couple was sure that we never went to the bathrooms since they were seated near them."

He pointed to the table closest to the bathroom doors but didn't pull his gaze from the kitchen.

"Two different patrons saw William Reiner leave through the front door while we were still inside," he continued. "But of all the people in here, staff included, no one saw *us* leave through the same doors."

Millie stepped back as Foster stood and, without any more of an explanation, seemed to follow his invisible line of thought. She followed him wordlessly to the kitchen door, where he stopped so quickly that Millie ran into him.

A blush burned its way up her neck and singed her cheeks.

"Oops, sorry."

Foster didn't flinch as he looked to the bar.

"Deputy Lawrence said that everyone in here confirmed everyone *stayed* in here except for Reiner."

"Well, drugged or not, I'm pretty sure we didn't just disappear into thin air," Millie pointed out. Though she knew he wasn't implying that they had.

Foster Lovett was in his element.

And he was building up to something.

"You're right. Someone would have seen us if we left through the front door. There were too many people for everyone who had been interviewed to be sure we hadn't gone out that way. So—" he pointed to the kitchen door in front of him but kept his gaze on the bar "—the only other way to leave would have been to go through the kitchen door, and only one person had direct sight line to that at all times."

"June Meeks, the bartender," Millie finished. "But

wasn't she questioned extensively while we were missing and in the hospital?"

He nodded. "After they realized we'd been drugged, she was brought in for more questioning. The sheriff himself headed it up. He said he didn't think she had anything to do with it, but I also haven't had a chance to ask her myself. Until then I'm going to trust his call."

Millie thought that was absurd, but she didn't say as much. They were drugged through their drinks, and yet the bartender wasn't suspect because the sheriff said so? And now Foster thought June had seen them leave through the back but lied about it?

Then again, why in the world would June Meeks drug and lie about them?

It made no sense.

Not that much made sense recently.

"So you think June saw us go through the back and then the cook didn't see us?"

Foster shook his head and pushed into the kitchen in question.

"The cook left right after we got here. I remember seeing him when we were at our table. Apparently, his wife had car trouble so he ran out to help and didn't get back until deputies were here."

Millie had never been in the kitchen of Rosewater before, at least not when she remembered it. It wasn't that big of a room but it had three doors. One had a scratched plaque that read Office, the other had an exit sign, and in between them was a freezer door.

"So let's say we *did* come in here, with or without June knowing." Millie motioned to the doors and shrugged. "Why? You said earlier the owner wasn't here at all and now neither was the cook. So why did *we* sneak back here?"

For the first time since Deputy Park had dropped them off, a look that wasn't wholly professional crossed his expression.

He glanced down at her lips.

All at once the kitchen felt like it had shrunk to the size of a shoebox. In it, the space between Millie and the detective became nearly nonexistent. She was still so close to him that she could feel the heat from his arm radiating toward her own.

So close.

And Millie was feeling the urge to get closer.

There was no denying the attraction between them. Not anymore. Not for her.

Millie had been struggling with it since she'd sat down in his office, even after she'd left, angry at him.

She was *attracted* to him.

Plain and simple.

But did he feel the same? Or was he simply following every avenue of thought about the night before?

Millie and Foster in the kitchen with an unspoken attraction instead of a candlestick?

The blush from earlier flared back to life but, regardless, Millie had to set the man straight.

"Listen, if I wanted to *sneak around* with you there would be a lot easier ways and a lot better places to do it." She caught herself with a stammer. "I—I mean not 'do it' but, you know, *seek privacy* with you. I'd pick your truck, if anything. Especially over the Rosewater kitchen, and that's assuming you somehow sweet-talked me into not worrying about the gossip if we got caught."

Foster's lips turned up at the corners. He was trying not to laugh. Which made it only slightly adorable when he finally did. It was a deep, rumbling sound.

He held up his hands in defense and was still chuckling a little as he continued.

"Okay, okay so if we weren't back here for *personal* reasons, then the only other reason I can think of would be because of maybe something Reiner said to us before he left. Or maybe we came in to look for something?"

They lapsed into silence as they split up and searched through the kitchen. Foster went into the office and Millie into the freezer. She didn't know what they might be looking for, but there wasn't anything but food and containers inside. She backtracked and shut the door behind her. She let Foster finish his own search solo and turned her attention to the door leading to the exit.

There was no fire alarm warning attached to it, so she took her chances and pushed it open.

No alarm went off but heat, wrapped tightly in humidity, hit her as hard as the noise would have. Millie growled at it as she walked out onto the concrete pad. A dumpster for the bar sat against the wall, and trees from the overgrown lot that bordered the old motel was opposite, blocking the back lane from being visible to patrons and the parking lot.

Millie went to the edge of the concrete pad and looked down at the ground that continued on from its edge to the back of the middle section of the building. Cigarette butts and footprints were pressed into the damp dirt. They looked relatively new, probably belonging to deputies in the department who were asked to comb the area.

Still, Millie followed, she thought, two different sets of footprints until she was behind the rooms that had been used as storage since the bed-and-breakfast had shut down. Since all the doors to enter the rooms were positioned on the front of the building, she started to look in the windows. They'd been put in during the renovation but looked as worn and stained as the old rooms had been. One of the windows was even missing a screen altogether. Whoever owned the middle section of the building sure hadn't been around to maintain or clean it in a while, Millie decided.

She looked back down the narrow lane toward the bar's

back door and then past it to a patch of grass just before it transitioned to the street.

"Why were we out here?" she asked herself out loud.

According to the Good Samaritan, and then according to Foster who heard it from the sheriff, Millie and Foster had been put in a truck in the parking lot in front of the business offices side of the building.

What had happened between the time they had gone into the kitchen to when they'd gotten into the truck?

Why had they been taken in the first place?

Who had Foster fought?

And, with a resounding frustration, Millie came back to the general why of it all.

"Millie?" Foster's voice carried to her, along with its worry.

It was touching.

When she met his gaze, he visibly calmed.

"Did you find anything?" she asked.

He shook his head.

"Nothing remotely out of place or interesting. You?"

Millie motioned to the window closest to them.

"Nothing other than the thought that whoever owns this part of the old motel should probably invest in some Windex."

Foster agreed.

They walked the rest of the length of the building and rounded the corners until they were in the parking lot in front of the business offices.

Nothing popped out and yelled a clue at them.

Which was probably why Foster had gone more tense than when they'd first walked into the bar.

"At least we have our things back," Millie said as they stopped between two yellow painted lines. He was surveying the lot; Millie was surveying him.

Even in profile the man was a sight.

His jaw hardened. Then it was all cool green eyes on her. "Millie, I need to tell you something about when we—"

"Foster Lovett, I swear to everything holy!"

A woman's voice shrieked through the air behind them. Millie jumped. On instinct she grabbed Foster's arm. The detective, however, looked less startled.

He turned so they were both looking at a woman coming out of one of the offices. He groaned.

"Why is Mrs. Zamboni charging over here at us?" Millie asked. "And why is she so angry?"

Foster made a noise. She couldn't place its emotion.

"Because she's my former sister-in-law and likes being a pain." He lowered his voice and finished in a rush. "And she's like The Hulk. She's always angry."

"I HAVE SPENT almost sixteen years of my life not giving a dog's behind about you, Foster Lovett, and I'd prefer you'd keep it that way."

Helen wasn't wearing her crown of flowers like the day before, but her stomach seemed even more round in her flower-print dress. Her eyes, though, were wide. Foster hadn't seen her so grumpy since she'd turned sixteen and failed her driver's test. Twice.

"Well, how do you do too, there, Helen," he replied.

Millie let go of his arm. Foster wondered if they already knew each other. Being a palm reader in small-town Alabama was pretty close to celebrity status.

But Foster wasn't going to take his chances on not being polite, so he went ahead with introductions before getting to the current root of Helen Mercer's problem with him.

"Millie Dean, meet Helen Mercer. Helen, this is Millie."

Helen stopped with a huff but nodded to Millie. Then she was quickly back on him.

"I do not like feeling anything for you other than some

good ole dislike, so you better watch your back around here because I certainly can't keep doing it."

Foster's eyebrow rose.

Helen wasn't her usual mad.

"What are you talking about?"

"I'm talking about being eight months pregnant and trying to chase you two down after you were taken! Philip nearly had a hay day when he saw the damage I made to the car after popping the curb trying to speed after y'all."

Foster put his hand up to slow the woman's rate of words per millisecond.

"Wait." Then it dawned on him. "*You're* the Good Samaritan who saw us get taken?"

Helen gave him a *well, duh* look.

"Not only did I see it and call the department, I chased after that dang truck until it lost me in the back roads! Nearly went into labor over how stressful it was."

Foster could barely believe it.

Helen had saved them, and now? Now she was upset.

She cared.

"Helen, if it wasn't for you, no one would have known we were missing until the next day most likely," he told her. "You saved us."

Foster would have extended a hug had it been anyone else, but he didn't want to invade her personal space, especially her pregnant, personal space. They'd never had that relationship.

But Millie took it into her own hands.

She wrapped her arms around Helen within the span of a blink.

"Thank you," Millie said into Helen's silver hair. "I don't know what would have happened had Deputy Park not gotten to us when he did."

Foster agreed.

Helen's look of grumpiness softened. Discounting her

interactions with him, she was a polite, well-liked woman in the town. She patted Millie's back and nodded to her when the embrace was finished.

"Well, I can't very well go on disliking Foster if he's not around to tick me off." Her words had gone softer too. "Plus it looked to me like he was the one doing all the heavy lifting." She glanced down at his hands. They were still bruised and scabbed from his fight.

"You saw me fighting?"

She nodded. "Or trying." Helen pointed to the corner behind them. "The streetlight blew months back and it was dark. Plus you two were on the other side of the truck. Like I told the sheriff, I couldn't make out who you were tussling with, but I could hear, and vaguely see you, hitting him. You seemed slow, though. It didn't look like it took too much to put you in the truck too."

Foster looked down at Millie.

"So then that's definitely our guy," she said, guessing at his thoughts. "The one you bloodied your knuckles on."

The one who might be Fallon.

That's what he'd been about to tell Millie before Helen had interrupted.

The truck they'd been taken in? Fallon's.

Which meant one of two things and neither of them good for Millie.

That's why he kept quiet now.

He wasn't about to give her those two theories in front of Helen.

Despite it being his job, it felt like something he should do in private. Something to talk about with just the two of them.

Helen cleared her throat. Her hand went over her stomach in what must have been a soothing motion. She met Foster's eye with a severe expression and tone.

"You might not be family anymore, but I've grown used

to disliking you. If you go up and get killed on me, then I won't have someone to complain about anymore," she said. "Whatever is going on, I need you to figure it out and get it settled. Without getting kidnapped again. Okay? I need this town to go back to normal."

Foster had thought the last week had already been strange enough, but it took another turn as Helen waited for him to confirm he would, essentially, try to stay safe.

"I'll try my best."

Helen nodded. Then she went back to her shop.

They watched as she walked away. Millie was the first to speak. There was no humor in her words.

"I don't think this town has been normal since Annie McHale went missing."

# Chapter Fifteen

The water was warm, a gentle hand against the skin of someone who needed to relax. To reflect. To heal.

To try to feel an emotion that wasn't so complicated that she'd pushed away the only man who had been helping her.

Millie slid farther down in the tub, a sigh escaping as she went. Her shower cap crinkled. Water lapped against the back of her neck. The bubbles had already started to dwindle, though their scents of vanilla and lavender had long since coated her skin.

If she closed her eyes and tried to the best of her abilities, she could almost forget about the last week. The last six months too.

*Almost*.

But that was putting too much pressure on a bubble bath.

Millie opened her eyes and looked at the tile wall opposite her. It wasn't intentional and it certainly wasn't hard to do, but she imagined the house on the other side of that wall.

She sighed again.

Foster had taken them from the parking lot of Rosewater to her front porch, all while staying as quiet as a mouse. Millie had known he was gearing up to say something, something she probably wasn't going to like. It was only after he'd made sure her house was empty and that the deputy at the road was alert, did he circle back to her standing on the front porch and finally said what was on his mind.

"Helen saw and described the vehicle that took us from Rosewater. She even got a partial license plate."

Hope had sprung eternal. A lead!

But then he pulled the cord on that hope with four words.

"It was Fallon's truck."

Millie had felt excitement and anguish all at once.

It hadn't helped that Foster had told her his thoughts on the topic.

"The man who took us could have been Fallon or been working with him, meaning he's not just missing but he's involved in something and choosing not to come forward." Then he'd softened. Sympathy had drenched his expression. Millie's stomach had gone cold. "Or something happened to Fallon and his truck was stolen."

Millie hadn't wanted to sit there and listen to reason or theories. After everything she'd been through in the last week? The last twenty-four hours? Her entire adulthood? Finding out about Fallon's truck—his beloved truck that he'd never give up without a fight or consent—was too much for Millie.

So she'd focused on the part that shouldn't have mattered the most, if at all.

"Why didn't you tell me earlier? Why didn't you tell me when you found out?"

Foster had done his detective thing again. Just like he had in the interrogation room. He'd gone from a man who looked at her with concern and depth to a professional who had deemed her nonessential. Or a threat. His mouth had tightened, his stance had hardened and even his voice had gone almost flat.

"I wanted to know more before I did that."

Millie's heart had been hurting and scared and she knew she'd misplaced her emotions. Still her voice had raised and the corners of her eyes had pricked with tears.

"You wanted to figure out if I had something to do with it too, didn't you? You wanted to see if Millie Dean was just as much trouble as her brother."

Foster had shaken his head. "Millie, that's not it. I just wanted to—"

But Millie had reached the point of no return. She'd interrupted him by raising her hand to stop whatever it was he'd been about to say to her.

"We're not a team. We're not partners. I'm just your neighbor and a suspect. And I'm tired. I'll make sure my phone is on and all the doors and windows stay shut and locked, but I'm going inside now. I'll talk to you later."

The words had rushed out, but there had been power behind each syllable. Maybe it was that power that kept the man from responding past a nod of acknowledgment and a quiet "okay."

Then he'd gone and now, as night fell, Millie was in the bath, wondering if he was home or not.

Before Foster had come to town, before Fallon had disappeared, Millie had lived a life of routine and normalcy. Now it felt wrong to not be with the detective, sleuthing at his side and waiting for those green eyes to land on her.

The idea of a simple life stayed elusive as Millie refused to give thought about what Fallon's truck did or didn't mean. Fallon was, and always had been, a good kid. A great kid. One with heart and a strength that not even he probably realized he had.

He wouldn't be part of something malicious or bad.

But what did it mean if he wasn't involved in whatever it was going on?

Tears started to prick up again.

Millie ran a hand over her face, water catching in her eyes. She shook her head.

Her brother was still alive and, until she was given proof otherwise, Millie decided she was going to stay optimistic.

She finished her bath with new resolve and slipped into her robe with purpose when the doorbell rang.

Fear and adrenaline went to every area of her body. The power of the bubble bath washed away. She checked her phone to make sure she hadn't missed a call or text.

She hadn't.

Millie tied her robe tight and tiptoed to the living room. She peeked out of the front window, barely moving the curtain. Flashes of Jason Talbot with a gun went through her mind, followed by Foster with a smile.

However, the person standing on the welcome mat was neither.

"Amanda?"

Amanda Alvarez was still wearing her colorful patch-work clothes from earlier at the hospital. She had a paper bag in one hand and held it up and out to Millie in greeting.

"I promised Dr. McCrushing On Me that I'd check on you and the detective, so I'm keeping my promise. *With* the addition of greasy burgers and fries because A, I haven't had a chance to eat yet and B, I'm a big believer in it being good for everyone's mental health to have some guilty pleasure food every now and then." She shook the bag. On cue Millie's stomach growled. Amanda laughed. "Could I come in?"

Millie looked out to the street where her assigned deputy babysitter was still sitting. He made no move to get out of the car. Not that Millie thought the coroner was a threat, but it was still nice to know she wasn't even a suspect.

Plus Millie *was* hungry.

"Yeah, sure. Come on in. Just don't mind the mess."

Amanda followed her in and through to the eat-in kitchen. The other woman laughed as they walked.

"This? If you think this is messy then you'd have a melt-down at my place," she said. "I took this job before I found a place to live, so I'm currently staying in the apartment over the pharmacy on Main. It's the size of a shoebox, a shoebox filled to the brim with boxes of crap I don't need but can't let go of."

She took the seat Millie offered and started to dump the bag out.

"I didn't realize that apartment was even livable," Millie replied. "I work across the street from it at the grocers and haven't seen anyone come or go in years."

Amanda laughed. "The parking is in the back alley and, before me, I don't think anyone had lived there in a while. Let's just say my first week in Kelby Creek was spent elbow deep in cleaning supplies and frustration."

Millie grabbed some plates and napkins and nearly sat down before she heard a crinkle.

"And I'm still wearing my shower cap. Please excuse me while I go change." Millie laughed at herself before going to her room and changing into something less comfortable than her robe but comfortable all the same. She had no plans to leave the house that night. Maybe not even leave the house the next day either. She hadn't decided.

When she padded back into the kitchen, Amanda had set both plates and was chewing on some fries.

"Sorry, I'm starving," she said, waving a fry in the air. "And for all of their grease and calories, fries are my weakness."

"No judgments here," Millie assured her. "My weakness is pie. Like entire pies. I have a frozen one in the freezer as we speak."

"My kind of people."

Millie took the seat opposite and tore into her burger

with enthusiasm she hadn't had before. It was like her appetite had come back all at once. She was done with half of the burger before Amanda could ask the question that she'd come over to ask in the first place.

"So other than your love for pie, how *are* you feeling? Any pain or weirdness? Sudden and new superpowers? The urge to eat human flesh?"

Millie snorted. Even though the coroner was joking around, she could see the concern. Millie appreciated the brevity.

"No superpowers unless you can count my undying optimism," Millie joked back. Then she gave a more serious answer, losing her smile for a more thoughtful demeanor in the process. "My head still feels kind of groggy. Like the aftereffects of taking a Benadryl. But it doesn't hurt like it did earlier. I've also been drinking a lot of water like I was told and taking it easy."

"Nothing else? No paranoia or increased anxiety or depression?"

"Well, in the last week I've had someone break into my home and try to kill me, been drugged and woke up on a boat and lost hours of memory." Millie bit into a fry and smirked to show she wasn't taking what she said as seriously as it was. "Aside from the paranoia, anxiety and depression that goes along with that, no, nothing extra."

Amanda held up her own fry and tipped it to Millie.

"Touché."

They ate a few more bites. Millie glanced over Amanda's shoulder. Once again she imagined the house just beyond hers.

And the man who might or might not be in it.

"So, do you need to go check up on Foster next or was I the second stop?" Millie tried not to blush but probably didn't succeed.

She felt like a schoolgirl fishing for information on her crush.

Amanda didn't pick up on it, or at least didn't take it that way. She shook her head and spoke around a bite of her burger.

"You're my second stop. I went to the department first to see him since it was next to my precious fries' connection."

So Foster was at the department and not home.

Millie felt a pang of anxiety at that. And something else she didn't have time to think on.

"Is he doing okay too? No more headache or sudden superpowers? No signs of being a zombie?"

There she was, fishing again.

"Nope. He answered about the same as you, actually. The whole anxiety and stress thing was 'just a part of the job.' Very macho with his gun on his hip and the files piled on his desk. So I told him I was on the way to get food and see you. He said he'd call ahead to the guy out front, and I told him he needed to head home soon too."

"Let me guess, he took the suggestion under advisement but didn't say he actually would," Millie guessed.

Amanda laughed. "Actually he said he'd already done his resting at the hospital but would head home when he found a stopping point."

"I haven't known Foster more than a week but that seems to be his way. He's really dedicated to his job. Which is definitely something Kelby Creek needs after The Flood."

Millie dipped into the town's past without meaning to. The Flood had just become so ingrained in residents that it was hard not to hit on the topic on occasion.

Amanda picked up on the mood change. She didn't brush it off or make jokes anymore.

"You know, I thought the first person I heard say 'The

Flood' was being dramatic, but that's what everyone here in town calls it, isn't it? Everything that went down?"

Millie finished her burger with a last bite. She nodded. Amanda waited until she was done chewing to press on.

"You were here for it? The Flood?"

"Yeah." Millie was also there before it had happened long enough to feel the burn, the hurt, the betrayal.

The anger.

"I don't know who started the name, but it's been the easiest way to refer to what happened," she added. "Plus the flood *is* what really changed everything."

Amanda's brow rose high.

"It's not just a metaphorical name?"

Millie shook her head and paused in the process of getting more fries. She knew the look that crossed Amanda's face just as she'd seen the same one in her reflection over the last six months.

"Do you not know what happened?" she asked. "You replaced someone who was fired because of it."

"I only know the highlights that the news gave out. And, well, that my predecessor was fired for fudging reports, but I never got the *details* details. Not the up close and personal ones."

Amanda's expression was searching. Since Millie had already decided she liked the woman, she relented and told the story of The Flood.

Well, after she got out the frozen pie to let it thaw.

*Then* she told the coroner to buckle up because she was jumping right on in.

"There are two really wealthy families in Dawn County. The McHales were one of them and had lived in Kelby Creek for generations. They had family money and then they made more by having a hand in half of the town's businesses. But, for all the stereotypes of the rich family being small-town royalty, the McHale family was actu-

ally very beloved. If you didn't know they had a verita-
ble mansion in the woods, you might not know they were
filthy rich at all. That went doubly for their only daughter, Annie McHale."

Millie paused to do some math, trying to remember
the exact timeline.

"Everyone refers to the beginning of the end for a normal Kelby Creek when Annie went missing, but the truth
was she was actually kidnapped," she continued. "It's just
that no one knew for sure until a few days had passed and
missing, I suppose, sounds less menacing compared to
what actually happened. Annie went missing on a Sunday and by Wednesday a ransom call was made to her parents. The kidnappers wanted five hundred thousand dollars
within twenty-four hours or they'd kill her."

Amanda made a noise. "That's some kind of action stuff
you see on a TV show."

Millie had to agree with that.

"It only gets more intense from there. See, the McHales
were really close with the sheriff. He was actually the kids'
godfather. So when the call came in and a drop for the
money was set up, he convinced the McHales to let him
be the one who handled it. He took some undercover deputies with him and led them and Mr. McHale right into a
trap." Millie didn't say it, but she remembered hearing the
gunfire from the store that day. Like fireworks popping
in rapid succession until there was nothing but an eerie
silence. "In total five people were killed, some deputies
and some civilians while a few more were wounded. Mr.
McHale even took a bullet to the leg and nearly bled out."

"What about the kidnappers?"

"They managed to stay hidden, is what everyone said
at the time. But after that the kidnappers became openly
angry and pulled the stunt that put the town on national
news and finally brought in the FBI."

"I know this part," Amanda said excitedly. "The town website got hacked."

Millie nodded. "A video of Annie McHale was posted on the website and stayed up for half an hour until someone could get it down. It went viral across the internet."

"I saw it. She was just sitting there all bloody and beaten tied to a chair while some guy spoke next to the camera. He asked for more money, didn't he?"

"A million dollars this time," Millie answered. "And three days to do it in."

"Let me guess. After her parents saw the video, they were definitely in."

"Oh yeah. But they didn't get the chance to actually do it." Millie couldn't help but lean in a little, as if she was conspiring with Amanda. This part of the story always felt a little unreal. "Two FBI agents came in as part of a small task force to help and, the day after the video was posted, one of the agents, Jaqueline Ortega, left a message on her partner's phone that she was following up on a hunch. But then she went missing too."

"What? I never heard about that part."

Millie shrugged. "Jaqueline Ortega, as far as I could see, never made the news. *But* her partner did," she continued. "He was out looking for her the next day, driving through some backroads, when a nasty storm hit. It created a flash flood and by the time he had decided to go back to his hotel room, he came up on a car that had wrecked out into the ditch. Being the good guy he was, he stopped to help them. Turns out, it was the mayor. Good friends with the sheriff and the McHales. He was unconscious but alive and while the FBI agent saw to him, he spotted something shiny in the floorboard. A necklace specifically designed for Annie McHale."

Amanda sucked in a breath. "Man, this story needed

popcorn, not fries! So that's how everyone was caught? The mayor wrecked because of a flash flood?"

Millie nodded. "Apparently the wreck dislodged the necklace and it was all the FBI guy needed," Millie confirmed. "He launched his own investigation, and then all the pieces started to come into place. The sheriff and the mayor had been the masterminds behind the kidnapping and ransom. They'd also been behind the ambush and the video."

"And they weren't alone."

"Nope. Not by a long shot." This part of the story was widely known, but Millie recapped it for completion sake. "A new FBI team came and started a town-wide investigation of local law and government to see how deep the corruption went. Annie McHale was just the tip of the iceberg. Several people were fired, some were incarcerated and a few even ran. It took nearly a year to sort everything out and, then, the FBI just left. The town hasn't trusted local law or government since."

"That's why Foster and I are here," Amanda added.

"Yep. The town needs redeeming, most especially the sheriff's department."

Amanda let out a long, deep breath. She finally stuck her fork in the piece of pie Millie had offered.

"That's a tall order," she said. "Trying to get an entire town to trust you."

At this, Millie felt a coldness in her.

"It doesn't help that Annie McHale and Jaqueline Ortega were never found."

Amanda didn't disagree.

After that the two women ate their pie in silence.

# Chapter Sixteen

Foster dropped his keys on the kitchen counter and tried his best not to swear.

It wasn't like anyone was in his house to hear him if he did. The AC was the only thing that stirred when he came through the front door, and a beer from the fridge was the only thing calling his name.

He put away his badge and gun and got that beer, popping the cap with a little too much force and a whole lot of frustration.

Kelby Creek had gone from his hometown to home of his most complicated case. He couldn't figure it out and he couldn't escape it. Not that he wanted that. Foster went to the dining room window and peered out into the night.

From the driveway he'd been able to see Millie's living room light was on, but he couldn't see any movement. He had no idea what she was doing or *how* she was doing.

And it bothered him.

And it bothered him that it bothered him.

*We're not a team. We're not partners.*

Millie had been right. She was his neighbor. She was also a victim or a suspect, depending on who you talked to. But in his eyes? Millie hadn't asked for any of this to happen to her. She hadn't planned any of what they'd been through. Foster felt that truth in his bones. Now he was looking for answers, justice, and a way to give the woman who deserved some good, some kind of peace.

Foster should have told her that on the porch. Should have hammered home that she wasn't a suspect to him, but the way Millie had looked at him? It was like he'd watched a piece of her break right there on the same spot he'd been shot the week before. Foster hadn't known how to react because he hadn't known the cause. So, what did you do when you didn't know what to do?

He hadn't done anything at all.

Which meant now he shouldn't have wanted to update her on what he'd found. He shouldn't have wanted to talk through everything that had happened to her. He *definitely* shouldn't have wanted to go next door and forget about the case for a while.

But he did.

"Women are trouble, Foster," he reminded himself and the still-somewhat stale air of his new home around him. "That one with a capital *T*. Pull it together. Do your job."

The pep talk carried him to the hallway bathroom. He turned the shower on and put his beer on the counter. The reflection in the mirror showed him a man who was tired but wasn't about to sleep. Not until he had answers.

Just one.

That was why he was in Kelby Creek. To help the department, to help the town. Not to stumble through his first investigation since he got back.

*For Pete's sake, you got shot and drugged within the first week!*

Foster shook his head at himself. This time he did curse.

It was back to the drawing board when he got out of the shower, he decided. He needed to rethink everything from tip to tail.

He could do this.

He *had* to do this.

Foster nodded his affirmation to himself and started to pull up the hem of his shirt to undress. Instead, he watched his reflection flinch. Without any pain meds in his system, his bruised ribs had become angrier. Painful. Especially since Donni Marsden had used him as a punching bag on the boat. Donni might have been older, but he'd had force behind each blow. It also didn't help Foster's case that the sheriff had grabbed a casual T-shirt and not a button-up to put in his hospital bag.

"Can't solve this case, can't take off your shirt," he grumbled.

He switched sides, hoping that would help the pain.

It didn't.

He was considering getting the scissors when the doorbell rang.

"Coming!"

Foster glanced at his phone on the kitchen counter on the way to the door—no new messages—and went right for the peephole. He imagined the sheriff being on the other side, ready to share a beer and frustration. Maybe talk over the case some more and discuss how to deal with Donni Marsden and Fallon's still-missing truck.

But the sheriff and his cowboy hat weren't on the other side of the door.

All at once, Foster went on alert and quickly pulled open the door.

"Millie? Are you okay?"

Millie didn't appear to be in any physical pain or trouble—in fact, she looked like she'd been getting ready for bed in a worn cotton tee and a pair of sweatpants—but there was nothing but distress written across her face.

Foster looked over her shoulder. Deputy Calloway's cruiser was still at the curb. No one else seemed to be in the street or around the yards.

"What's wrong?" he prodded when she still hadn't answered. Foster pictured his gun locked in the nightstand next to his bed. Too far away if he needed to act fast. He'd just have to use his fists.

Millie's wide eyes managed to widen a bit more.

"Oh, no. I'm okay," she hurried to say. "I just wanted to talk. Sorry. Can I come inside?"

Foster didn't lower his guard just yet. He stepped aside, not moving until she was past him.

"Sure, yeah, come in."

The smell of lavender and something else mixed in surrounded him. Foster tamped down the urge to enjoy the scent. It was one he was becoming used to. He instead focused solely on the woman and whatever it was that had her upset.

Which wasn't hard considering she stopped in the middle of the open room and whirled around to face him with such acute worry, Foster went right back to high alert.

"Is that the shower going?" she asked, voice pitched higher than normal. Her gaze trailed down to the beer in his hand. He hadn't realized he'd swiped it from the counter next to the sink. "Oh, are you not alone? Is someone else here? Am I interrupting?"

The way she said that made it sound like Foster had a lady friend lying in wait. He laughed the idea off.

"No, no one's here. The only thing you interrupted was me about to drink in the shower and, honestly, that's probably a good thing."

Millie looked a little less distressed, but not fully relieved. Foster sidestepped offering her a beer to get to the reason behind the late visit.

"Millie, what's wrong?"

The AC revved to life and the ice maker in the refrigerator dropped some ice cubes. Foster even heard some frog chirping outside the window. All before Millie worked up enough courage to saying what she'd come to say. She opened her mouth then closed it. She did it again.

There were tears in her voice.

"Annie McHale was gone for two hours before Kelby Creek turned upside down. Less than a week later the entire country wanted to find her, to know what happened." Those tears warbled her normally calm voice. "Fallon was gone for three days, and I had to *beg* for someone to listen to me. Fallon has been gone for six months and no one seems to care about what happened but me. That is, no one until you. But, honestly, if I hadn't gone to the woods that night? If Jason Talbot hadn't come for me? I'm not even sure you would have given Fallon, or me, another thought."

Foster tried to interrupt but she kept on. She wrung her hands.

"I mean no disrespect or lack of appreciation for what you've done so far. It's just that when you told me about Fallon's truck, I couldn't figure out what to feel." She took a step closer to him. "Ever since my dad was killed, life hasn't stuck to any plan I've ever made. School, a future career path, serious relationships, my mom? I learned to roll with the punches as a way to survive because I know things could always be worse. Then, eventually, the only constant in my life became Fallon. He's been my person since he was that ten-year-old boy sitting on his bed practicing cursive."

She took a breath. When she spoke again, her voice was not as tremulous.

"I have tried very hard to make sure he has the stability that we never had growing up. I've tried to make Kelby Creek a real home, to build a foundation that he can always come back to when he's ready. But then? Then he was just gone. And nothing I had done, nothing I *have* done, seemed to matter anymore." She paused. Foster was surprised to see one of her hands fist at her side. "I've spent the last six months trying to find Fallon because I love him, because I want him to be safe, but—in a small way—I don't know who I am without him. Every choice I've made, every decision I've come to in the last several years has been as a sister, as a surrogate mom, as a moral compass. It's been for Fallon, for our family."

Millie stood straighter. Like she'd been zapped by a sudden surge of electricity. Her hands relaxed though her gaze sharpened.

She was no longer on shaky ground.

She was determined.

"But it wasn't until today when I stood in front of you and felt like a suspect that I realized how much your opinion matters to me. How, even though you wouldn't be the first and probably won't be the last person to not believe me, to not trust me, you're the first person I've actually wanted to prove wrong. Not out of spite but because I like being around you. Not as a sister. Not as a guardian or teacher. Me as Millie. I know that probably seems a bit weird considering I barely know you, but it's the truth."

She put her hands on her hips, determination mounting.

"So, all of this was to say, I'm sorry I snapped at you earlier when you were just doing your job. I just— Well, for a lot of reasons, I didn't want this to end. I'm sorry."

Foster watched as Millie let out an exhale that relaxed her rigid stance. Instead of defeat or embarrassment, she seemed relieved.

Then she was waiting.

Waiting for him to respond.

Little did she know that Foster had already come to a conclusion about Millie before she ever set foot inside his house.

Foster smiled. He hoped she saw how genuine it really was.

"Millie Dean, I have never thought you were anything

other than extraordinary," he said, honest. "You're too good for this town, for me, and certainly for anyone who has the gall to think you're less than. I wouldn't keep my distance from you unless you told me to do so. Case or no case."

There it was. The truth. It wasn't as eloquent as Millie's or as deep, but it was how Foster felt.

He might have only known Millie a week, but in that time she'd spent every moment they had together proving that she was a woman to be reckoned with. A warrior with a heart of gold. Someone you were lucky to have by your side in thick or thin or otherwise.

Foster figured he should say that, but Millie made a fool of his detective skills. In a move he truly didn't see coming, Millie closed the space between them and covered his lips with hers. Bruised ribs be damned, Foster didn't move an inch as she pressed against him.

Then it was like she was electrocuted again. She ended the kiss and backed up in a panic.

"I—I'm sorry. I just wanted to do that and realized that maybe you were just being nice and professional and then here I was lunging at you after invading your house!"

In that moment Foster could have done a lot of things.

He could have been professional and told her not to worry but yes, they should focus only on the case for now.

He could have been friendly and assured her that it was just a kiss in a high-pressure situation, and not to read anything into it.

He could have lied and told her that she'd misread his compliments as something more than they were.

He could have told the truth, spelled out the fact that, as much as he admired Millie, he was attracted to her too. That he was a bit upset he hadn't been the one to kiss her first.

Yet Foster didn't want his words to do the talking.

So he asked her a question instead.

He grinned. When his words came out, they were low and filled with unintended grit.

"Millie Dean, why don't you help me take my shirt off and I can show you just how I feel?"

Millie, God bless her, didn't take long to pick up what he was trying to put down.

Instead of being shy about it, though, she surprised him with a smirk that nearly made him lose his cool right then and there.

"Well, considering I helped you put it on this morning in the first place, I guess it would only be fair to help take it off."

And boy, did she do just that.

# Chapter Seventeen

The shower became background noise.

Millie barely registered it. She'd only noted it at all because she expected them to trail that way. Not that she had thought helping the detective take his shirt off because of an injury would lead them directly into the steam together.

Though she'd be lying if her mind wasn't already playing through the logistics of it. Chief among them the fact that there was a good height difference and that her curls would get wet.

But the synapses firing in her head, trying their best to piece together coherent thought, decided whatever happened next with Foster, she was good with. She didn't mind if it was on the floor, in the bedroom, or on the roof.

She wanted him.

More than she'd wanted anyone else in the same sense.

Thankfully, the feeling seemed to be mutual.

The second Millie had his shirt off, Foster was cradling her head in his hands, pulling her close and keeping her against his lips. Millie ate it up. She put her arms around him, steadying them, while her hunger burned through her and out to him.

What started as a warm, introductory kiss deepened. He parted her lips and her tongue searched him out. A moan escaped her lips as he moved his hands down her body, looping one around her back while the other anchored at her hip.

For several blissful moments they were caught in a whirlwind of movement and gasping for air.

Then Foster made a noise.

Millie stopped in an instant.

With hooded eyes and swollen lips she was all concern. "Are you okay? What's wrong?"

Foster still had his arm around her but dropped the one from her hip. He used it to give her a dismissive wave.

"I'm good. I'm fine."

Millie shook her head. "No one who is good or fine says they're both good and fine. Tell me."

Foster sighed. Then he made a face.

"If I tell you then we might stop, and I don't want to do that," he said.

Millie gently wiggled backward out of his grip. She felt guilty in an instant as she realized what was happening.

"Foster! Am I hurting you?"

She had to give it to the man, he was able to look sheepish and devilishly sexy all at once. Beneath Foster's shirt was a lean but muscled body. Something she'd already seen in the hospital but, after feeling its power against her, a work of art she appreciated much more now. Yet among those muscles and smooth skin was an awful smattering of color.

Bruising from Jason Talbot's bullet.

And from Donni Marsden's fists.

That wasn't even accounting for what she couldn't see.

Not to mention, she'd just had to help take his shirt off.

"I'm fine," he repeated. "The pain caught me a little off guard, is all."

Millie shook her head then traced his side again with her eyes.

That's when she saw the scar farther down, right above

the brim of his jeans. It looked like it had once been deep. It was also shiny. Millie had only seen a scar like that once before on her former manager's arm at the store. It had been made by a deep cut. She ran her index finger along the line, like a moth to a flame.

It was a clear reminder that she didn't know much about the man. But that she also wanted to learn.

"That happened a long time ago." His voice had gone low again. Millie absently wondered if it was because of her touch. Even her own tone had changed.

"From Seattle?" She imagined the man in a wild fight with fancy men in suits with misting rain and clouds as a backdrop. Foster, the brooding detective ready to dispense justice. It was an image right out of a television show.

It also was being muscled out by another thought. Foster, however, spoke first before it could fully form.

"I actually got it here in Kelby Creek." He smirked. "From our very own Mrs. Zamboni. Before she was all-knowing, she was a teen with really bad aim and—"

Foster stopped talking. His body went rigid and his green, green eyes widened.

Millie wasn't much better.

The thought that was teasing her fully formed.

It was only the luck of timing that she spoke first.

"When Jason was in my house, he told me that he'd been watching me for weeks and he specifically said in the woods that he'd seen me at the store." She felt a smile pull up her lips, excitement breaking through. "Does that mean we could look at the security camera footage to see him and use that to help us figure something out?"

Foster laughed.

*Really* laughed.

Millie would have been offended had he not hurried with an explanation.

"That could definitely help us get a lead," he said. "Just like the realization I just had might help us."

"You thought of something too?"

Foster placed his hand over hers, still touching his scar.

"You've got the magic touch, apparently."

Millie laughed. "First time I've heard that but I'll take it. What did *you* realize?"

To say the man was excited was an understatement. He looked like a boy in a candy shop with his mom's credit card.

"Helen, the all-knowing Mrs. Zamboni," he said simply.

That surprised her.

"Wait, you want to ask her for psychic advice?"

This time Foster laughed.

"No, but *William Reiner* went to her with questions about his brother after he left town."

Millie raised her eyebrow. "You think that Reiner is looking for his brother?"

"He was then," he said. "Maybe if we know what questions he asked, we can figure out what he did next when he didn't get any answers from her. Maybe we can find out what he's been up to since, and where he might be now."

Millie nodded.

"Or this could be just what we needed to finally get us on the same page as everyone else," Millie said.

They lapsed into a thoughtful silence. To any outsiders they might have looked odd. Standing in the middle of the living room, Foster shirtless and Millie pressing against his scar, both with red lips.

But they were both invested in everything that had happened so far. More so than anyone else.

They'd been attacked, drugged, questioned and confused.

Finding two new avenues to look down? Well, that was two kids in a candy shop combined with a toy store. The possibility that they might find exactly what they needed was thrilling.

Millie wanted to get started now, and she couldn't imagine that Foster felt any differently. That said, she also was well aware that the time was nearing eleven at night.

Foster had already found his way to the thought, it seemed. He answered her next question aloud.

"I'll make some calls first thing in the morning," he said. "There's nothing we can do with either point tonight."

Millie nodded. Then she asked a follow-up question.

This time she knew the answer. Still, it gave her a thrill to ask it.

"So, what do we do now?"

Foster's mouth quirked up at the corners. When he took her hand and started to walk to the hallway, it felt like a thousand butterflies were fluttering around Millie's stomach.

"I can think of a few things."

Pain? What pain?

Foster didn't seem to feel anything other than Millie once they made it to his bed.

She felt curiosity and appreciation from him as he watched her throw off her shirt to match him. She felt excitement and anticipation as she took it a step further and stripped down to her black silk undies that she'd put on by sheer luck. Then it was wide-eyed, grinning fun as he did a two-step and showed her he was a boxer briefs kind of man.

Nothing but strength followed.

Foster picked up Millie's mostly naked body and brought her with him into a swath of fabric. His hands moved just as fast as his mouth covered hers.

He tasted like beer but also something more. Something she liked.

And Millie wanted more.

His hand found her breast, his fingers her nipple. He teased her, kissed her, and the entire bedroom heard her feelings on it all as another moan escaped. It seemed to hit the right note in the man.

Things escalated and it wasn't one-sided at all.

As Foster's hands went exploring again, Millie decided she was ready for the main adventure. She wrapped her legs around him and spun. It broke their kiss but earned a surprised laugh from the detective.

Her curls shifted as she looked down on the man she was now straddling.

Green eyes searched her face. Then he cupped her cheek, running his thumb along her jaw.

"See?" he said. "Extraordinary."

And that was the magic word.

Millie was smiling as she pressed her lips back to his.

SHE WENT INTO the house and didn't come out until it was morning.

He knew because he was at her kitchen table for hours. Waiting.

*You could go next door*, he thought. *If you take her, then the detective will follow anyway. Eventually.*

But, ultimately, he decided against it.

Getting into Millie's house without being seen had been easy. Getting into the detective's house would be trickier.

He couldn't change it.

Not now.

So, he waited instead.

When the birds started chirping and the sun started to paint the sky, he admitted defeat. It was only when he was back in the car and driving past the house and the deputy's cruiser that he saw a glimpse of the two, now going into Millie's.

It was a good thing he hadn't stayed, he realized.

There was no way the detective would let Millie go without a fight.

He'd already proven that by killing Jason Talbot.

Now the plan would have to change.

And his boss wasn't going to like that.

Not at all.

"So, Deputy Calloway probably knows what we did last night, doesn't he?"

Millie started the coffee maker, sliding the thermos Foster had brought with him to her house into the holder. The blissful smell of coffee was enough to give her a zip of energy. Though after spending a good portion of the night *not* sleeping, she'd need a bit more than a zip to make it through the day.

Foster, now dressed to impress in a flannel button-up that was open to show his dark undershirt, a pair of Levi's that hugged, and black-and-white Converse running shoes that gave off punk band vibes, chuckled at her comment. Mostly because he probably knew it was true.

She'd walked to his house in the middle of the night and hadn't come home until the morning. Foster was wearing new clothes, and she was wearing his shirt instead of the one she'd arrived in.

Law enforcement or not, that didn't take much detecting skills to figure out what might have happened behind closed doors.

"According to the sheriff, Calloway is a good guy. Professional," Foster said. "I trust that he won't gossip on what he thinks might or might not have happened."

Millie shook her head. Her curls were a different level of wild. Their time spent in bed, then the shower, then back in bed hadn't helped. Foster's hair, however, was model-worthy. Golden, wavy and nothing but complimentary to the rugged handsomeness of a man who was ready to save the day.

Even if it was barely seven in the morning.

"While this brews, I'm going to go get decent," Millie announced.

It earned a sly smile from the man.

"I think you're already more than decent right now."

Millie rolled her eyes.

The level of comfort with the detective had more than risen in the last few hours. Not only physically. Admitting that she hadn't been living for herself had opened up the floodgates for a lot of pent-up emotion for her. Emotion she hadn't realized had tangled up with Foster as much as it had.

He might not have had any big breakthroughs with her in turn, but that didn't matter.

Not last night.

Not right now.

If Foster needed time to lower some of the walls that seemed to always be present, then that was okay.

Millie might want to live for herself, but that didn't mean she was over finding Fallon.

If anything, she was more determined than ever.

Somewhere between talking with Foster and sleep the night before, Millie had decided on one thing and one thing only.

Fallon wasn't involved in what was happening.

He was a good kid. A good man.

Which put even more fire in her to finally get the story. Finally find her brother.

And Millie believed that Foster was the key to it all.

Even as she retreated from the kitchen to go to her bedroom, she could see the detective going from charming to focused.

Their night together had been great but now it was time to get back to work.

*What happens when it's all done?* The thought was surprising and loud as it rang through Millie's head without warning. *When the danger and mystery are gone, will Foster go with them?*

## Chapter Eighteen

The day started out calm enough.

Deputy Park and Millie went to the grocery store to ask for the security camera footage from two weeks before she met Jason Talbot in the woods, then returned to the department to go through it. Foster meanwhile went to talk to his ex-sister-in-law about her time with William Reiner. For all the resentment Helen had harbored through the years at Foster, she was more than willing to help.

"If knowing what Reiner asked will help you stop whoever drugged and kidnapped you and Millie, I'll tell you everything," she'd said. Then, like it was a tic, she'd run her hand over her pregnant belly. "I love this town and I just want it to be safe for my kids."

Helen had taken him into her office, and among colorful tapestries and crystals had broken down the four questions William Reiner had asked.

It was only after he was leaning against the wall of the break room at the department that he was able to repeat them to Deputy Park and Millie.

"Where did Cole Reiner go the day before he left town? Where was Cole now? Did Cole find what he was looking for? Was Cole in danger?"

Foster finished off his coffee and waited for the two to mull over the questions. A laptop was up between the pair, and both had notepads in front of them. Millie might not have been in law enforcement, but she sure was getting to work like the rest of them. A lot more thrilling than her shift at the grocery store. One that Larissa had been kind enough to cover for her.

"It almost sounds like Reiner is treating his brother like a suspect," she said, head tilted to the side and brows drawn together. "But he wasn't found guilty of anything to do with The Flood, right?"

"There was never any evidence found," Foster stated. "Just suspicion with the timing and how fast he left."

Deputy Park shook his head. "No way was Cole mixed up with any of that," he said. "I came into the department with Cole, and he was a straight arrow. He had to be to live up to William's hype, especially once he had to retire." Millie squirmed a little in her seat, but the deputy went on without noticing. "Even you would have liked him, Love. He was trying to make detective before he left."

Foster pushed off the wall. "Cole Reiner wanted to be a detective?"

"Yeah," Park answered with enthusiasm. "I caught him looking into cold case files one day after his shift ended, and he said he was trying to show initiative. I asked what for, and he told me he wanted to make detective."

"That was absolutely not something I knew."

Foster had up until then been on the same wavelength as Millie when it came to Reiner. He had suspected his brother of being involved in The Flood. But now? Now he was switching gears.

"What if we've been looking at this all wrong?" he asked. "What if *Cole* wasn't a suspect during The Flood but instead he was playing detective?"

Millie was quick. "You think he might have been looking into a cold case?"

Foster shrugged. "He could have actually found something in an old file and followed it. Followed it until he had to leave town. Or was forced. It might account for why he left so suddenly."

"Like Fallon."

Millie's voice was small. Deputy Park looked between them. Foster pressed on through the line of thought.

"Let's speculate wildly for a second here." He took a seat in the chair across from them, hands already up and moving with enthusiasm as he worked through the new theory aloud. "William Reiner asked Helen where Cole went the day before he left town. He must have known, or at least suspected, that Cole was working *something*. Which is why he asks her the follow-up questions of where Cole was then, did he find what he was looking for, and was he in danger. Since I got here, nothing about what's happened has really added up. It feels like we just keep getting curveballs thrown at us during this investigation into what happened to Fallon." Foster couldn't help but smile, knowing it was a stretch but one he felt good making as he said it. "What if *we're* the ones who are throwing a curveball into someone *else's* investigation?"

Millie's head was still slightly tilted in curiosity. He could tell she was working through his pitch. Deputy Park was more vocal with his thought process.

"You think someone else is investigating Fallon's disappearance?"

Foster shook his head. "It feels more like we stumbled onto something else *while* looking into Fallon. That's why nothing is fitting. It's not that we don't have all of the pieces, it's that we're not even on the same game board."

At that Millie started.

"'This ain't a game. If it was, we'd be losing to a much better player.' That's what Donni said on the boat," she recalled. "Maybe you're right. Maybe we're the ones who stepped in late."

Deputy Park shook his head this time. He crossed his arms over his chest and leaned back.

"I'd say you two were on the front lines. Someone did drug and kidnap you. Why else would they do that?"

Millie's eyes widened in excitement as an idea took shape.

"To buy them time," she stated. "We weren't hurt, when we woke up we were unsupervised, and since all of our belongings were fine back at Rosewater, all we lost was the time it took for you to find us."

This time the excitement moved to Foster.

He leaned in. "It was like we were put in time-out. We were sidelined."

Millie mimicked his movement. Her leaning in would have frayed his concentration now that Foster knew what she felt like, tasted like, but them being onto something together was a different kind of excitement that was hard to resist.

"Which means that someone didn't want to hurt us, they just want us out of the way."

"But who *is* that someone?" Deputy Park joined them by rocking forward in his chair and leaning closer. "William Reiner? Cole Reiner? Fallon? And how does Jason Talbot fit into any of that?"

At that, Foster lost some of his enthusiasm.

But not all of it.

"We need to keep digging," he decided. "Did you find anything on the security footage so far?"

Deputy Park sighed but Millie answered.

"No. Jason said he saw me the day I was wearing an orange hair clip but, if he came into the store, he did it through the back. We couldn't find him on the street either. We still have two days before that to go through, though."

Foster stood up, a to-do list updating in his head.

"Let me know if you find anything. If you don't, come get me when you're done."

Millie uncapped her pen. Foster focused on the deputy.

"Do you happen to know which cold case file Cole Reiner was looking at when you walked in on him?"

The department had an outstanding amount of cold cases, and that was before all the town-wide corruption had been uncovered. Since then several closed cases had been reopened and then rerouted to cold case status. Dealing with the sheer volume of them was one of Foster's main goals within his new job.

"I never saw the name of the specific one, but I did see the box. Fall 2012." Park snorted. "And the only reason I remember *that* is because we talked about how dumb it was for someone to label the boxes by seasons and not dates."

Foster might have found the humor in that had he not already guessed finding a file that might or might not have been of interest to Cole was going to be a long shot.

Still, it was an actionable lead since everything else had hit dead ends.

Donni still refused to talk, Wyatt was still in a coma, Jason was dead, the boat had been stripped and searched with nothing of value found, and Fallon, William Reiner, and both of their trucks were still missing.

Cole Reiner felt no more or less attainable as a lead as the rest to Foster.

"I'm going to go see if any cold cases pop out at me. Best case, we get lucky and can tell what he was looking at. Worst case, if he found anything in those files, he took it with him."

"And what happens if it's worst case?" Millie asked. "What happens next?"

Foster didn't realize he already knew before his gut said the words for him.

"I'm going to figure out what the hell happened with Cole Reiner."

FOSTER HADN'T FOUND any cold cases that he thought Cole would have found interesting and, according to the list assigned with the box, there were no files missing. From there he'd gone to trying to find out what Cole had been up to since leaving town.

Based on how much he swore when he didn't think Millie could hear him, that hadn't gone well. Foster went from online searches and phone calls to reaching out to current and former sheriff's department employees who might have seen or heard something like Deputy Park had.

Millie hadn't had much better news.

The security footage of the grocery store had shown several locals and residents going into the store but none had been Jason Talbot. The only familiar faces she and Deputy Park had seen belonged to June Meeks, the Rosewater's bartender, Detective Gordon, the sheriff and Larissa. Not as significant as finding Talbot would have been. It was a small town, after all. Familiar faces weren't uncommon.

Since then Deputy Park had been reassigned to help Foster's search for Cole, and Millie had been given clearance by the sheriff to stick around Foster's office. There she'd decided to do what she'd become good at in the last six months.

She wrote down notes and created timelines, much like she'd done on the whiteboard in her kitchen at home.

If Foster's feeling was right—that it was the two of them who had stumbled onto another investigation entirely—

then assuming everything so far had been connected was as bad as assuming everything wasn't.

Millie was now looking at Fallon's name, which she'd put in the middle of the paper. Arrows branched off from his name in several directions.

If Millie and Foster really were putting a kink in someone else's investigation, then what did that mean for Fallon?

How was he involved?

If he was, why hadn't he reached out to her?

And where had he been?

The cold and creeping worry that Fallon had found something worse than trouble pulled Millie's heart down.

Just as quickly she shook her head to get rid of even the possibility that Fallon's truck was in play because he'd been a victim.

*You haven't thought like that in the last six months. You can't start now*, she mentally chided herself, eyes focusing on the paper between her hands. *There's got to be something you're missing.*

Missing.

Millie tilted her head. A new thought entering.

If Fallon was involved, who was he involved with?

Jason Talbot? Donni or Wyatt? William or Cole Reiner?

Millie grabbed her purse and slung it across her shoulder. She left Foster's office with purpose and didn't slow until she found him leaving the interrogation room.

Even without speaking, she could tell his frustration had been turned up to extra high.

Still, concern lit his features at the sight of her.

"What's wrong?" he asked without preamble. "Did you find something?"

Millie didn't waste time either.

"It might be nothing, but there was a screen missing off one of the Rosewater's back windows when we were looking there the other day. Maybe that wasn't just bad maintenance." She lowered her voice. "We know that Reiner wasn't the one who took us since he was spotted leaving the bar before us, so whoever drugged us and took us from the bar had to be close, right? Did anyone from the department search the midsection of rooms at the motel? If not, can we?"

Foster shook his head. That frustration stretched into something else.

"No, but, Millie, Wyatt Cline just woke up and he said he wants to talk."

# Chapter Nineteen

The hospital was quiet.

Somehow, that made being there exponentially more unsettling.

At least that's what Millie told him, shoulder against his as they walked side by side down the hallway and toward the elevator. Since their unexpected time together, he'd realized their orbit had gotten smaller around one another.

Little moments.

Leaning in toward her, touching the small of her back or her elbow to lead her in the direction they needed to go, looking at her when she was doing something else.

It was an odd feeling.

It also wasn't a logical one.

Foster had known Millie for a little over a week. Within that week they had been put in high-pressure situations that weren't run-of-the-mill by any means. Danger, fear and violence had created a bond between them. An understanding and relatable thread.

But when they found Fallon?

When they figured out what happened with Cole and William Reiner?

Well, Foster imagined they'd have to talk about what he and Millie meant to each other then and if that thread between them had severed.

Foster wouldn't be mad about it.

He'd been with Regina for a decade and known her for a decade more. She'd been a great woman and they'd had all the tools to have a great life together.

But they hadn't.

Foster knew deep down that that wasn't all on him, that they'd been too young when they'd married and then kept on with their mistake just to prove everyone wrong. Yet there had been another factor that had put pressure on their marriage.

Foster loved his job and, when it came to solving a case, to getting justice, he kept going until it was done.

Right now, that worked for Millie and him. She wanted to know what had happened to her brother and wanted justice for their abduction. The truth was, though, that Fallon wouldn't be his next case, nor the one after.

Would Millie still be accepting of his job then? Of him? Of his inability to let go?

*Maybe you're the one who's trouble, Love*, he thought to himself as they moved into the elevator. *Here you are with a lead and you're wondering if Millie will still want to kiss you after it's been followed.*

Millie, unaware of yet another series of thoughts pertaining to her rattling around in his head, eyed the elevator around them with blatant hesitation.

"What I like less than a hospital that's eerily quiet is a metal box that has the ability to plummet back down to the ground with me in it."

There Foster went smiling again.

"Just think of it like a car going uphill." He pressed the button for the third floor. He didn't say it, but he suspected the quiet of the lobby would disappear once they made it to Wyatt's room.

At least he hoped.

Any information Wyatt might give was probably more than they had.

Millie lobbed a side-eye at him. Warm amber.

"Watch out there, Detective," she said with a smirk. "You might make me afraid of cars too."

Foster mirrored the smile but quieted. When the elevator stopped at the third floor, there was a lag in the doors opening. Like a switch had been flipped, the teasing stopped.

"What if Wyatt doesn't know anything?" Millie's voice wasn't just small. It was broken.

Foster knew that that wasn't the question she really wanted to ask.

*What if Wyatt knows something and it's not good?*

A lack of answers had so far hurt and saved Millie. She had no idea what had happened to Fallon, which meant she could blissfully stay away from the worst-case scenario. Wyatt could keep her in the dark or he could shine the light on an uglier truth.

And there wasn't anything Foster could do about it.

"You don't need to be in there, Millie," he reminded her. "I'll repeat every word he says to me."

Millie shook her head. "We're a team," she said with purpose. "I want to be there. I need to be there."

The elevator doors slid open and they walked out onto the floor. At the end of the hallway stood the sheriff. He had waited for them.

"I didn't think we were a team," Foster teased, trying to diffuse as much of the mounting tension as he could before they were at Wyatt's room.

Millie played ball.

"We won't be a team long if you keep telling me things like pretend elevators are cars. Next thing I know you're going to tell me to imagine a clown the next time I'm at the dentist."

"So you're afraid of clowns? Or you're afraid of the dentist?"

Millie laughed. "If you value this partnership, then you'll avoid both topics."

"Fair enough."

The walk to the sheriff was a short one. All jokes and teasing were left at Wyatt's door. Sheriff Chamblin tipped his cowboy hat to both of them before taking it off all together.

"The doc said he's stable and not resisting or anything," he told them. "He wouldn't let me handcuff him, but he's had hospital security on him the entire time one of us couldn't be here."

"Good," Foster said. "Has he talked to you or anyone about what's going on?"

The sheriff shook his head. "Since he's not going anywhere and you're lead on this, I wanted to wait." He looked to Millie, then back to Foster. If he was about to try to talk him out of letting Millie come in too, he was going to have a hard time of it.

Thankfully, he didn't.

"I'll let you keep the lead on this," he said instead. Then he held the door open for him and Millie. "Let's get us some answers."

The hospital security officer gave them a nod as Foster, Millie and the sheriff set up in the room. They each took up a spot around the hospital bed. Millie to the left, the sheriff to the right and Foster at the end. Despite their closer proximity, Wyatt's gaze went to and stuck to Foster.

"Wyatt Cline, I'm Detective Lovett with the sheriff's department and I have a few questions."

MILLIE HAD SEEN Foster naked, felt him against *her* naked, yet seeing him command the absolute attention of a man who had tried to shoot him days before brought out a different kind of attraction in her. It was like seeing someone in his element and being in awe of him.

Respect mixed with admiration and a big pinch of passion added in.

It was easy to stand there, quiet, and watch him do his job. Even the sheriff remained silent as Foster dove in without further preamble.

"Why were you out on that boat?"

Beneath the fluorescent lights of the hospital, Wyatt Cline appeared harmless enough. He was round and young and had dark rings beneath his eyes. A young man who looked like he was working himself to the bone for some corporate bigwig and a promotion he probably was never going to get. And now he was in the hospital for it, an older man of the law ready to give him a stern talking-to.

He didn't fit the image of intimidating. He definitely didn't fit the image of Donni Marsden's partner in crime.

Wyatt rolled his eyes, only adding to the impression of youth Millie got from the young man.

"I'd always wanted to go night fishing," he responded, voice a bit on the scratchy side. "Seemed like as good of a time as any to try it out."

Foster stopped the story by holding up his hand.

"We heard everything you said before Deputy Park showed up. You were looking for me and Miss Dean. Why and how did you know where to go?"

Wyatt didn't respond this time.

It only made Foster lean in more.

"Wyatt, you pulled a shotgun out and aimed at a member of law enforcement. That's attempted murder, bud. It was also caught on Deputy Park's body camera so it's not just hearsay. It's a provable fact." Foster took a beat, letting his words settle in a little. "This conversation right now doesn't keep you from going to prison. It only decides on how long you'll be there. So, if I were you, I'd start cooperating while my patience is still intact. And let me tell you, after the week I've had, that patience is paper thin and only getting thinner."

All of the defiance and snark seemed to deflate right on out of the younger man. He shared a look with Millie and the sheriff before going back to Foster.

He came to a decision quick. "I want immunity," he declared. "Immunity or I don't say anything."

The sheriff spoke up on that. "We can only start to talk about talking about a lesser sentence if you give us actionable information, just so you're clear."

Wyatt didn't like that. Foster was quick to slide back in.

"That's the only shot at a good deal you're going to get during all of this, Wyatt," he said. "If that works out then, add in good behavior, and it could mean the difference of years."

Millie didn't know if that was necessarily true—she'd seen on cop shows where they'd stretched the truth to *get* the truth—but she found she didn't care at the moment. Wyatt knew something.

They needed to know that something too.

Wyatt gave them all another passing glance.

Then defeat was all that showed on his freckled face.

"Fine. I'll tell you what I know."

The sheriff pulled out a notepad and pen. Millie didn't mean to, but she took a small step closer. Foster, ever the detective in charge, stayed as sturdy as a statue.

"Why did you go out to the boat?" he repeated.

Wyatt sighed and surprised her yet again. He lifted his arm slowly and pointed in her direction.

"Donni called and said he'd heard that her and some cop had been taken. He said we could use that to finally get what we wanted."

Foster didn't miss a beat. "What was it that you wanted? And how would Millie help you get it?"

Wyatt was a little more hesitant. "We thought that since he was finally making a move, we could use that to force him into a trade for her."

"Who's he?"

This time Wyatt was the one who looked surprised.

"William Reiner," he said matter-of-factly. "Y'all were taken to the boat to be delivered to him. You know, he's the bad guy, right?"

For the first time, Foster faltered.

Millie didn't know why yet—or maybe she did—but her blood started to turn to ice in her veins. A creeping cold that began to freeze her in place atop the tile floor.

"Do you know who drugged and kidnapped us to take us to the boat?" he asked, recovering.

Wyatt gave a half-shrug, then flinched. For a moment Millie had forgotten they were in a hospital, talking to a former gunshot and coma patient still attached to hospital equipment and an IV.

"Never seen him myself but I'm guessing Cole Reiner, you know, his brother."

"We would have noticed if Cole Reiner had been around to drug us." Foster's voice had gone even. No inflection, just powerful monotone.

Wyatt shrugged again. "I mean, that's probably where June comes in."

"Say again?" the sheriff spoke up. "You're talking about June Meeks?"

"Yeah."

"And why would June drug anyone?"

Wyatt snorted. "Well, she was pretty hot and heavy with Cole before he 'disappeared.'"

Sheriff Chamblin looked at Foster. His jaw set. Hard. He was angry.

He'd been the one to vouch for June and, Millie was guessing, he'd had no idea about her former relationship with the younger Reiner.

Foster, however, stayed on point.

"So you're saying that June drugged us so Cole could take us out to an abandoned boat in the middle of the creek. Where we would then wait for his brother to come and collect Millie. Why would William Reiner go through all of that trouble and why would he go for Millie?"

A monitor beeped.

Someone made noise out in the hallway.

Air came out into the room from somewhere.

Millie could have sworn she heard her own heartbeat.

"Donni said he guessed it was because, after all of this time, she was still poking around to find out what happened to her brother. She even got a new guy, you, to help her. Some hotshot detective from the big city."

Millie took a small step again. This time backward.

Foster didn't volley back a question quick enough.

She knew it then, right then, that he'd already finished the conversation with Wyatt in his head.

That he'd already reached the end of the road.

That he already knew that her brother hadn't left Kelby Creek at all.

"William Reiner didn't want Millie looking for Fallon?" Foster had to ask.

Wyatt snorted.

Actually snorted.

He shook his head. "Considering he killed Fallon, no, I'm guessing he didn't want her, or anyone else, looking for him."

There it was.

The end of Millie's world, coming from the mouth of a man with shadows beneath his eyes.

This time Millie could have sworn that, instead of her heartbeat, she heard her heart break.

# Chapter Twenty

Millie spent a good while tucked into Foster's chest.

She didn't know how long, and she didn't care who saw. For a while it was just the two of them. His heartbeat against her ear, his arms holding her together.

But, then, Foster had to go.

He had a bad guy to catch, he had a mystery to solve.

He had to get justice for someone who had been unfairly taken.

Fallon.

Every time his name echoed in Millie's head, she felt like she was falling deeper down into a hole. She saw the man he'd been, the child she'd loved, and the person she'd hoped to see him become.

Happy, healthy, and no longer struggling beneath the weight of his past.

Then came the awful sense of despair right after.

The churning and curdling heat of anger and hate came next.

Millie let herself attach to those ugly feelings to get her through everything that had to happen next. Then? Later on? She would go back to that deep, dark hole and cry into it until there was nothing left to give.

So, while her eyes might have been red and swollen already, when Foster pulled her into an empty hospital room half an hour later, Millie's words were running on default mode. She looked up at the man who had caught her the moment Wyatt Cline had destroyed her world.

Those green eyes—which now Millie was sure reminded her of tall grass on a cool day—searched her face with nothing but empathy. He stroked her cheek and then dropped his hand to her shoulder. The pressure felt nice, comforting. At least for a second.

Then it was gone and Foster was talking.

"There's a few things I need to do, so Amanda is going to take you home and keep you company until I'm done. Is that okay?"

"Did Wyatt tell you anything else?" Millie's voice was hoarse. Not too badly but enough to remind them both that she'd sobbed hard for a bit.

Foster looked like he'd rather not say, but he surprised her and said it anyway.

"He said he works for Donni, but Donni answers to someone else. Wyatt swears he's never known who that is, but that the Reiner brothers took something of theirs that they need to get back."

"Something? Like what?"

Foster rubbed his hand along his jaw. Millie hadn't noticed the stubble that sprouted along it until now.

"I don't know. The easy guess? Drugs or money. There's not much else usually good enough to entice the aggression of drugging and kidnapping a civilian and a member of law enforcement."

"Donni and Wyatt wanted to trade me to William Reiner to get back their boss's drugs and or money," Millie stated.

"That's what Wyatt's claiming."

Millie shook her head. It wasn't meant to be a disagreement. Instead, it was more disbelief than anything.

"That's a long, winding way to go to just kill me," she said. "I don't understand the trouble of it all."

Or the senselessness.

Killing Fallon for—what?—revenge? Then trying to get Millie to keep her from getting answers?

It was the last few dominoes of tragedy falling, the first one to be pushed over being her father's death.

Foster's hands were back to positions of comfort. They wrapped around her upper arms and steadied her.

"I will get every person involved and every answer we need. Okay?"

Millie nodded. She believed him.

Which was why she wanted him to leave.

"And you can't do any of that while worrying about me," she said. "I'll go home with Amanda."

Foster didn't look relieved but he nodded.

"Deputy Calloway is already outside your house, and his partner will come in and check on you two every half hour. There's also an updated all-points bulletin out on Cole. And June, who the sheriff is personally very invested in finding considering what Cline said about her involvement in our abduction." He used his finger to gently push her chin up so that her gaze was fully wrapped in his. "I'll be home as soon as I've ended this."

Foster's kiss was brief. The feeling it stirred within her wasn't. When he stepped back and helped her out into the hallway, Millie realized she'd have to unpack the complicated emotions tearing her up from the inside.

But now wasn't the time.

Amanda met her at the elevator, blue hair bright and frown severe. She didn't say anything. Just put her arm around Millie's shoulders on the way down.

She didn't need to pretend the elevator was a car anymore.

Not after her worst fear had come true.

DETECTIVE LEE GORDON lived in a part of Kelby Creek that Foster was unfamiliar with. A hard feat, given the size of town and the fact that he'd been adventurous growing up within its borders. Yet while driving up the long, twisted dirt road that led to a surprisingly large one-story house with a field behind it and woods on either side, Foster had to reorient himself a few times. He knew roughly where they were but, as he got out, it felt like he was on an island.

Total seclusion.

Foster just hoped that didn't translate to a man who was as helpful to him now as he had been to Millie when working Fallon's case.

*Fallon.*

Foster had known there was a good chance that the conversation with Wyatt wouldn't go the way they wanted. Still, hearing him say that Reiner had killed Fallon... That had hit hard.

Mostly because he could tell Millie knew it was coming.

The more Wyatt spoke, the more Millie seemed to build her defenses. Her body language kept changing from the first word until the last.

Yet all of those defenses—mental and otherwise—hadn't been enough.

And all Foster could do was catch her when they had come down.

When the tears came, they'd come from six months of worry. From years of love. From a life that should have been lived to one that didn't seem possible.

Foster had seen it before throughout his career. He'd seen hope and devastation all within one conversation. Yet Millie's body shaking against his, racked with sobs, felt different to him.

Rage and anguish and protectiveness had vied for top emotional position within him.

He didn't want to just console Millie, he wanted to change the world for her.

Something the sheriff seemed to pick up on.

"Remember what you told me about Regina and why your marriage didn't work out?" he'd asked after Millie had taken a seat in the hall so they could have a private moment. Foster had been more than surprised at that remark, but he'd nodded. "Tell me again," the sheriff added.

So Foster had.

"We were restless and young and got married to get away. Then we wanted to prove everyone who had told us it was a bad idea wrong so badly that we became people who liked each other but hated being married to each other." Foster had looked at Millie then. She was out of earshot but still he quieted. "Regina never understood why I loved my job and why I couldn't give it up."

"And why can't you give it up?"

"Because every case I work is about someone else's life," he'd answered. "And it's hard to give up on a life."

The sheriff had clapped him on the shoulder and smiled. It was a quick thing, but Foster couldn't help but be reminded of his father.

"*That* right there is the reason why you're one of the best people I know," he'd said. "And why we're going to help her life by giving her peace about Fallon Dean's death."

It was a pep talk, true as true could be, and it stuck its landing. Millie giving him the okay to keep going down the rabbit hole only strengthened Foster's feeling of purpose.

Of determination.

That focus was now drenched into his every movement. He took his badge and gun and hopped up the front porch stairs two at a time.

Detective Gordon had questioned the lead suspect when Fallon had disappeared. Gordon's statement on William Reiner had been short and had said in less than one paragraph that William hadn't done it and was a good man. There was no mention of an alibi or reason to drop suspicion in Gordon's file. Just like there had been no mention of Millie and Fallon's backstories and why Fallon's note should have been in cursive.

The retired detective had been incompetent.

Now he was going to have to answer for it, as well as where his former colleague William Reiner might be.

Foster knocked against the door, already feeling his face harden in anticipation of an ornery man. According to Deputy Park, Gordon spent most of his retirement golfing, hunting and frequently bringing a new date to the country club in the city. Being questioned by the detective in between those activities probably wouldn't be something he'd appreciate.

Then again, maybe it was Foster's feelings for Millie that were coloring his opinion of the man he'd never met.

Either way, the longer Detective Gordon didn't answer the door, the more frustrated Foster became.

He walked around the porch and peered into the open garage. A small, sporty car in fire-engine red sat inside. Retirement sure was looking good for the man.

Foster backtracked to one of the front windows of the house and looked inside. A curtain obscured the view. He took a moment to listen. When nothing and no one made a noise, he decided to take a better look around.

He went back down the porch steps and walked around to the garage. Foster unbuttoned his holster and kept his hand hovering over his gun as he moved past the expensive ride and to the door that led inside the house.

This time he didn't knock.

The door was splintered at the lock.

It had been kicked in.

The gun came out of its holster in a flash.

He should have waited or called in backup, but all he

could think about was Detective Gordon being in danger. No matter how incompetent he was, it didn't mean he deserved that.

Foster pushed the door open while doing his best to be quiet. It led into a galley-style kitchen, long and narrow. Sparse but high-end. Metal backsplash and granite countertops. A double oven and a beast of a refrigerator. Foster's gut started to wake up, but it wasn't the time to listen to it.

He moved through the room and turned into the living area. Foster's mind went through two different tasks.

*Details.*

Leather couches, large, flat-screen TV, a bricked fireplace with a mantel of law enforcement memorabilia, a high-end sound system and an honest to goodness self-portrait of Detective Gordon in uniform.

*Defense.*

There were three exits that led out of the room. The one he'd come through, one to the left that led into a hallway and one straight ahead that led to the front porch and outside. No one stood in the room or at any of the exits.

Foster continued on his tour.

The hallway had four doors that branched off to make up the right side of the house. The first door was open and showed a bathroom.

It looked like it came out of catalog, same as the next room. Foster opened its door and would have whistled had he not been trying to keep quiet. It was a home office but unlike any he'd seen in real life. Not even the *sheriff's* office at the department was as decadent.

One wall was nothing but a bookcase. Half of it was filled with books while trinkets and knickknacks were interspersed between. The desk in front of it was slick metal and glass, the computer on its top slim and expensive. Two armchairs were set up much like the standard layout at the department but, unlike the department, there was a small table between them with an ashtray, a cigar cutter and the ends of two cigars.

Foster stopped a second and listened again. He heard no movement anywhere else, so he did what his gut was whispering to do and went to the desk. There, with gun in one hand, he used the other to open the top drawer.

Paper, pens, thumbtacks. Sticky notes.

Nothing out of the ordinary.

He opened the second drawer.

It was empty.

The third drawer wasn't.

There were more office supplies. But a bundle of black zip ties was what caught and kept Foster's attention.

It wasn't unusual for those in law enforcement to have them, even retirees, but, still, Foster's gut wasn't buying it.

He was about to go to the fourth drawer when the sound of a door squeaking made him pause. Footfalls from, he guessed, the bedroom.

Foster took a few long, quick strides to the side of the door, just in time to get out of view from whoever was coming. His grip tightened on his gun.

It could have been Gordon.

If it was, Foster should have announced himself.

He *was* trespassing.

But his gut had gone from whispering to yelling so Foster didn't say a word.

A good choice, considering the man who walked into the office and right past Foster wasn't the man who owned the house.

Foster raised his gun and pointed it at the newcomer as he got behind the desk.

"Move and I'll shoot," Foster warned.

To his credit, William Reiner remained calm.

"I told him I heard someone," he said. "He said no one would come out here because no one had done it before, but I've seen your résumé, Lovett. And I know you're better than that."

The footsteps came out of nowhere. Foster barely had time to spin around.

For the first time in his career, he hesitated. *Truly* hesitated.

The young man's face was busted and bruised.

Foster lowered his aim, despite self-preservation and years of honing his instincts telling him to do otherwise.

Instead, he said the first thing that came to mind.

"What in the hell is going on?"

THE WHITEBOARD WOULD have undone her all over again had Millie not already felt numb. It was like gaining distance from the hospital had put space between the awful truth of her brother being gone and her current situation.

Denial.

That's what it was.

Deep and reaching denial.

Amanda walked the line between being supportive in silence and asking if she could get Millie anything. Past that she split her time between hovering and talking to Deputy Waller, one of the two deputies who had been assigned to Millie until the Reiner brothers and June were caught.

It was during one of those conversations where Amanda was on the front porch with the man that Millie ventured into the kitchen with the idea of finding something sweet to lessen the pain. Instead, she looked at one of the only things in the house that could take her denial and break it down completely.

The whiteboard had seemed like such a good idea after Fallon had disappeared. Sure, it didn't match the decor of the kitchen—or the house for that matter—but it had helped Millie straighten her thoughts, all leads and the timeline of what had happened. The story of Fallon's life, written by the sister who was willing to do anything to fight for his future.

Now the marker was a violent contrast, but Millie couldn't look away. She wrapped her arms around herself and traced the date that Fallon had disappeared through Detective Gordon's barely there investigation to side points listing Fallon's friends, his job and then to the people who might want to do him harm.

Kelby Creek, written in all caps.

Beneath it was Deputy William Reiner.

Or it used to be.

Millie took an uncertain step forward.

The name hadn't only been erased, it had been replaced. "Dobb's stockroom. Come alone."

The words spilled over into notes about the Kintucket Woods and would have raised alarm in Millie, realizing that someone who wasn't her had written them.

But all Millie could do was cover her mouth with one hand and touch the marker with the other.

Every new word was written in cursive.

Fallon's cursive.

Something she knew by heart.

"Hey, Millie?"

Amanda's voice carried in from the living room.

All at once Millie made a decision. She didn't have time to wonder if it was a good one.

"In here."

She managed to get to the edge of the kitchen counter and lean against it before Amanda and her blue hair came into view. Instead of repeating the question asking if she was okay, she kept to a more neutral route.

"Deputy Waller just had some food dropped off, and I was wondering if you were hungry. He's out on the front porch with a smattering of choices."

Millie was touched, but she was also working on her

maybe-not-the-best plan. Guilt spread across her conflicted heart as she feigned exhaustion.

"Honestly, I'd really just love to lay down," she lied. "I haven't been getting a lot of sleep lately and, well, today's been a lot."

Sympathy pure and true wrapped around every part of the coroner. She nodded, understanding.

"You do what you need to do," she said. "I'll get Waller to bring the food in and maybe we can eat later when you're feeling up to it?"

"That sounds good. Thank you." Millie paused as she walked by. "I mean it, Amanda. Thank you for being so kind."

Amanda shrugged. "I've found it's easy to be nice to good people."

Millie gave her a small smile, and they went in opposite directions. She wondered if Amanda would still think she was good people when she realized Millie had sneaked out.

Because that's exactly what Millie was about to do.

# Chapter Twenty-One

Dobb's Grocer always smelled like cinnamon.

Millie had thought that the first time she'd walked through its front door past the Help Wanted sign and she thought it now as she used her keys to sneak in through the back.

The bike she'd "borrowed" from a neighbor down the block was resting against the brick wall that extended across the back alley. Main Street might have been out front, but the small alley that ran behind the buildings felt like a world away.

So did the back section of the grocery store.

For a small town, Dobb's was quite large. The main store spanned two buildings and always had two cashiers and one manager out front. The stockroom was the first door once inside and ran the same length of the two buildings but was narrow and filled to the brim with boxes, crates and product not yet shelved. Past that were the doors to the freezer where the meats were kept and the break room and employee bathrooms. If you kept straight on then you entered the shopping section of the store, right between the medicine aisle and the small toy aisle in the main room.

If Fallon wanted to meet her, there was only one room in the building that would give him the best chance of privacy.

Millie paused outside the stockroom door, hand hovering over the handle.

That morning Fallon had been dead; now he was waiting for her in the stockroom?

Was it naive of her to think that was true or was she back to being hopefully desperate and walking into a trap?

While she was sure the note on the whiteboard at her house was new within the last few days, that meant that Fallon would have meant her to find it after he'd written it. Was she too late now?

*Standing here won't get you answers*, her inner voice said. *The only way through it is through.*

Millie looked around the open area between the back half of the store. A part of her felt overwhelmingly glad that Larissa was off and that she hadn't told Foster where she was going. Also that the manager's office was at the front of the store so the chance of Robert walking back and finding her would be slim. Same for whoever the two cashiers on shift were.

Millie didn't rightly know who they were other than they weren't Larissa. She had, admittedly, not had her mind on work for the last week or so. Her thoughts had, instead, run between Fallon and Foster.

Two men she felt she needed but for much different reasons.

Millie flexed her fingers. The weight of her cell phone in her back pocket was like an alarm that never went off.

It was like when she'd gone out to the Kintucket Woods. There was nothing but hope on this side of the door, and the last time she followed hope into the woods, she'd been pulled into a series of threats, danger and the unknown.

*Was* it the totally wrong move to risk it all for even the chance of finding Fallon there? Fallon in perfect health and William Reiner nowhere near them?

It was.

Millie knew that.

She also knew that if there was any chance at all that Fallon was waiting for her, she'd always choose to go.

So Millie opened the door and went inside.

The fluorescents buzzed to life and illuminated the long room. No one and nothing jumped out at her as out of the ordinary. Shadows scattered across the floor-to-ceiling metal shelves and the various packages and goods on each. Toward the back half of the room sat a stack of four pallets with empty, open boxes. It was a recycling pile. Employees took it out only when it nearly touched the ceiling.

Millie approached the cluster of boxes, heart hammering away.

She already knew what was supposed to be on the other side of them—two lawn chairs and a pillow where their youngest employee sometimes sat and played on his phone when he was supposed to be stocking—but she hoped there was something else.

Someone else.

She held her breath and made her way around the pallet.

Fallon wasn't there.

No one was.

Millie let out that breath in defeat.

Maybe she'd just missed him or maybe he hadn't come yet.

*Or maybe you're reaching.*

Millie shook the thought out of her head and started to search the area. The toolbox beneath one of the chairs that housed the store's box cutters, a hammer, and occasionally a candy bar, was partially opened.

Millie dragged it out and pushed the lid up. A folded piece of paper with her name written on the top was the first thing she saw.

It was written in cursive.

Foster's cursive, much like the note on the whiteboard.

The message inside was short. "I'm okay. I promise."

And there it was.

Millie might not have known all the answers to what was going on, but that was enough hope to lift the weight that had been crushing her since Wyatt had spoken to them. A glimmer of light in the dark.

She could work with that.

Millie slipped the note into her pocket and felt new resolve flood through her. Now it was time to rectify her mistake. Foster needed to know what she'd found, she decided, pulling out her cell phone.

They were partners, after all.

Better intentions or not, Millie didn't get far.

"Where is it?"

Millie spun around at the new, deep voice behind her, instantly terrified.

It wasn't Fallon.

It wasn't Foster.

It wasn't even Aaron, the teen who did their stocking.

Much like in the woods, all at once Millie realized just how badly she'd messed up. Her desperation had led her into danger.

No one knew where she was.

No one but the last man she'd expected to see.

FALLON DEAN STOOD in front of Foster like it was the most normal thing in the world for him to be there. Like him, William Reiner and Foster were just three men socializing in a home office on a nice, warm afternoon.

Not at all like a man who had been missing for six months. Definitely not like a man who had been supposedly killed by a Reiner.

A Reiner who spoke up quickly.

"We can explain," he said.

Foster, who hadn't even entertained the thought that Fallon would be who he found in Detective Gordon's house, rebutted with the first thing that came to his mind.

"You better have a good damn reason why this one here has made his sister worry for the last six months."

Fallon winced, but that might have had more to do with the bruises across his cheek or his busted lip. He gave the older Reiner a look caught somewhere between guilt and anger.

It heralded in a new tone for William. One that oddly sounded fond.

Two seconds into the conversation and Foster was already reevaluating everything they had thought they'd known.

"He does," William said. "But I can only tell you so much before we start having to make decisions."

Foster took a step back so he could look at both men. He didn't like that he was outnumbered. He also didn't like that he was the only one who didn't seem to know what was happening. Still, he kept his gun down and aim away from both men. A part of him knew that he wouldn't have been able to point his weapon anywhere near the grown man Millie had basically raised.

It didn't help that there was no denying the resemblance between the Dean siblings. Fallon's complexion was a match to Millie's, along with his dark hair with some curl. His eyes, the same shape but a different shade of brown, searched Foster's expression with a curiosity that Foster bet the man carried with him always. A trait that, no doubt, was thanks to his father's influence and belief in always learning.

Still, just because he wasn't going to aim his gun at Fallon didn't mean he wasn't going to lob some accusations at him.

"It was you," Foster said, sure of it in that moment.

"You were the one I fought. You took us from Rosewater and put us on the boat."

"Yes, he is but there's a reason—" William started.

Foster wasn't having it. "We're about to get really acquainted in a second here, bud," he interrupted Reiner. "I want Fallon to answer me now."

"Fine," the older man replied. "But make it quick, Fallon. We're in a hurry."

Foster let that one go simply because he wanted to hear how Fallon could possibly make what he'd done okay.

Millie's brother or not, he'd made some bad choices. Ones that could only lead to being arrested.

Something Foster should have been doing now.

Fallon let out a breath that was long and tired. Then he was talking a mile a minute.

"William asked you to meet him in the kitchen a few minutes after he left through the front door so no one would suspect that he was involved. That timed everything right for Millie who passed out pretty quickly from the meds. You too, but when we were loading Millie in, it was like you came back awake and ready to fight. It didn't last long but, obviously, long enough." Fallon motioned to the bruising. "It might not have been the best or well-executed plan, but we didn't expect you two to team up to solve all the mysteries."

"So you sidelined us."

Fallon nodded. "We needed you and Millie out of the way just for a little while, especially after Jason had already tried to hurt her."

"Kill her," Foster corrected. "Jason Talbot tried to take her, and then when she ran he tried to kill her."

Fallon tensed all over.

"Which is why when you two kept at it it made a less than ideal decision," William interrupted.

"To drug an innocent woman and cop and dump them

on a boat to only then get attacked by two criminals? Less than ideal is a less than apt description of that plan."

"We didn't know who was watching," Fallon told him. "We—"

"We don't have time to tell you all the details." William cut him off. There was palpable tension in his shoulders. Time was running out.

Foster just didn't know what for.

"Why are you two here?" Foster pivoted to his most current question.

"Why are you?" William threw back. It, like his body language, was filled with mounting anxiety.

Foster didn't see the harm in telling the truth. Something he hoped the other two men would reciprocate with more clarity than the vague explanations they were giving him.

"I was hoping to ask Lee Gordon about the statement he took from *you*—" he pointed to William and then thumbed back to Fallon "—about *your* disappearance after Wyatt Cline said *you* were killed by *him* for revenge six months ago." He reversed his motions. Both men seemed surprised.

"He said I was dead?" Fallon's worry showed in his tone of voice. Foster knew where this was headed.

"Yep. He told me *and* your sister that a few hours ago."

Both men cussed.

William Reiner walked around the desk, closer to them. Not at all worried about the gun still in Foster's hand.

"If Wyatt Cline woke up and is talking, then there's a good chance Lee Gordon is about to pull a disappearing act," he stated. "Which means if he isn't already gone, he'll be coming back to pack to leave soon."

"You're going to have to give me a lot more than that." Foster turned his gaze to Fallon. "Start with what you've been doing for the last six months and how Reiner here is involved."

Again, Fallon didn't get a second to even open his mouth to respond. Instead, it was William who answered.

"He's been helping me look for my brother, the only place we knew to look. Which brought us a whole lot of nothing until we ran smack-dab into trouble last week." A look of disapproval moved across the older man's face. It was aimed at Fallon. "When both Fallon and his sister decided to do something impulsive."

"Give me more," Foster ordered.

Fallon sighed. "I took a chance and stole something from someone I shouldn't have. Then apparently Millie went to the woods to look for me and found Jason instead."

The pieces, as wild and unpredictable as they'd been since Foster had met Millie, started to vibrate in his gut. Like magnets sensing their partner, getting ready to connect.

"That's why Jason went after Millie," he said, realization dawning. "He was trying to get back what you took? Then Wyatt and Donni went after it after Jason was killed?" He looked to William, who didn't correct or argue the questions. "Wyatt said that you'd want Millie for revenge because of your accident and that you would trade her for whatever it was that was taken."

William nodded.

"But Wyatt was under the impression that Fallon was dead and that Cole and June Meeks were helping you," Foster added.

He didn't miss that at the mention of Cole's name, William's expression turned pained.

"June helped us because she loved my brother, but... but Cole... He's not a part of this."

That didn't sound good.

Not at all.

Foster thrummed his fingers along the butt of his gun.

If he had misread the intentions of the two men too close to him in a small room, he'd have to act fast.

"What happened to Cole?"

A look passed between William and Fallon. The former gave the other a small nod.

Fallon let out a breath of regret. "After The Flood happened, Cole suspected that there was someone still dirty in the department who didn't get caught. Someone who had taken a lot of money through the years to doctor files and cover up certain misdeeds. But Cole didn't know who exactly that was and decided to try to find out on his own just in case." He gave another look to William.

"And he didn't come to you?" Foster asked the older Reiner.

That pained look sunk in his frown.

"Not every sibling pair can be as close as the Dean children."

Foster wasn't about to argue that as Fallon continued.

"Cole disappeared completely soon after he quit, and that's when William started trying to figure out what was going on. We never found Cole but a few months back heard talk that a former young deputy from the department had been killed for trying to stop a massive drug deal out in Riker County."

"Cole," Foster surmised.

Fallon nodded.

"So, how does Cole go from quitting to being in the middle of a massive drug deal several counties over?"

William took this question. "When Cole was new to the force, a friend of his was killed in a drug bust that, according to the file, his friend facilitated. The case always bothered Cole because he didn't believe his friend could do that, but it wasn't until The Flood happened that he questioned what actually went down. Cole started looking into every member of law enforcement and official involved in the case, all the way down to the coroner. Then he quit and then he disappeared. My guess is he found his way from who he suspected to the drug supplier who had supposedly sold to his friend who was killed. Then he died trying to stop them."

"So you *have* been investigating Cole's investigation," Foster said. "And we've been investigating Fallon, which ran right into you."

William nodded. "I tried for months to figure out where Cole was and who he suspected. Then one day I was drinking myself dumb when this one here showed up at my door."

Foster had been waiting for this. The connection between the man who supposedly hated Fallon the most and Fallon himself.

"It was the anniversary of his retirement and the paper did a story on it. Like a recap," Fallon said, taking over. "I realized, after all of the years, that I never actually apologized for my part in the accident. Or explained why I was out there at all. But when I showed up he was clearly upset about something else. And, well, he told me everything he knew and I offered to help if I could."

"And he did." William smiled. It was brief but genuine. "He gave me the idea to go a different route than my brother did to try and find the dirty cop. Instead of looking into law enforcement and town officials before, during, and after The Flood—"

"—you looked into the drug supplier's side," Foster concluded.

William nodded. "Everyone knew me so I couldn't ask a lot of questions without raising suspicion, but Fallon had a history and a town whose law enforcement largely disliked him. It was easy for him to dig deep in that side of life."

Foster couldn't believe it. "You left town to go undercover into a drug operation to try and find a dirty cop," he said.

Fallon shrugged. "When you say it out loud it doesn't sound as great but, yeah."

Foster put his gun into his holster and ran a hand along his jaw.

"And I'm guessing you didn't tell your sister because she would have shut that down really quick." He looked at William, realizing one of the errors of their plan that had led Millie and Foster into it. "You wrote the note, didn't you? You did it before he told you that he always writes in cursive to Millie."

William sighed. "Yeah. If we went back and fixed it, it would have only added more questions. So we left it alone and hoped to figure out everything as quickly as possible."

"Okay," Foster said after a moment. "Okay. So there are still some more detailed answers I want, but I have to ask again, why are you *here*?"

"Because, dumb or not, what I stole finally gave us a name," Fallon answered. "Lee Gordon."

Foster should have been surprised but ever since he'd seen the sports car, his thoughts on the former detective had started to change from a man who was possibly incompetent to a man who might not be as cut-and-dried as he'd once seemed.

William motioned around the room. "You tell me if you think this house should belong to a single, retired small-town detective with no family money or investments to be had."

Foster couldn't, but he was ready to ask more questions when his cell phone started to vibrate in his pocket. It was loud enough that it drew the attention of two set of eyes. He answered without hesitation when he saw the caller ID read Dr. Alvarez.

Foster didn't care about Fallon or William or even Lee Gordon anymore.

All he could think about was Millie.

"What's wrong?"

Amanda didn't hesitate either.

"Foster. She's gone. Millie's gone."

# *Chapter Twenty-Two*

The gun bit into Millie's back, pushing her out of the stock-room like she hadn't already wanted to leave it and the man holding the gun behind.

"Why are you doing this?" she cried out.

Lee Gordon was dressed like he should have been out on the golf course. He had on a nice button-down and slacks and brown loafers. None of which went with the gun or the severe anger marring his expression.

Anger clearly aimed at her.

"If you would have let that no good brother of yours go, none of this would have happened. But *no*. You, like him, are more trouble than you're worth."

Millie let out a small noise as Gordon pushed her through the door. She spun around but not before taking a few steps away for distance. The back door to the gro-cery store was behind her, but the door to the main room was closer.

Gordon held the gun up and stepped between her and the closest escape.

"I don't understand," Millie said again. "What do you want?"

It had been almost four months since Millie had seen Lee Gordon. She'd imagined on occasion that he'd be lounging on the couch, beer in hand, and watching TV, living stress-free and not thinking about Fallon ever again. He'd barely showed interest when he had the case, after all.

But standing there now, Lee Gordon looked like he hadn't enjoyed an ounce of his retirement. There were bags beneath his eyes, stubble along his jaw and a frown that seemed to drag his entire face down. He didn't look like the man Millie had loathed after he'd officially closed the investigation into her brother's disappearance.

"You know, I worked my tail off for *years* for the chance to not have to work at all," he said. "I did what I was supposed to and then I did a bit more, just so I could leave it all and not worry about a thing until the day I died. But then you show up and get everyone in a tizzy over a boy who wasn't even worth the gum on the bottom of a shoe *before* he got William Reiner mangled." He shook his head. "I should have said no to it, retired early, but I figured what harm would it do to just tell everyone what they already knew? That Fallon Dean was a runaway."

He took a moment, but the aim of his gun stayed on her. Millie wasn't near anything she could use as weapon. Her best hope was to hear the man's rant and try to stretch it long enough to find a way to escape *without* being shot.

Gordon laughed.

There was no humor in it.

"That's where I messed up," he continued. "I went to talk to Reiner and saw Fallon's truck under a tarp. Knew it then that he had killed the boy. Justice, if you ask me."

Millie's heart squeezed.

She clung to the hope that the note in her pocket had been from Fallon and not an elaborate hoax by Reiner.

"I guess it didn't matter if I reported it or not. Just being there must have put me on the younger one's radar."

"Cole," Millie couldn't help but say.

Gordon snorted. "I'd heard he was sniffing around former law enforcement, especially those who hadn't been caught up in The Flood. But it wasn't until I had some former acquaintances of mine show up, asking me to fix everything or else, that I realized just how close he'd gotten. That's when I had to outsource."

Millie didn't know why he was giving her a rundown but had to admit she knew from experience how cathartic it felt to vent. She also wanted answers.

"You're who Donni and Wyatt were working for?"

Gordon made a face. Like his laughter, humor wasn't the cause of it.

"Working for me would suggest they listen to what I say," he answered. "All they were ever supposed to do was get back the damn ledger that Cole stole from Jason *The Idiot* Talbot. But, no, they thought it was a great idea to step in the middle of whichever Reiner-sibling plan involved you and that overblown detective and a boat."

He shook his head with more force than before.

Then he shook the gun at her.

"But if William wants you so badly, then I'm going to cut through all of this madness and deliver you myself. If he won't give me the book for covering up the murder of your whiny little brother, then I'll sweeten the pot with the opportunity to finally destroy all of the family that destroyed William Reiner's." He motioned his head to the back door. "The only choice *you* get now is to come quietly or I'll make a pit stop to kill your Detective Lovett, since I've heard you two have become so close."

Millie went from standing still, wondering what the heck the ledger was all about, to making another not-so-great choice that day.

She ran.

Right at Gordon.

It caught the man so off guard that he didn't pull the trigger until Millie's hands were already pushing his wrist and arm up.

The shot exploded overhead and made an awful noise. Glass shattered. Someone in the store screamed.

Millie didn't slow down.

Her momentum took them both backward, much like her fight with Jason. This time there was no wall right behind them. There was also a gun in play from the get-go. The ground caught Gordon just as he squeezed off another shot.

Millie recoiled on reflex as the sound pierced her ears.

It was all Gordon needed to throw her off him.

She tried to scramble back but it was too late.

Gordon turned the gun on her—

Then yelled as a man tagged in and threw a punch that redirected Gordon's aim. The gun dropped from his grip and skidded across the floor.

Millie had hoped her savior was one of two men. Yet, as the newcomer turned, it was neither Foster nor Fallon.

"Cole?"

Millie had never seen Cole Reiner in person, but she'd seen his picture. There was no doubt it was him, dressed down but fiercely focused, and ready to tussle with the former detective.

When he looked her way and yelled, "Run," Millie decided to let him have that tussle.

She scrambled to her feet and ran half-bent and stumbling to the double doors that led into the store. Once on the other side, she was met by nothing but the sound of '80s music that looped on the overhead speaker and a commotion from, she guessed, the street. Any employees or shoppers must have run at hearing the obvious shots.

Millie was about to follow.

She tore through the toy aisle as another shot went off behind her.

She didn't have time to wonder where it hit.

The sound of squeaking tennis shoes against the recently buffed floor shot another dose of adrenaline into her veins. Someone was coming toward her from the front of the store.

More than one someone.

Millie stopped and readied to pivot, going back a few feet to the midstore opening that cut across the middle of the space and aisles, but she ran out of time.

She watched, heart in her throat, as the two people she'd wanted to see most came into view.

Foster looked her up and down in an instant. He held his gun down at his side, and focus unlike any she'd seen yet was evident across his features. He ran toward her, saying something, but Millie didn't hear it.

Her own focus homed in on the man who she'd been told that morning was dead.

But he wasn't.

A look of relief and guilt washed over Fallon's face.

If Millie had the time, she would have cried right then and there.

Instead, the world turned to chaos.

Everything that had slowed when she saw her brother, alive and well, sped up in a whirlwind of violence and sound.

The three of them came together just as the doors to the back banged open.

Millie didn't look back but knew it wasn't good.

Another gunshot sounded.

Millie went from trying to run to being caught off guard as Fallon tucked himself around her. Both staggered as Foster yelled out.

One last gunshot went off, but Millie couldn't tell from where.

Instead, she fell to the ground beneath the weight of her brother.

The deadweight.

She held on to him as pain lit up her backside from hitting the floor.

Fallon wasn't moving but Foster was.

She watched in what felt like an out-of-body experience as the detective ran down the aisle and right up to Lee Gordon, his discarded gun and the blood around both.

Foster had shot him, just as he had Jason to protect her.

But this time, he hadn't been the one to take the bullet meant for her.

This time Millie did cry as her brother lay limp in her arms.

FOSTER SPENT A portion of his life not believing in good luck or bad luck, yet, three months later he was starting to decide it was okay to change his mind.

The bad luck had already happened, but no one realized how much until Foster had finally managed to get all parties together for a chronological and lengthy explanation of the last six to eight months.

And it had happened to the exact people who deserved it.

It was bad luck for Lee Gordon that, after years of helping a drug supplier in exchange for cuts of the money— which he had used to live an expensive lifestyle after retiring—that he'd covered up the death of none other than Cole Reiner's childhood friend. A man Cole had decided to avenge by getting justice, even when it included dropping off everyone's radar to find whoever was the dirty cop.

It was bad luck that William Reiner, who had realized the value of family in the last few years, had become so determined to find his little brother that he'd accepted the help of another little brother who had been looking for redemption.

It was bad luck again when both parties, looking for the same dirty cop, had gone about it by opposite routes.

Cole had learned everything he could about those who had been a part of the corruption of The Flood and those who had managed to run from it while William and Fallon had infiltrated the drug scene that stretched across South Alabama to find the exact supplier who had worked with the same dirty cop.

It was bad luck that Millie Dean had refused to give up on her brother, no matter what anyone said, which led both to her and eventually Foster to confuse all sides involved.

And it was an extra dose of bad luck that Millie and Fallon had both missed each other so much near the six-month anniversary of him leaving that both had made impulsive choices.

Fallon had befriended and then stolen from Jason Talbot the one piece of evidence that eventually led to proof that Gordon had been involved in several transactions, deals and cover-ups, while Millie had gone to the woods, making Jason think she was working with her brother.

Everything else that had followed eventually turned into good luck for everyone who deserved it in the end.

William Reiner was reunited with his brother and Cole was able to provide leads to several cold and closed cases that had potentially been tampered with before The Flood happened. He also accepted a job back at the department with every intention of going for detective in the near future. June, his now fiancée, had been beside herself at his homecoming. So much so she'd announced she was ready to go to jail for drugging Millie and Foster.

It was an admission no one accepted and the only area of transparency everyone involved believed could stay a little opaque.

Then the focus turned to Fallon.

For all the trouble he'd put Millie through, Foster should have felt some anger at the young man. Yet the moment Fallon had shielded his sister from Gordon's last shot in the grocery store, Foster had decided he could never do wrong by him. He'd been as brave as his father had the day he'd shielded Fallon.

And it was only after Millie realized that Foster had given her brother the Just in Case bulletproof vest to wear before they'd gone into the store, that she pulled Foster down to their level with a strong embrace and a passionate kiss.

The good luck had continued from there on by way of the town, county and state covering the intricate story of two sets of siblings fighting for justice and each other with the help of the sheriff's department. It didn't make anyone forget about the town's past, but it was a step in the right direction.

"Keep it up and we might turn this place around yet," the sheriff had told Foster on the way out.

Foster aimed to do just that.

But not without doing a few things first.

Foster parked outside his house but walked up his neighbor's drive instead.

The front door opened before he could knock.

Fallon was grinning. "I'm not supposed to say anything yet," he confessed hurriedly in a whisper. "But Millie just got accepted. Full scholarship. She told me it wasn't a big deal but when she tells you, make sure to hype it up."

Foster did a little dance of excitement. Fallon joined in. After the world had settled around her, Millie had decided that she wanted to become a social worker and had applied for an online program that, according to her, was exactly what she hoped to get.

"I love where I am right now," she'd told him. "And I love the people I'm with. If I can do both, I'd like to try."

Now Foster didn't need to promise to be excited for her. He genuinely was.

Both men went quiet as Millie herself appeared in the

doorway. She leaned in for a kiss that Foster turned into a dip.

"And that's my cue to go gag inside," Fallon said around a bite of laughter. He went inside and told Larissa and Amanda, loudly, that his sister was making out with her boyfriend on the front porch.

Millie shook her head, smiling when the kiss was done.

"Are you sure you want to switch houses with him?" she asked for the fifth time that week. "Living with me and having my brother as a next-door neighbor? That's almost a comically bad idea."

Foster grinned. "Don't you know? I eat bad ideas for breakfast."

Millie rolled her eyes. "The only thing you eat for breakfast is scrambled eggs with spoons because, for whatever reason, you keep throwing away your forks."

He let out a howl of laughter at that.

"You caught me doing it *one* time and now I'm marked for life!"

"All I'm saying is that when you officially get all moved in, I'm going to make sure my forks are already counted up," she said, hands going onto her hips. "I will not stand a fork thief!"

Foster got a squeal out of her as he pulled her in against him. The kiss they shared next quieted them both in the best way.

He wouldn't say it for three months—the night they'd get engaged—but in that moment Foster knew one thing with absolute certainty.

His luck had changed for good the moment he'd met Millie.

\* \* \* \* \*

# COMING SOON!

We really hope you enjoyed reading this book.
If you're looking for more romance, be sure to
head to the shops when new books are
available on

# Thursday 8th
# July

To see which titles are coming soon, please visit
**millsandboon.co.uk/nextmonth**

## LET'S TALK
# Romance

For exclusive extracts, competitions
and special offers, find us online:

- facebook.com/millsandboon
- @MillsandBoon
- @MillsandBoonUK

**Get in touch on 01413 063232**

For all the latest titles coming soon, visit
**millsandboon.co.uk/nextmonth**

# MILLS & BOON

## THE HEART OF ROMANCE

---

## A ROMANCE FOR EVERY READER

---

### MODERN

Prepare to be swept off your feet by sophisticated, sexy and seductive heroes, in some of the world's most glamourous and romantic locations, where power and passion collide.

### HISTORICAL

Escape with historical heroes from time gone by. Whether your passion is for wicked Regency Rakes, muscled Vikings or rugged Highlanders, awake the romance of the past.

### MEDICAL

Set your pulse racing with dedicated, delectable doctors in the high-pressure world of medicine, where emotions run high and passion, comfort and love are the best medicine.

### True Love

Celebrate true love with tender stories of heartfelt romance, from the rush of falling in love to the joy a new baby can bring, and a focus on the emotional heart of a relationship.

### Desire

Indulge in secrets and scandal, intense drama and plenty of sizzling hot action with powerful and passionate heroes who have it all: wealth, status, good looks…everything but the right woman.

### HEROES

Experience all the excitement of a gripping thriller, with an intense romance at its heart. Resourceful, true-to-life women and strong, fearless men face danger and desire - a killer combination!

---

To see which titles are coming soon, please visit

millsandboon.co.uk/nextmonth

# JOIN US ON SOCIAL MEDIA!

Stay up to date with our latest releases, author news and gossip, special offers and discounts, and all the behind-the-scenes action from Mills & Boon...

 millsandboon

 millsandboonuk

 millsandboon

*It might just be true love...*

# Start your free trial now

## Available at
## weloveromance.com

# MILLS & BOON
## MEDICAL
### *Pulse-Racing Passion*

Set your pulse racing with dedicated, delectable doctors in the high-pressure world of medicine, where emotions run high and passion, comfort and love are the best medicine.

# MILLS & BOON
## *Desire*

Indulge in secrets and scandal, intense drama and plenty of sizzling hot action with powerful and passionate heroes who have it all: wealth, status, good looks…everything but the right woman.